Time Stryder

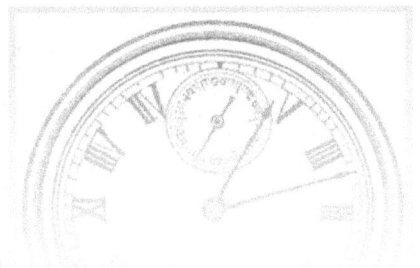

A NOVEL

J. W. Kingsley

Lindenleaf Books

First published in 2011 as the podcast
'Time Stryder – Storm Warning'

Further released in 2012 in the following formats:
Hardcover – ISBN 978-0-9813123-2-3
Trade Paperback – ISBN 978-0-9813123-3-0
EPUB ebook – ISBN 978-0-9813123-4-7

Completely reworked, rewritten, and relaunched in 2015 as

Time Stryder

Kingsley, J. W.
Time Stryder
ISBN 978-0-9813123-7-8
I. Title

For Evie, whose writing inspired me
even before I could read

TIME STRYDER

The past has yet to happen,
and the future haunts us all

"The human mind, no matter how highly trained,
cannot grasp the universe…"

— *Albert Einstein (1930)*

Contents

Appendices

Epilogue

A Moment of Your Time

Behind this story are some ideas that may seem quite strange to you, since they not only go against current theories in physics, but also, perhaps more unforgivably, go against well-established tropes of science fiction. If this double heresy tempts you to skip over some parts of the story, or even avoid this book altogether, I must warn you that if you do so, you may miss the devil in the details – and trust me, there is more than one monster to be found lurking within these pages.

Ultimately, if you do read this book, and you do like it, I ask only that you take a moment to share it with your friends.

However, if you do *not* like it, then I suggest using it in large quantities to confound your enemies.

Volume discounts gladly provided for book burnings.

Enjoy.

Chapter One

Storm Warning

The wind blew hard as massive waves battered the rocky coast. Rain came down in torrents and lightning stabbed out from dark clouds as thunder crashed in a deafening barrage. In the middle of this violence, a young boy tumbled out of nowhere onto the narrow beach. This was George Stryder, when he first came to our world, broken, bloody, and utterly lost.

From out of the clouds high above, a thing made of shifting shadows, a creature that looked like no more than a wisp of smoke, flew down from the centre of the storm and landed on the beach. It glanced around nervously as it grew more solid. It looked like a gargoyle, a grotesque statue from an ancient cathedral, and yet now appeared to be a creature of flesh and bone.

Fighting to keep from being swept away by the storm, it crouched low as it crawled across the sand to where George lay, face down at the edge of the surf. It rolled him over and removed a gold watch from George's coat, placed it within a small wooden box, and then returned it to George's pocket.

The creature suddenly tensed, as if it had heard something, and then, wary of unseen danger, it faded back into shifting shadows, spreading its ghostly wings and rose back into the storm. It circled overhead once or twice like a vulture, then vanished as lightning flashed and the clouds folded in on themselves.

Then, in a most peculiar way, the wind just seemed to die away, while the rain diminished to a faint drizzle, and a heavy mist settled over everything.

As he slowly became conscious, George felt like his head was going to explode, and when he moved, everything just seemed to spin. After waiting a moment for everything to settle down, he tried to move again, and eventually, he was able to roll over. Then, with great difficulty, because his right arm felt strangely numb and refused to work, he dragged himself up the beach, and away from the surf. He struggled to prop himself up so he could look around.

He could see that he was on a narrow strip of sand, just below a low rocky shore, and he could just make out tufts of grass and the tops of trees above the rocky bluff. It reminded him of Kingscross on the Isle of Arran, when his parents had taken him to Scotland the previous summer, yet this place looked so much wilder, and stranger.

Where were his parents? He called out, but there was no answer, only the cry of the seagulls and the crash of the waves. He had a sense of great danger, of loneliness, and of fearing for his parents' lives as much as for his own, but no memories of what had happened.

Weakness and exhaustion swept over him, and when he rolled over onto his back, his injured arm struck a rock in the sand. The shock of intense pain made his world go black once again.

It was early in the morning on the last day of Alicia Henderson's family vacation on Hornby Island, and while her father made pancakes, she was busy tagging photographs on her computer.

Alicia was eleven years old, and a pretty cool kid... at least, she was somewhat cool in a geeky, nerdy kind of way. The most important thing about her was that she didn't want to be defined by her strawberry-blond hair, or the fact that she wore glasses, or by anything else so stupid. She just wanted to be herself, and if that self was different from what everyone thought she should be, then that was their problem, not hers.

For instance, she really liked cactuses, and ever since she had first learned that there was a species of cactus that grew along the rocky shores of the island, she just knew she had to get a picture of it, but so far, she hadn't found even one.[1]

Her brother Matt, who was a year older, and way more normal, thought she was nuts for wasting so much time looking for some dumb plant, especially when there were such righteous mountain-bike trails on the island. And even though their older sister, Chella, loved nature just as much as Alicia did, she also thought that getting so worked up about some weird plant was totally lame.

It was only Alicia's little brother, Simon Toliver, who really seemed to understand her, but then he was only seven years old, so no one took his opinion seriously. And besides, he was a bit odd himself, with his one green eye and one blue, and hair that was light brown with patches of blond.

So, while the rest of the Hendersons were doing normal vacation things on the island, Alicia had spent the entire time searching the cliffs and rocky shorelines for a cactus. And now it was the last day they would be there, and she was tagging the hundreds of shots of interesting plants, wildlife and ocean vistas before making one last desperate expedition to find what she was really looking for.

'Did you get that picture you wanted?' her dad asked distractedly as he flipped a pancake.

'No, Dad,' she said with some frustration, 'you know I didn't... I told you all at supper last night... like, about ten times.'

'Sorry, I must not have been listening... so are you going to try again today?'

'Yeah,' she replied distractedly as she tagged a few more pictures, 'I think I'm going to try looking around the Point again...'

'Sounds good,' her father said, 'but take your phone with you, and remember: we all have to be back here and packed by 2:30 if we're going to make the 3 o'clock ferry.'

Mr Henderson was a solidly built man of modest height, with thinning sandy coloured hair. His nose had been broken in a rugby game long ago, and never quite set right, but that only added to his natural air of authority. 'Better eat this before you head out... whoa...

---

[1] *Opuntia fragilis* – the **Brittle Prickly Pear Cactus**, as it occurs on the west coast of British Columbia, is grey-green in colour, and blends in with its surroundings so well that finding it, at least when it's not in bloom, is very difficult indeed.

on second thought, you might want to hold off on your plans. Looks like a pretty bad storm coming in.'

Alicia adjusted her glasses as she checked the weather app on her computer, but according to it, the weather was clear and calm.

'Seriously, Dad, it'll be fine.'

'Yeah, well 'seriously' you should turn around and have a look.'

When she did, she could hardly believe what she was seeing. The blue water of the bay had turned steel grey as white-capped waves drove hard against the shore. Heavy clouds rolled in and turned the sky almost black, while a powerful wind howled through the trees. Lightning flashed brilliant white, followed by thunder that rumbled through the cabin walls. Hail began to clatter on the skylights.

Alicia walked slowly toward the cabin's big glass wall, transfixed by the strange storm. Her little brother, Simon Toliver, came running into the room.

'The sky cracked,' he said, as he ran into the room.

Despite being only seven years old, Toliver was not easily frightened, and usually enjoyed the spectacle of powerful weather, but something about this storm had unnerved him, and he clung to his father for reassurance.

They all watched as sparks of red and blue lightning crawled along underneath the clouds, the blue ones spiralling out, while the red sparks spun toward a gaping vortex growing in the centre of the storm.

'Dad, have you ever seen lightning do that?' Alicia asked, almost in a whisper.

'No... I've never seen *anything* like that.'

Rain and sea spray lashed across the cabin's large deck, splattering the glass and obscuring the view, and then, with a deafening crack of thunder, the cabin lights flickered and died.

'Damn,' said Mr Henderson, 'that was way too close for comfort.'

Just then, Alicia felt her little brother tugging on her arm, and when he spoke to her, his voice became muffled and distant. 'Allie... where are you going?'

The strangest sensation suddenly came over her. It was as if she was moving at great speed even though she was sure that she was standing perfectly still. The cabin seemed to fade in the distance, while the storm dissolved into a thick fog, and then, her surroundings became very quiet.

She was standing at a fork in the forest path, facing a battered old sign directing her to the point where she had planned to go that morning, but she had absolutely no memory of just how she got there. This must be a dream, she thought, that's the only explanation that makes sense.

She started to walk down the path, the fog swirled around her, and although she thought she knew the trail well, it looked so strange now. The trees were larger and older than she remembered them being, and the path was tangled with undergrowth as if no one had tended it for years. The way had been clear when she had been here only yesterday, but now it looked as if time had run wild for decades.

Through the thinning fog, she could see the outline of a big redcedar tree that she had admired just the day before, but it looked so much older than she remembered, and so battered by the storm. As she approached, she looked up at one of its largest branches, twisted and damaged by the wind. Then the branch broke free with a terrible crack, and an invisible hand grabbed Alicia's shoulder, throwing her back violently as the branch landed with a heavy dead thud, right on the path where she had been standing.

She fumbled for her glasses, looking for the person who had saved her, but there was no one there.

She called out, but there was no reply, only the faint sound of rain dripping from the trees while the mist continued to swirl around the forest path. She looked everywhere as the strangest sensation of being watched crept over her.

Then she saw it.

An almost human-shaped void in the mist.

No, she thought, it's just a shadow, a trick of the light, nothing to freak out about.

The shadow raised an arm and moved toward her.

She ran.

"There's no such thing as ghosts, there's no such thing as ghosts," she frantically repeated to herself as she fought back the panic.

No way, she thought.

She had outgrown the monsters under her bed, the shadows in the night, and the unseen terrors that reached out from under the basement steps. So, no way was she going to give into such childish fears again.

She stopped suddenly.

'Just so you know,' she yelled defiantly as she turned around, 'I don't believe in ghosts!'

The forest was just as calm as ever, and now the mist had started to dissolve in the morning sun, while the overgrown tangle seemed to fade away, and her surroundings became familiar once again.

Alicia stood for a moment and looked around, glancing back over her shoulder once or twice, and then she laughed a little nervously, amused by how her imagination could still get the better of her. It had just been a trick of the light, a stupid shadow, she thought. Of course, that's all it was. She relaxed, took a deep breath of the fresh morning air, and continued on her way.

It was turning into a beautiful day, and she might as well head down to the Point to see if she could finally locate one of those elusive little cactuses growing along the cliffs.

The last of the fog dissolved quickly in the warm morning sun, and the smells in the air were sweet, crisp and clean. The old-growth firs and red cedar soon gave way to wind-contorted Garry oak and arbutus, and the ferns of the forest floor gave way to wild grasses that rippled in the breeze, mirroring the ocean waves beyond.

She turned when she heard Simon Toliver's laugh in the distance, and saw him running down the eastern path, with her parents following close behind. Her mother using a cane to steady herself, and her father walking beside her, with the baby in a carrier strapped to his chest.

Okay, she thought, this is more like it, no big deal. The freaky storm, the missing time, and the thing in the forest, all that seemed unimportant now.

Anyway, she was getting used to things being a little weird these days, especially with her mother getting sick and the new baby and everything.

In fact, Alicia could still remember every detail about that day, the day when everything had changed.

It had been early in the autumn of last year, and her parents had called a family meeting, something that they almost never did. Alicia could still see her mother sitting on the sofa, a woman of such certainty and calm determination, suddenly looking small and vulnerable, almost defeated. Her mother's hazel-green eyes downcast, and her hands clasped nervously, silently speaking of an unfamiliar fear.

It was then that she had told them all the terrible news. She had been diagnosed with multiple sclerosis, a condition that would slowly rob her of her strength. A disease that would change everything.

At first, there had been silence, and then Rachael, the eldest, had nervously asked what treatment would cure it, and how long her recovery would be.

'Chella, honey,' her mother had replied, hesitantly, 'there is no cure.'

A painful knot had formed in Alicia's gut as she asked, 'Are you going to die?'

'No, no,' her mother had tried to reassure her, 'I just have to be careful not to make it worse...'

'What that means,' her father had cut in, 'is that we're all going to have to pitch in around here, and help keep your mom's stress to a minimum.'

'So, are you going to quit being a doctor?' Matt had asked, 'like, your job's got to be pretty stressful.'

'No,' her mother had answered firmly, 'there won't be any big changes around here because of this.'

But Alicia soon learned that wasn't really true, because things *had* changed – a lot. But not nearly as much as they would change, just a few months later, on a cold January afternoon.

Alicia had been walking Simon Toliver home from school, when she saw her mother sitting in her car in the driveway, staring blankly ahead. Alicia tapped on the driver's side window. 'Mom... are you okay?'

When her mother didn't respond, Alicia opened the car door, and it was then that she saw the blood. She quickly closed the door, but it was too late, her little brother had seen. 'Toliver, go inside, get dad.'

'What's wrong with mom?'

'It just mom's surgical scrubs,' Alicia tried to reassure him. 'She didn't change before coming home. Now go and get Dad, okay?'

While Simon Toliver ran inside, Alicia tried once again to get her mother's attention. 'Mom, you're scaring me... what's going on?'

'I tried...'

'Tried what?'

'What's going on?' Mr Henderson asked impatiently as he came outside, 'I'm in the middle of an important conference... what the...?' He knelt down by the open car door, and gently cupped his wife's face in his hand. She then turned to him, a deeply haunted look in her eyes.

'Gil, I tried to stop it... I did...'

'Are you hurt, is this your blood?' he pleaded, almost demanded.

'It's not mine, but it's on my hands just the same, Gil... so many people dead... and for what?'

With a level of strength that surprised Alicia, her father lifted her mother directly out of the car, and tenderly cradled her as he carried her into the house. 'Allie,' he said, without looking back, 'take care of your little brother.'

Worried, and needing a distraction from her own fears, Alicia tended to Simon Toliver, and tried to reassure him. It was only hours later, after she had seen Toliver off to bed, that her father finally came out of her mother's office. His face was pale and drawn.

'Your mom's okay,' he had said, too casually to cover the tension in his voice. 'She just needs a good rest. Listen, Allie, can I rely on you to make sure Toliver gets to school okay in the morning?'

'Yeah, of course, Dad... but what's going on?'

'Nothing,' he smiled, unconvincingly. 'Are Matt and Chella home?'

Alicia nodded, 'yes.'

'Good... I'll need to talk with them.'

It was the next day, late in the afternoon, when her parents called another family meeting, and although Alicia had braced herself for some terrible news, when her parents made their announcement, she couldn't believe what she was hearing.

'What baby? Coming to live with us... when?'

'This is so totally stupid!' Chella cut in, 'seriously, mom, what were you thinking... making a promise like that?'

'Rachael,' her mother replied very firmly, 'this is not up for a vote, it's going to happen, and that's final.'

'There's no freakin' way,' said Matt, 'that I'm going to change any dirty diapers.'

'You won't have to,' she sighed, obviously disappointed by her son's unwillingness to help, 'I'll be giving up my position at the hospital so your father and I can do this together.'

'No way!' shouted Chella, 'Mom, that's your career... why would you give that up? Seriously, there must be tons of people looking to adopt... Let someone else take care of it... like... don't be so stupid!'

'Chella!' Mr Henderson barked, his voice unusually deep and hoarse, 'you will *not* speak to your mother like that!' But then his voice softened, 'listen, Princess, this is what your mom wants, it's a promise she made, and it's up to all of us to help her keep it.'

'Anyway,' her mother had added, 'we all knew that I'd have to eventually quit.'

'Yeah, because of your MS,' Chella snapped, 'but why take in a baby as well... it totally makes no sense!'

'It's just something I have to do... something we all have to do... besides,' Dr Henderson had added with an oddly hollow laugh, 'it's not like it's the end of the world.'

No, it hadn't been the end of the world, thought Alicia. In fact, here they all were, almost five months later, and although her mom still wouldn't talk about what had happened at the hospital, in every other way, things were actually pretty cool. Her mom was way less stressed, and her dad was getting way more exercise, especially since he hardly went anywhere without the baby carrier strapped to his chest, and even Matt and Chella had started to accept the changes.

Alicia hesitated for a moment more as she watched her parents and Simon Toliver approach. Yeah, she thought, since Anessa has come to live with them, things were not too bad, after all. She waved to them in the distance, and her mother smiled while her father waved back. And then Alicia was gripped with a sense of just how fleeting time really was, so she pulled out her camera and took picture after picture of them, wanting to anchor the moment in her memory.

Simon Toliver suddenly shouted, 'there's someone on the beach!' as he excitedly pointed to the base of the low rocky cliff.

'It's probably a harbour seal sunning himself,' Mr Henderson called out, 'best leave him alone.'

'I don't think it's a seal, Dad,' replied Alicia as she looked where her little brother was pointing. 'It looks like a boy... he might have fallen.' Without a second thought, she scrambled down the rocks to the thin strip of beach below.

'Alicia! Wait!' her father shouted back as he struggled to remove the baby carrier and hand it to his wife, angrily muttering, 'great... what family vacation is complete without at least one random body washed up on the beach?' He broke into a run, but Alicia was already down on the beach. 'Dammit, Allie, I said *wait!*'

Alicia, however, hadn't heard a thing. Her father's voice and even the sound of the surf faded into nothing, all she could hear was the shallow breathing of the boy lying face up on the narrow strip of sand.

He was about the same age as her, wearing clothes that were torn and dirty, and she could see ragged red claw marks on his chest.

'He's hurt, please help him,' she called back to her parents.

The boy's eyes were closed, and Alicia wondered what colour they might be. She knelt down beside him and reached out to brush his pale cheek, but as she did so, a deep chill ran through her, as if a doorway to winter had suddenly been thrown open. She pulled back instinctively, and the feeling faded, but not nearly as fast as it had rushed in.

The boy took a gasping breath, and Alicia instinctively grabbed his hand, wanting only to comfort and reassure him, but once again, a cold and empty feeling wrapped itself around her. She looked back to her father, desperately seeking his help, but he appeared to have stopped in mid stride. In fact, except for the air shimmering and rippling in a most peculiar way around her, the whole world seemed to have frozen.

But then red and blue sparks spiralled across the ground toward her, and a hollow wind spun into a tight vortex as her world vanished into an overwhelming nothingness. There was nothing below, nothing above, and as she tumbled into this opening void, she felt as alone as she had ever been in her life.

Chapter Two

A Stumble in Time

Alicia cried out, but her world had disappeared and no one could hear her. The wind grew into a gale, roaring like a freight train past her ears. It forced its way into her tightly closed eyes, making tears stream back on her cheeks and up over her forehead.

The storm felt empty, dark, and devoid of hope, but then she felt a warm hand grasp her own. At first, she wasn't sure if she had imagined it, but there it was again, that trace of human contact that meant the world to her, and she held onto it for dear life.

The storm died away quickly, and the air around her became very still and heavy, the darkness lightened to a dull grey as a thick fog wrapped around her. She took a step forward and cracked her shin against something hard.

The fog thinned to a mist, and it was then that she could see ghostly silhouettes start to form around her – a small tree here, a hedge there, and even garden beds full of planted rows of vegetables, divided by gravel paths and all surrounded by brick walls covered with carefully sculpted fruit trees. In the distance, she could see the outline of an old manor house, which loomed like a ghostly presence at the far end of the garden.

She felt another squeeze, and turned to see the boy from the beach standing beside her, and she was still holding his hand. His clothes were dry, he didn't have the bloody claw marks on his chest, and she could see his eyes now, which were an unusual deep blue.

'Where am I?' was all she could think to ask.

'I'm not exactly sure,' he replied in a crisp English accent.

'However, do you mind terribly... letting go of my hand? You're rather crushing it.'

'Sorry... so... who are you?'

'Stryder, George Stryder... And you are?'

'Alicia... Alicia Henderson.'

'Well it's very nice to make your acquaintance, Alicia Henderson, welcome to... well, I really don't have the foggiest notion where this actually is, but I must say, you are most welcome, nonetheless.'

Unsure of how to reply, Alicia said nothing as she continued to look around, but finally said, 'this is totally weird,' as she turned back to George. 'I don't think I've ever had a dream that felt so real before.'

'Neither have I, but then, I don't think this *is* a dream.'

'Seriously? I just found you on the beach.'

'On the beach... on the Isle of Arran? When was that?'

'No... Hornby Island... just a couple of minutes ago.'

'What the deuce do you mean? I've never been to Hornby Island.'

'What*ever*,' said Alicia dismissively, 'I saw you on the beach just a couple of minutes ago,' she hesitated, 'and then I was, like, here, in this... dream.'

'I assure you that this is no dream,' George said, although he was less sure of this than he wanted to admit. He looked around as well, and then in a burst of inspiration he said, 'you cried out when you banged your shin on that bench, and if this were a dream you wouldn't have hurt yourself.'

'Okay,' she admitted, a little reluctantly, 'but if this isn't a dream, then what is it? Like, seriously, how else can you explain how I got here from the beach so fast?'

George stammered for an answer, but no good one came to him.

'Well,' continued Alicia, 'wherever this is, I want to get back in time for lunch.'

'Why,' George asked, 'are you hungry?'

'No... not really,' she replied slowly as she thought about it, but then suddenly added, 'I didn't feel pain either – I was just startled when I bumped into that thing, but it didn't hurt – so this *is* a dream!' She then climbed up on the bench and raised her arms above her head, which caught George by surprise.

'What on earth are you doing?'

'This is how I fly in my dreams,' she said in a perfectly matter-of-fact way, 'I want to have a better look around.' She then made a little hop from the bench, and landed awkwardly on the ground in front of him.

'That *was* impressive.' he said with a smile, 'although I think I shall stick to walking, myself, if it's all the same to you.'

'What*ever*,' she said with as much dignity as she could muster, and then straightened her glasses and began to stomp toward the old manor house, which seemed to her like the first logical place to check out.

'You can look around 'til you're blue in the face,' he called after her, 'but you won't find a way out.'

Alicia stopped and turned, and even though she didn't want to give him the satisfaction, her curiosity still got the better of her. 'Why would looking around make my face turn blue?'

'I don't know,' said George. 'It's just an expression, I suppose.'

'Well, it's a stupid one... Anyway, why do you talk like that?'

'Like what... precisely?' George asked, taken aback.

'Well, saying things like 'blue in the face' and 'what, precisely,' and stuff. It sounds weird.'

'Weird? And I suppose you think the way you talk is all just tickety-boo?'

'Wow... like I was saying,' Alicia muttered as she turned back to the garden path. This totally has to be a dream, she thought, as she looked at the fruit trees covered in spring blooms, surrounded by drifts of daffodils and bluebells. None of this made sense, because she knew perfectly well that it was now summer, and all those flowers should have finished long ago.

She continued down the path, and then, just as she walked past an old wooden wheelbarrow, a small red fox jumped out in front of her. The little creature looked at her very carefully, but then turned and trotted quickly up the path toward George.

'Is that your fox?' she asked, 'she seems very tame.'

'She is rather, isn't she?' he replied, 'been here as far back as I can remember, but she isn't mine.'

'So you've been here a long time?' Alicia asked.

'I... I don't know,' he answered, a little reluctantly.

George was trying very hard to understand this reality that Alicia insisted must be a dream. For him, the sound of the English robins singing, and the crunch of the gravel as he walked over it, were absolutely real. The smell of the flowers and the rich earth, and even the sight of the sun glinting off the morning dew, and yet he had no memory of how he had arrived, or real idea of where he was. He wasn't hungry, but had no recollection of eating; wasn't tired, but could not recall sleeping; and wasn't bored, but had no memory of doing anything at all in the garden.

Finally, he had to ask the only question that really mattered to him, 'you didn't happen to see my parents on the beach did you?' He walked up to where Alicia was inspecting the excellent crop of spring vegetables.

'No... just you,' she replied, 'so you really can't remember how you got here... or when?'

'No... it's the oddest thing, but I honestly couldn't tell you if I've been here an hour... or for days.'

'Do you do the gardening here?' she asked as she looked around thoughtfully.

'No...'

'Well, this garden is too well tended,' she reasoned, 'so I'm pretty sure you'd have seen the gardener if you'd been here for days.'

'I suppose that makes sense,' he agreed, 'but I do wish I could remember more.'

'So what's the last thing you *do* remember?' she asked. 'Maybe if you concentrate on that, then the rest of it will come back to you.'

George tried, but his memories were oddly fragmented and broken. He could recall the fear in his father's voice, as he had spoken of the coming war, and the sadness in his mother's eyes when she had heard the news... and he could remember them talking about leaving their home in London, but nothing else after that seemed to make much sense.

Then, just as he thought he could remember something desperately important, the air began to shimmer and crackle as red and blue sparks spiralled along the ground toward them.

Alicia watched in amazement as the water dripping out of an old brass tap stopped in mid-air. 'Wow, it's like the water is frozen.'

'Something's about to happen,' said George as he tried to grab her hand, but he clutched only air as a hollow wind whipped around them, and they were plunged into darkness.

'Are you even listening to me?' Mr Henderson demanded.

Alicia looked up, suddenly aware that she was back on the beach, kneeling next to George. Her father was glaring at her. 'Look, Allie, when I say *stay put*, I mean it. It's for your own good. Understand?'

'Yeah... of course,' she mumbled, unsure if it was still a dream.

'Seriously... you've been walking around like nobody's home all morning.' When she just shook her head and made no other reply, he grumbled something inaudible and then called out to his wife, 'Gayle, the boy's got a pulse, but he's unconscious... so we're going to need your medical expertise down here.'

'A little help, then maybe,' she called back.

'Oh, right... Sorry, hon, I'll be right up.' He bounded back up the low bluff, strapped the baby carrier back on, and took his wife's hand, and then together, they slowly made their way down to the beach.

Alicia stayed with George, transfixed by how pale and damaged he now looked compared to how he had looked in the garden. It was only when her mother awkwardly knelt down beside him that Alicia even took her eyes off George.

'Be very careful, Allie, you can hold his hand, but we can't risk jostling him in case he has a neck injury.' Dr Henderson tried to smile reassuringly, and then began to examine the boy carefully, mumbling to herself as she noted the details. 'Head trauma... pulse weak... breathing appears very shallow.' She had the professional manner of a doctor, but the expression on her face was still that of a concerned mother. 'He has a probable dislocation of the right shoulder,' she paused, 'and those look like *claw* marks on his chest...

poor thing... I wonder if he came between a mother bear and her cubs.'

She brushed his hair away from his face and found a small sprig of something that looked oddly familiar. 'Rosemary... but where on earth would that come from... way out here?'

'Mom, will he be okay?' Alicia asked, hating to see George so battered and broken.

'I don't know dear... I'll do everything I can.' Dr Henderson then turned to her husband, who was talking with the Search and Rescue dispatcher on his phone, 'Gil, how long 'til they get here?'

'It'll be at least an hour to fly the crew up – you'd better fill them in on the boy's condition.' As he handed her the phone, he added, 'this is going to make things tight if we're going to make the 3 o'clock ferry.'

'Actually Gil,' Dr Henderson said as she took the phone, 'the boy's in rough shape so I'd better fly out with him... and I'm afraid that means you're going to have to drive back without me.'

Alicia felt a sudden panic at the idea of being apart from George. 'Mom, I want to go with you,' but her mother was too busy with the dispatcher to answer.

'Allie,' her father said, 'I don't think the paramedics will let you fly with them.'

'But Dad, I don't want to leave him... he needs me,' she pleaded, and then turned back to her mother for support, by which time Dr Henderson had finished, and now looked at Alicia thoughtfully.

'It's okay, Gil, it'll be an adventure for her, and besides, that way you'll have one less kid to wrangle.'

While they were waiting for the rescue team, Alicia would some-times take George's hand back in hers, but no matter how she tried, she could not make his strange world return.

'There it is!' shouted Simon Toliver as the helicopter, a large Sikorsky S-76, came into view. It landed in the meadow above the bluff, while below the blast from the rotors blew away the silver emergency blanket that Dr Henderson had used to cover George. Alicia watched as her little brother chased it, while their father ran up to the meadow to greet the rescue crew.

There were two paramedics, a man and a woman, and they worked very quickly. The woman placed a collar around George's neck, and then together they carefully slid a backboard under him.

The woman then turned to Dr Henderson, 'are you related, do you know the boy's name, or where his parents are?'

'No, we've never seen him before, and there was no sign of his parents anywhere...'

'His name is George Stryder,' said Alicia, 'and he's a very long way from home.'

'Allie,' said Dr Henderson, as she looked at her daughter with some surprise, 'how could you possibly know that?'

Chapter Three

An Exotic Land

For most people, a first helicopter flight is either a wonderful adventure, or a terrifying ordeal, but for Alicia, it was nothing compared to the storm. The drumming pulse of the rotors and the whine of the powerful engine all faded into background noise as she sat beside the stretcher and held George's hand. She was trying to make sense of how unnaturally real the garden had felt, and the more she thought about it, the clearer the experience was in her mind, and that, she was sure, wasn't like a dream at all. But then if it hadn't been a dream, she wondered, what *had* it been?

When the helicopter was preparing to land, Alicia watched the grass around the landing pad ripple in a pulsing spiral, and it reminded her of the sparks that had come before the storm. She braced herself, fearing, but also hoping, that she would be carried away once again. Yet the red and blue sparks did not appear, and she remained steadfastly in the real world.

A medical team ran out from the hospital, and one of the doctors greeted Alicia's mom as the medical staff tended to George. Perhaps it was because her mother was well respected at this hospital, or perhaps it was Alicia's look of absolute determination, but no one asked her to let go of George's hand, even as they wheeled him into the emergency department. There was the usual flurry of activity as George was assessed, examined, poked and prodded, and all the while, she did not leave his side.

Eventually, however, when the ER doctors and Dr Henderson were all satisfied that George was stable, Alicia was very tired.

'Hey, Allie,' Dr Henderson said, looking exhausted from the long day, 'the boy's in good hands now, so I think we should go home.'

It had been a very long day, and George was safe now, so Alicia nodded, and followed her mother out of the ER. However, as they walked down the corridor toward the exit, the further they went, the more difficult it became for Alicia to continue.

'Allie, are you all right?'

'Mom, I feel weird.'

'Well I'm not surprised, it's been a long day, but we'll be home soon.'

'Seriously... I can't move.'

'You're just tired,' her mother smiled and held out her hand for her, but as their fingers touched, Dr Henderson suddenly felt something pushing her back, and she slumped against the wall.

'Mom!' Alicia cried out, holding her mother's hand tightly, all at once having to offer support, when seconds ago it was she who had sought it.

'It's... it's okay Allie... it's just my MS,' her mother said as she struggled to right herself, letting go of Alicia's hand as she did so. 'There,' she said, as she stood up straight, 'I'm feeling a little better already...' Dr Henderson had grown used to the fickle nature of her disease; how on some days it would almost disappear, and on others it would make even the simplest tasks almost impossible, and as a doctor, she knew what that meant. She knew that while sometimes it might seem to get better, the disease would nonetheless slowly rob her of all her strength, before it took her life. 'I'm sure I'll feel much better when we get home. Come on, let go...'

'Mom, I can't.'

'That's enough, Alicia!' snapped her mother, 'I'm not feeling well right now, and we *are* going home.'

'But I can't!' protested Alicia as she wanted desperately to explain what was happening to her, but she simply didn't have the words to describe what she felt. She didn't know how she could tell her mother in a way that an adult would understand, or even believe, so she just mumbled, pleadingly, 'seriously... I can't leave.'

'Stop fooling around,' Dr Henderson said as she grasped her

daughter's arm, but as she did so, she once again felt the massive pressure pushing her back. 'Dammit, Alicia, can't you see I'm sick right now? I need your help.' Once again, Dr Henderson let go to steady herself against the wall, and almost instantly, the pressure vanished.

'I can't go, Mom!' Alicia insisted, as she found it harder to fight back tears of frustration. 'Mom, I – I want to go home! I do,' she stifled a sob, 'but I can't... I... I really can't move.'

It was then that Dr Henderson saw the genuine fear in her daughter's eyes, and she instinctively reached out to brush the tears away. But as soon as her fingers touched her cheek, the pressure returned. Dr Henderson pulled back reflexively. 'Alicia... what's going on?'

'I don't know,' Alicia said as she awkwardly pulled off her glasses and wiped her tears away with the back of her hand, 'Mom, I'm scared.'

'It's all right,' her mother said, desperately wanting to hold her child, but fearing the return of the inexplicable force. 'I'm here...'

Dr Henderson's years of scientific training could offer no explanation, no comfort, for what she had just encountered, but her practical medical experience told her that whether she understood what was happening or not, she had to do something about it. 'All right, Allie, do you think you can go back? There's a coffee shop down the hall... we can get a little snack... perhaps then we'll both feel better.'

'Uh huh,' Alicia nodded as she smiled weakly. She knew that there were things happening that she couldn't explain, not to her herself, or to anyone else, but she was grateful for her mother's strength and reassurance.

Then, as soon as they began to walk back down the corridor, Alicia felt the pressure fade away into almost nothing.

It wasn't much of a meal: An egg salad sandwich and an apple juice for Alicia, while her mother had only a cup of coffee. They sat in silence for a while, but eventually Dr Henderson spoke, and when she did, it was as if nothing unusual had happened at all. 'Well, if we're going to be stuck here,' she said, 'I'd better call your father and let him know.' Her voice trailed off as she fumbled through her bag looking for her phone. 'I must have left it in the ER... Allie, you stay here and finish your sandwich... I won't be long... you'll be okay alone here for a moment?'

Alicia rolled her eyes, but smiled, 'yeah, Mom, I'll be fine.' She knew perfectly well that her mother was incapable of going to an emergency room without stopping to consult with the other doctors.

After her mother had gone, Alicia looked distractedly through a nearby stack of magazines. Just as she found an old National Geographic with an interesting article on the building of the pyramids, red and blue sparks spiraled along the floor toward her.

The sun was blinding and the air was thick, heavy, and oppressively hot. Alicia was standing beside George at the intersection of two dusty streets, and she felt just as dazed and disoriented as he looked. She shielded her eyes, and tried her best to look around.

Down the road, she could see a ragged collection of buildings, some made of stone, others of brick, and yet others made of wood. In front of these structures was a confusion of shops that crowded the edges of the main street. In some of the stalls, baskets of pungent cinnamon, turmeric, cardamom, black pepper, and all manner of spices and dried foods were offered for sale. In other shops, exotic fruits and vegetables lay on large woven mats in enticing displays, while still others were draped with colourful silks and cotton fabrics. At the end of the street, there was even a tinsmith's stall with a jumble of pots and pans glinting in the sun.

While none of this was familiar to Alicia, the truly strange thing, the thing that made her almost dizzy, was how the people looked as they moved. They were oddly blurry, as if each person was preceded by an image of where they were going, and followed by blurs of where they had been. The result was that it appeared almost as if one individual blended into the next, so that the crowds seemed to ebb and flow like a river. To test if it was her own vision causing this strange effect, Alicia waved her hand in front of her face, but she didn't seem to blur the same way as the other people did. 'Wow... that is so weird... so where are we now?'

'I have no idea,' said George, 'this is all very strange... who was that shining the light in my eyes?'

'Uh, I don't know,' replied Alicia, but then quickly added, 'oh, yeah I do, it must have been one of the doctors in the ER.'

'In the what?'

'The emergency room.'

George didn't have any idea what she was talking about, and looked at her in disbelief.

'You know, like in the hospital,' she prompted.

'Why on earth would I be in a hospital?'

"Cuz when I found you on the beach, you were totally unconscious, and my mom, she's a doctor, she said you had a concussion and had to go to the hospital, so we took you there...'

'Wait a tick, what do you mean I had was unconscious?'

'Well... you were injured... banged your head and stuff.'

'And *stuff*? Why didn't you mention that before?'

'I don't know... I guess I didn't want to scare you.'

'Really... didn't want to scare me?' he said sarcastically, but then added, 'mind you... I suppose a good bang on the noggin might explain why everything looks so blurry now.'

'No, I see the blurs too, so I don't think it's that,' said Alicia, 'and besides, you don't look blurry to me... do I look that way to you?'

'No,' he admitted, a little surprised by how very different from the other people she did look. 'No... I suppose not.'

'Then it's not us, it's them. Like, I can see where people have been, and where they're going,' she said, but then added, 'wait a minute...' She squinted in the bright sunlight and watched the fronds of a tall palm blur back and forth in a light breeze. 'Oh wow, okay, it's like anything that moves is blurry... except you and me. It's actually kinda cool... but the big question is: Where are we?'

'If I had to guess,' answered George, as he continued to watch the river of humanity flow by them, 'I'd say we're in India. My mum was born just outside Bombay... and this looks just as she described it.'

'Hey, look at *those* guys,' said Alicia, pointing to a couple a men wearing khaki coloured pith helmets. 'They don't look like they fit in here any better than we do.'

'I don't know about that,' replied George, 'I think they fit in perfectly well, and if anyone can tell us where we are, I would think that they can.' With that, he grabbed Alicia's hand and together they tried to keep up with the men while weaving through the crowds.

Just when it looked like they were about to lose sight of the men, George took a shortcut through one of the stalls where great lengths of brightly coloured sari cloth hung from poles overhead. He lost his footing and stumbled into the shop owner, 'sorry, sir,' he said, but the man did not seem to notice that anything had happened. George turned to Alicia, utterly amazed, 'it's as if I'm not even here. He can't see me – see us – at all.'

'I don't think anyone can,' replied Alicia, 'it's totally weird... like we're in this kinda in-between place.'

'Well, whatever it is, it's all very peculiar,' muttered George as he backed out of the stall, watching for some hint that the man was actually aware of them.

'Hey, watch where you're going!' Alicia laughed.

George turned around to find himself face to face with what was surely the largest creature he had ever encountered; a full-grown Brahma bull.

'Wow,' said George, 'I've seen pictures before, but I had no idea they were so big.' He looked at the creature more carefully, and he thought for just an instant that it could see them, but then the bull simply turned its head, flicked its ears indifferently, and lay down in the middle of the street. Now that it remained still, the bull was not at all smudged as it sat contentedly ignoring the world around it. Then, like water in a river that encounters a rock too large to wash over, the surrounding blur of humanity in the streets divided and streamed around the creature, respectful of its right to be there.

Just then, George caught sight of the men in pith helmets again, moving through the streets like a khaki smudge against the colourful current of the street. 'Hurry up,' he urged, 'we don't want to lose our quarry again.'

'Our what?'

'Hurry up! They're getting away from us!'

The men blurred against the flow of the crowds until they finally stopped in front of a rather imposing structure. The building, looking oddly out of place and time, was constructed in the style of an ancient Grecian temple whose tall marble pillars stood like mute giants, guarding its occupants from the world outside.

'I know this place!' exclaimed George, 'my mum told me all about it, it's the officers' club where my granddad used to come.'

As the men went inside, George looked around to be sure no one was watching him, and then quickly dashed up the wide steps behind them.

Alicia called after him in a loud, clear voice, 'You remember no one can see us or hear us, right?'

He looked back at her a little sheepishly, but then said impatiently, 'Oh, do come on, then!'

George was feeling a growing sense of excitement with what was turning into a rather grand adventure and did not notice that high above, clinging to one of the pillars, and blending almost perfectly in the darkness of the portico, was a shadow with a hunched back, ragged wings, and glowing red eyes. The thing was watching their every move as it cautiously crawled along the portico's ceiling to follow them into the building's cavernous interior.

The air inside the main hall was surprising cool, but there was also a cold opulence about the place that gave Alicia an uncomfortable chill. The dark marble floor was polished to a mirror shine, which reflected the ornately carved, over-stuffed red velvet furniture. The only light in the room came from outside, reflected from the street below, casting faint shadows of blurred humanity onto the interior walls.

A number of important looking men in khaki uniforms stood around in small groups, and unlike the people out on the streets, their blurs seemed rather faint, as if they had nowhere in particular to go.

'My mum told me about how granddad used to hate the officers' club,' said George, 'but she never saw the inside of it herself.'

'It feels kind of dead in here,' said Alicia.

'Mum told me that granddad always described this place as cave full of silly blighters who didn't even have the good sense to know that they were prisoners of their own machinations.'

'What does that even *mean*?'

'To be honest, I never quite knew... but now that I see this place,' George felt a shiver run through him, 'I think I know what he meant... You know, my mum was just a girl when she lived in Bombay, and she loved it. But, when my gran died, my granddad rather lost his will to live, so he sent my mum back to England, and she never saw him again.'

'I wonder,' said Alicia slowly, 'if that's why we came here... I mean to India.'

'You say that,' said George, with some frustration, 'as though you think that I have some control over where we go.'

'Hey I'm just trying to make sense of all this,' said Alicia, 'but I admit it's kind of stupid trying to make sense of a dream.'

'Would you kindly stop with that drivel about this being a dream?'

'So, you think zapping in and out of different places is normal?' she asked defiantly.

'No... of course not, but if this is a dream, is it yours, or is it mine?' demanded George, 'at least tell me that.'

'I hadn't thought about it that way,' replied Alicia, thoughtfully, 'but it must be my dream, since if it was your dream, I wouldn't be having it.'

'But I'm having it too,' protested George.

'Yeah... this must be a dream,' Alicia continued, ignoring him and trying to convince herself, 'I mean, seriously, if this was real, then it would be pretty scary that no one can see or hear us.' She then went over to a large window that opened onto the verandah, where she noticed a man who was sitting in an old-fashioned winged chair, reading a newspaper. She bent over and tried to read the date, 'it's the 'The Times of India,' she said, 'but I can't make out the date.'

George looked around at the army officers, the businessmen, and the turbaned drink-wallahs serving them, and he couldn't help but feel that he had fallen into an almost forgotten past. Then he glimpsed a man in a black suit standing in the shadows.

George nudged Alicia, 'do you see that man over there?' he whispered, 'The one who looks like an American gangster, you know, from the cinema?'

'Huh? Oh yeah… a bit creepy looking.'

'Only, he's not like the others; he's not at all blurry when he moves… and I think he can see us.' George then began to walk toward the strange man. 'Excuse me sir,' he said, but the man only pulled down the brim of his hat to hide his face as he vanished back into the shadows.

The sound of distant thunder rumbled through the room, followed by the patter of heavy rain. A monsoon was sweeping over the city.

'Over there!' Alicia cried out as the man ran out the door. George scrambled to follow him out into the street, but before he could catch up, the man had disappeared into the crowds. Even though George had lost him, he lingered a moment to watch the hypnotic tide of humanity in the street, with one individual flowing into the next, like watercolours dissolving in the rain.

As George turned and slowly walked back to where Alicia stood at the top of the wide steps, a strange thought occurred to him. 'Can you feel the rain?' he asked as he walked up toward her.

'Yeah, of course I can.'

'Then why aren't we getting wet?'

Before she could answer, the air shimmered and crackled as red and blue sparks began to spiral, hugging the wet ground as they moved closer. Then a strangely hollow wind began to blow, and the crowd slowed down as the people froze in place.

A small movement in the corner of Alicia's eye drew her attention, and she looked up to see a shadow with blazing red eyes and ragged wings. It turned to smoke as it moved toward them, but before she could cry out to warn George, the storm had swept them both into its darkness.

Alicia felt something grab her. Not the warm clasp of George's hand, but a cold dead thing that took hold of her. It wrapped itself around her, and squeezed until she couldn't breathe. She fought hard, but even as she did, a sense of fear and hopelessness coiled around her. An emptiness darker than the deepest night. The thing in the storm was spinning her world out of control, but just when she thought she couldn't fight it anymore, she heard her mother's voice reaching out to her. 'Allie... are you all right?'

Light spilled back into her world. She could just see her mother beside her, but everything was still spinning with a sickening speed, so all she could do was lean forward, and vomit.

Perhaps it was an hour or two later when Alicia awoke, but she opened her eyes only slightly, and did not move from where she lay on the waiting room sofa. Her mother was sitting near her, nervously thumbing through a magazine, when her husband arrived.

'Hey there, hon, so what's going on?'

'I'm not sure,' said Dr Henderson as she embraced her husband, 'but I think Allie might be coming down with the flu or something, and that's why she's been acting so odd all day.' She held him tight, unable to voice her fears.

He wrapped his arms around her in return, speaking softly, almost inaudibly, 'whoa there... are you okay?'

Then, when she seemed to regain her strength, she let go, and only answered his question with one of her own. 'So, where are the rest of the kids?'

'They're safe at home... I left Chellie in charge, but she's insisted on making some vegetarian thing for dinner, so the boys weren't exactly thrilled about that...'

'What about the baby?'

'Nessa's fine. I fed her, changed her, and put her to bed as soon as we got home... You know, she cried the whole way back, so she's completely exhausted, and she'll probably sleep for hours... but if she doesn't, Chellie can take care of her.'

'Are you sure? You know she still resents her.'

'Hey, give your daughter a little credit... she'll be fine.' Mr Henderson then walked over to where Alicia lay on the couch, still pretending to sleep. 'So let's see if we can get this one home as well.' He gently scooped Alicia from the couch, and then, with quiet, steady strides, carried her toward the main exit. But as he made his way down the corridor, he could feel the air become heavy, almost liquid, as if he were walking through water. Then the air seemed to thicken until it was like pushing against a wall of foam rubber. He leaned hard into it.

'Honey,' he whispered, 'look at this! This is amazing!'

Dr Henderson, who had walked ahead with no difficulty, turned around to see her husband leaning forward at an impossible angle.

'Gil,' she said, her frustration tinged with fear, 'If you're going to pull a stunt like that, at least put our daughter down first.'

'I'm not kidding, it's like I'm leaning on something solid!'

'Dad,' said Alicia, as her father put her down, 'it's like I already told Mom... I can't leave... I have to stay near George.'

Mr Henderson kept his hand on her shoulder, even as he continued to lean into the invisible force, but as soon as he let go of her, he crashed to the floor. He quickly jumped back to his feet, his eyes wide with amazement. 'Wow, it's gone now, but it was so *real*, so solid! What the hell was that?'

Chapter Four

A New World

'Hey kid, how're you doing?' George heard a man's voice. He blinked hard against the bright light, and for just a moment, he wondered if this was another dream.

In fact, the night before, he had experienced a rather frightening nightmare where he kept getting pushed up against the bars of the fence outside his school, even as terrified nurses and doctors tried to hold him down onto a bed that was being dragged across the floor.

Dream or not, he still felt a little bruised from that incident.

As George's eyes slowly adjusted, he could see that he was indeed in a bed. One with the most peculiar sort of heavy railings on either side of it, and he wondered if these were the railings he had been thrown against the night before. But there was new and more immediate mystery before him: Strangers, a man and a woman, standing at the foot of the bed. He suddenly felt alone and exposed, but when saw Alicia standing at the side of the bed, he felt a rush of relief.

'Hi George' she said 'Are you feeling any better?'

'I-I do have a rather beastly headache,' he replied slowly, 'but otherwise, I am well... I suppose.'

'George,' said Alicia, 'this is my mom and dad, and these are my brothers Matt and Simon Toliver.'

George hadn't noticed the two boys standing at the other side of the bed at first. One was taller and looked to be about a year older than Alicia, while George thought the other boy was probably only about seven.

'So, you're a bit of a mystery around here,' her father said, 'even though Alicia seems to know you... Is your name really George?'

'Yes,' he answered hesitantly, 'Stryder... George Stryder.'

'Do you remember what happened?' asked Alicia's mother. 'You've had a bad bump,' she added, 'a concussion, but luckily no sign of a subdural haematoma.'

'I told you my mom's a doctor,' said Alicia, 'so she talks like that a lot.'

'Are my parents here?' asked George, 'I would very much like to see them now.'

'Oh, George,' Dr Henderson answered, somewhat hesitantly, 'dear... there was no sign of them.'

'Where am I?'

'You're in Children's Hospital,' replied Mr Henderson, 'in Vancouver.'

'How... how... did I get here?'

'We brought you here,' said Dr Henderson, 'after we found you on the beach.'

'I told you that already,' said Alicia, 'don't you remember?'

'Memory problems,' said Dr Henderson, 'are to be expected when you've had a bit of a bump to your head.' She smiled at George reassuringly. 'So, to test for that, we usually ask people if they know what the date is, or if they know who the Prime Minister is.'

'I'm not entirely sure of the date, but everyone knows that Neville Chamberlain's the Prime Minister,' said George, yet when the Hendersons looked surprised, he added, 'Oh, sorry. Did you mean the Prime Minister of Canada? I'm afraid I don't know who he is.'

'Do you know the year?' Dr Henderson asked, looking a little more worried.

'It's 1939, of course,' said George, surprised by such a silly question.

'I'm sure you're just a little confused,' said Dr Henderson. 'You just need some more time to rest. Why don't you try to get some more sleep?'

'No thanks,' he replied, 'I feel as though I've been asleep far too long as it is.'

In fact, although George's mind felt thick and strange, and he was deeply tired, the last thing he wanted to do was sleep. He wanted to shake off this fatigue, get back to reality, and find his parents.

Dr Henderson looked unconvinced, but then Mr Henderson said, 'we're just going to go and see if there's any news about your parents... so you kids'll be okay for a minute or two?'

'Yeah, dad, of course,' said Matt.

'I do hope,' said George, 'that there's good news. I should very much like to see my mum and dad soon.'

'Oh, and kid,' Mr Henderson quickly added, 'you might want to keep that stuff about 1939 and Neville Chamberlin to yourself. Some people might get the wrong idea.'

'Yeah,' agreed Alicia, 'it *is* pretty freaky.'

'I don't understand,' said George, turning to Alicia as her parents left the room, 'is it 1940 already... was I out that long?'

'Like, seriously, dude, this is the twenty-first century,' laughed Matt, 'does this look like 1940 to you?'

Indeed, as George looked around, he realized that almost nothing was familiar. However, he had never actually been in a hospital back home, so how was he to know? Perhaps all hospitals looked like this, or maybe it was just the hospitals in Canada that looked this alien. Some sort of colonial quirk, he thought. Yes, that must be it. Ever so much more believable than being thrown an entire lifetime into the future.

'Does that hurt?' Simon Toliver asked in a small voice, pointing to George's bandages.

'Well, as I said... I have a headache,' he replied, distractedly. 'It comes and goes, but it's not intolerable.'

'Hey, maybe it'll leave a scar,' said Matt, 'and it'll only hurt when your evil nemesis is near – that would be pretty wicked.'

'Mom said he probably wouldn't have a scar,' said Alicia, matter-of-factly.

Matt just rolled his eyes, and then, wanting to change the subject, asked George, 'so, like... what do you do for fun?'

'What do you mean?'

'I mean, what do you do for fun? Like, with your friends.'

'Nothing extraordinary, really,' replied George, 'I like to ride my bicycle, read books, play conkers...'

'What are conkers?' asked Alicia.

'It's a game,' said George, 'but you need to find a good solid one first...'

'But what *are* they?' Alicia asked again.

'They're horse chestnuts,' said Matt as he looked up from his phone. 'You tie them to the end of a string and try to bash the other guy's conker without breaking yours. Actually looks pretty cool... you know... in a primitive sort of way.'

'What's that?' asked George, pointing to Matt's phone.

'This?' Matt asked casually, brimming with pride that someone had noticed his most recent acquisition. 'It's the latest in human connectivity,' he said, quoting the manufacturer's slogan.

Alicia rolled her eyes in exaggerated frustration, 'it's just a stupid phone.'

'This is way more than just a phone!' said Matt, defensively, 'this is the coolest smart phone around. It has 256 gigs of ram, 20 meg cameras back *and* front – capable of full 4K-res. It's totally 5G ready for massively multiplayer games – has 750 ppi resolution, full voice recognition, and, like, millions of available apps.' [2]

'Which is kinda stupid,' said Alicia, 'since the screen isn't even true 4K... and besides, the voice recognition software's garbage. Dad says that until they improve the ambient noise filtration, the dependant aps are totally useless.'

'Do you even know what that means?' snapped Matt.

'Of course I do,' sneered Alicia. 'It means your 'voice' texting makes you look like a complete moron.'

'I still don't understand,' said George. 'What is it... exactly?'

'It's just a phone,' replied Alicia, a little surprised. 'Like, seriously, haven't you ever seen a phone before?'

'You mean like a telephone?' asked George in complete disbelief. 'But it doesn't look anything *like* a telephone. Where's the cord,

---

[2] Back then, these were very impressive features indeed, even though they might seem primitive by today's standards.

where's the mouthpiece?'

'Phones haven't needed cords in, like, ages,' laughed Matt.

'But I've never seen such a thing,' said George, unable to take his eyes off the unfamiliar device's colourfully glowing screen.

'Then how do you talk with your friends?' asked Matt.

'When I see them, I talk with them, and if they're not there, I don't.'

'That's what I do,' said Simon Toliver, 'I don't talk to my friends when they're not there, either.'

'Well, duh,' said Matt, 'it'd be pretty creepy if you did, since you don't have your own phone yet.'

'But, don't you want to keep in touch,' Alicia asked George, 'like, with your friends?'

'I have a few mates at school, but no one I'd go out of my way to talk with when they're not there.'

'Your mates? You live on a pirate ship or something?' joked Matt as Alicia rolled her eyes once more.

'However,' said George, 'that still doesn't explain how you just found out about conkers using your telephone. I certainly didn't hear you talking with anyone else.'

'He just searched the 'Net,' said Alicia. 'Here, I'll show you.'

'Hey,' protested Matt, 'I thought mom and dad said you couldn't have your own smart phone until you're twelve.'

But Alicia ignored him as she pulled something out of her backpack. The device reminded George of a large scallop shell.

'Ooo,' said Matt, mockingly, 'a Princess of the Sea™ laptop… '

'Oh grow up,' snapped Alicia, 'it's just one I'm testing for dad… some movie tie-in, or something.' When she opened the device, the inside was an eye-straining pink, and inside it, George could see rows of buttons that looked vaguely like the keys on a typewriter. Then, when Alicia pushed one of the buttons, the upper half of the clamshell came to life, and an animated mermaid rose out of an azure blue sea on its screen. It was a scene that reminded George somewhat of Botticelli's 'Birth of Venus', but then that image dissolved to black, and a new scene appeared, a sunset over the ocean.

'Blimey... what is that?' he whispered in amazement.

'I took that the night before I found you on the beach,' said Alicia, always pleased when people admired her photography.

'Hey Bright Bulb,' said Matt, 'he means the whole thing. You've never seen a computer before, have you?'

'Well... perhaps... My mum was going to be a computer... at the War Office... but I've never seen a computing *machine* before.'

'What do you mean your mom was going to be a computer?' Alicia asked in complete disbelief. 'People aren't computers, like, only computers are computers.'

'Of course people are computers,' replied George, a little surprised. 'By definition, someone who does calculations, someone who computes, is a computer. Certainly no machine can do complex calculations as well as a human can.'

'Oh wow, you really are from another century, aren't you?' laughed Matt. 'Even that stupid mermaid laptop can do more calculations per second than any human ever could.'

'You're telling me that thing can think?' George asked in disbelief.

'Of course not,' said Alicia. 'No computer can think... well at least not this type... I guess the human ones can, but then I've never really thought of people as computers before.'

Simon Toliver was sitting on the floor quietly playing with one of his small toy cars. 'I'm a computer,' he said without ever looking up.

'Well, that's because you're a freak,' said Matt.

'You mean you *have* a computer,' Alicia corrected her little brother.

'No, I *am* a computer. I can come up with all the answers you want, beep-beep,' he said as he began to make noises like a robot in an old science fiction movie.

'So what sort of complex maths,' asked George, 'could you possibly be doing, for which you would need your very own computing machine?'

'Nobody calls it a *computing machine*, it's just a computer, and I don't use it for math... well, not unless I'm doing homework,' said Alicia. 'Like, seriously, a computer can do all kinds of different things. I use mine to play games, or get new music, but mostly I use it to link up with my friends. Oh… and I also use it to organize my pictures and make slide shows and stuff.' She touched the screen and more images appeared, glowing on the screen. 'For instance, these are the photos I took last week.'

'That's brilliant!' remarked George.

'You think that's cool? Watch this,' she touched the screen again, and the display changed to show the home page of Wikipedia.

'Whoa,' said Matt as he came closer to get a better look, 'that's supposed to be a totally walled computer, like for little kids. How'd you unlock it so fast without bricking it?'

'Actually,' replied Alicia, clearly pleased with herself, 'it was a pretty easy hack – the OS has an exploitable app that's just supposed to be for updates, but I got around the code pretty easy…'

'Impressive,' said Matt, in genuine admiration for his sister's skills.

'That's why,' added Alicia, 'dad's gonna give the company a failing grade on their new kids' platform.'

'I'm sorry,' said George, 'I don't understand any of what you're saying.'

'Well,' said Alicia, 'I help test the little kids' computers for my dad's company, and this one was pretty easy to break.'

'But it doesn't look broken.'

'Nah, I only crack the software, the programming… so the client company knows that they have to make the computer safer for kids.'

'Why?' asked George, 'is there some risk of electrocution?'

'No,' said Alicia, trying hard not to laugh, 'it's just that the 'Net can be kinda dangerous for little kids to surf.'

'The net? What do you mean… like a fishing net?'

'No, not *a* net, *the* 'Net… like the Internet… just think of it as like all the information in the whole world available in one place… but of course, a lot of the stuff out there isn't safe for little kids to see… so I test these things first, because I'm way more careful than little kids.'

'Yeah, right,' laughed Matt, 'you mean 'careful' like the time you gave your BFF your password? After that big fight you had, she made you look pretty stupid with some of the stuff she posted.'

'No way!' snapped Alicia, 'That was so totally last year!'

'You both realize,' said George, 'that I'm still not following any of this?'

'Oh... it's complicated,' said Alicia, embarrassed by the turn the conversation had taken. 'Anyway, I just wanted to show you some of the cool things a computer can do... like, here's something... it's a game I like to play – you can join in, if you want.'

Fascinated by the new experience, George joined Matt and Alicia as they spent the next hour or so in a virtual world of blocks, where they worked together to build stockades to keep out mobs of animated zombies. Simon Toliver, however, continued to play alone on the floor, beeping like a computer from the imaginary past.

Meanwhile, their parents were out in the corridor, talking with the police and a social worker or two, when eventually, Mr Henderson's voice could be heard to rise in growing frustration.

'Look, the kid needs a place to stay, so what's the problem?' Someone tried to get him to lower his voice. 'Oh don't shush me, I'm sure the kids have heard every word anyway, and frankly, they should have as much say in this as anyone.' He leaned into the room and added, 'Hey, George, you wanna get out of this hospital and come stay with us, at least until your parents get here?'

'Yes,' said George, 'yes please!'

'And you kids, how do you feel about that?'

'That'd be cool,' said Matt.

'That computes,' said Simon Toliver.

'Yeah, of course,' said Alicia, but then mumbled, 'like, that's the only way I'm gonna get home, anyway.'

'There,' Mr Henderson said to the unseen people in the corridor, 'What more do you want?'

That evening in the hospital, George's dinner tray had on it a lump of something Mr Henderson guessed was probably supposed to be tuna casserole. 'Whoa, kid, why don't I order in some pizza instead?' He then pulled out his phone, 'What do you want on yours?'

'I'm sorry,' said George, 'I'm not really sure what pizza is...

precisely.'

'Seriously, kid? You don't know pizza? I've been in London a few times, and they had pizza joints all over the place.'

'Daaad,' said Alicia, rolling her eyes as if to say parents can be so dumb sometimes, 'things were different back when George lived there.' She then turned to George, 'so, it's basically a flat bread with all kinds of good stuff on it, like cheese and ham and pineapple and stuff.'

'All right, I'll trust your judgment on that,' said George, looking once again at the unappetizing lump on his tray, 'but isn't it a dreadful waste of perfectly good food?'

'Nah,' said Mr Henderson, 'anyway, I don't think that really counts as food... perfectly good, or otherwise.'

It wasn't long before the pizza arrived, and since George was very hungry, he tried a slice from each of the two different boxes that Mr Henderson had ordered; one called 'Ham & Pineapple' which sounded terribly exotic, and one called 'Meat Lovers Madness', which sounded quite peculiar, but was otherwise rather delicious. To his great surprise, it was the more exotic ham & pineapple that he enjoyed the most, and so he politely asked for another slice.

'We don't stand on ceremony here, kid; just help yourself,' said Mr Henderson, and then, after taking a few bites of his own slice, he added, 'So... kid... Alicia seems to know an awful lot about you... I mean, even before you were awake. So, what gives... how is that possible?'

'It's okay,' said Alicia, 'Dad's pretty cool... you can tell him.'

'Um, well... sir...'

'Whoa, kid, you're not in the army here; call me Gil... or Mr H, or even Mr Henderson, if you prefer, but please don't call me sir.'

'Sorry, s... Mr Henderson,' George stammered, 'I really don't remember much.'

'Well, how come Alicia knew your name before you were awake?'

'It was in a dream, Dad,' said Alicia. 'I met George in a dream. We were in a garden... like, I mean, an actual real old fashioned walled garden, with trees and flowers and stuff.'

'Wow... really?' Mr Henderson raised an eyebrow in disbelief.

'It's true,' added George, 'but I think it was all too real to just be a dream... but, then again, I suppose that there's really no other way of explaining it.'

'You see, Dad,' Alicia began, 'when I found George on the beach, it was like a tornado came and carried me away, and then I was, like, in this big fancy garden, and George was there...'

'Kind of like the 'Wizard of Oz',' mumbled Mr Henderson to himself, but neither George nor Alicia seemed to notice.

'And then we were in India,' said George, 'in Bombay.'

'Right, but that was later, like after we got you to the hospital...'

'Really, because to me, it seemed like just a moment later...'

'Whoa... really?' asked Alicia. 'Like, when we met up again, I didn't realize that it was like no time had passed for you...'

'Well, I wouldn't say *no time*,' replied George. 'I did find myself alone in the garden briefly... but then, before I could even turn around, I was in India with you...'

'Damn,' said Mr Henderson, 'I don't believe it.'

'No, seriously, Dad, that's really what happened...'

'Sorry Allie,' said Mr Henderson, looking up from his phone, 'I'm going to have to go... the order-processing servers are down in Philadelphia.' He then turned to George, 'Look, you two have some wild imaginations... but keep all this to yourselves, okay? Otherwise, people will think you're nuts... and if they think that, then they won't let you out of this place.'

'But, sir, it's the truth.'

'Kid, it's only because my wife is a doctor that she was able to convince the staff here that you'd be okay to come stay with us.'

'Dad,' said Alicia, a little hesitantly, 'what *about* mom? Like, even when you were leaning against that invisible wall, she acted like it wasn't real.'

'Really... I did what now?' asked her dad, but before Alicia could recount the incident, he added, 'I guess that sometimes it's just easier if we ignore the things we don't understand... Anyway... I really have to go,' he said as he quickly grabbed another slice of pizza. 'You'll be okay 'til your mom gets here?' he asked as he headed for the door, not waiting for an answer.

Chapter Five

The Lost Letters

George yawned, stretched, and lay in bed as he listened to the unfamiliar birdsong outside. The Hendersons had given him a room on the top floor of their house, and while it was very comfortable, with a wonderful view of their big backyard, it just wasn't the same as being at home in his own room.

He closed his eyes, and for just a moment, he could almost convince himself that he was back home in London. He could imagine his mother downstairs, preparing the family breakfast, while his father read the morning paper, just as they always had. But no matter how much he wished to go back, he couldn't seem to make it happen.

He missed his parents terribly, and he wondered if they were safe, and if they were worried about him. He knew that he would have to find them, but he didn't know how, or even where he would start, but he knew he had to do whatever he could. So, with fresh determination, he got out of bed, but had to slow down when a painful twinge in his right shoulder forced him to move more carefully.

He looked around the room. Beside the bed was a small pile of clothes and on top was a note from Matt that read, 'Hope there's something here you can use.' These are some rather peculiar clothes, George thought. There was a pair of faded trousers with ragged holes in the knees that had a large manufacturer's label, which nobody had bothered to remove, that said something about being 'designer jeans', whatever that meant. There were also some canvas trousers that were too long to be called short pants, but too short to be proper trousers, and they also had a very large manufacturer's label, but this one read; 'Sharkfood™ Surf Wear' – and he had no idea what that meant, either.

Perhaps Matt was playing a joke on him, he thought, but then again, maybe the Hendersons had fallen on hard times, and these ragged old clothes were all that they had to spare. In either case, he decided that it would safer to play along with the joke, rather than risk offending the family's generosity.

First, he put on the canvas trousers, since they looked less ragged than the 'designer jeans' did, and then put on a faded Madras shirt, which he carefully buttoned to the top and tucked neatly into the short trousers. Next, he pulled on a clean pair of white socks and a pair of heavy black sandals. Then, as he looked at himself in the mirror he thought, with some grim satisfaction, that at least now nobody would be able to tell that he didn't belong in this strange new world.

It was still very early when George went downstairs for breakfast, and only Mr Henderson was there, sitting by the window, feeding the baby. 'Hey, kid, hope the room was okay.'

'Uh, yes… it's very nice. Thank you.'

'Glad to hear it,' said Mr Henderson as he prepared to burp the baby, 'just help yourself to cereal in the cupboard by the fridge.'

'This cupboard?'

Mr Henderson nodded, then after a moment, said, 'look, I don't know what happened… how you got separated from your parents, or how you got so banged-up… but if you ever want to talk about it, I'm here for you… and until your parents show up, you have a home here. I want you to know that.' The baby fussed, and Mr Henderson returned his attention to her, but after a moment, added, 'oh, and there's going to be someone from immigration coming to talk with you this morning, but nothing to worry about.'

However, George didn't pay attention, as he was too distracted trying to figure out how to open the plastic milk jug.

'You really aren't from around here, are you?' Mr Henderson chuckled as he reached over and peeled away the security tab.

'Frank Erlanger,' said the man whom Mr Henderson greeted at the front door. When George first saw him, he thought that the man looked rather haggard, like someone who was much older than his years.

After brief introductions, they went back into the kitchen, where Mr Erlanger sat down, and said nothing for a moment as he looked at George over the top of his wire-framed glasses. He then opened a small laptop and typed a few things, and then looked at George again.

'Well, you're quite the celebrity now, aren't you?' he said as he began his interview.

'Sorry, I don't understand,' replied George, 'why would I be a celebrity?'

'We've tried,' Mr Henderson quickly answered, 'to keep the media out of this... we figured George has enough to deal with.'

'Ah,' said Erlanger as he typed something more, and then looked pointedly at George. 'Well... George, is it? I need to find out more about you. After all, a mysterious boy who washes up on a beach with no sign of his parents anywhere,' the immigration man said with the hint of a smirk. 'That's the sort of stuff that the media thrives on... and then the rumours that you claim to be from 1939. A real cry for attention, that.'

'I think that someone must have misheard,' said Mr Henderson, 'The number was part of an address, or something like that, not the year... Isn't that right George?'

'Uh, yes... I must have been trying to remember my address... or something,' said George, as he noticed Mr Henderson visibly relax.

'Ah,' said Erlanger as he typed in a few more things, 'Well, George, could you tell me your full name and address now?'

'Yes, of course... my name is Stryder... Arthur George Edward Stryder, and my address is... was,' George stammered, knowing that the lie about 1939 was about to be exposed, but he didn't know what else to say. 'My address is 148 Auriol Road, Hammersmith... in London.'

'Ah,' said Erlanger, 'Really... I thought...'

'The boy got bashed in the head pretty hard,' said Mr Henderson as he rested his hand on George's shoulder, 'so he's bound to have some confusion.'

'Uh-huh,' said Erlanger, 'And I suppose that you're a doctor, then?'

'No, he isn't,' said Dr Henderson as she came into the kitchen, 'but I am, and my husband is quite correct, the boy has had a considerable blow to his head, to his right temporal lobe, in fact, and that can muddle memory, even distort his perception of time.'

'Ah,' said Erlanger as he examined the screen of his computer more closely, 'I didn't see that part of your file. Yes, there you are... a doctor indeed. Well, I think that will be all for now.'

'I can go?' asked George with considerable relief.

'Oh... no,' said Erlanger, 'you and I still have a lot to talk about, but Mr and Mrs... ah, *Doctor* Henderson, it's probably best if George and I speak alone.'

Mr Henderson clenched his jaw and seemed to be fighting the urge to say something, while Dr Henderson made a point of ignoring the man. 'George,' she said, 'if you need me, I'll just be in my office.' She then turned to go, but when her husband didn't follow, she added, 'Gil, didn't you have a conference call scheduled a few minutes from now... something about the Philly outage?'

'Right,' said Mr Henderson, trying hard not to glare at the immigration man, 'I'd better see to that... but George, if you need anything, just call.' But before he left, Mr Henderson added, 'sorry kid, but bureaucrats live on data, and if you don't feed them what they want, when they want it, they'll just come back when you're not looking, and eat you alive to get it anyway.'

Mr Erlanger watched over the top of his glasses as Mr Henderson left the room, and when he was sure that both they were gone, he turned his attention back to George. 'So, what can you tell me about your parents?'

'My father,' George stammered ever so slightly, 'my father is a researcher ... some ministry or another... and my mum works for the Bodleian Library... well... that is, she did, but when my dad was transferred to London, she had to resign.'

'Uh-huh,' said Erlanger, as he typed. 'Do you have a passport or visa?'

'Um... no... at least, I don't think so.'

'Hmm,' said Erlanger, 'and what is your citizenship, and that of your parents?'

'British.'

'All of you?'

'Yes.'

'Do you have any documentation to support your claim?'

'Well... no... I'm afraid that I don't...'

'Are you aware of the immigration status that your parents may have applied for?'

'Um... no...'

George was never quite sure what Erlanger really wanted, but the interview continued for almost an hour, and so he was very relieved when the man finally closed his computer, and indicated that he was done.

'Well, I'm glad that's over,' said Dr Henderson after she saw him out the door.

'So am I,' agreed George. 'Bit of a bureaucratic blighter, really.'

'I suppose he is,' she said, 'but he's just doing his job, *and* as annoying as he is, I think he just has your best interest at heart.'

'I didn't realize that he had a heart,' replied George, which made Dr Henderson laugh.

'Has anyone told you that you have a very grownup way of talking?' she asked.

'No,' said George, 'not that I recall.'

'Well, it just makes you sound like a very old soul, that's all.' She smiled at him and then added, 'Alicia is out in the backyard working in her garden. Why don't you run and her fetch her in, so the two of you can have lunch together.'

Later, in the heat of the afternoon, Alicia pulled a couple of frozen pops from the refrigerator and suggested that they sit on the front steps in the shade.

It was the first time that George had a really good look at the outside of the Henderson house. It was a grand old shingle-style building, nearly a century old, and nothing like his house in Auriol Road. The house in London had been the smallest on the street, a forgotten little building jammed between grander homes, but the Henderson house had an unmistakeable presence on the street.

'So… you like it?' asked Alicia.

'It really is rather impressive.'

'Mom and Dad said you could stay as long as you need to.'

'I'm ever so grateful, but I would much rather be back with my own parents.'

'Yeah… well I'm not really sure how that's going to work.'

'What on earth are you talking about?'

'I mean,' said Alicia, 'haven't you noticed that we're stuck together? Like, ever since I found you on the beach, if I get too far away, it's like I'm running into a wall.'

'Don't be absurd. What on earth do you mean?'

'You were in the hospital for three days. Didn't you wonder why I never left, why I never went home?'

'I… I just assumed that you were worried about me.'

'Look, George, it's not like I don't care, but I'm not so crazy about you that I'd stick around for three days. I was totally stuck there, and every time I tried to go home with my parents… I couldn't.'

'Why didn't you mention this before?' he asked.

'Dad told me not to,' she hesitated, 'Seriously, I think he and Mom know something, but they're not saying…'

'The idea that we're stuck together simply makes no sense.'

'Okay, then,' Alicia said, crossing her arms defiantly, 'if you don't believe me, why don't you try running away – let's see how far you can get.'

George said nothing, but shook his head in disbelief as he walked out to the front sidewalk. Whatever it was that she was playing at, he thought, he'd soon put it to rest. He began to trot, and then to run, up the street.

The huge silver maples offered some protection from the hot sun, but soon the heat, the humidity and a persistent ache in his shoulder caused him to slow down. Then, just as he was starting to think how pointless this whole exercise was, his legs began to feel as if they were getting heavier, while the air in front of him seemed to be getting thicker. With great difficulty, he found that he could push against it and still move forward, but when he turned around, he saw Alicia buffeted as if he were pushing her directly. He laughed at her struggle to resist, and leaned back as he called out, 'so this is what you were talking about?'

In a burst of angry inspiration, she ran toward him, and it was with some satisfaction that she watched as he lost his balance and fell back. He landed badly on his right side, and struggled to get back up.

'What the deuce was that?' he asked as she approached.

'That,' she replied, 'was what I was talking about.' However, her sense of triumph soon vanished when she saw how pale and unsteady he was. 'Come on, I think my mom had better have a look at you.'

Dr Henderson was not pleased. She shone a light in George's eyes and asked if he felt like he was going to be sick. When she was satisfied with his answers, she put away her doctor's kit.

'I know that it's summer,' she said, 'but George, you need to take it easy. You're still recovering from a concussion, so even little bumps can make it worse. And as for you, Alicia, I want you to stay with him and let me know right away if he starts feeling dizzy or sick.'

'But mom...'

Her mother gave Alicia a look that said enough that she didn't bother to argue the point. Reluctantly, she then led George into the great-room, where she flopped down on one of the big sofas, picked up a magazine and said nothing in protest.

The great-room occupied most of the back of the house, and was a full two storeys high. In the northwest corner, a spiral staircase led up to an interior balcony that overlooked the main area below, while in the southwest corner, a baby grand piano stood surrounded by a number of very comfortable looking seats and a rather large kentia palm. The southern wall was filled with windows that extended from floor to ceiling, while the eastern wall was open to the dining room and kitchen. All the other walls, it seemed to George, were covered in bookcases. It reminded him of a music hall, a library and a rather grand sitting room, all rolled into one, and he had never seen anything quite like it before.

Alicia continued to ignore him as she thumbed through the pages of an old geographic magazine.

'This really is a rather grand place,' said George, as he looked around at the impressive room.

'Yeah, well, so what do you want to do?' she asked, a little petulantly.

'So many books...'

'Knock yourself out,' she said, feeling less than generous at having yet another beautiful summer day taken away from her, so she didn't bother to explain all the many options for entertainment the room contained.

'So your mum stayed home from her surgery today?' he asked, trying to change the subject.

'No,' said Alicia, 'Mom's retired – she said that if she was going to waste what little energy she had left, she wanted to waste it with us.' She paused, and when George said nothing, she asked, 'so, what do your parents do?'

'Well, my mum was going to work at the War Office... but when my father's contract with the Council was terminated, he said we should leave England altogether... so I suppose it would be fair to say that they were both redundant when I was last with them.' He paused, and then asked, 'so what does your father do?'

'Dad was a systems developer, like, way before I was born, but then there was this crash he always calls the dot-bomb, and so he decided to give up, and just be a stay-at-home dad when Chella was born. But then he started to blog about being a stay-at-home dad, and then he started reviewing software and hardware as well... but then things just kinda took off, and his blog turned into a company, and then it kept growing. And since my dad runs the whole thing from his study, he's always around... and now that my mom's quit her job at the hospital, she's always here, too... So, with my parents always around, it's like I have no freedom anymore.'

'I suppose,' said George, 'but it's better than not having them around at all.'

'Sorry... I didn't mean,' Alicia said, suddenly feeling rather awkward. Then, after a long pause, she said, 'okay, so it's all a big mystery what happened to you and your parents, right? So let's look at the clues.'

'What do you mean... what clues?'

'I don't know, but there must be something.' She thought for a moment more, 'do you still have your stuff... like the clothes you were wearing when I found you?'

'Yes... but I can't imagine that there's anything useful there.'

'Look, if we have to stay inside, we might as well do what we can to find out what happened, and your clothes are a good place to start.'

George quickly retrieved what was left of his old clothes and returned to the great room. Together they emptied all the pockets and found a few wads of paper, a sticky mass that had probably been a lemon drop or two, a rusted pocketknife, and a small wooden box.

The box was curious, very old, and appeared to be hand-hewn from a single piece of wood. The lid had swollen closed with seawater, but George was able to carefully pry it open, and was surprised to find a gold pocket watch inside.

He took it out of the box and flipped the watch open and it chimed softly. 'It's still running!' he said as he checked it against the clock on the wall, 'and it's still keeping time.'

'May I see it?' Alicia turned the little watch over in her hands, and as she did, the back sprang open, exposing the inner mechanical workings, which were protected from dust by a glass crystal. Then she noticed an engraving on the inside cover, which she read aloud; "For Ages, For All Time'... what do you think that means?'

'I honestly haven't the foggiest notion.'

She handed the watch back to George, and once again, it chimed as he touched it. He looked carefully at the inscription.

'Actually it says 'For A. G. E. S., for all time'. Those are certainly my initials, so I suppose it must be mine,' he then looked at the newly exposed inner workings, 'and this doesn't look like any watch I've ever seen before.' He closed the back and opened the front again, only to see a completely different watch-face. 'That is really most peculiar.'

The watch face glowed a faint blue, and then above it, out of thin air, a scroll of paper unrolled and floated in front of them. But when George tried to touch it, his fingers passed right through the page.

'Wow,' said Alicia, 'it's a hologram.'

'A hollow what?'

'A hologram – like, you know, a 3D picture... but this one looks totally real.'

Then, as if written by an invisible hand, a message appeared.

'It's a letter... and it's addressed to me!' George could hardly contain his excitement as he began to read aloud.

'London, 31st October, 1939

My Dearest Boy,

I am hoping with all my heart that this letter finds you safe and well. I have been searching frantically for both you and your mother for days now, so when you receive this letter, please write back as soon as you possibly can, and let me know that you are safe.

My scans tell me that your 'node is still active, so I can only hope that you are safely with your mother. The readings are confusing, however, as the time and geo-locator signatures make no sense...'

Before George could read any more, the letter vanished. 'No!' he shouted, 'I hadn't finished!'

'Hadn't finished what?' asked Matt as he came into the room.

'Oh go away,' said Alicia.

George frantically opened and closed the watch, hoping to make the letter appear once more. Matt caught a glimpse of the strange little watch, and he marvelled at how it kept changing its face; one moment glowing a faint green with peculiar symbols, then the next turning yellow, and then, finally, the watch-face returned to blue and a paper scroll began to unfurl out of thin air.

'Whoa, that is so totally wicked! What is that thing?

'It's George's pocket watch.'

'No way - that thing's way more than just a watch!'

George carefully placed the watch on the coffee table, hoping not to disturb it so that he could finish reading his father's letter before it disappeared again. But this was an entirely new letter...

'London, 24th December, 1939

My Dearest Boy,

It is Christmas Eve now, and I am still waiting to hear from you and your mother. I am hoping that you are together. Scattered reports suggest that more than a few survivors made it to New York, as several lifeboats were recovered by American vessels, and so it is my dearest hope that you and your mother may yet be found there.

I have been conscripted by The Council once again, and so find myself bound to their service here in London, and can do little else in my search but write letters and wait for your reply.

The Council has arranged reasonable accommodation for me in Saint James Square, and while the flat is little more than a servant's loft, it's comfortable enough, and has sufficient space for all of us when you return.

I've settled in for the war ahead and...'

Once again, the letter disappeared. George reached for the watch at the same time as Matt and Alicia did, and as their hands collided, red and blue sparks spiralled around all three of them.

Chapter Six

London Calling

George looked around, and felt a massive wave of relief. He was home, in Auriol Road, in Hammersmith, in the London of his memory.

As he watched, men in heavy woolen overcoats and flat caps strode along the street purposefully, while mothers walked with their children, and tradesmen pedalled their bicycles down the road. It all seemed so very familiar, and yet at the same time, so very strange. As it had been in India, the people were surrounded by blurs of where they had been, and where they were going, which was not at all how he remembered his neighbourhood being. For just a moment, he had the impression of looking at old photographs, where the people had moved before the camera had finished capturing their images.

'No... way... no freakin' way,' Matt said as he held his hands to his head and turned around.

'Oh Matt, get a grip,' said Alicia, wanting to hide her own excitement. She had always insisted that the things she and George had experienced were only dreams, but now that Matt was there with them, it all seemed so much closer to reality.

As Matt tried desperately to get his cell phone to pick up a signal, and Alicia marveled at the blurring crowds of people, George turned to see the ghostly image of a small brick townhouse standing over a smoking pile of rubble. The houses on either side still stood, but only as burned-out shells of their former selves.

'George, where do you think we are now?' asked Alicia, but when he didn't answer, she turned to look at him. 'George, hey... are you all right?'

'This was my house... this is where we lived,' he trembled ever so slightly as he spoke, 'I was just thinking about coming back here... My mum, my dad... what if they were here when this happened?'

'But didn't your dad's letter say he'd found a new place?' Alicia took his hand and squeezed it, 'Oh, George... I don't think they were here.'

'Right... of course...'

'What happened... where is this?' asked Matt, as he gave up trying to text his friends.

'This,' George answered quietly, 'this was where I lived with my parents... I must say... it's a dreadful wrench to see it like this.'

'Does somebody have it in for you and your family?' Matt asked as he looked over the pile of rubble.

'No,' said George, fighting to control the tremor in his voice. 'My mum and dad, they used to talk about the coming war... they would talk in whispers and thought that I didn't hear them, but I did... Yet I never thought... I didn't think it would happen... not really... not like this.'

'But how did we get here, anyway?' asked Matt, 'like seriously.'

'It's a long story,' said Alicia, knowingly, even though the truth was, she didn't know any better than anyone else did. But then she thought of something. 'All right... George, so you wanted to start looking for your parents... I think that's exactly what we're doing. I think you brought us here somehow, kind of like you did before.'

'What? Me? I don't see how I could have... perhaps it's the watch... I think that makes more sense.'

'Sense? Dude, speak for yourself,' Matt said, 'none of this makes any sense.'

'Okay,' said Alicia, 'so what do we know? We know that your dad mentioned that he'd found a new place here in London.'

'Yes... I suppose... but he wrote about things I have no memory of... something about a ship sinking and that he was looking for my mum and me... so if he says that my mum's still missing... what if she was here... alone... when this happened?'

'Hey, this is weird,' said Matt, 'have either of you noticed that the people here are all blurry… and… like, I don't think they can see us!'

'Seriously, Matt? Do you mind? Right now we're trying to find out what happened to George's parents.' Alicia turned back to George, 'I don't think she was here. Look, we know that your dad said he's still looking for your mom, right? And I bet this would have been the first place he would have looked.'

'Yes… I suppose you're right.'

'Seriously, you two, this is freakin' weird! Nobody can see us!'

Alicia said nothing, as she was secretly enjoying the sight of her older brother nearly panicking in a situation that she had almost become accustomed to herself.

'Right, that does it,' said George, 'we daren't stop here. We simply must find my mum and dad. Where did the letter say he was, again?'

'James… Saint James something,' said Alicia as she tried her best to remember.

'Well, St James covers a rather large area,' said George, 'I only wish I still had the watch so I could read the letter again.'

'What? This?' asked Matt, as he held out his hand.

'Yes!' George laughed with relief, 'thanks!' He took the watch back and flipped it open, 'I just wish I knew how to get that letter back.' The watch face, which had appeared green when he had first opened it, immediately changed to blue, and then the very letter he had wanted, unfurled right before their eyes.

… The Council has arranged reasonable accommodation for me in Saint James Square, and while the flat is little more than a servant's loft, it's comfortable enough…'

'Brilliant, but I'm not sure precisely where St James Square is,' said George, 'or have any idea how we might get there.'

The little watch chimed softly as if in reply, and the face changed from blue to green as a map of the neighbourhood unrolled in front of them. Then, a thin red line traced out a path: down the street toward Barons Court Station, up the line to Piccadilly Circus Station, and from there down a couple of short streets to Saint James Square.

'Oh, wow,' said Matt, 'pretty wicked app.'

'Yeah,' said Alicia, 'but how did you activate it?'

'I haven't the foggiest notion.'

'It's pretty obvious, isn't it? It uses voice commands,' said Matt, 'and since it only chimes when George touches it, it probably only responds to his voice.'

'You mean all I have to do is ask the watch for what I want?'

'Well, yeah, just don't make it too wordy, and it should work.'

Alicia was embarrassed that her brother might have worked out the puzzle of the watch before she had.

'But why did it shut off at the house before, even though George wasn't finished reading? Huh... why?'

'I don't know,' Matt shrugged, 'Maybe because he wasn't touching it at the time, I guess.'

'Actually,' said George, 'that makes a lot of sense... and, dash it all, I really do think that it *was* the watch that brought us here.'

'So how'd we get to India?' asked Alicia. 'You didn't have the watch then.'

'Well, yes... there *is* that little matter... so, really, we're back where we started... so to speak.'

'Whoa, what do you mean?' asked Matt as he looked from George to Alicia. 'What *about* India... when were you there?'

'Just the other day, really... I think,' said George, 'it would seem that I've been strutting around in time without the slightest idea of how I'm doing it...'

'Oh, wow,' said Alicia, 'you know, we should totally call it time *striding*... you know... 'cuz that's like your name and all.'

'Clever as that may be, it really doesn't matter what we call it,' said George, 'if we still don't know how.'

'I think it's the watch,' said Matt.

'And I agree,' said George.

'Well I don't,' insisted Alicia, 'I think it's you... I can just feel it.'

'Only one way to find out,' said Matt, 'let's test it.'

'Right you are,' said George as he held the watch out, 'grab hold, and I'll ask it to take us to St James Square.'

Matt and Alicia reached out to touch the closed watch, staring at one another, each daring the other to be wrong.

'Take us to St James Square,' said George as the watch chimed softly.

Nothing.

'Well... that was pointless.' said Alicia, with just a hint of triumph in her voice.

'...please?' added George.

'Maybe the watch has to be open to work,' Matt suggested.

George quickly flipped open the cover and spoke a little more deliberately, 'Take us to Saint James Square... please.'

The watch chimed softly, and its face glowed a faint green as the map appeared once again, and as before, a red line silently traced the route.

'Well, that was kinda useless,' said Matt, but then added, 'by the way... just wondering... If you guys have done this before... how did you get home again?'

'Um, well, it just sort of happens,' said Alicia, and then said suddenly, 'Okay, so what if this is a quest, and we have to do something or find something before we can go on to the next stage... or even go home?'

'Like a game? [3]' laughed Matt, 'Get serious, this is the real world!'

'Well, real or not, we're not getting anything done by standing around,' said George. 'One way or another, we might as well see what we can do.'

He closed the watch, took one last look at the smouldering ruins of his old house, turned, and then began to walk down the street.

'Um, George?' asked Alicia, 'Do you think we'll have enough time to do this? Like, I mean before we get swept away again.'

'We either do, or we don't, but we should at least try,' he replied.

Matt responded by imitating the voice and expression of one of his favourite characters from the movies. 'Do, or do not... there is no try.'

'That's a rather silly thing to say,' remarked George.

'It's not silly,' snapped Matt, 'Yoda's advice is totally wise.'

---

[3] Video games were an early form of interactive electronic entertainment that were the primitive forerunners of the ARIES (Alternate Reality Immersion Entertainment Systems).

'I beg to differ,' insisted George. 'I mean, it's just so dreadfully simplistic, really, isn't it? Why on earth would anyone...?'

'Seriously, dude,' Matt cut in, 'you can be such an old man sometimes.'

After a few minutes more, Matt turned to Alicia, 'what about mom and dad? This is freakin' amazing and all, but won't they miss us?'

'Nah, it doesn't work like that. It's like no time has passed when we get back.'

'Hah! Wicked excellent!'

Along the way, Matt couldn't help but comment on how old the cars looked; while George said that he thought the autos actually appeared to be reasonably new. However, Alicia didn't care about the cars at all, as she was too distracted watching for signs of the air shimmering or sparks flying.

It was only a few blocks to the Underground Station, a route that George knew well, so he stowed the watch in his pocket and didn't refer to it again.

When they reached the station, Alicia was uncomfortable with slipping past the ticket sellers.

'It's like we're invisible,' Matt laughed, 'do you seriously think we can *buy* a ticket?'

Alicia just rolled her eyes, and then followed George and Matt as they slipped under the turnstile and headed down the stairs, and then out onto the long Barons Court platform.

'Alright,' said George, 'we want the Piccadilly line, not the District line... oh do come on, Matt, we can't afford to get separated.'

'Sorry, it's just that it's so cool to see all this retro stuff.' Just then, a very large man crashed into him, and Matt was thrown so hard that he slammed face first into one of the metal pillars. The heavyset man stopped dead in his tracks, looking as though he had just seen a ghost, but then shook his head and continued on his way. However, Matt did not recover so quickly.

'Whoa, are you okay?' asked Alicia.

'Yeah,' said Matt, 'no big deal,' but then a telltale trickle of blood ran out of his nose. Alicia gave him some tissue, which he quickly jammed into his bloody nostrils.

'All right,' said George as he looked around, 'so despite the fact that people can't see us, it's not as if we're invulnerable.'

'You know,' said Matt, 'it felt totally weird, like the guy was made out of solid rock or something,' he said, impatiently brushing his sister away as she tried to inspect his injury more closely.

'Crikey,' said George, as he looked toward the tracks, 'I don't remember the trains ever going this fast.' While the station looked as he remembered it and the tracks next to the platform were clear and solid, the trains themselves were blurred to the point of being almost invisible.

'Well, this is stupid,' said Matt, 'like, how are we supposed to get on?'

'You know,' said Alicia, as she watched the people in the station very carefully, 'I don't think they're moving any faster than they usually do.' She continued to study the faded lines of people as they blended into the blur of the trains, and then, when she figured that the time was right, she jumped.

For just a moment, it looked to George and Matt as if she were standing in midair, suspended a foot or two above the tracks. She beckoned frantically, 'Come on – we don't have a lot of time!'

'Brilliant,' laughed George as he quickly followed.

'Are you guys nuts?' Matt asked, as he took the leap himself.

The interior of the train suddenly appeared as solid as the platform had been, and now it was the station that dissolved into a blur of motion.

'How did you know it was safe to go?' asked George.

'I noticed when someone walked in front of us,' Alicia tried to explain, in a single excited breath, 'that they looked more solid than someone walking *past* us. So, when I saw someone standing around waiting for the train, they looked pretty solid, but then they turned into blurs when they moved to get on the train. So I figured that if I followed someone, I could see when to get on the train.'

'Well I'll be a monkey's uncle,' laughed George, 'I didn't really follow that, but it was nonetheless bloomin' brilliant!'

'Yeah... well,' said Matt, reluctant to admit that his sister was capable of such cleverness, 'So how are we going to get off, huh? Now everything outside looks like a muddy smear, so like, it's totally impossible to see where the stations are.'

'If you'd bothered to look up,' said Alicia, defiantly pointing to the diagram of the Piccadilly Line above the carriage windows, 'then you'd have seen the map. I'm counting the times the doors open, and right now we've just left Earl's Court Station.'

'I must say,' said George as he looked at her with genuine admiration, 'I'd be pretty chuffed to have a sister like you,' but when he saw how angry she suddenly looked, he quickly added, 'chuffed... that's... that's a good thing... it's a new word, and I'd have thought it would've caught on by now.'

'What*ever*,' she said, dismissing him as she tried to suppress a smile, then continued with counting the number of times the doors opened, while Matt distractedly read the names of the stops marked out on the map. Suddenly, he could hardly contain himself.

'King's Cross Station! We totally gotta go there!'

'What's so dashed exciting about King's Cross Station?' asked George.

'Oh, it's something from a book Matt's been reading, but I think we should keep to where we're going.'

'Sometimes it's like you have no imagination, Allie,' said Matt. He then pulled out his phone and tried once again to send a text.

After a few minutes more, Alicia said, 'okay, I'm pretty sure that last stop was Green Park, so the next one's Piccadilly Circus... get ready...' She focused on a man in front of her, since she could see that he was starting to form a blur toward the door. 'Okay... GO!'

George and Matt followed as the train vanished and the platform at Piccadilly Circus solidified around them.

'It worked! Brilliant!'

'Let's hope it's that easy on the way back,' grumbled Matt.

'Why would we need to go back?' asked George.

'Well, I'm totally new to this whole space-time freak-out thing,' said Matt. 'But doesn't it screw things up if we don't go back to where we started from?'

'Nah,' said Alicia, 'we just sort of end up back home no matter what... at least, we have so far.' She looked around at the interior of the station and decided that the wide circular concourse had too many directions to choose from. 'Okay George, you better show us the way out.'

George, for his part, was surprised to see how different the place looked as they walked up the last stairs of the north entrance. There were now sandbags stacked around the iron railings, and a most peculiar line of people patiently waiting by a sign that read: 'Please form a queue here. The station will be open for use as a shelter at 4 p.m. sharp.'

He looked around at this new mix of strange and familiar things: There was no mistaking Piccadilly Circus, with its confusion of traffic and giant signs, but the place simply did not look as he remembered it. He had last come here with his parents to see a pantomime last Christmas. And then the place had seemed so alive and festive, but now, despite the heavy traffic and blurring crowds of people, it felt somehow empty and subdued.

To the north, the familiar Bovril sign still stood high above the intersection, and next to it, the Guinness clock still ticked away the hours, but their lights had been extinguished, and their once warm glow was replaced with the flat cold pallor of late afternoon.

The people too, were different. It wasn't so much those mysterious blurs, but it was more that the people themselves seemed to be driven by a new desperation, hurrying through the now dull streets.

In the middle of the intersection, George had expected to see the familiar bronze fountain with its winged statue, but the fountain had been replaced with a giant eight-sided grey cone, which was topped with an ugly black cap.

He remembered that when he had first seen the fountain, his mother had explained that most people thought that the statue was supposed to be Eros, the god of passionate love, but she knew that it was really his brother, Anteros, the god of reflected love. That was just the sort of thing his mother knew, the sort of detail that most other people tended to ignore or forget.

He felt a pang in his heart and wished that she were there.

'What *is* that thing?' asked Matt.

'It looks like a space capsule,' said Alicia, 'you know, like they used to have.'

'But this is Piccadilly Circus,' protested George, 'and there's supposed to be a fountain there... only some silly blighter's gone and bunged-in that ruddy great monstrosity in its place.'

'Hey,' said Matt in a moment of inspiration, 'it totally looks like a Dalek... you know, like, from Doctor Who.'

'Sorry,' said George, 'I'm afraid I don't get the reference.'

'Seriously, dude? There's nobody more British than him, and he's been around for, like, forever... and you haven't heard of him?'

'Don't mind Matt,' said Alicia, 'he's a total fan-boy.'

'Hey, I'm just saying,' muttered Matt, but then burst out, 'okay, so like, we don't know why we've come back in time... but what if that thing is some weird alien device that's making all this happen?'

'I suppose it's at least worth looking into,' said George. He saw a man hesitating at the edge of the road, and on an impulse, he followed him across the wide street, leaving Matt and Alicia scrambling to keep up.

They were now on a large traffic island in the middle of the intersection, standing next to the strange gunmetal-grey cone, which now seemed so much larger than before. Surrounding the strange object was a hastily constructed wooden railing, as if someone had made a half-hearted effort to protect the public from its great menace.

'Whoa,' said Matt, 'that thing looks totally alien.'

Alicia climbed through the railing to get a better look, but when she inspected the thing's surface, she could tell that it was made of plywood. It sounded solid and heavy, then she noticed a trickle of sand leaking out of a piece of burlap caught between two boards, and she suddenly understood. 'It's filled with sandbags – they must have put this up to protect the fountain.'

'I still think it looks like some sort of time travel device,' insisted Matt.

'Yeah, well, if it was,' said Alicia, dismissively, 'I hardly think that they'd have decorated it with a bunch of old war bond posters.'

'Right, then,' said George, as he pulled out his watch and flipped it open. 'Enough with these distractions. We still need to find my mum and dad.' Once again, the map materialized, and the route traced itself down Regent Street, took a right along Charles II Street, and then went on to St James Square.

With careful timing, they were able to follow another pedestrian safely back across the street, and then past the Clydesdale Bank building. Unnoticed behind them, in the middle of Piccadilly Circus, the air shimmered ever so slightly above the grey cone, a thing with huge ragged wings of smoke and shadow formed out of nothing. The creature, invisible to the people below, carefully surveyed its surroundings with glowing red eyes, and then slowly beat its strange wings as it lifted off and flew to the top of a nearby building. It perched high on a stone ledge, and turned its head ever so slightly to listen.

George felt a chill run through him as a hollow scream echoed in the distance. 'What's that?' he asked, feeling strangely aware of something watching him.

Then the world around them became deathly quiet.

'I... I'm not sure,' said Alicia.

Just then, a different scream started low and grew louder, rising and falling in a deafening wail.

'What's that?' demanded Matt.

'Air raid siren!' shouted George over the growing noise.

'It's the most horrible thing I've ever heard!' cried Alicia as she held her hands over her ears, 'What should we do?'

People from all over came out of the surrounding buildings and poured onto the street, some walking fast, others running, and all headed back toward Piccadilly Circus Station. The blur of traffic ground to a halt, as drivers pulled to the side of the road and abandoned their vehicles to follow the crowd.

'They're all heading to the Tube station – it's an air-raid shelter!' George yelled. The three of them had to press themselves against the building in order to avoid being trampled by the streaming crowd.

But then the people on Regent Street slowed down before stopping completely.

'Guys, I think we're leaving!' Alicia shouted.

Sparks began to crawl over the frozen people and along the ground in wide spirals, and it was then that Alicia saw a large bat-winged shadow, and even though the rest of the world seemed to be frozen in place, the creature moved with ease as it crawled down the side of the building toward her.

'What is that thing?' she cried out, and the creature's eyes blazed red when it heard her, but then the sparks converged and the spiraling wind grew to a deafening roar as the storm carried them away.

Chapter Seven

The Watch

'What on earth are you screaming about?' Dr Henderson's voice echoed in the distance as the darkness of the storm faded.

Alicia heard Matt answer, 'sorry, Mom, we were just goofing around.'

'Well, keep it down, okay?' I really need Nessa to sleep so I can get some work done.'

'Sure, yeah... sorry,' Alicia heard him call back, as the great-room came back into focus, although her head felt like it was still spinning in the storm.

'What was that thing?' she asked, her voice trembling.

'That... Was... Freakin'... *Amazing!*' said Matt, but then realized that Alicia was talking about something else, 'what thing?'

'How could you not have seen that?' asked George in disbelief, 'that thing... that creature?'

'*Creature*? Are you kidding me?' Matt could hardly contain his excitement. 'Really? We totally have to go back now! What did it look like?'

'Like a grotesque, or a gargoyle,' replied George, even as the memory of the thing faded unnaturally fast, although the dread it had left in him did not fade nearly so quickly. 'But it was as if it was made out of smoke rather than stone.'

'What are you talking about?' asked Matt.

Alicia tried to control the tremble in her voice, 'it was crawling down the wall.'

'*Seriously*? Yeah, we have totally got to go back!' insisted Matt, but then he narrowed his eyes and added, 'unless you're just messing with me.'

'Sorry,' said George as he shook his head as if waking from a nap, 'what was that?'

'Did you really see that creature that Alicia was just talking about?'

'Was she?' asked George, unsure of what he could remember, 'perhaps I did see something... but no, no... on second thought, I don't think that I actually did.'

Alicia felt confused and tired, as if she had just awoken from a dream, and like a dream, the memory of the creature was fading rapidly, yet all the other memories of London remained fresh and clear in her mind.

'Come *on*, guys, let's go again!' said Matt. 'You gotta admit that was *amazing!*' But when neither George nor Alicia seemed the least bit willing to try, he flopped into one of the big armchairs in exaggerated defeat. 'Wow, you two are total downers.'

'Sorry, Matt,' said George, 'but I really don't know what's going on... or even how this blasted watch actually works... although, I am ever so grateful that you figured out how to open my dad's letters... thanks.'

'Yeah, sure,' Matt grumbled, 'glad I could help.'

'Hey,' said Alicia, noticing the trickle from Matt's nose, 'you're bleeding again.'

'Crap,' he said as he pinched his nose, 'so this means that stuff that happens to us there... like, it really happens?'

'Yeah, I guess so,' said Alicia, as she handed him a tissue, which he stuffed up his nose.

'So, where did you say you got that thing... the watch?' asked Matt.

'It was in my coat pocket... Alicia and I found it there earlier,' said George, 'but I certainly don't remember it from when I was living in London with my parents.'

'Okay,' said Matt, as he stuffed another wad of tissue up his nose, 'so, no question that this is the most advanced tech I've ever seen... but what else does it do?'

'I really don't have the foggiest,' replied George.

'Alright,' said Matt, 'so, like, is it the watch or not? I mean, is it the thing that took us back in time?'

'It's the only thing that make sense to me,' said George.

'No way,' said Alicia. 'It just doesn't make any sense that it would be the watch doing that.'

'Well, whether it is or not,' said George, 'it really is the most confounding piece of kit I've ever encountered... it would be so much easier,' he said as he flipped open the case again, 'if there were an instruction book of some kind.' The watch chimed softly as its face turned amber, and then a large book appeared above it. 'By jingo, that's it!'

'That is so cool!' laughed Matt, with growing excitement, 'we have the freakin' users' manual!'

It was the middle of the afternoon, and Mr Henderson needed a break. He had been struggling with a particularly difficult database problem for some time, and decided that a quick snack was just what he needed to clear his thoughts. He went to the kitchen, and while he was making himself a sandwich, he happened to glance over to the great-room where he saw Matt, Alicia and George. He did a double take when he thought he saw a large book open in front of them, *floating in mid-air*.

But it was when the book turned into a fully-grown lion, roared, and shook its huge mane, that he sprang into action. In a single motion, he jumped over the kitchen counter, and then threw himself between the lion and the children, but as he did this, the lion simply vanished.

'What... the... *hell*... was... that?' he panted as he felt his heart pounding hard in his chest.

'It's George's watch,' said Alicia, 'pretty amazing, huh?'

'Seriously, Dad,' added Matt, 'you have to see what this thing can do – it's totally the shiniest tech I've ever seen.'

Mr Henderson looked at the three of them in disbelief, but said nothing.

'George,' said Alicia, 'show him some of the other things it can do.'

'Um, are you quite sure?' asked George, 'only it seems to me that he's had rather a shock.'

'Start with something simple,' said Matt, 'I don't think he could take another scare like that,' he laughed. 'Show him the mail.'

'Another smartass remark like that,' said Mr Henderson, as the shock wore off, 'and you'll find yourself cooking tonight's dinner, *and* doing the dishes.'

'Well, sir... um, Mr Henderson,' said George, 'I just hold the watch open like this, and asked it if I may see my mail, and then...' The watch chimed softly, while above it, a handwritten letter unfurled out of nothing.

'That's... that's amazing,' said Mr Henderson, as he bent down to have a better look. 'It looks absolutely solid... Allie, get me a piece of paper... I want to see where this thing is generating the image from.'

As he tried to touch the letter, his fingers passed right through it, but then, as he passed the sheet of paper between the image and the watch, the letter simply disappeared. 'That's odd,' he muttered.

'Dad, look,' said Matt, 'the letter!'

There it was, on the paper as if hand-written by George's father.

'This,' said Mr Henderson, 'is truly one of the most astounding things I've ever seen. George, may I hold the watch?'

'Yes...yes, of course.'

Mr Henderson tried to smile reassuringly as he took the watch and examined it. 'It's so small... there's no way... nothing like it... anywhere.' He flipped open the lid to expose an ordinary looking watch face, and when he opened the back, the device still looked like a perfectly ordinary, old-fashioned, mechanical pocket watch. He handed it back to George, and as he did, the watch chimed softly.

'A capacitive signature?' Mr Henderson asked no one in particular. 'So, it actually recognizes who's touching it.'

'Honey?' said Dr Henderson as she came into the room, cradling the baby in her arms, 'What was all that noise a few minutes ago? You woke Nessa.'

'Sorry... the kids and I were just playing,' he quickly replied. When she left the room, he whispered, 'look, your mother has enough to deal with at the moment,' he then paused as he looked at the watch again, 'so just keep this thing to yourselves, okay?'

'Oh for pity's sake, Gil, I'm not deaf,' she said with a frustrated laugh as she came back into the room. 'So, what is it that you don't want the kids to show me?'

'Uh, well,' Mr Henderson stammered, but then remembered the paper in his hand, which he held out for his wife to see, 'this; it's a letter from George's father.'

'Why on earth wouldn't you want me to see that? That's wonderful news, George. So I suppose you'll be back with you parents soon.'

'Yes, I do hope so,' said George with an awkward smile.

'See,' said Mr Henderson, 'that's all it was, I didn't want you to be disappointed that he'd be leaving us so soon.'

'Oh, good,' she said, but then added, 'for a minute there, I thought you didn't want me to see that amazing little device that he's hiding in his hand.'

Supper that night at the Hendersons was quite an experience for George. He could hardly believe the great bounty of food available, in both volume and choice, and he wondered how the family could possibly manage to eat it all. And since so much of the meal had been prepared on the barbeque, he couldn't help but wonder if it was only the Hendersons, or indeed all Canadians, who liked their food somewhat charred. However, after trying each dish in turn, he found that the flavours were far more appetizing than he would have ever believed, and after his third helping, the matter of how they dealt with the excess food was far less of a mystery as well.

George may have been focused on the food, but the rest of the family was captivated by his watch. They all wanted to see the lion again, and so he flipped open his watch, selected 'Defense Strategies; Distraction; Display Sample; Lion' from the instruction manual, and once again, the book turned into a fully-grown lion, which sat right in the middle of the table as it let out a mighty roar.

For an encore, he tried 'Display Sample; Review Random', and this time, the lion appeared at the side of the room and began to pace around the table. Within seconds, it morphed into a brown bear that ambled up to his side before rearing up on its hind legs.

'That's amazing!' said Mr Henderson, who had been eyeing the watch as much as the show itself, 'the images are stabilized relative to the environment, not the source.'

The bear then became a gorilla, which thumped its chest before it dropped to all fours and morphed into a unicorn. Then the unicorn reared up and whinnied, and with a flick of its head, jumped over the table and turned into something else – a creature that looked vaguely human, except for its shadowy grey-black skin, long sharp claws and its bat-like wings. The creature let out an oddly quiet and distant sounding scream, and George reflexively snapped the watchcase closed, which caused it to vanish.

There were whoops and applause from the family, except for Alicia, who shot George an uneasy look. Unwelcome fragments of a nightmare had been awakened in both of them, recovered pieces of something they had somehow forgotten. Nobody else however, was bothered by the sight of this last creature, and even though Matt and Chella were calling for more, Dr Henderson had had enough.

'Alright,' she said with a tired smile, 'let's try something a little less scary for the baby.'

'Ah, come on, Mom, protested Matt, 'she doesn't care – look at her.'

Indeed, Nessa was giggling and cooing, and seemed completely unconcerned with what she had just seen, but Dr Henderson was insistent. 'George, why don't you tell us about your dad's letters?'

'Yes... yes, of course,' said George, still haunted by the strangely familiar winged creature. 'Well, Alicia and I found them in the watch, but it was really Matt who discovered how to properly open them.'

'It's not just letters,' cut in Matt, 'that watch has really cool maps, too, and somehow it took us to London, like back in 1940... and we saw George's old house – and it was totally bombed out.'

'Whoa, wait just a minute,' said Mr Henderson, looking very concerned. 'What do you mean, it took you to London?'

'Seriously, Gil, you've seen that device work. It's all a wonderful illusion, nothing more, and certainly nothing to look so worried about. Now George,' said Dr Henderson, 'why don't you put away your watch for now.'

'Uh... yeah... illusion,' stammered Mr Henderson, but then he seemed to put it out of his mind as his face brightened. 'Anyway, good idea to put it away for now... Hey why don't you kids get the cleanup done, and then maybe we'll make popcorn and watch a movie.'

Later, as they were doing the dishes, George admitted to Matt that he had only seen one colour film before, the Wizard of Oz, and he had enjoyed it very much.

Matt, however, held a low opinion of that film, 'yeah, it was okay, I guess, but the special effects were pretty primitive. These days, they're way better... like, the movie we're gonna watch tonight... it's kinda like,' he paused as he tried to think of a film old enough that George might be familiar with it. 'It's sorta like the original Superman, but way better. You know Superman, right?'

'You mean Shaw's 'Man and Superman'?' asked George. 'My mum loves that play, but I wouldn't have thought it would appeal to you.'

'Uh, yeah... whatever, dude, my point is that Ironman is way better than Superman.'

It wasn't long before the smell of fresh popcorn wafted enticingly through the house, and the family gathered once again in the great-room. When Mr Henderson simply pushed a button and one of the bookcases slid aside, exposing a large television screen, George couldn't help but be impressed.

'Yeah, not bad, eh kid?' said Mr Henderson, with a certain self-satisfied pride as he looked around the room. 'It's kinda like having my own kick-ass man-cave, but for the whole family, so I guess you could call it our family-cave.'

'I... I suppose so,' agreed George, although he couldn't think of a less rustic or cave-like space. However, when Alicia dimmed the lights, the darkened room did seem rather cavernous, and then as everyone gathered around the glowing screen, to share food and partake in stories, the place did seem to take on a wonderfully primeval feel.

When the movie began, it was not so much the images, but the sound that impressed George the most, making his heart race as it travelled right through him. The music was so utterly different from anything he had ever heard before: pounding, harsh, relentless, and even painful to listen to, yet undeniably exciting.

At times, it was altogether too much, and George had to look away to catch his breath. Once, when he turned away from the screen during the excruciating final battle scene, he thought he saw something move across the wall.

'Did you see that?' he whispered to Alicia.

'What?' she asked impatiently, not wanting to take her eyes off the movie. 'Seriously, you're missing the best part.'

But when George looked back, the hulking shadow with ragged wings had vanished, and his memory of the thing soon faded into nothing.

It was very late when George finally went up to his room, but after the intense excitement of the movie, he just couldn't sleep, so he sat on the edge of his bed, flipped open his watch, and continued to study its instruction book.

The first thing he looked up was time travel, but all he found was a long boring article about how difficult and expensive it actually was. There were also several articles about the brave pioneering researchers who travelled back in history to operate data scanners, and who would never be able to return to their own time, because, as the book mentioned time and again, traveling against the flow of linear time was a one-way journey.

But George wanted to read about people who could move back and forth through time as easily as he could, not about people who could never return home.

However, everything that he read told him that what he wanted was simply impossible. He kept reading, hoping for more answers. However, as he read, he learned many more things about his little watch. He learned that it was a device called an acnode, and that it could send letters to anyone else who had a similar device. The book also mentioned that most people just called them 'nodes, and that they could be hidden inside watches, books or even walking sticks.

The book also explained that the name for the device came from the fact that it contained a small amount of a rare and valuable substance called acnodinium. It was a substance that was neither matter nor antimatter, but composed of exotic particles that existed outside the curvature of space-time, despite the fact that they were still able to satisfy all known dimensional equations for matter within space.[4]

As he kept reading, he learned that as well as sending letters, his 'node could retrieve historical maps, but he also read a very important footnote that warned him that scanned history and printed history were often different, and that only scanned history should be trusted, so he was very glad that he always read the footnotes.[5]

He continued to read a particularly long and boring chapter on 'Communications: Reciprocating Correspondences' before finally reaching the instructions that he actually needed.

He spoke the commands to open his father's letter, and then gave the command, 'Use primary link: Reply.' His father's letter turned into a blank sheet of paper; 'Dear Dad,' he said, uncertain what was supposed to happen next, and much to his amazement, the words appeared on the paper in his very own handwriting. 'How could it possibly know what my handwriting looks like?' he wondered aloud. 'No, no, don't write that, blast it! Erase, restart reply: Dear Dad; I am safe and well, but I miss you and Mum terribly. I have met some wonderful people who have very kindly taken me in, but this place

---

[4] And, no, he didn't understand that explanation any better than you or I just did, but at least he learned the proper name for his watch.

[5] Not subtle enough?

is strange and confusing. I don't belong here, but even when I was back in London today, that didn't seem quite right, either.'

Seeing his thoughts written out on paper made them feel strangely more real, even if the paper itself was only an illusion.

He couldn't think what else to say, so he finished the letter, 'I hope to see you both very soon. Love, George. End reply.'

He then closed the little watch and sat on the edge of his bed, lost in thoughts of home, but then he suddenly remembered something, so he flipped opened the watch, and said, 'send mail.' The watch chimed softly to confirm his command, and then... nothing.

He had hoped that there might be a new letter, or even a reply to read, but there was nothing. He reasoned that if his father had replied, he would have done so years ago, and therefore the reply would be ready and waiting for him to read now, but that was not to be. It was strange and confusing to think about how these things might work, and the whole business just seemed so exhausting that he lay back on his bed, and soon fell fast asleep.

Outside in the garden, the night air shimmered ever so slightly, and a shadow with large ragged wings formed in the blackness. It rose up and landed silently on the side of the house, and then slowly, cautiously, its eyes glowing red, it crawled toward the bedroom window.

George awoke suddenly. He could sense something in his room, but when he turned on his bedside light, nothing seemed out of place. He then looked out his window, but could see only the blackness of night through streaks of fresh rain. So he rubbed his eyes, and dismissed his hollow uneasy feeling as the remains of a bad dream.

He heard the sound of thunder in the distance, and then downstairs, the baby started to cry. He fumbled for his watch on the bedside table, and it was just past three in the morning. He felt oddly empty, so went downstairs to get himself a drink of water, or a snack, or anything to help him feel better and hopefully sleep once more.

As he approached the dimly lit kitchen, he could hear the Hendersons talking in hoarse whispers.

'...look, Gil, it's not that I don't appreciate your utterly misguided good intentions, but this has got to stop.'

'I was just trying to keep your stress levels down.'

'And you think telling the kids to keep secrets from me is going to do that?'

'No... no, of course not... it's just... it's just that all this stuff with the kid... what happened at the hospital with Alicia... and now all this... Dammit, Gayle, I just don't want your MS to get any worse than it already is, okay?'

'I get it, and I love you for it, but you've got to stop being so damned over-protective.'

'How the hell do you do it, Gayle?' Mr Henderson asked, still whispering. 'Seriously... I'm totally freaked out by all this stuff, and yet none of it seems to faze you.'

'You're just going to have to trust me on this, Gil.'

'What are you looking at me like that for?' He said as the tone of his voice changed to one of disbelief, 'what... you've been protecting *me*?'

'Let's just say that I know things,' Dr Henderson said, no longer bothering to whisper, 'for instance, I happen to know that a certain someone is lurking out in the hallway right now... Aren't you, George?'

He wasn't sure what was more embarrassing, hearing the Hendersons arguing, or being caught listening in.

'I'm sorry... I didn't mean to,' he muttered. 'How did you know?'

'I could see your reflection in the window,' Dr Henderson replied with a little chuckle. 'It's okay, dear, come on in.' She was sitting in the big chair by the window, holding the baby, while Mr Henderson was by the kitchen island, preparing a bottle of formula.

'Hey, kid,' he said, 'did the storm wake you?'

'Yes, sir, I suppose that's what it was... the storm.'

'Perhaps some warm milk,' Dr Henderson suggested, 'that should help you get back to sleep.'

Mr Henderson gently took the baby from his wife, 'alright, now that George is here, he can help me with Nessa, so why don't you go back to bed, and I'll be along in a few minutes.' He then brushed her cheek tenderly, before giving her a lingering kiss on the lips.

'Alright,' she smiled, and turned to go, 'but don't take too long.'

After watching his wife with an enthusiastic intensity that made George feel even more awkward, Mr Henderson then turned to him. 'Okay... so, kid, why don't you hold the baby while I warm up some milk. Sound good?'

'Uh, yes... but I've never held a baby before.'

'That's okay, just sit in the rocking chair over there, and I'll hand her to you.' George did as instructed. 'There you go... that's it. Just be sure to support her head... that's it. Perfect... see kid, you're a natural.'

The baby looked at George carefully, and then cooed softly as she nestled into his arms.

'You'll make a great father someday,' said Mr Henderson as he continued to prepare the formula.

'Um, thanks.'

'George,' he began, changing the subject a little hesitantly, 'I work in the tech industry... you know, computers and the like, and I've dealt with some pretty shiny bleeding-edge stuff... I've even consulted on some defence contracts... but I have *never* seen anything even *close* to what that watch can do.'

A timer beeped and Mr Henderson tested the formula on his wrist, and then handed the bottle to George, who, with just a little guidance, soon had the baby contentedly feeding.

'See, kid, I told you – you're a natural... now, about that watch...'

'I have no idea where it came from,' said George as he looked up, 'that was what you were going to ask, wasn't it?'

'I suppose it was,' said Mr Henderson, smiling a little awkwardly. He then seemed to think a moment more as he poured a couple of mugs of milk. 'Seriously, kid, holograms today, even the very best ones, can only be viewed from limited angles, or require the viewer to look through a lens of some kind. Yet that watch of yours generates images that appear to have solid *reflective* surfaces that can be viewed from any angle. Not to mention the fact that it can generate animated characters that respond to their surroundings. I can't even begin to understand the programming, let alone the physics, involved in doing that.' He then paused to search for the right words, 'look, what I'm trying to say is this; you might be from 1939, but that watch sure as hell isn't... and it's not from this century, either.'

'I really wish I could remember more,' said George.

The microwave beeped and Mr Henderson pulled out the two mugs of milk. 'I'll take over feeding Nessa, and then you can have your milk.' At first, the baby was not pleased with this change in arrangements, but soon settled down again.

'Son,' said Mr Henderson, 'the technology in that watch is worth a fortune, and there are many, many people in this world who would do you grievous harm to get their hands on it... so I want you to keep it to yourself. Don't - *under any circumstances* - show it to anyone outside the family... and I'll tell the kids the same thing.'

The thunderstorm drew closer. A deep hollow scream echoed in the distance. George felt a chill run through him.

'What was that?' he asked.

'Not sure. Could have been a coyote... they've moved into the city in the last few years... but actually, you know what?' Mr Henderson laughed, 'it sounded just like that damn gargoyle thing from your watch last night... Seriously, kid, what the hell was that thing supposed to be anyway?'

Chapter Eight

The Gathering Storm

When George had been living in London with his parents, weekday breakfasts had been a relatively quiet affair.

His mother would have her copy of the Daily Mirror, which she would glance at while she prepared the meal, and his father would have his morning tea as he perused his copy of the Times. Then, when breakfast was ready, they would all sit down together and discuss interesting items in the news, or their plans for the day as they ate. It was all so civilized.

At the Hendersons', however, things were considerably more chaotic, as each family member came down at different times to grab whatever was easiest to fix, and fastest to eat, before they disappeared to do their own thing. However, this morning was different, as Mr Henderson stopped each of the kids when they came into the kitchen, and he made them wait until they were all there. Then, when everyone was assembled and impatient to go, he made his announcement. Everyone, but everyone, was to keep quiet about George's watch.

Matt protested that he had already texted a bunch of his friends, inviting them to come over and meet George.

'Sure, Matt, introduce him to your friends,' his father replied, 'but I don't want you mentioning the watch to anyone, under any circumstances.'

'What's the point then?' asked Matt as he took a particularly angry bite of toast.

'Gee, thanks,' said George, 'that makes me feel just splendid.'

'I didn't mean that,' Matt sputtered defensively, toast crumbs flying out of his mouth, 'I just meant…'

'Whatever you meant, Matt,' his father said, 'the fact is that there are things going on here that we just don't understand, and until I get a better handle on it, I don't want *anyone* outside the family knowing about that watch.'

'But, Dad, what's the big deal?' asked Chella, not looking up from her phone.

'Let's put it this way,' he said, '*none* of you will mention this watch to anyone… and you'll stop texting or tweeting your friends about it *right now, Chella*…'

'But, Dad,' she protested, 'I've already told Marcie.'

'Then you will tell her that you were mistaken, that it was nothing more than… than vaporware that some client company of mine had totally overhyped, so there is nothing to see.' He then made eye contact with each of his children in turn. 'If you still want to be involved in testing or reviewing new prototypes, software, *or whatever* for my company, you will do as I say, or you will be cut off. Understand?'

This was, by far, the most serious threat that he could possibly make, as it was generally agreed that testing new stuff was easily the coolest thing about being a Henderson kid. So, despite a few resentful grumbles, he had made his point.

By mid-afternoon, the air had grown oppressively hot, and Alicia found George in the back yard, still studying the instruction book for his watch. 'Come, on,' she said, 'Simon Toliver wants me to take him down to the corner store for a slushie… you can try one too.'

'No thanks,' he said, barely looking up, 'I have rather a lot of reading to do… you go on without me.'

'Yeah,' she said, rolling her eyes, 'like, that's going to work. Remember?'

'Oh, right… of course,' he said, looking up. 'So… what exactly was it that you wanted?'

'It's a drink… no big deal… basically just pop with crushed ice,' replied Alicia, 'but it can be really cool, like nice, on a day like today.'

'Well,' said George, 'then I suppose it's worth a try.'

The big maples that lined the street offered some shade from the direct sun, but the neighbourhood was filled with the heavy sort of quiet that comes when it's too hot to be outside. As Alicia, George and Simon Toliver walked down the street, they saw a few kids jumping through a sprinkler, but otherwise the place was oddly empty.

Then, when they turned the first corner, they came across a yard sale. George was fascinated by all the things that looked so very modern to his eye, yet nonetheless bore the stains and marks of great age. It all seemed so wonderfully curious, but nothing took his fancy quite so much that he wanted to buy it. That is, until he saw an old pith helmet, just like the ones he had seen when they had been in India. Just for a lark, he tried it on, and it fit surprisingly well.

'Whoa,' said Alicia, 'isn't it kind of early to be looking for a Halloween costume?'

'Considering this heat,' replied George, as he checked himself out in a nearby mirror, 'I think that this will be rather practical for keeping cool.'

'Trust me, there's nothing cool about it. Seriously, if the wrong kids see you wearing it…'

The old woman tending the sale came over to where they stood.

'I think it suits him beautifully,' she said. 'Did you know that they used to call that a Bombay Bowler? And that particular one belonged to my great uncle… when he was stationed Ceylon… before the war.'

'Is it for sale?' asked George.

'Yes… it all is, I'm afraid,' she said as she looked wistfully at her lifetime of objects, spread out on the tables and across the lawn. She then turned back to George and smiled, 'however, I wouldn't want to let that hat go to just anyone… but it does suit you rather well.'

'I promise to take good care of it,' he said. 'How much?'

'Well young man, it's yours for a loonie.'

'I'm sorry, a what?'

'A dollar,' said Alicia, 'it's a one dollar coin.'

George fumbled around in his pocket and pulled out some of the change that Mr Henderson had given him, but the coins all looked so foreign, and he didn't know yet which was which.

'It's the gold one,' said Alicia as she took the coin from George's open hand and gave it to the woman. Then, before he could find anything else even more embarrassing to wear, she dragged him away while she kept an eye out for any kids who might take exception to George's new hat. 'Come on, Toliver,' she said, 'you don't need any more stuff, either.'

'Thank you,' said George, over his shoulder as they hurried away.

When they entered the corner store, a small brass bell rang out to announce their presence, which was an odd note of familiarity for George in such an otherwise foreign world.

The interior of the shop was well air-conditioned, more for the sake of the many brightly wrapped chocolate bars than for the comfort of the customers, but it was wonderfully refreshingly, just the same.

As George entered the little store, he felt almost overwhelmed by the abundance of treats. So many choices of sweet and savoury items to choose from, even a glass hotbox containing a variety of warm snacks beside the counter, from which wafted out the smell of pizza and burritos, blending with the smell of chocolate and bubble-gum, confusing and teasing his senses.

Alicia knew exactly what she wanted, and went straight to the back of the store, to where the slushie dispenser was.

'I'm making you a root beer and orange,' she explained as she layered brown and orange mush in the cup. 'It's a pretty safe combination for someone who hasn't had one of these before.' She then handed him the cup and proceeded to make one for Simon Toliver. 'And be really careful drinking it, otherwise you'll get brain freeze.'

'I'm not daft,' said George as he took a sip. It tasted sweet and cool. But the day was hot, and he was thirsty, so then he drank deeply, and the coolness in his throat felt wonderful. Then his forehead began to ache ever so slightly, and within seconds, the pain grew into an explosion of agony as his eyes watered and he felt himself stagger.

'That's brain freeze,' said Alicia as she took a delicate little sip of her own drink. 'I told you to take it slowly.'

'I don't like brain freeze,' said Simon Toliver.

'Really?' asked George as his ability to speak slowly returned, 'why ever not?' He then shook himself, 'that was genuinely unpleasant... so you drink these blasted things on a regular basis?'

'Only when it's really hot out,' said Alicia as she took another delicate little sip and then paid for the drinks before heading out the door. 'Come on, I want to show you my school.'

'It's my school too,' said Simon Toliver.

Just around the corner, Drysdale Elementary was an old four-storey red brick building, with a huge gabled roof and was much older than most of the neighbourhood that had grown up around it. Built on a south-facing slope, its grounds were large, occupying four city blocks, with a couple of sport fields, and a small wooded area in one corner.

They walked along the school's circular driveway, around the side of the building, and then down to the swings in the woods, where they sat and sipped their slushies in the cool shade.

'Are you leaving?' asked Simon Toliver.

'Well,' George hesitated, 'I suppose I will... eventually. I do like being here, but I would really rather be back with my parents.'

'I don't want you to go,' said Simon Toliver.

'Anyway,' said Alicia, 'you can't go back until you hear from your dad. Anything yet?'

'No... not a word.'

A light breeze came up from the lower field, and brought with it the shimmering heat of the open ground. George felt the hair on the back of his neck stand on end, and as he reached up to brush it down, he felt a spark. Suddenly, he felt weak and groggy from the heat.

'I meant,' said Simon Toliver, his voice sounding muffled and distant, 'are you leaving now? 'Cuz I think something's trying to take you away.'

The sun-baked air from the field came rushing at them, while heavy clouds began to form as the hot wind collided with unnaturally cold air above. Then, little red and blue sparks began to circle and snake towards the three of them as the breeze became a strangely empty wind. The trees began to creak and sway.

Alicia felt a shiver run through her, not from the cold, but from the sense that something was watching her. She looked behind her, and hidden in the woods, she thought she saw a shadow sitting on a low branch. Fragments of lost nightmares came racing back into her mind, and memories of things both familiar and strange awoke within her. 'George,' she whispered hoarsely, 'that thing... it's back!' but he could hardly hear her, as if her voice was muffled by great distance.

'I don't think it's alone,' he replied, as he watched several shadows circling under the clouds, and then swoop out of the storm to land in the trees nearby. A deep hollow scream echoed in the distance as rain began to pelt down. Lightning flashed and thunder rolled.

Alicia pulled off her glasses when the rain made it near impossible to see, 'we've got to try to get home,' she shouted. 'Come on!' She wasn't sure what it was that she was running from, only that it was something terrible as whispers of dread grew to shouts in her mind, while fragmented memories never quite formed. Something... wicked... had attacked her before, and she was determined to keep that evil away from her little brother.

'What are they?' cried Simon Toliver as sparks began to circle around them.

'And where in blazes are they all coming from?' George shouted.

'Run! Go!' Alicia called back as she grabbed her little brother, and as they ran, the tight circle of sparks seemed to lose focus.

'Crikey, I think we might just be able to outrun it!' George called out, but then something moved behind him, and as he instinctively glanced around, he tripped and fell. Alicia stopped, torn between coming back to help, and getting her little brother to safety.

'Keep going!' George shouted. The sparks appeared to focus again, and a funnel cloud formed directly above him.

Alicia knew that at moment, there was nothing more she could do for George, but she was determined to keep her little brother safe from the shadows.

Simon Toliver stumbled more than once, and his knees were scraped and bloody, but he refused to cry. He could see the fear in his sister's eyes, but more than that, he could feel something truly malevolent in the storm.

George could feel it, too. Thoughts of winged creatures clawed at his mind, and now the danger seemed clearer than ever. These things were real, and he was not going to let his memories fade as they had so many times before. Because now he could remember. There *had* been times before, many times before, in which these things had come into his life, creeping, howling, shrieking.

He sprang to his feet and ran.

'I will not forget, I will not forget,' he kept muttering to himself, but then he shouted, 'I will not forget you, you blasted bloody monsters!'

The storm grew stronger and more furious as lightning streaked overhead. There was another hollow shriek, and a tree across the street exploded as a bolt struck it. The resulting thunderclap left George stunned, almost deaf, and even though he stumbled, he refused to fall again. He knew that if he did, there would be no second chance.

It was only three blocks away from the school, but it felt more like three miles as they ran, pursued by the shadows in the storm. When they finally reached the house, Alicia fumbled with her key as the things drew closer. As the door opened, they tumbled into the kitchen. Alicia slammed the door shut, and bolted it.

'Caught playing in the rain?' Dr Henderson asked as she came into the room, but her smile faded as Simon Toliver ran over and clung to her. 'What's wrong?' she asked, 'are you all right?'

'We were running... to get away,' said Alicia as she fumbled to put her glasses back on. She wanted to say the words, she wanted to tell someone what they had seen, but the thoughts wouldn't organize, 'Toliver fell...'

'It was the lightning,' added George, 'it hit a tree... it left us all a bit shaken.' He could remember the shadows, but try as he might, he could not speak of them.

'Well, Toliver,' said Dr Henderson, 'we'd better get those scrapes cleaned up... Allie, could you fetch me the first aid kit... Alicia, honey, are you okay? You look like you've seen a ghost.'

George could see Alicia struggling to answer, to form the words and speak of what they had seen. But he knew she could not, because neither could he.

'It's... it's nothing, Mom,' she finally mumbled.

'Alright, then, if you're sure... why don't you and George go get dried off, while I take care of Simon Toliver.'

As George went up the stairs to his room, he could feel the memories start to fade, and more than once, he had to stop to concentrate on keeping them. Then, after he put on dry clothes, he headed back downstairs, and found Alicia, sitting on the bench on the landing by the window that overlooked the back yard. The sun was beginning to shine through cracks in the clouds, but rain still tapped on the window.

'Are you okay?' he asked when she didn't look up.

'Um... yeah... sure,' but the truth was, she wasn't sure at all.

'I saw them,' said George, 'those shadow creatures... like the one in London... I remember now.'

'Yeah, but I don't... not really... it's just like a really bad dream, you know, little bits... but nothing real.' When she heard her little brother come up the stairs, she fell silent.

Simon Toliver sat down on the bench next to her, and as he inspected his freshly bandaged knees, he asked, 'are you talking about the storm?' But then he seemed to lose interest in his own question, and said, 'come on, Mom made us hot chocolate.'

'Get serious,' Alicia laughed, but when they went down to the kitchen, there were three warm cups waiting for them. 'Wow, mom, you really *did* make hot chocolate.'

'Hey,' said Dr Henderson, a little defensively, 'I can be just as domestic as your father.'

'This really hits the spot,' said George. 'Thanks.'

'It's been the oddest weather, hasn't it?' said Dr Henderson as she watched the clouds clear away. 'Boiling hot one minute, and then raging storms the next... I've seen this out on the prairies, but not here on the coast.' She then turned, and added, 'well, I'm going to see if I can get some more work done, so bug your dad if you need anything more.'

George was about to say something to Alicia, but she shook her head as she looked over to Simon Toliver. 'Let's not talk about it now.'

'It's okay,' said her little brother, 'I saw the shadow things too.'

'Um... you saw them?' asked Alicia.

'Yeah... I could hardly see them,' he said, 'and now they're going away.'

'Just a tick,' said George, 'my watch must have information on those things.' He pulled out his watch, flipped it open, and called up the instruction book. He tried several questions, but the search results were all frustratingly vague.

The memories of the afternoon were not gone, just obscured and strangely unimportant, but somewhere, deep inside, George felt a part of himself fighting to keep the fear alive. However, there was a fog in his mind now, and through it, the creatures seemed less important.

There had been something, to be sure, but now he was certain that it had been nothing more than childish imaginings, and it was time to grow up. The struggle had ended.

After a couple minutes of searching, George asked, 'what were we looking for again?'

Alicia shrugged, 'I dunno... but I don't think it could have been very important.'

The watch chimed softly, and a letter appeared in front of him. It was from his father.

My Dearest Boy,

When your letter arrived, I was so relieved to hear that you are safe and well. It's as if a great weight has been lifted from my shoulders.

I am well myself, and though London has been bombed
terribly, my building remains unscathed. I have continued my
scanning for the Council, and have made some fascinating
discoveries in the process, but we shall have plenty of time to
discuss all that when I see you next, on St Swithin's Day.

–   As ever, your loving father, Alex Stryder

George let out a sad little laugh.

'What's wrong?'

'As far as I've always known, when someone says something will take 'til St Swithin's Day, it means that it'll take... forever'

'So... when is St Swithin's Day?' asked Toliver.

'I haven't the foggiest,' said George. 'Is it even a real day?'

'Well... then,' said Alicia, 'ask the watch.'

'Fine,' he said, half-heartedly, 'When is St Swithin's day?' A little calendar appeared, showing July 15th highlighted, and he laughed in surprise. 'It's real! It's a real day! My dad's going to be here in just a couple of days!'

'How's he going to know our address? Maybe you'd better write him back and tell him,' said Alicia.

'Of course! Right then... Recall last letter, use existing link: reply.'

A message appeared stating 'Link no longer viable. Create new link?'

'Yes please.'

The watch chimed again, 'Target unavailable. Please try again later.' George's heart sank.

'Hey,' said Alicia, trying to be reassuring, 'I'm sure when he gets in range of a cell tower... or whatever it is that those things use, then you can write to him again. I bet this happens all the time, kind of like a dropped call.'

'Dropped call?'

Alicia rolled her eyes, 'never mind.'

George shared the news of his father's letter with the rest of the Hendersons during dinner that evening.

'We'll have to make a special meal,' said Mr Henderson. 'How does roast beef and Yorkshire pudding sound?'

'Seriously, Dad,' Chella groaned, 'why do all our meals have to be about meat?'

'Hey, Princess,' said Mr Henderson, 'I'm a carnivore at heart, and I can't help the way I eat.'

'Really?' she asked in disbelief, 'would it kill you to make at least one cruelty free meal?'

'Look, this is for George and his dad, and a good old English meal always has meat in it. Isn't that right, George?'

George had the uncomfortable feeling that this was an old argument between Chella and her father that he now found himself in the middle of. 'I'm ever so sorry, but my father does so love roast beef,' he said, hesitantly, 'and it's been ever such a long time since I've had some, myself.'

'Fine, eat your dead animals, see if I care.'

George was stung by this remark, and he felt that he had let Chella down. From the moment he had first seen her, he had thought her to be one of the most beautiful girls he had ever known, and now he wanted desperately to say something to make it all right again, but when she just glared at him, the words stuck in his throat.

'Well, then, that's settled,' said Mr Henderson. 'So, how is your dad getting here?'

'I'm not exactly sure,' replied George, grateful for the change of subject. 'I wasn't able to send him a message with the address, but I'll keep trying.'

'Do you know where he's coming from,' Mr Henderson asked, 'or when?'

'No... I-I'm not sure.'

'Any idea how he'll travel?'

'Gil, don't grill the poor boy,' said Dr Henderson, giving her husband a slightly frustrated smile. 'It's a lot to take in, and he's clearly excited by the prospect of seeing his father again.'

'Hey, hon, just trying to make interesting dinner conversation...

So, then... what did the rest of you kids do today?' Chella didn't feel much like talking, and the look she gave her father told him to try elsewhere. 'So, Matt, what about you, what did you do today?'

'Uh, you know... the usual... chilled... tried my new mountain board down at the skate-park. Pretty sweet ride, but then there was that freaky storm, so I came home.'

'That *was* a strange storm, wasn't it?' said Mr Henderson. 'So, Allie, I hope the rain didn't ruin your tomatoes.'

'No,' said Alicia, 'they should be okay.'

'Well, that's good,' Mr Henderson said as he then turned to his youngest boy, 'and Simon Toliver, what did you do today?'

'I was with George and Alicia, when the monster storm came for us.'

'Monster storm?' Mr Henderson laughed, 'why would you call it that?'

'Because,' said Simon Toliver, in a very small voice, 'the monsters made it.' His tiny remark cut through the fog in George's mind, strengthening faded memories that were once again clear. Suddenly, George could recall the terror of the afternoon, and when Alicia gave him a pained look, he knew that she had recovered her own memories.

George felt a surge of anger at his own recklessness. How could he have forgotten yet again? He forced himself to remember, he needed to remember, he *must* remember. He swore to himself that he would never forget the shadow things again... those creeping, crawling, howling, shrieking things... and their flying... yes... he needed to remember that they could fly.

Chapter Nine

A Familiar Stranger

Although it was only two days, for George it felt like an eternity, but when it was finally the afternoon of the fifteenth, he still had not heard from his father.

'Hey, kid,' said Mr Henderson, 'why don't you help me with getting the roast ready? I could use the help, and you could use the distraction.' He then winked and added, 'though I have to warn you that Chella has demanded equal time... wants to give you a lesson in vegetarian cooking... probably something about trying to make tofu taste like real food.'

'Sorry, I don't know what tofu is.'

'Neither do I kid, neither do I... However,' said Mr Henderson as he pulled a large brown paper parcel out of the refrigerator, 'this roast is absolutely real food, so let's get it on the barbeque.'

The barbeque, as Mr Henderson called it, was a timber-framed building with no walls, except for the giant brick chimney that occupied the entire back of the structure. This over-sized outdoor kitchen, built of bricks, steel, granite and wood, was surely large enough to cook for an entire army, George thought.

'Pretty, cool, eh?' asked Mr Henderson as he dropped the package on the granite counter. 'Some people thought it was over-kill, but seriously kid, when a man wants to cook, he really needs a proper place to do it.' He then unwrapped the heavy butcher's paper to expose the biggest beef roast that George had ever seen, but then he stopped, and added thoughtfully, 'you know, it just occurred to me... you were asking me about my man-cave the other night.'

'Was I?'

'Yeah... I guess you could say this barbeque is my real man-cave. Other guys can have their big screen TVs and their cushy chairs... but me... just give me a roaring fire and a big hunk of red meat, and I'm a happy camper.'

For the next hour, Mr Henderson gave George a comprehensive lesson on trussing, seasoning and preparing a large joint of meat for the roasting spit, and although cooking had never really appealed to George before, Mr Henderson had definitely piqued his interest.

'Okay, kid,' he said as he finished up and wiped the counter, 'you better go in now, and give Chella a chance to win you over to her hippy-dippy way of thinking.'

So then George went into the kitchen, where he found Chella already hard at work, her tablet computer propped up on the counter, playing a video on preparing an authentic Indian masala. He was a little nervous at first, since although he was drawn to her beauty, he was also a little wary of how vehement she could be in defending her beliefs.

'Hey, it's okay, I don't bite,' she said, as she must have sensed his uncertainty. She then brushed a stray blond hair away from her blue-green eyes with the back of her hand, exposing her fingertips stained orange with fresh turmeric. 'Seriously, I just wanted a chance to show you how good vegetarian food is... you know, not just to eat, but how it's totally better for the environment and stuff. Like, my dad just doesn't get it – people are chewing up this planet faster than nature can repair it, and if we don't stop soon, we're gonna be totally screwed.'

'I'm sorry,' said George, a little flustered. 'I thought you were more concerned about the animals...'

'Yeah, of course I am,' she replied, 'like, what gives us the right to eat other creatures? Seriously, how would you feel if they started eating *us*?'

'I shouldn't think,' he replied, shivering as if a long forgotten nightmare had just crawled out of the depths, 'that I would like that at all.'

'*Exactly*,' she said triumphantly.

Chella was relatively new to cooking, and so she was still a little awkward in the kitchen, but George saw none of this. He saw only a vision of loveliness gliding effortlessly about her business, and although he had never given vegetarian food a second thought, at that moment, there was nothing in the world that was more important to him. It was important to her, and that was all that mattered. He watched intently as she threw her masala spices into a hot pan, and suddenly, there was an explosion of exotic scents. Unexpected, he was overtaken by the image of his mother cooking, and was soon lost in a reverie of great warmth, and yet equally great loss and longing.

George could remember how his mother had loved to make the dishes of her childhood in India, but then, in England, the ingredients were usually too difficult to find, or too expensive to buy, so it was only very rarely that she was ever able to make her favourites. Yet those few occasions were all the clearer in his recall, as the memory of seeing his mother so contented, so very happy, had imprinted deeply in his mind.

'Did you hear anything I just said?'

'Sorry... what?'

'I was saying that it's stupid to keep cutting down the forests and depleting the oceans of fish... like, soon there won't be anything left for our kids, and becoming vegetarian is just one way we can reduce our impact on the planet.'

'Right, of course,' agreed George, somewhat distractedly.

Chella may have been new to cooking, but she was very good at following recipes, and so when she was done, George was surprised by how rich and savory the dish actually was. 'Oh my,' he muttered, almost to himself, 'who needs meat with food this satisfying?'

'Well, yeah... that's kinda my point.'

The afternoon faded into evening, and yet George had not been able to contact his father, so eventually, the Hendersons decided to serve dinner, even though George's dad, the guest of honour, had not arrived.

The meal itself was wonderful. The roast was done perfectly, the gravy and Yorkshire pudding were rich and savoury, and the green peas, straight from Alicia's garden, were fresh and naturally sweet. Chella's curry, her practical protest against her father's carnivorous habits, was also delicious. So good in fact, that even he had to admit that vegetarian cooking might not actually be the complete culinary wasteland that he had always believed it to be. However, Chella was still disappointed when he and the rest of the family still had generous servings of roast beef and gravy.

George, however, found that he could hardly eat anything, worried that his father had not arrived as promised. He had tried several times during dinner to re-establish a link, and then again after the meal, but all with no success. Eventually, he went up to his room, where he flopped onto his bed, and just stared at the ceiling.

It might have been minutes, or even hours later, but he awoke with a start at the sound of muffled voices downstairs. He could recognize the Hendersons, but there was also an unfamiliar voice, gruff and elderly. He listened for a moment, but soon curiosity got the better of him, and he started downstairs, only to run into Mr Henderson bounding up toward him.

'Hey kid, your dad's here.'

George ran down the stairs and just as he was about to head toward the great-room, Mr Henderson called after him.

'Front parlour, kid.'

George changed directions so fast that he almost fell over, but when he reached the door to the front room, he stopped when he saw the back of an unfamiliar grey-haired man.

'George, come on in,' said Dr Henderson, 'I was just introducing Nessa to your father.'

When the man turned around, George could see that he looked very much as he had always thought his grandfather might look, except with the addition a neatly trimmed grey beard and glasses, but surely, this man couldn't be his father.

'Hello, son.'

George hesitated; this man was so much older, and his voice was so different.

'I must look so very strange to you,' the man said as his voice trembled ever so slightly, 'it's been too long since I last saw you, Arthur m'boy.'

But it was only his father who ever called him by that name, and it was then that George also noticed a familiar spark in the man's eye. There was no mistaking, this was his father, but somehow older, greyer and oddly spent. George ran over and hugged him, almost knocking the wind out of the man. His father seemed to be so overwhelmed that he had to sit down as he tried to catch his breath. 'Sorry, m'boy... temporal dissonance... they say it gets easier over time... just give me a moment.'

Matt and Chella stood off to the side, uncertain what to do, while Simon Toliver, who woken with the commotion and had come down in his pyjamas, watched from behind Alicia, who herself stood out in the hallway.

'So,' Mr Henderson started uncomfortably, 'uh, is it true... that... well... George tells us that you and he are from 1939?' His wife shot him a look, but he ignored her.

Mr Stryder hesitated, and seemed to be considering very carefully how to answer. '1939... is that what he told you?'

'And that watch,' Mr Henderson added, 'that thing is absolutely amazing.'

'Ah, so you've seen it, have you?' said Mr Stryder, almost relieved, 'well then, I suppose that there's no sense in denying it... yes, I'm afraid that it's true.'

'How the hell did you manage that?' Mr Henderson asked.

'It's all rather a long story,' George's father replied with a sigh, 'and I'm afraid the journey took rather more out of me than it did my boy.' Mr Stryder then added with a tired smile, 'he looks exactly like he did the day I lost him. Quite disconcerting, really.'

'Where's Mum?' asked George, hopefully.

'M'boy,' Mr Stryder's smile faded, 'a lot of time has passed, and it's a big world... and I have not been able to find her.'

'I don't understand,' George muttered. The past two weeks had seemed like an eternity to him, and yet also as if no time at all had passed. It was all so confusing.

'I know, I know m'boy… but now I've found you, and that's more than I had ever dared hope for,' his father sighed, 'I do wish I had better news for you.' Then, after a long awkward silence, he added, 'It's the strangest thing… All those years ago, thinking of all the things I regretted not saying to you before… if I'd only had that one last chance… and now, here you are, seven decades later, and I find myself unable to think of even one of those things.'

There was another long pause, but Mr Henderson could no longer resist, 'So what actually happened… How did you all get separated?'

Mr Stryder took a deep breath, and seemed to take a moment to gather his thoughts. 'I don't really know… the only thing I *do* know is that I woke up on a sinking ship, and my wife and son were missing. I searched the ship but couldn't find them… my only hope was that they had already escaped in a lifeboat… so I abandoned ship.' He fell silent for a moment, the pain of the memory visible on his face.

'And then,' he continued after a moment, 'my lifeboat was picked up by a British merchant ship. It was only much later, when I was back in London, that I found out that some of the other passengers and crew were adrift for much longer… Then, all I could do was wait… but there was no news. My son's watch still emitted a weak signal, life readings, and that was the only hope I could cling to,' Mr Stryder looked exhausted, and didn't go on.

After a long pause, Mr Henderson asked, 'so, what exactly is that watch… really?'

'Seriously, Gil,' Dr Henderson cut in, 'the man has just told us about what was probably the most harrowing day of his life.'

'I would be just as curious myself,' said Mr Stryder, smiling weakly, 'if I had never seen such a thing before. It's called an acnode, and it's a communication device… and I have no doubt that you've already seen that it can to do some rather amazing things.'

'Yeah,' said Matt, 'we even used it to go back to London to look for you.'

Mr Stryder looked confused, 'A 'node can no more take you through time and space than your cell phone can drive you to the corner store.'

'But we did,' said George, 'we did go back... to look for you.'

'You're having me on. You really went... That's impossible.'

'It was sort of like a dream,' said Alicia as she spoke up for the first time, 'we could do all kinds of things, but it was like no one could see us.'

'I'm sorry,' Mr Stryder smiled and shook his head, 'this is really too much to take in. I'm... I'm far too jet-lagged to make sense of anything right now.'

'You get jet-lagged from time travel?' Mr Henderson asked.

'I suppose that's possible, but in my case, it's from nothing more exotic than travelling on a jet. My flight from London was delayed several hours in Toronto,' he then paused, before adding, 'I did so desperately want to see my boy today, so I came despite the late hour, and for that, I must apologize... however, now I must go.' He then pulled out a rather old looking flip phone, 'do you have a local number for a taxi?'

'Gil,' said Dr Henderson as she turned to her husband, 'why don't you and Matt pull out the sofa in my office,' then she turned back to Mr Stryder, 'you brought a bag with you?'

'Yes... but I have a room booked... I really shouldn't impose... but, then again, I'm too tired... so, for the sake of decorum, let's just pretend that I protested strenuously, yet eventually gave in to your generous offer.'

'Come on Alex,' Mr Henderson said with a laugh, 'this'll just take a few minutes, and then you can get all the sleep you need.'

Thunder rolled in the distance as another storm drew near.

George awoke early, unsure of what had been real, and what had been a dream. He went downstairs to the kitchen, looking for confirmation of the reality of what had happened, and there he found Dr Henderson. She was in the big rocking chair, feeding the baby her morning bottle.

'I'm not disturbing you, am I?' George asked.

'No, not at all... I'm actually grateful for the company. Nessa's a sweet baby, but her conversation skills leave something to be desired.'

'Nessa,' George liked the sound of the name, but couldn't quite place it. 'Is that short of Vanessa?'

'No, Anessa,' said Dr Henderson as she gently rocked the baby, 'I think that I read somewhere that it's Greek, and that it means 'complete'... but I'm not sure why her mother gave her that name.'

'Sorry,' said George, suddenly feeling awkward, 'I didn't know that she wasn't your own...'

'Oh, don't look so embarrassed, George.' said Dr Henderson with a bit of a laugh. 'Giving birth to four of my own was quite enough.'

'Then... um,' George stammered. He wasn't used to talking with adults about such personal things, but then, mercifully, Alicia walked into the kitchen. 'Hey, sleepyhead,' he said, perhaps a little too enthusiastically, 'good morning!'

'What's with you?' she asked.

'Oh, nothing to worry about,' Dr Henderson chuckled as she rose awkwardly from the rocking chair. 'Anyway, the baby needs changing, so I'm just going to take her into the other room... unless, of course, you two would prefer to watch the whole thing while you eat.'

'Eew, Mo-o-om, don't be so gross!' Alicia protested.

'Suit yourselves.'

Alicia rolled her eyes but then, after her mother had left the room, lowered her voice to a whisper, 'so, did you talk with your dad yet... you know, about the freaky jumping around in time stuff?'

'No... I didn't have a chance,' said George as he fidgeted with his toast. 'It's the oddest thing... I know he's my father, but it's as if I don't know him anymore. He's the same person... but different.'

'I kinda know what you mean,' said Alicia, 'like, it's not the same thing at all, but each year when I go back to school, and see all the kids I knew before the summer break... it's like I don't even know them anymore... But you were only away from your dad for a few days.'

'A few days for me, but more than seventy years for him,' said George, 'I simply can't fathom what that might mean.'

'Wow... yeah, that's almost a whole lifetime,' agreed Alicia, 'I mean, is he even the same person? Like, *really* the same?'

'Well, whether he is or not, I must say, it felt ruddy peculiar when I first saw him.'

'Okay, but now that he's here, you really have to ask him about some of this freaky time stuff.'

'Yes, I know, but now that he's here, I'm sure that we'll have all the time in the world to do that.'

It was almost noon before Mr Stryder came out of his room, and although he was so much older than George remembered, he was not as tired, nor as worn, as he had been the night before, and now he seemed to be a little more himself. More like the father George had known back in London.

'Hello Arthur m'boy,' he said as he ruffled George's hair.

'Hey Alex,' said Mr Henderson, 'can I offer you a coffee, or would you prefer tea?'

'I think coffee's what I need. I could use an extra kick to get me going.'

'Dad,' said George, 'what happened?'

'Well, m'boy,' Mr Stryder answered with an unexpected laugh, 'that's a rather loaded question.' He then nodded appreciatively when Mr Henderson handed him a cup, 'ah, that's the stuff.'

'When can we go home?' George asked, 'I mean, since the war is over.'

'The war... oh good lord, of course,' Mr Stryder laid a hand on George's shoulder, 'my dear boy, I am sure that you have many questions, but first, give me chance to ask a few questions of my own, and let me get my bearings back, and then I promise to answer what questions I can.' He smiled, 'so, how long have you been here?'

'I think about two weeks,' George answered.

'Ten days,' said Mr Henderson. 'We were on Hornby Island, and Alicia, my daughter, she found him on the beach.'

'That's not possible,' George's father said, looking altogether shocked.

'I was there,' said Mr Henderson with an uncertain smile, 'and I assure you that's what happened… George was injured, so we called Search and Rescue… my wife's a doctor, so she flew back to Vancouver with him… brought him to Children's Hospital.'

'I went too,' said Alicia.

'But what about the entanglement?' asked Mr Stryder. 'It should have kept him tied down to the emergent location for weeks, months, really.'

'Like quantum entanglement?' asked Mr Henderson.

'It's similar, I suppose, but rather more involved. In fact, when you took George from the beach, it should have felt like hitting an invisible wall.'

'Whoa, so that's what it was,' said Mr Henderson, 'it was the strangest thing, Alicia seemed to know that she had to go with him in the helicopter… but when we tried to take her home from the hospital… she couldn't leave without him.'

'But, that… that's impossible… the largest mass in the vicinity, usually the ground itself, is the anchor,' Mr Stryder turned to George, 'Is it true… that you can't be apart from one another?'

'Um… yes… well, we don't have to be right together,' said George, 'but we can't be very far apart, either.'

'Yeah,' said Alicia, 'it just feels like wading upstream in a river, until you can't wade any more… but I think we can get farther apart now… like, we were more than half a block away when we last tested it… a lot further than when it started.'

'The bond will wear down in time,' said Mr Stryder, thoughtfully, 'but I've never heard of the entanglement forming between two people before.'

'How long will it take?' asked George, 'I mean before we can truly be apart?'

'The half-life of the bond is just about a year.'

George and Alicia shared an uncomfortable glance, and then George asked, 'Dad, what does that mean… precisely?'

'Normally, that would mean that you couldn't leave this place for a long time… but, in your case… I suppose it means that you and

Alice...'

'Alicia,' she quietly corrected him.

'Alicia, will have to be careful not to get too far apart. So traveling in separate cars or planes is out of the question. The bond is unbreakable, and more than powerful enough to cause crashes. I just assumed that you'd be entangled with the location... not another person.'

'What... what causes it? The bond, I mean?' asked Mr Henderson.

'It's an effect of accordant gravitation,' said Mr Stryder as he answered somewhat distractedly. Then he thought about it for a moment, and added, 'the theory is that accordance keeps events stabilized, and it does so by acting on temporal mass... very much as regular gravity acts on physical mass.'

'Dad, now that you're here, shouldn't we travel back and change things so Mum doesn't get lost.'

'No... m'boy,' his father sighed, 'I'm afraid that's just not how it works.' He then reached out and squeezed George's shoulder, 'but don't worry... I'll do everything I can... I promise.'

'So, if that's not how it works,' said Mr Henderson, 'how did you travel through time to get here now?'

'I simply grew older,' replied Mr Stryder. 'We all travel with time... it's traveling against it that's the challenge... and it's pretty much a once in a lifetime journey for those who do... When I was first assigned to Oxford in 1925, I knew that I would never be returning.'

'But... but that was over eighty-five years ago,' Mr Henderson almost stammered, puzzled by what he had just been told. 'You look like you're in your late fifties, early sixties... how...?'

'In my time, people live a bit longer than people do in this time,' replied Mr Stryder. He then paused to take a sip of coffee, before adding, almost casually, 'I was already seventy when I became a father back in 1928.'

'Seriously?' asked Mr Henderson, sounding doubtful.

'When George and his mother, Emily, were lost,' said Mr Stryder, 'I never expected to see either of them again. My only hope was that I might get a letter,' the words seemed to catch in his throat and he paused, gently rocking his cup back and forth, watching the coffee swirl around inside. After a moment more, he added, 'when I did hear from my boy, well, that was a glorious day... and when I saw the time stamp, I knew that I just might have a chance to see him once again... but only after seven decades of waiting.'

There was another long silence, as the meaning of what he had said hung heavy in the room.

'All those years,' said Alicia, 'alone.'

Mr Stryder's face flushed ever so slightly. 'Well, not quite alone,' he said quietly, and then added, 'Arthur m'boy, you and I will need to talk.'

'Dad,' began George, not quite understanding what his father had just said, 'if people can only travel in time once... how are we going to get Mum back?'

'M'boy,' his father replied, 'as I said... we will need to talk.'

'So,' Matt blurted out, 'if you're saying I can only travel in time once, that totally means that I wasted my one trip going to London? HEY!' He yelped as Alicia kicked him under the table. She then gave him an angry glare.

Mr Stryder looked at him with some confusion. 'You mentioned that last night,' he said, 'and I was sure that I had misheard... but you honestly believe that you travelled back in time?'

'I... uh... it might have been a dream... I think,' stammered George.

'My wife thinks it was just an illusion,' said Mr Henderson, 'something conjured up by the watch.'

'I always said it was a dream...' began Alicia.

'When we were in London,' Matt cut in, 'you were talking like it was all real!'

'What*ever*,' she snapped back.

'One thing that's puzzling me,' said Mr Henderson, ignoring his arguing kids, 'is how you managed to travel back in time yourself... I mean, without totally screwing up the past... or the future, for that matter. What about the butterfly effect?'

'Accordant gravitation pretty much keeps things in order,' replied Mr Stryder. 'If you throw a ball into the air, physical gravity will bring it back down. Accordant gravity works in a similar way, but on what we perceive as events: You might change things, but they will eventually balance out.'

'So,' said Mr Henderson, with a tone of challenge in his voice, 'if I were to go online right now, and tell everyone what you just told me, then you're saying that that wouldn't totally wreck the future?'

'By all means, try it,' replied Mr Stryder, his voice becoming oddly cold, 'tell the world what you think you know... and see if anyone will listen. There are a million crackpot theories out there; all claiming to be the truth *writ large*... What makes you think that your ideas will have any more impact than those?'

'My company website has tens of thousands of daily visitors.'

'You think I don't know that?' asked Mr Stryder. 'I've studied the profile the Council has on you, and I know that your company stands to grow significantly over the next few years – that is, assuming the CEO is not dismissed for being mentally unstable.'

'I'm not sure,' said Mr Henderson, his voice growing tense, 'if you intended that as a threat or not.'

'I did not,' replied Mr Stryder flatly, 'it was merely a statement of fact.' George's father seemed to relax a little as he added, 'the fact is, my dear fellow, supressing information is near impossible... But why even bother to try? There's really no need to supress anything, since your claims, no matter how close to the truth they might seem, will simply drown in the veritable sea of misinformation that's already out there... That's just the nature of accordant gravitation. It is only with hindsight in the future that people will be able to look back and determine what was real.'

'But it sounds like you're talking about this 'accordant gravitation' as if it's fate,' said Mr Henderson, 'and I don't believe in fate... or destiny. I believe that we absolutely determine our own futures, which at most is controlled by the laws of probability.'

'By all means, the future is yours to change,' replied Mr Stryder, with a dismissive wave of his hand. 'People once believed that the future was fixed and unchangeable, and they called it fate, and people in your time still believe in the immutability of the past. However, in my time, we know that the future *and* the past can be altered, it's just that accordance keeps both of them from changing too much.' He paused, and then added, 'which is not to say that events are controlled by probability, because that assumes that there is a single correct point of view. There is not – my probability is not the same as yours. For instance, one of the stranger aspects of accordance is that because your future is part of my past, I have less ability to change it than you do.'

Mr Henderson was about to say something, but then stopped, unsure of what he had just heard.

'And how are you to know,' asked Mr Stryder, 'how much of what I've just told you is the actual truth, and how much is misdirection designed to keep you quiet?'

Mr Henderson puzzled over this a moment more, and then finally said, 'you're enjoying this... aren't you... confusing the hell out of me?'

'A little,' admitted Mr Stryder, with an odd grin. 'In fact, my dear fellow, if you are truly determined to share these ideas and test the nature of accordance, then why not bury what I've told you in a dry philosophical treatise. Something impenetrable and grand, something that only a few misguided university students might debate, but never quite resolve, until such time as accordance allows it? Or perhaps, even better,' he added with a chuckle, 'a work of fiction. Something with plenty of teenaged angst, set against a backdrop of zombies and vampires, with just a hint of existential nonsense to help make it all palatable.'

It was turning into a long afternoon, and an even longer discussion, as the two men continued to talk this way for a very long time. However, when they started to debate even more obscure concepts, Alicia had had enough, and she nudged George. 'Hey,' she whispered, 'you wanna go get a couple of slushies?'

'Yes please... I'm really not following any of this, anyway.'

'Daddy,' she said quietly, 'this is all very interesting and everything... but it's also really boring, so George and I are going to go down to the corner store. Okay?'

Chapter Ten

An Unexpected Parting

It was just past midday, and the air beneath the large maple trees was growing hot and humid as George and Alicia walked down the street on their way to the corner store.

'So why didn't you want Matt to ask my dad about travelling to London?' asked George, as he adjusted his pith helmet.

'I don't know,' said Alicia. 'This might sound weird... but it just didn't seem right...your dad's been alone for so long, stuck in one place, and here you are, able to move around in time so easily.'

'Well... when you put it like that,' said George, 'but I suppose there'll be plenty of time to work this all out. My dad's here now, and it looks like we're both going to have to stay for a while yet... at least as long as I'm still glued to you.'

They had walked about a block, when they heard Matt rolling up behind them on his mountain board.

'Yo, freakazoids, watch out!'

'What do *you* want?' Alicia demanded.

'I dunno,' said Matt as he swerved to an expert stop, 'Just wanted to chill... got a problem with that?'

'No... I suppose not,' said Alicia, unable to think of a better comeback.

'We were just going to get a slushie,' said George, 'and this time, I rather think I should like to try it without the brain freeze.'

'Yeah... brain freeze is no fun,' said Matt as he picked up his board and took off his helmet. 'By the way, I have to wear this for safety... so what's your excuse?'

'What? The Bombay Bowler?' asked George, mistaking Matt's question for admiration, 'rather dashing, isn't it?'

'Um... yeah,' Matt looked sideways at Alicia, 'yeah... that's what it is... 'dashing'.'

'I think it looks good on him,' Alicia said, defiantly.

'Yeah, right,' said Matt, 'so, anyway, why'd you kick me when I asked George's dad about London?'

'I don't know,' replied Alicia, frustrated at having to explain herself yet again, especially since she really wasn't sure why she'd done it in the first place. 'It just didn't seem like the right time.'

'But aren't you at least a little curious?'

'Of course I am, but Mr Stryder seemed so upset by the idea, sort of like he thought it was impossible... but also very wrong, too. I don't think people from the future like hearing that they don't know what's happening, any more than we do.'

'I still think it's stupid not to ask,' muttered Matt – then added, 'there's another thing that's bugging me; when Simon Toliver was talking about the 'monster storm'... he wasn't talking about the size of the storm, was he? You guys saw that gargoyle thing again... the one from London... didn't you?'

'I think so,' said George, shivering as he recalled it, even though the memories seemed so faint, so distant. 'And I'm sure that there's more than one of them.'

'Cool!' Matt said in a sort of hushed awe.

'It is *not* cool!' Alicia snapped, 'those things are real, not like your stupid zombie comics!'

'Hey,' replied Matt, a little defensively, 'those are graphic novels... shows what you know.'

'So,' George turned to Alicia, 'you're finally admitting that this jumping around in time isn't a dream? Only, you didn't sound so convinced back in the kitchen.'

'I don't know,' Alicia replied, 'but there's been so much weird stuff since you got here.'

'Yeah... it's been pretty cool,' said Matt, 'but I guess you'll be leaving now that your dad's here.'

'No,' said George, 'no, I don't believe that I actually can, at least not for some time.'

'Sweet,' said Matt, but then quickly added, 'I mean, like, it's not so great for you, but...'

'I know what you meant,' said George, with a bit of a smile.

It wasn't long before they were at the corner store, and after they got their drinks, they sat outside the shop on a bench. This time, George took very small, very careful sips, and it was cold and refreshing. But then the heat that reflected off the pavement, the dust from the road, and the noise of the cars, still made them all a little uncomfortable.

'Come on guys,' said Matt, 'let's go to the woods and get out of the sun.'

'No way,' protested Alicia, 'you just want to go there because you think those things might come back!'

'Fine, then,' said Matt, rolling his eyes in frustration, 'we'll go to the basketball court instead... you know, the one behind the school ... that's a decent place to chill.'

She still hesitated.

'Oh, come on, Alicia, do,' said George, 'I refuse to let fear of those things rule my life.'

With some reluctance, Alicia followed as the boys led the way. At the school, George and Alicia sat on a grassy bank and sipped their drinks, while Matt practiced some basic moves with his new mountain board on the blacktop.[6]

'So, what are you going to do now?' she asked.

'I don't know,' said George, 'there's just so much to take in... but at least now that my dad's here, we can start looking for my mum together.' He gently rocked his slushie so that its contents swirled around, and he smiled to himself as he remembered how his father had done the same with his coffee cup. 'We'll find my mum... and then everything will be back to the way it was.'

'I hope so, I like you and all, but this being stuck with each other is getting old pretty fast.'

---

[6] It may be hard to believe, but back then, mountain, or all-terrain, boards were barely known, and most kids Matt's age were still using skateboards that only rode on pavement. I know it sounds too primitive to be true, but that's really how things were.

'Oh, ho,' he laughed, 'so you think it's been a jolly day at the beach for me?'

Alicia just smiled, and for a while, neither of them said anything as they sat and watched Matt struggling to master his new board. He was not yet used to its eight-inch outboard wheels and larger deck than his regular skateboard.

'Do you mind if I have a go,' asked George, 'only, I've never seen a contraption quite like that... and it looks to be rather a bit of fun.'

'Yeah, sure,' said Matt.

'You gotta put on Matt's helmet,' Alicia called over.

'Are you joking?' laughed George, 'you're mad if you think I'm putting on his manky equipment... besides, I've got my own helmet!'

'Stop worrying,' Matt shouted back, 'it's not like he's going anywhere.'

With only a little guidance, George was standing comfortably on the board.

'Okay,' said Matt, 'now, just kick off with your right foot... easy... don't lose your balance.'

George found that the board moved smoothly, and so he kicked again for a little more speed. He felt a rush of excitement, and looked back over his shoulder, 'this is fantastic!'

The thing about Drysdale School is that it was built on the side of a hill. The school and the basketball court are on the highest ground, while the woods and sport fields are at different levels further down. Alicia was suddenly aware of what was about to happen, and fearing the unique danger that accordant entanglement posed for her and George, she called out, 'DON'T...!'

But it was too late – George had overshot the edge of the blacktop, and was rolling at an ever-increasing speed. Alicia ran after him, fearing the consequences of their entanglement.

As the thrill of the moment overcame him, George couldn't hear a single thing as he flew down the slope, the wind rushing past him. As he headed directly toward two very large Douglas fir trees, without even thinking about what he was doing, he instinctively shifted his weight, leaned into the turn, and carved a clean line around them. He felt another rush.

But the grassy slope quickly gave way to the hard-packed clay of the woods, and the board's big wheels went even faster. Diving, weaving, carving left, then right and left again, his legs tightened with each turn, but finally, it was too much, and he lost it near the swings. He tumbled across the soft woodchips and banged into the support post where he lay for a moment, amazed more than stunned. He pulled off his pith helmet to look at the large new dent in it.

Alicia had felt the pull of entanglement as it threatened to wrench her off her feet, so she had run as fast as she could, and was relieved when George had tumbled to stop, because she knew she wouldn't have been able to keep up if he had gone any farther.

'That was amazing!' Matt shouted as he ran to catch up to them.

Alicia was laughing in spite of herself, 'are you... okay?' she asked while gasping for breath. 'You wiped... out pretty... good!'

'I'm fine,' said George as he sprang to his feet, 'in fact, I'm ready for another go!'

'No... way,' she puffed, 'it's your turn to... run behind me!'

'Whoa,' said Matt, 'later, when we get both of you your own riding gear. Mom would kill me if she found out that I let you go without it.' Matt handed George his slushie, 'anyway, it's almost supper time, and we should probably head home.'

'Are you mad? That was ruddy brilliant... and I want another go,' said George as he took a big slurp of his ice-cold drink. Then, soon as the pain of a fresh brain freeze subsided, he added, 'although... perhaps I shouldn't press my luck...'

With Mr Stryder finally in attendance, supper that night was a time for celebration, and Mr Henderson had almost everyone help with the preparation. He put George and Alicia in charge of washing the greens and making the salad, while Simon Toliver worked the salad spinner. Chella made another of her vegetarian curries, and Matt, who preferred not to cook at all, practiced his guitar, while Dr Henderson sat nearby and fed the baby.

Mr Stryder was sitting at the bar of the big outdoor kitchen as

Mr Henderson tended to the barbeque, and the two men continued their discussion about the effect of accordance on the nature of free will and self-determination.

It all sounded like very grand and important stuff, so neither George nor Alicia felt particularly comfortable asking their own questions. Questions about things like gargoyles, strange shadows, and jumping around in time. However, later in the evening after supper, while the light was golden and the air fresh, they took Mr Stryder on a tour of Alicia's garden.

'When I was a boy,' he said, a little wistfully, 'my grandfather grew his own vegetables... but that will be such a very long time from now.'

'Dad, can we have a garden when we get our new place? I'm finding it such a treat to grow things.'

'We will see, m'boy, but I can't make any promises.'

A cool breeze blew through the yard, and above, clouds formed out of the clear sky. At first, the setting sun was golden across the undersurface of the steel grey clouds, but its light was soon extinguished as the storm grew with unnatural vigour. A flash of lightning, a deafening crack of thunder, and then the rain began to pelt down.

'What the devil is going on?' Mr Stryder growled, but then his eyes grew wide. He spoke in a hoarse whisper as he saw the winged shadows circling above, 'bloody hell... not sappers!'

'Dad! You know what they are?'

'Get inside! Both of you!'

'Dad, I'm not leaving you!'

'Come on!' Alicia shouted as she tried to pull George toward the house, but he refused to leave his father's side. Then Mr Stryder roughly pushed him away, just as a shadow swooped down so close that Alicia could feel its wings brush her face.

Another blinding flash and crash of thunder, and then red and blue sparks began to snake across the grass while more winged shadows circled above.

As the storm grew, the air pressure dropped so fast that Alicia cried out in pain as her ears popped. Then a noise like a freight train came roaring out of nowhere.

A shadow crashed into Mr Stryder and he was knocked flat. The tornado then roared over him, and in an instant, he was swallowed by the spinning mass of cloud.

Fighting against the force of the wind, Mr Henderson struggled to reach George and Alicia. He grabbed them both, and pulled them back into the house.

'My dad!' cried George, 'my dad's still out there! I'm going back out!'

Mr Henderson slammed the door shut. 'No way kid. You stay here... I'll go.'

'Dad! No!' Alicia yelled, the roar of the storm almost drowning her voice.

Through the window, the two watched as Mr Henderson tried to fight his way across the deck and down toward where George's father had fallen, but then there was another flash, and the whole house shook with the impact.

Then the storm simply fell apart, and through its dying shreds Alicia could see her father, sprawled on the ground, unmoving.

'Daddy!' she cried as she threw open the door and ran outside.

George ran past her, to the blackened patch of grass where his own father had fallen. There was nothing left of the man but his shattered acnode, lying in pieces on the edge of the patio bricks.

The whole world seemed distant, muffled, and utterly unreal to George as he watched Alicia huddle over her own father, while Matt ran from the house to join her. George didn't even notice as the air started to shimmer – it was Matt who realized that something was about to happen, and he instinctively grabbed his sister's arm as everything went black and a hollow wind roared up around them.

When the blackness faded and the light returned, it was the dull grey light of winter dusk.

George heard Alicia pleading with her father to get up, and turned to see her and Matt still huddled over their father.

Where are we now? George wondered, as he looked around at the vaguely familiar city street. There were a number of grand old buildings on one side, and the remains of a park on the other. Around the park, traces of old wrought iron fencing remained hanging in the air, like ghostly images of what had once been, while the lawns and flowerbeds had all been dug up and overturned.

'Why is Dad here?' Matt asked as he crouched down next to her.

'I was holding his hand,' Alicia said quietly, 'I didn't see the sparks until it was too late.'

'Where do you think we are now?' Matt asked.

George walked over to a small sign posted next to the square, and read aloud 'Managed by the St James Square Victory Garden Committee.' He looked around, 'so I suppose we've finally made it.'

'So all that crap about travelling only once is totally bogus,' said Matt. 'Okay… so what should we do now?'

'I don't know what *you* want to do,' said George, 'but I'm going to find my dad and warn him about what just happened.'

'No way!' Alicia snapped, 'we're not leaving dad just lying here on the street.' She quickly looked around and saw a large ornate doorway behind them. 'There,' she said, 'give me a hand moving him over there… to the doorway with number 16 on it.'

'Are you kidding, Allie?' Matt protested, 'you want us to carry him? Dad's no lightweight!'

'He's not fat, if that's what you're saying!'

'Let's at least try to wake him up first,' said George.

'What do you think I've been trying to do?' demanded Alicia. 'Look, George,' she said with the sort of authority that her father usually asserted, 'you and I will each get an arm, and Matt, you get his legs.' It was awkward, and definitely not pleasant to watch, but eventually they were able to lift, drag, carry, roll, and otherwise manoeuvre Mr Henderson into the doorway. There they propped him up on the steps, and when his head lolled forward, Alicia gently pushed it back to rest against the wall.

'All right… good,' said George, 'now I'm off to find my dad.'

'You're not going anywhere,' said Alicia, firmly, 'we have to stick together.'

George turned to her in disbelief, 'so we're supposed to just sit around here and do nothing?'

'I'm not leaving my dad, and we can't be apart,' said Alicia, 'anyway, nobody can see us – remember? Your dad won't be able to see or hear you, so you won't be able to warn him about anything, anyway.'

'Well, this is stupid,' said Matt. 'What's the point of coming here, then? What's the point of having an adventure if we can't, like, have a decent adventure?'

George looked surprised and just stared at Matt for a moment, and then burst out laughing. Alicia looked annoyed at first, but found it difficult to keep a straight face, and soon she was giggling with nervous tension.

'What?' demanded Matt, 'what's so funny?'

'It's just... it's just all so... so *silly*, so utterly absurd,' said George. 'By all rights, we should all be scared out of our wits with what's going on... and instead, you're complaining about the relative quality of the adventure.'

'Well... yeah,' Matt began defensively, 'but it is really stupid to come here and then do nothing. I mean, what's the point?'

'Maybe there never was a point,' Alicia joked.

'Now that's the scariest thing of all,' laughed George, 'what if none of this means anything?' He laughed again, but the emptiness of what he had just said sank in, and the smile faded from his face. 'Well, that's an unhappy thought. No, there simply must be a purpose to it all... we just haven't worked out what it is yet.'

With that thought hanging in the air, they sat on the steps and waited for Mr Henderson to wake up, or for something, anything, to happen. The dull light of dusk faded into night as the full moon rose over the city, but there was not even a hint of artificial light visible anywhere.

'Why is it so dark and empty here... so dead?' asked Matt.

'It's the blackouts; they started in the summer before we left London... along with the curfew.'

'Oh, George... look,' said Alicia as she pointed across to the garden, toward where a small shadow sat quietly in the moonlight, 'it looks like that little fox from the garden.'

'It can't be,' said George as he craned his neck to get a better look, 'I mean it couldn't be the same one... could it?'

'Well, it seems to be watching us,' Alicia said, 'and it sure looks the same.'

In the distance, an air raid siren began its mechanical wail, and soon other nearby sirens joined in the unearthly chorus. Then, a series of rapid explosions echoed across the city, followed by small explosive puffs high over East London.

'What're those?' Alicia shouted over the sirens.

'Anti-aircraft fire,' George replied as he scanned the sky for signs of any shadows blocking the stars. 'We'll need to get to a shelter.'

'We can't... I'm not leaving my dad!'

George felt something brush against his leg – it was the fox. She pawed at him as she looked up at him expectantly. 'Go away, shoo you silly thing!'

'What do you think it wants?' Matt asked.

The rumble of hundreds, if not thousands, of airplanes drew closer as the anti-aircraft fire grew louder. Nearby, a strange whistling sound was followed by a deafening explosion, and a cloud of fire erupted in the next street.

Just then, a muffled volley of creative swearing came from the doorway behind them. 'What the hell is going on?' demanded Mr Henderson.

'Daddy!' Alicia called out, 'you're okay!'

'I am damn-well *not* okay! Where are we?'

'We're in London,' Matt shouted.

'What the hell are you talking about?' Mr Henderson shook his head and blinked hard.

'We need to get into a shelter...,' shouted George, as the planes roared overhead and more bombs fell and fireballs erupted throughout the city. The fox snapped and pulled on the cuff of George's jeans. 'What is with this ruddy fox?'

'We have to follow her,' shouted Alicia.

The fox nodded vigorously, and then ran to the side of the building, where she indicated a deep stone stairwell descended to the building's ground floor.

'We gotta go down there,' Alicia called out.

Wave after wave of bombers roared overhead, and the anti-aircraft artillery grew more desperate, peppering the sky with flak, while the moon was blotted out by smoke billowing up from hundreds of fires in the East End.

In the near total darkness of the stairwell, they felt their way down into the relative safety of its depths, but then a building on the other side of the square exploded, and debris crashed into the wall above, raining down onto them. Mr Henderson took most of the glancing impacts of falling rubble on his back, but he could not keep the others safe from the choking clouds of dust that rose up.

It may have been an hour, or two, but eventually the roar of the planes faded, and the wail of the sirens died away, only to be replaced by the shouts of men battling the fires.

'You stay here,' growled Mr Henderson, his voice hoarse with dust. 'I'm just going to have a look.'

The world seemed to be spinning out of control beneath him as he made his way up the stairs. Through the balustrade, he could see men from the volunteer fire brigade blurring back and forth, fighting to keep the fires contained.

'You stay here,' he called down the stairs, even as the spinning kept getting worse, 'I'm going to see if I can help.'

'You can't, Dad, there's nothing you can do for them,' Alicia ran after him as he staggered into the street, 'they can't even see you.'

'What the hell do you mean?'

'Dad, we can't change things,' Matt said as he bounded up the stairs to his father, followed closely by George.

'Sir, it's true, there really is nothing that we can do.'

'So, what *is* this? Some sort of illusion... like, from your watch?' Mr Henderson asked, 'there's no way that thing could be generating this level of... of... reality!' he protested. It all seemed too much for him to take in, his head began to swim and he fell to his knees.

The air began to shimmer as red and blue sparks started to snake along the ground toward them. Mr Henderson teetered and fell over, his eyes rolled up, and the last thing he was aware of was the sound of his daughter's voice echoing in the distance.

'Dad, hold on!'

Mr Henderson opened his eyes, only to see his wife kneeling beside him. 'Gil, take it easy, the paramedics are on their way.'

Chapter Eleven

Leaving Home

Mr Henderson propped himself up on his elbows as his world was starting to come into focus again.

'Hon,' he said, 'you'd better call the paramedics and tell them not to come.'

'Why on earth would I do that?' she demanded.

'I feel fine,' he lied, as his head felt like it was going to explode. 'And besides,' he added with some difficulty, 'you're a doctor and you can check me out... please call and cancel.' He looked around and saw Alicia, Matt and George standing over him. 'Where's Alex?'

'Uh, well,' Dr Henderson hesitated, 'he's gone... it looks like... like he took a direct hit from the lightning... and...'

Mr Henderson struggled to his feet, but found that he was less steady than he expected. Chella and Simon Toliver came bursting out the back door.

'Daddy!' Chella cried, 'Are you all right?'

'Fine, Princess, just fine,' he looked down at the scorched lawn where Mr Stryder had fallen. 'Gayle, you have to cancel the paramedics right *now* – do it before they get here!'

'But why?'

'Because all this has to do with that damn watch, and the Stryders... there's some genuinely weird crap going on here, and having the paramedics here won't help a bit. The last thing we need is to get more people involved.'

'Gil, you've been hit by lightning and I want to make sure that you're okay!'

'But how are we going to explain Alex's disappearance? He spontaneously exploded? There should at least be a body.'

'Gil!' Dr Henderson snapped, 'show a little sensitivity! His son is standing right there!'

'So then, what the hell *did* happen to him?'

'The shadows took Mr Stryder,' said Simon Toliver.

Dr Henderson's face went pale as she turned to her youngest son. She didn't say anything, but quickly pulled out her phone and called to cancel the ambulance.

Mr Henderson rubbed his neck and looked back at the scorched lawn. 'So what the hell could have made him completely disappear like that?'

'It was the shadows, Daddy,' said Simon Toliver.

George, Matt and Alicia exchanged glances, but Mr Henderson did not seem to hear his youngest. Before the others could ask Toliver any questions, Mr Henderson barked. 'You kids, inside,' he gestured toward the house. 'Your mother and I need to talk to you. That means you too, George, as long as you are under our roof, you're one of ours.'

Dr Henderson looked uneasy. 'Gil, I need to check on the baby first.'

'Huh,' Mr Henderson glanced over to her, the bark gone out of his voice, 'of course... are you okay?' but when he saw the kids hesitating, he turned back to them and snapped, 'move it!'

Once they were all in the great-room, Mr Henderson looked at each of them in turn. 'I have no damn idea what's going on, and that's not how I like to operate, so I want some answers.' He paused, as if wanting to start again, 'look, there's some *very* freaky stuff going on here... George, let's start with our unexpected little trip to London. Is that the sort of thing you were talking about... before... at the hospital, and again at dinner the other night?'

'Uh, yes, sir.'

'Well... that was way more than an illusion,' said Mr Henderson, 'we were really there... in another time.' Then, his voice softened as he asked the next question, 'So, George, just now... is it possible that's what happened to your dad... could he have been pulled into another time and place... sort of like we just were?'

'Yes... but I think,' George wasn't sure how to say it in a way that sounded believable. 'I-I think the creatures took him.'

Mr Henderson looked puzzled. 'Alright,' he said with an odd tone of increasing anger, 'what do you mean 'the creatures took him'?'

'Simon Toliver saw them,' Alicia said, a little nervously, 'he saw them take Mr Stryder.'

'I see,' said Mr Henderson, with a certain forced calmness. He put his hands behind his neck, as he would when he did sit-ups, but this time he was trying to stop the throbbing pain in his head. 'Dammit, kids, this is serious stuff... first we get thrown into London during the Blitz...' He suddenly dropped his voice to a whisper, 'which, by the way, you are not to mention to your mother under any circumstances. And now,' he continued, 'you're telling me that some *creatures* took us back in time? '

'Well,' Alicia began hesitantly, 'I don't think they're the ones actually making us... stride... they just seem to be there... sometimes.'

'There? Where is 'There'?' Mr Henderson demanded.

'It's where we just were,' said Alicia.

'You mean London during the war?'

'Sometimes,' she replied, 'but... but it can be other places too... it's like in a dream... or an in-between place.'

Mr Henderson turned away and punched the air rapidly to release his growing frustration, but then he stopped and let his arms fall to his sides and took a few deep breaths. It was all just a matter of needing more information, he figured, and there was nothing he couldn't handle if he could just understand the details.

He then turned to face the kids once again, 'look, in case you hadn't noticed, I'm trying to help, but I can't do that unless you help me, too.' He again looked at each one of them in turn. 'I need you to tell me everything. Allie, why don't you go first?'

'Well,' Alicia spoke hesitantly, 'we were in my vegetable garden... and then there was this cold wind...'

'And we heard thunder,' added George, 'and the clouds seemed to come out of nowhere... and then I saw the creatures flying over us...'

'These gargoyle things?' Mr Henderson prompted. 'Toliver, are those what you saw?'

Simon Toliver looked at the floor and spoke in a very small voice. 'They just look like shadows to me.'

'But I think George's dad could see them,' said Alicia.

'Matt, did you see any of this?' asked Mr Henderson.

'Me? No I was stuck inside doing the stupid dishes, remember?'

Alicia turned to George, 'your dad said something... he called the creatures something...'

'Right,' said George, 'what was it... it sounded like 'raptors'...'

'Like birds of prey?' asked Mr Henderson.

'Or dinosaurs?' Matt suggested, hopefully.

'No... that wasn't it,' said Alicia, then she burst out, 'I remember! It was 'sappers', he called them sappers, and that's when he made us run to the house.'

'Okay, now we're getting somewhere,' said Mr Henderson, 'Do you still have your watch with you?'

George pulled out his watch, and flipped it open.

'Good,' said Mr Henderson, 'ask it for as much information as it has on sappers.'

George made the query and the watch face glowed a faint gold colour as the big book appeared to open up and hover in front of him. An entry on the page was highlighted, and he read it aloud;

'Sapper (noun), 1. Military specialist in constructing trenches and tunnels, or in conducting trench warfare. 2. Specialist in mines; deploying, locating and or disarming landmines. 3. Individual with the rank of private in the British Army, Royal Engineers...'

'Well, that's not much help,' said Mr Henderson, 'anything more?'

'4. Short for Time Sapper, mythological being of darkness and shadow, which is said to stalk human prey...'

'Bloody hell,' muttered George as he closed his watch and tried his best to keep from trembling. 'Is that what's going to happen to my dad?'

Mr Henderson crouched down in front of him, 'listen, kid, we'll do everything we can... but right now, you might want to use that watch of yours to write to your dad... in the past... and give him a warning. Ask him what he knows about these things.'

'Of course,' said George, with some relief, 'why hadn't I thought of that before?' He had been so focused on finding his father in London, and so distracted with everything else that had happened, that he had completely forgotten about simply sending a letter. He flipped open his watch once again. 'New letter, Alex Stryder, use primary established link.'

The watch chimed softly and a piece of paper appeared to float in front of him:

'Alex Stryder: Primary, secondary and tertiary links unavailable. Would you like to create a bottle or a balloon instead?'

'Uh,' George hesitated a moment, as he had to think back to what he had read about the different types of messages, 'balloon... no change that... create a bottle: Dear Dad, When you come to meet me in Vancouver, there will be some creatures, Time Sappers, that will attack us. Please take whatever precaution...'

The watch played a flat chord and a new message appeared:

'To prevent congestion in the message-sphere, bottles are limited to 144 characters (including spaces), you are about to exceed that limit, would you like to send the message as is, or do you wish to revise?'

'Send... no, revise...' The watch chimed softly.

'Message sent. Your account has been billed. Would you care to review your statement?'

'No... thank you.' George said as he closed the watch.

'What the heck is a bottle?' asked Matt.

'It's a message that just floats out there until a link reforms,'

George replied, distractedly, 'it's not sent to any particular time.'

'Give it time, kid,' said Mr Henderson, trying hard to sound reassuring. 'I'm sure your dad will get the message... and then everything will be all right.'

'Yeah... he'll get it,' said Alicia, 'and then he'll know what to do.'

'I hope so,' said George, 'because the book said that those things *eat* people...'

The feeling that night in the Henderson house was uneasy, although memories of the evening's events were fading unnaturally fast.

It was very late, and George had spent hours reading the big instruction book, but was frustrated by how very little it contained on the subject of sappers. With all that had gone on that day, he couldn't sleep, so he went down to the kitchen.

The stairway was dark, except for the moonlight that shone through the large window and pooled on the landing, and in that dim blue light he was sure that he saw the fox's white-tipped tail flick around the corner, but when he looked again, there was no sign of her.

As he approached the kitchen, warm light flooded into the hallway, and when he entered, he found Dr Henderson sitting in the big rocking chair feeding the baby.

'Trouble sleeping?' she asked.

'Yes... so I was rather hoping that a cup of warm milk might help.'

She smiled, 'That always works for me... You know where everything is?' She then hesitated before adding, 'George... ever since I was diagnosed with MS, my husband has developed the really sweet, but incredibly annoying, habit of trying to shelter me.'

George was surprised by this admission, but said nothing.

'I know there are some very strange things going on... and I know what you saw today was terrifying.' She then paused as she gently shifted the baby to a more comfortable position, 'so if you ever want to talk about it, that's okay. Despite what Gil might say, you can talk to me about anything... I'm here for you.'

'Th-thanks... but I'm fine,' he lied.

'Yes,' she smiled, 'I can see that... and I'm sure that when you drink warm milk, you always shake like a leaf.'

'D-d-do I?' George stammered. 'N-no, I'll be fine... I just need to get a grip. Stiff upper lip, and all that... what? Why are you laughing?'

'I'm sorry, George, I just didn't think anyone actually said that anymore.' She paused as the smile faded from her face. 'Seriously, I want you to remember that you don't have to go through this alone.'

'Thanks... I'll... uh... I'll be fine... and so will my dad... I've sent a letter to warn him.'

'That's good... it gives you good reason to hope, and that's always important.'

George finished his milk, thanked Dr Henderson, and returned to his room. However, once there, sleep still eluded him, and the night seemed to drag on forever. He watched the moon slowly trace its arc across sky through his bedroom window, then, when it seemed like he would never be able to sleep again, there was a gentle rustling, and he looked over to where the moonlight fell on the middle of his bedroom floor. As first, he wasn't sure if he was imagining it, but soon the pale blue light started to ripple, and then the air above it shimmered. Silently, gracefully, the air seemed to form into the fox, and then the little creature looked up, and jumped onto his bed and curled up right beside him. This ghostly occurrence might have seemed strange, but at that moment, it all seemed completely natural.

'I've missed you, you know... so who *are* you, anyway?'

The fox made no sound, but simply nestled closer to him, and then closed her eyes and went to sleep.

When George awoke in the morning, he stayed in his bed and kept his eyes closed, listening to the sounds outside. His mother was gone, and his father had vanished, but now, for just a moment, he wanted to pretend that he was safely back home with them. In London.

In fact, he could almost hear the familiar early morning sounds of his neighbourhood. The gentle clatter of the horse-drawn milk-wagon as it ambled down the street, with the horses' hooves clopping along unhurriedly as the glass bottles rattled in their racks. It was a familiar sound that reminded him of the time when the old milkman, Tom, had told him that he didn't trust motorcars, and that his horse, Walter, would never forgive him if he went modern. George smiled to himself, and for just a moment, he was sure that it sounded real once again.

He opened his eyes and to his astonishment, he was back in his old bedroom. The sounds *were* real. He quickly got out of bed, and moved very carefully, as if tripping, or bumping into something, might break the spell or wake him from this wonderful dream. He cautiously washed up, and then got dressed, and as he slipped on his old woollen trousers, he was surprised by how heavy they felt, compared to the cotton jeans he had been wearing at the Hendersons. But of course these clothes feel heavy, he thought, because they're real, while everything at the Hendersons had been nothing more than a dream.

As he went down to join his parents for breakfast, as he always had in the past, doubt suddenly clouded his mind, and he stopped before he reached the bottom of the stairs. He paused and closed his eyes as he made a silent wish. Only then did he continue toward the cramped little kitchen at the back of the house. And just like any other morning, his parents were there, waiting for him.

His father, once again a younger man, was sitting at the little kitchen table reading the Times, while his mother was fixing breakfast on the old hob. She was just as he remembered her, a short, slightly plump woman, with a warm smile and a glint in her hazel eyes that her friends and neighbours could never quite describe, except to say that she had an intriguingly exotic air about her. He ran and embraced her.

'My, that's a big hug, Georgie.'

In the past, George had never really liked it when his mother called him Georgie, but right at that very moment, it was the very dearest thing she could possibly say.

'Chin up, m'boy,' said his father as he put down the paper, 'it's not the end of the world.'

His mother then brushed his cheek with a reassuring hand. 'I know you were disappointed when we left our house in Oxford last year, but we managed... didn't we? And I know that it's terribly upsetting to have to leave our home once again, but your father and I will still be with you... and soon we'll be able to make a new home in Canada'

'It's not that,' replied George, barely able to find the words, 'it's just that... I had this terrible dream...'

'It'll fade soon enough, then,' said his father as he stood up to go, folding his paper under his arm and picking up his umbrella and old leather briefcase. 'Well, I'm afraid I have some business to take care of, so I'll have to leave the two of you to finish packing. However, I shall be back before tea.'

'All right, love,' said Mrs Stryder, 'we'll be busy enough here.'

'Dad,' said George, a little hesitantly, 'do you know what sappers are?'

'A rank in the Royal Engineers, aren't they, m'boy?'

'Yes... I suppose... it's just that in my dream there were these things... Time Sappers.'

'Those? But they're just a myth, m'boy,' his father said as he casually flipped on his bowler hat. 'Right now, the only monsters we have to worry about are the Nazis... and unfortunately, they are very real.'

'You best hurry, Alex,' said Mrs Stryder, 'or you'll be late.'

'Right you are m'dear,' Mr Stryder said as he turned and gave her a quick peck on the cheek before heading out the front door.

George ran to the window and watched his father as he strutted up the street, confidently swinging his umbrella.

'Now, Georgie,' said his mother, 'your father will be back soon enough, and we'll be so busy that you'll hardly notice the time fly by.'

It was late afternoon, and George's footsteps echoed off the bare walls as he walked through the newly empty rooms. His mother had asked him to make one last check for anything they might have forgotten, while she went to the neighbour's to return some borrowed items and there was almost nothing left in the house now, barely a trace that his family had ever lived there.

To pass the time, George pulled his favourite book from his suitcase, sat on one of the steamer trunks, and began to read. It was just as he reached the part where Rupert Bear and Bill Badger were about to enter an enchanted wood, when out of the corner of his eye he saw the air start to shimmer. He dropped his book in astonishment.

'You can see me?' asked Alicia, 'Finally! I've been going nuts trying to get your attention.'

'What are you doing here?' he asked in disbelief.

'Duh, we can't be separated.'

'But you were just a dream,' he protested as he bent down to pick up his book, '... just a dream.'

'Hey, I thought the same thing about you.'

'So what happened?' he asked as he sat back down on the trunk.

'I don't know, like, I went to bed last night like always, but when I woke up... I was here and you couldn't see me... or hear me. It was really weird,' she paused, and then added, 'but then again, since I met you... I've kinda gotten used to weird.'

'I'm not going back,' said George, defiantly, 'I'm home, with my parents, and I'm going to stay here.'

'Well, if you think I'm going to stay stuck here, you're nuts!' snapped Alicia. 'Besides, it looks like you're getting ready to leave anyway.'

'Well, yes... we're sailing for Canada tomorrow... just as we were supposed to... in my own time... but now, what about you, how are we going to get you back home, to your time?'

'Well, something's gotta happen... eventually,' said Alicia as she looked around, 'so this is your house before it got bombed? It's... nice.'

'Well, it's not so grand, but it is – or at least it was – home.'

Alicia felt awkward comparing their homes, so she wanted to

change the subject. 'So, what are you reading?'

'The Adventures of Rupert,' replied George as he held up the book for her to see. 'My mum can't stand the newspaper it's in, so I just get the annuals instead.'

'So, like, what's it about?'

'Well, Rupert and his friends have all sorts of grand adventures,' said George, but then he paused a moment before adding thoughtfully, 'you know, whenever Rupert gets back home, everything is right with his world once more... I've always liked that about his stories.'

Just then, the front door opened and his mother came in. 'Hello Georgie, I'm back,' she said, 'who were you talking to, dear?'

George was surprised that she couldn't see Alicia at all, even though she was standing right there in front of him. 'Uh... no one, I suppose,' he answered, 'just talking to myself.'

'Oh, I know what that's like, dear,' his mother replied, closing the door and taking off her headscarf, 'I have some of my best conversations that way.'

'This is totally freaky,' said Alicia, 'so your mom can't see or hear me at all... but you can?'

'Uh... yes, I suppose so,' said George, answering both his mother and Alicia at the same time.

'I stopped at the baker's,' said Mrs Stryder, 'and picked up a couple of Cornish pasties for us to have now, and some custard tarts for tea when your father gets back.' She smiled at him, 'so why don't we have ourselves a little picnic now. That'll be nice, won't it?'

'Yes... thanks, Mum.'

'My,' said Mrs Stryder as she looked around the empty room, 'it's freezing in here. Well, there's no sense saving any of the coal in the scuttle. We might as well use it up, since we certainly won't be packing *that* off to Canada.' She opened up the coal stove and placed a particularly large lump on the dwindling fire. 'It's a shame we've already sold the wireless, it would have been nice to have had a little music to listen to.'

'Wow, so you had wireless stuff back then, I mean now?' asked Alicia, 'what is it... like, Wi-Fi?'

'It's a radio,' answered George.

'Sorry, Georgie, what did you say?' his mother asked distractedly.

'A... a radio, Mum... in Canada, I think the wireless is called a radio.'

'Oh, I do believe you're right,' she smiled, 'well, I can see you'll have no trouble fitting in when we get to our new home. You wait here and I'll just pop the kettle on for a spot of tea.'

As Mrs Stryder went to the small kitchen, Alicia turned to George. 'Your mom is a really nice lady.'

'I know, and I don't want to lose her... not again,' he whispered, 'but I have no idea how I'm going to convince my parents not to get on that ship... especially if they've already paid for the tickets.'

'Yeah,' agreed Alicia, 'that might be tough.'

'My dad should be back soon,' he said, glancing toward the kitchen where his mother still busied herself. He then lowered his voice to only the faintest of whispers, 'the problem is, we can't stay here, either, since you and I know perfectly well that this house gets bombed.'

'Why don't you show them the letters from your watch?' suggested Alicia, 'that might convince them.'

'Of course... I'd completely forgotten about those,' said George as he fumbled through his pockets, but the more he looked, the more frantic he became. 'I can't find it! I've lost it!'

'What's that, Georgie? What have you lost?'

'My watch, Mum, my pocket watch!'

'But Georgie, we haven't given it to you yet,' replied his mother as she came into the front parlour carrying a small tea tray. 'How ever did you find out about that? I thought your father was saving it as a surprise for tonight.'

'Sorry, Mum,' said George, 'I-I must have dreamt about it.'

'Oh, dear,' she said as she poured the tea and handed him a cup, 'then I've just gone and ruined the surprise, haven't I? So you must promise to be surprised when your father does give it to you.' She then hesitated before asking, 'this dream... is it anything you wish to talk about, anything in particular?'

'Mum... I can't remember it all, but I think something terrible happened to the ship we were on... will be on... and you were lost.'

'Oh, love, I know that you're worried, but your father has looked into this very carefully, and he knows that we'll be safe. I can't tell you how, but your father knows these things.' She smiled, and then added, 'we really don't have a choice... we simply must move to Canada.'

'Whoa,' Alicia yelped, 'something's happening...'

George watched in disbelief as the air in front of him rippled and swirled, and then Alicia was gone. 'But I don't understand,' he mumbled, 'I thought we couldn't be separated.'

'Oh Georgie,' replied his mother, 'I promise... we won't be...'

Alicia awoke to find her own mother sitting on the edge of her bed, holding her hand.

'How are you feeling?'

Alicia thought that was an odd question, because she was fine, but then she realized that she wasn't really fine at all. She actually felt sick, really sick, and it was difficult for her to focus.

'You've still got a bit of a fever,' said her mom, 'but it's not as bad as it was this morning.'

'Where's George?' Alicia asked as her voice came out hoarser than she expected.

'Who?'

'George... you know... George Stryder... the boy we found on the beach.'

'I think you're just going to have to rest a little more,' said Dr Henderson as she stood up slowly, 'at least until your fever comes down a bit more. Would you like your dad to bring you anything, maybe some chicken soup?'

'No... no thanks.'

'Okay, sweetheart... but call if you change your mind.'

'Why don't you remember George?'

'Oh, honey, I've got a lot of work to catch up on right now. Maybe you can tell me about him later...'

Chapter Twelve

A Change in Travel Plans

The threat of losing his parents hung heavy in George's mind. He sat at the front window of the house and watched the steady rain as he waited for his father to return. It was late in the afternoon when George finally caught a glimpse of his father hurrying down the street, struggling against the bitterly cold wind.

Before Mr Stryder had even doffed his hat and hung up his greatcoat, he greeted George with a big smile. 'Arthur, m'boy, the world is changing, and... well... I want you to be prepared,' he said as he pulled the little gold watch from his breast pocket, holding it up for his son to see, 'do you know what this is, m'boy?'

'It's my watch!' George said as he hugged his father, 'thank you!'

'Well m'boy,' said his father, clearly pleased by his son's reaction, 'it's so much more than just a watch.'

'I know,' said George excitedly as his father handed it to him. 'It's a 'node... and I can use it to send you letters.'

His father's smile vanished. 'How could you possibly know that?'

Just then, Mrs Stryder came into the room and kissed her husband. 'Did you get all your business with the Ministry done?'

'Uh... yes, dear... Did you tell George about the watch?'

'No my love, I didn't want to spoil your surprise... but he did seem to know about it, so I thought that perhaps you'd already told him about it.'

'M'boy,' said Mr Stryder, turning back to George and looking rather stern, 'we need to talk.'

'I didn't mean to spoil your surprise,' said George, 'it was just a dream.'

'No, I don't think it was.' His father said as he sat down on one of the large steamer trunks. 'Look, m'boy, I'm not angry with you, I'm just very concerned, and I need you to tell me everything you know.'

'Listen, son, I need to ask you... Did Mr Sikes tell you about the watch?'

'Who? No, not that I recall... it was a dream... or at least it felt like a dream at first... sometimes... but then it was all so dreadfully real.'

'Arthur,' Mr Stryder spoke in low, even tones, but George was sure that he saw fear in his father's eyes. 'M'boy, where I work, we get used to some damned peculiar things, things that seem to make no sense... that is, until one little detail is uncovered... and that's when things begin to fall into place... Dream or not, I need you to tell me everything that you can about how you came to know about the watch.'

George was confused by his father's sudden intensity, and found it hard to concentrate, but then decided that the best thing was to show his father one of his own letters, so he flipped open the watchcase and said, 'retrieve all correspondence: Alex Stryder,' but the watch did nothing.

'M'boy, how could you possibly know the commands?'

'I thought I did, but now it won't work. I wanted to show you some of the letters you wrote to me.'

'That *I* wrote to you?'

'Yes.'

'Well, you won't be able to do anything until you register your 'node,' said Mr Stryder. 'Hold it up so that it can see your face, and then say 'activate authorization' and then say your name – your full name.'

George did as he was instructed, a little uncertain of what to expect. 'Activate authorization, Arthur George Edward Stryder.'

The little watch chimed softly and a message appeared to float above it:

'Activation request sent: Processing... authorization for Arthur George Edward Stryder is confirmed.'

The watch then made a different chime and a new message appeared:

'To begin personalization, please place this device on a sample of your handwriting.' George looked to his father.

'Yes, yes, fine,' said Mr Stryder, impatiently. 'Do you have something you've written?'

George snapped up his Rupert Bear book, and flipped it open to where he had written his name and address inside the front cover. He then placed it on his handwriting, and the watch chimed softly as it produced a new message:

'Sample processed. Would you like to view your account options?'

'That's enough for now,' snapped his father, 'I need to see those letters now.'

This time, when George repeated his request, the watch face glowed a faint blue, and then a small stack of pages appeared and his father began to read them.[7]

'This says that the ship sank,' his father mumbled, 'and that you and your mother are lost.'

'I wanted to tell you,' said George.

'Who's lost?' asked Mrs Stryder as she came back with the tea. She placed the tray on one of the big trunks and then wiped her hands on her apron. 'Oh, love, is it bad news from the future?'

'Mum... you know about this?' George asked in amazement.

'Dear boy, I've known about what your father does since before you were born.'

---

[7] Because the letters were composed and sent through George's acnode, they actually exist in the broader landscape of time, and therefore his acnode is able to navigate to their location regardless of when in *linear* time they were written, or even when in linear time the request might be made. However, that is not to say that one can simply request to see *all* the letters that one might write in one's lifetime, as one has to know about individual letters in the first place, before one can request to see them. This is because the physical addresses have not been established, and therefore the acnode is unable able to discern which probabilities will solidify and become affixed to the landscape. For even more confusing information on the nature of time's broader landscape, see *Appendix C – The Paradoxical Grandfather*

'I'm afraid,' said Mr Stryder, 'that we're going to have to change our plans, my dear, it looks like the boat we've booked passage on was sunk after all... or at least... it will be sunk.'

'Oh, Alex, how are we ever going to come up with the money for new tickets... and a hotel... we need to be out of the house by tomorrow – the new tenants will be moving in.'

'I hate to do it,' said Mr Stryder, 'but I'll have to call my superior.' He then spoke into his wristwatch, 'new message, set contemporary link, encryption high: Mr Sikes; Dear Sir; Requesting assistance with changed travel plans – please advise. Signed, Alex Stryder. Send mail.'

'Alex, don't worry,' said George's mother, 'I'm sure he'll be able to help. Didn't you once tell me that the Council gives Continuity Managers so much more leeway to change things?'

Alicia was having a perfectly wonderful dream about riding a flying bicycle, when she felt a nudge, and suddenly she was standing in the schoolyard, alone. A storm was forming, and from it emerged strange shadows that circled around her. One flew down and bumped into her hard, but she was unable to move or run away. She struggled to remember how to make her arms and legs obey her thoughts, but they refused to work. Another shadow flew down and bumped into her, and again, she tried desperately to remember how to move, her panic growing.

She awoke.

Another nudge startled her so much that she jumped out of bed.

The little red fox was sitting next to her, looking up at her expectantly. Then the air in the room began to shimmer and sparks began to circle them.

'I'm sick! I don't want to go anywhere!' she protested, but it was too late. The wind rose up and pulled them into complete darkness.

The room that Alicia found herself in was large, dusty, and felt very old. The low ceiling was supported by heavy timbers, and the wooden floorboards were rough on her bare feet. Through the dirty windows, she could see out onto a grey city street below, and beyond that, to several large ocean liners berthed at industrial docks. Then, a ship's horn sounded in the distance, and countless seagulls took to wing, crying out in reply to its echoing blast.

An old red taxi pulled up to the curb on the far side of the busy road. Alicia watched as George and his family emerged, but then someone coughed close behind her, and she was so startled that she almost lost her balance.

It was an old man, sitting behind a large desk in the far corner of the room, hunched over his work between stacks of paper and old books. His rumpled grey hair and dishevelled clothes made him blend into his messy background so well that it was not surprising that she had overlooked him.

The office door swung open and a man in a dark suit and black fedora walked in, and Alicia recognized him as the man who had been lurking in the shadows in India.

'Parsons,' the man said, in a cold, oddly calm voice, 'there's been a change in plans. Stryder suspects something, and has grown nervous about the passage you booked for him – what else do you have available?'

'Good morning Mr Sikes,' the grey-haired man said as he brushed aside the papers on his desk, and then consulted a glowing device he had hidden beneath the mess. 'I assume you still want something leaving from Southampton... I suppose I might be able to book a cabin on the SS Cormorant... and there's a stateroom available on the RMS Helenia... if Stryder doesn't mind paying a premium.'

'I doubt he has the money for anything better than third class,' said Sikes, taking off his hat and running a hand through his slick black hair.

'Well, then,' said Parsons with an unpleasant laugh, 'I'm sure I can find something on a tramp steamer leaving within the week.'

'No good, I need him and his family on the open ocean in the next twenty-four hours.'

'You continuity managers,' the grey-haired man muttered as he consulted his device again, 'you do so love to be such a mysterious bunch. Never an explanation of what you're doing, but you expect everyone to follow your orders without question... Well then,' he added in a clearer voice, 'it'll have to be the Helenia. How is Stryder going to pay?'

'I'll cover it.'

'That's very generous of you.'

'Generosity has nothing to do with it.'

'What about their belongings? Aren't they already on the other ship?'

'Do I seem concerned about that?'

'No indeed, my dear Mr Sikes, the very idea of you expressing concern is absurd... but then that's why the Council has you do their wet work, isn't it?'

Alicia wanted to get a better look, but as she moved closer, she stubbed her toe and let out a little yelp.

'Damn and blast,' Mr Sikes hissed as he glanced around the room, 'I think we have company.'

'I assure you,' said Parsons, 'that I've scanned my office thoroughly for any eavesdropping devices.'

'Bloody sappers,' mumbled Mr Sikes as he put on his hat and prepared to leave. He then spoke more clearly as he added, 'just print out the damn tickets and I'll be on my way.'

'Sappers? You mean Time Sappers? Don't tell me you believe in that superstitious nonsense,' the man laughed as he handed Mr Sikes the tickets. 'So, how will you be paying for these?'

'I can't have you reporting back to the Council about this, so I was thinking of a little something to make you forget everything we've just discussed.'

'You don't seriously expect me to take a bribe, do you?'

'No, of course not,' said Mr Sikes as he grabbed Parsons by the shirt collar, and then slammed something against his forehead. There was a sickly green glow, and the grey-haired man fell forward on his desk, twitching and drooling.

Alicia froze, not daring to move, lest she draw Mr Sikes' attention again, but he left the room, with only the slightest glance back over his shoulder. The little fox, who Alicia had almost forgotten was there, ran after him, and so she reluctantly followed.

The street was crowded, but the fox ran directly across the road between the blurring cars, seemingly unconcerned by the danger. Alicia, however, remembered her brother's bloody nose in Barons Court Station, and waited for a break in the traffic. It seemed to take forever, and her feet were starting to ache from the cold rough pavement, but then, finally, she saw someone preparing to dash across the street, and so she followed close behind.

On the other side of the street, she found George and his mother sitting on their luggage, waiting for George's father as he was down the street having a heated discussion with Mr Sikes.

A light drizzle had started to fall, and Alicia couldn't stop shivering. 'This is stupid,' she protested, but George still could not see or hear her, and the fox just ignored her. 'I know what you're trying to do... you're trying to stick us back together, aren't you? B-b-b-but it doesn't work anymore, does it?' The fox glanced at her suddenly, as if surprised that she would understand this, but then returned her attention to George.

Time passed, too much time, and Alicia was growing dizzy and weak, and her shaking became almost violent. 'I-I w-wa-ant t-t-to g-go h-home,' she groaned as she sank to her knees.

The fox, suddenly aware of Alicia's rapidly worsening condition, ran up to her and nuzzled her face, but when Alicia did not respond, the fox looked back at the Stryder family as if trying to make up her mind. She then nuzzled Alicia once again, and the sparks began to circle.

Alicia was back in her bed, but it wasn't nearly as warm and inviting as it should have been. Her violent shivering did not stop, and her arms and legs ached terribly. The cold was so deep inside her that she couldn't even think clearly. She tried to get out of bed, but her arms and legs no longer worked as they should, and she fell to the floor with a heavy thud.

'Alicia! What's wrong?' her mother almost shouted as she entered the room. She then knelt down awkwardly and took Alicia's limp cold hand in her own. Deathly pale, Alicia's lips were now a strange shade of blue.

'Gil! Get up here now!'

'Coming!' Mr Henderson called from below as he took the stairs three at a time, and then burst through the bedroom door, 'did you fall?'

'No, it's Alicia... she's completely hypothermic. It's as if she's been in a freezer.'

'How the hell is that possible? We're in the middle of a heat wave.'

'You put her in the tub and fill it with warm water, and I'll get my stethoscope.'

Alicia was barely aware of what was going on, but then she felt a strangely painful warmth spreading in her arms and legs. Then the pain faded, and the sensation felt absolutely wonderful. She opened her eyes.

She was lying in a tub of water, still in her pjs, while her father held her hand reassuringly, and her mother checked her heartbeat with a stethoscope.

'Hey Allie, how you feeling?' asked her father.

'What on earth happened? I just checked in on you a few minutes ago, and you were fine,' said her mother as she brushed wet hair away from Alicia's eyes, and all at once, Alicia was aware of how much she had missed the tenderness of a simple human touch.

'I... I got pulled back to England with George. He's back with his parents, and I was there, and it was really cold... George can tell you... Where is he?' She was still groggy, and the warm bath did feel wonderful, if a little weird since she was still in her pjs. Even after she was all dried off and back in her bed, warm and comfortable, her parents didn't seem to understand her questions. 'Seriously, where's George?'

'Who's George?' asked her mother.

'Allie, we honestly have no idea who you're talking about,' said her father.

'But how could you forget him? I found him on the beach... He was injured, so Mom and I flew in a helicopter back to Vancouver with him... and then we couldn't leave the hospital, or at least I couldn't, because of some sort of tangle thing.'

'That's a pretty amazing sounding dream, but I'm afraid that's all it was,' said her mother. 'Are you sure you want this heavy blanket? After all, it's actually a pretty hot day.'

'Yes please... Mom, why don't you remember George? Like, remember when we were trying to leave the hospital? You said it was all in my head, but then later, when George's dad showed up, he told you it was real, that there was this force that kinda glued George and me together... entanglement, that's it. I couldn't leave because of the accordant entanglement. Don't you remember Dad? Mr Stryder explained that accordance is the part of gravity we've been missing.'

'Wow,' said her father, 'that really does sound like one hell of a dream.'

'Dad, you and Mr Stryder talked a lot – he told you all kinds of things about how time works and how it's not at all like what people think it is.'

'Hey, kid, that sounds pretty cool, but...'

'Daddy, you never call me kid, that's what you call George.'

'All right, dear,' her mother said, 'I need you to drink this juice, and then I think you need to rest a while.'

'Why won't you believe me? Why don't you remember George?'

'Listen, Allie, it's not that we don't believe you,' her father said, 'it's just that you've had a nasty flu ever since we got back from our vacation last week... and, well... sometimes a fever can make your dreams seem really, really... well... real.'

'Last week? Daddy, we got back almost two weeks ago.'

'Like your father just said, you've been very sick, and you need to rest. You can tell us all about this dream later.' Her mother kissed her on the forehead, and then her parents left the room.

Alicia couldn't understand why they didn't remember George, but then, as she thought about it, she figured that maybe it was because the world was all back to the way it was always supposed to be. After all, George was back with his parents, and now she was safely home as well, so just like in the Rupert Bear stories, everything was back the way it was meant to be.

As she lay in her bed, before she drifted off to sleep again, she tried to imagine what George might be doing now. She wondered what sort of life he might have made for himself... did he grow up and have a family of his own? Or what if he and his family had perished on their journey to Canada? She had a sudden empty feeling.

If this is the way things are meant to be, she thought, then it's really not like Rupert at all it's just very sad, and very lonely.

Chapter Thirteen

A World of Difference

It was late afternoon when Alicia awoke again. Her fever had broken, and she was feeling much better. It was almost time for supper, and she was very hungry, but before she went downstairs, she needed to do something. She went up to the top floor of the house to the room that had once been George's, but when she opened the door there was no sign of him.

But then, just as she turned to go, something caught her eye. It was a pith helmet, covered in dust. She brushed it with her sleeve and then put it on. When she caught a glimpse of herself in the mirror, she could see that it made her look even dorkier than it had made George look, but somehow, she didn't mind.

She slowly made her way downstairs to the kitchen, where the rest of the family was getting ready for supper. Her dad was outside, cooking on the barbeque, her mom was sitting in the big rocking chair taking care of the baby, and over at the kitchen island, Chella was making a salad, while Simon Toliver set the table, and Matt sat on a barstool, practicing his guitar.

'So what's with the weird headgear?' Matt asked.

'You look like a mushroom,' said Chella, 'I hope you don't plan on going out in public with that.'

'This is George's hat.'

'Yeah, so, who's George?'

'You know,' said Alicia, with growing frustration, 'George... the kid who's been living with us for the past two weeks... the kid I found on the beach.'

'Wow,' said Matt, 'you've totally lost it.'

'Allie, I thought you picked that hat out for yourself,' said her mother, 'last summer, at some yard sale.'

'It was this summer, and it was George,' protested Alicia.

Mr Henderson came in carrying a platter of barbecued chicken. 'Hey, glad to see you up and around again... I like the hat.'

'Why don't any of you remember George?'

'Who's that?' he asked.

'The boy Allie had the dream about,' replied Dr Henderson as she prepared to burp the baby.

'But it *wasn't* a dream,' Alicia insisted.

'All right then, why don't you tell us about him,' said her father, as the family gathered around the table.

Alicia knew that it wasn't a dream, but as she told the tale, it started to sound too fantastical even to her, and for the first time, she began to doubt herself.

'You should write all this down,' said Matt, 'it might make a half-decent movie.'

'Except for the part about it being a dream,' said Chella, 'that's always such a rip-off.'

'Yeah, that's so lame,' laughed Matt, 'and magical time traveling watches... that's kinda been done to death, too.'

'But it wasn't a dream,' Alicia protested, 'and I told you, it wasn't the stupid watch doing it... it was something else... I think it was the little fox.'

'The fox that doesn't talk?' asked Matt, 'well, it's kinda pointless if it doesn't talk.'

'But it's not like I'm making this up... I can't just change something because you think it would make a better story! Reality doesn't work like that!' Alicia insisted. However, by this time Matt and Chella were completely lost in a debate about who the best director for the project might be, and whether vampires were more clichéd than zombies, or if werewolves were really what the story needed.

Her family had been impressed by her story, but no matter how detailed her recounting of it, she still hadn't convinced anyone that it had been anything more than a fever-fueled dream, and now it was getting late, and she was tired. She went up to her room, changed into her pjs, flopped into bed, and soon fell asleep. But it seemed like only seconds later that the fox was nuzzling her side.

'Go away,' she mumbled, 'you're just a stupid dream!'

The fox continued to prod her, and as Alicia opened one eye to look at the annoying little creature sitting on her bed, she saw that the air in her room had started to shimmer.

'It *is* you!' she shouted as she jumped away, 'you *are* the one doing all this!'

Sitting on the bed, the fox almost seemed to smile a little, as if caught doing something wrong.

'No way!' Alicia shouted as the wind began to spin around her, 'I'm not going anywhere! I nearly froze to death last time!'

The fox looked at her, then closed her eyes and bobbed her head ever so slightly, and the wind disappeared. She then hopped down from the bed, trotted over to the closet, and impatiently pawed at the door.

'Seriously? No way, I'm not going. I'm tired of being pulled around... and now everybody treats me like it's all been some stupid dream or something.' Feeling sick, and tired of not being believed, Alicia flopped back on her bed, and just lay there.

She fully expected to be pulled away into another time, despite her protests, but when nothing happened, she sat up and looked over to the fox, who was still waiting beside her closet door. Of all the things she had expected to happen, this was not one of them.

'You know,' she said as she took her glasses from the nightstand and put them on, 'I'm not sure if it's really cool, or really creepy that you understand what I'm saying... So, what are you?'

The fox sniffed in apparent disgust, and turned away.

'Sorry... I mean... *who* are you?'

It took a moment or two, but the fox seemed to get over the insult and looked back at her, then very slightly shook her head and almost seemed to shrug.

'You know,' said Alicia, 'my brother thinks you'd be so much cooler if you could talk... I gotta say, I think he's right.'

The fox tilted her head to one side, but made no other reply.

So Alicia sat on the edge of her bed, and thought about the situation for a moment. If it was a dream, then it was totally the coolest, realest, dream that anyone had ever had, and what harm was there in that? And besides, she thought, dream or not, if she went, she would at least get to see George again.

'Okay I'll go with you,' she said, 'but I have to get ready first, alright?'

The fox seemed to nod ever so slightly, and then went to the window to look out at the back garden. Alicia put on a good heavy pair of jeans, a t-shirt and a sweater, then warm socks and her favourite pair of red canvass runners. Just as she finished tying her shoelaces, the air began to shimmer. She quickly reached into her closet, grabbed her yellow raincoat, and clutched it tightly as the red and blue sparks began to spin around the room.

The hollow wind died away and the light returned, but it was the flat grey light of a cloudy day. Alicia had landed on the deck of a large ship, it shuddered beneath her as its giant engines rumbled to life. Then the ship's horn blasted loud and deep, echoing off the nearby warehouses several times as the ship pulled away from the dock. The wind across the deck was cold, so she quickly put on her raincoat, all the time wishing she had grabbed her warm puffy coat instead.

The portside railing was crowded with hundreds of passengers waving goodbye to loved ones and well-wishers, but the fox seemed to know exactly where to go, and led the way to where George and his parents stood.

'It's the funniest thing, isn't it?' Mr Stryder was saying, 'we don't know a single soul down there, and yet we're waving as though we're saying goodbye to our dearest friends.'

'I suppose so,' replied Mrs Stryder, 'but it feels more like we're waving goodbye to the whole country... all so dreadfully final, somehow.'

'We'll be just fine,' said Mr Stryder, as he pulled his wife and son closer, 'as long as we stick together. Now, let's go find our cabin and get settled in.'

Alicia and the little fox followed the Stryders inside, and down the dark corridor as Mr Stryder looked at the tickets and checked the numbers on the cabin doors.

The RMS Helenia wasn't as big or fancy inside as Alicia had expected, but then again, everything she knew of the great trans-Atlantic steamships was from the movie *Titanic*, but George had never seen such a grand vessel before, and looked around in awe, trying to take it all in.

'Well here it is,' said Mr Stryder as he unlocked the door, 'our stateroom.'

'How can we possibly afford this?' asked Mrs Stryder.

'It's all courtesy of Mr Sikes... these are the accommodations he arranged, so we might as well enjoy them.'

'This is brilliant!' said George as he ran to check out the different rooms.

'But what do you owe him?' asked Mrs Stryder, 'is this going to make trouble for you with the Council? I can't help but think of what happened because of him back in Oxford.'

'M'dear, that's ancient history, so let's not worry about that now, shall we? We're together, and we're off on a great family adventure.'

'You know, love,' said Mrs Stryder, with an uncertain smile, 'calling it a great adventure doesn't make it any easier.'

It was only much later, when George was alone in the cabin while his parents attended an evening reception, that the little fox seemed to let their presence be known. With the slightest nod, the air began to shimmer, and she and Alicia became visible.

'What are you doing here?' he asked in complete disbelief, but then quickly added, 'sorry... I mean... it's good to see you, to be sure, but I thought the connection between us was well and truly broken.'

'All I know is that *she* keeps bringing me back,' said Alicia.

The little fox hopped up onto the bed beside George, and rubbed against his arm, but when he reached out to pet her silky red fur, she pulled away.

'Well, I'm with my parents now,' he said, 'and everything is back to the way it should be... so I really don't understand why you're here.'

'Yeah, well,' said Alicia, 'all I know is the fox really wanted me to come back here... I think she wanted me to see something.'

'What on earth are you going on about?'

'You know that guy we saw hiding in the shadows in India? There's something totally creepy about him. His name is Mr Sikes...'

'That's the name of my dad's governor at work!' exclaimed George, 'why ever would he have been in India?'

'I don't know,' said Alicia, 'but I really think the fox wanted me to see what he was doing... Seriously, like when he was getting the new tickets for your dad, he totally attacked the ticket guy... to make him forget.'

'I don't understand... how could he *make* him forget?'

'He said something to the guy about not wanting the Council to find out what he was doing, and then he had this glowing thing in his hand, and he used it to knock the ticket guy out,' Alicia explained, shuddering as she remembered the grey-haired man sprawled across his desk, twitching and drooling.

'The Council? Who the blazes are they?'

'I don't know,' said Alicia, turning to look at the little fox, who was now watching them both very intently. 'I just know that she really wanted me to see all that.'

'Right, that does it,' said George as he grabbed his overcoat, 'we need to find out what that Sikes blighter is up to!'

Then, with this new call to action, the little fox sprang off the bed, and ran to the cabin door, her eyes wide with excitement, eager to lead the way. There was no question now that the fox was eager to show them something. She moved swiftly, indicating what doors to open, what corridors to go down, and where to hide so George would not be seen.

Once they were out on deck, the night was dark and the wind harsh, cold, and powerful, but the little fox seemed not to notice. She led them to a narrow metal staircase, which led up to the bridge deck, but then the little fox vanished.

'It's ruddy unnerving when she does that,' mumbled George, 'though I suppose she wants us to go up there.' He looked around cautiously before opening the metal gate with the sign on it that said *Ship's Personnel Only.*

'Let me go first,' said Alicia, 'since no one else can see me, anyway.' George nodded in agreement. Alicia then climbed to the top of the steps to look around, and when she was sure that it was clear, she signalled for him to follow.

As they approached the ship's bridge, despite the howl of the cold North Atlantic wind, they could hear two men arguing. Then, as they drew closer, it became obvious that one of those men was Mr Sikes.

'...your concerns are noted, captain,' he was saying, 'but these documents make it perfectly clear – you are to follow my orders without question.'

'Dammit man,' the captain's deep voice rumbled, 'we have women and children on this ship, and I am responsible for each and every soul...'

'If you continue to delay, I will not hesitate to assume command of this vessel myself,' said Mr Sikes.

'I'll be damned if I'll let you take my ship!' roared the captain. 'Commander, you heard him, we are to run dark, following evasive manoeuvres, west nor'-west.'

'Sir,' the commander replied, 'it'll take the stewards some time to blackout the cabins and get the passengers to comply.'

'Then get to it now, man!' the captain barked, and then swore loudly. 'There... it's done, now get off my bridge!'

'My orders are to remain here until these actions are fully executed,' said Mr Sikes, in his quiet, even, voice.

'Executed is right... having been condemned without a trial,' the captain grumbled with another curse, 'all onboard this ship are now in your hands... and on your head be any deaths.'

'I take no pleasure in this,' said Mr Sikes, 'but I assure you that this is all for the greater good.'

From where George was standing, he could see Alicia, her face lit by the glow from the bridge, invisible to all but him. Then the lights went out, and her ghostly profile shimmered as she suddenly turned.

'We gotta get out of here!'

George nodded in reply, and Alicia seemed to vanish as she ran, only to reappear at the bottom of the stairs, where she looked around to make sure the way was safe for George. He moved as quickly as he could trying not to make a sound, but the metal steps still echoed as he ran down them.

'We need to warn my mum and dad,' whispered George as they came in out of the cold. The ship's lights were already going out as the stewards hurried to fulfil the captain's orders, and it was now getting difficult to see where they were going. In the shadows, George and Alicia could see passengers being directed to their cabins by crewmembers of all ranks.

'You there, laddie!' a man in uniform called out in a distinctive Northumbrian accent, 'Where do you think you're going?'

'I-I was just looking for my parents.'

'If they're not already back in their cabin,' said the man, 'they will be soon, so you had best be on your way.'

'Yes, sir,' said George, but then asked, 'Do you know why the captain would order the ship to 'run dark'?'

'Who told you that?'

'I... I just guessed it,' George said, 'I was just wondering...'

'Well, laddie, this is a time of war, and we might not always be able to make sense of the orders we're given, but we carry them out nonetheless. For instance, your orders are to return to your cabin right now, do you have a problem with that?'

'No sir.'

'Good,' the man said with just a hint of a smile, 'because I'd hate to have to explain to your parents why I had to clap you in irons... now, away with you.'

George hadn't memorized the corridors yet, and with the lights turned so low, it was near impossible to make his way around, but

Alicia was starting to notice that the darker it was, the more she saw. This was a strange effect, and she wasn't quite sure what it was that she was seeing, but in the darkest corners, there seemed to be light of a different kind, in colours she had never seen before.

'This way, George,' she whispered, even though no else could hear her, 'your cabin's this way, just at the end of this corridor.'

It was a relief to find the door, but an even greater one when he opened it, and saw his parents there waiting in the stateroom.

'Oh Georgie, there you are,' said his mother. 'Off on a bit of an adventure of your own?'

'Um, yes, well, no... Mum, Dad, do you know what's going on?'

'The steward told us that this was just a drill,' replied his mother, trying to sound reassuring, but the worry in her voice was unmistakeable.

'Drill or not,' growled Mr Stryder, 'it's a damn foolish thing to be doing.'

'Only,' began George, hesitantly, 'I overheard Mr Sikes order the captain to turn out the lights and to follow evasive manoeuvres.'

'Damn and blast!' barked Mr Stryder, 'now the enemy will think that this is a battleship on the hunt for U-boats!'

'Alex, you don't think that Mr Sikes is trying to make things happen the way they were destined to, I mean, before we changed our travel plans?'

'I have no idea what that damnable blighter is really up to,' said Mr Stryder, 'however, he is subject to the orders that come down from the Chronology Council, and there's simply no telling what they might want done.'

'The Council doesn't give Mr Sikes that kind of power... to act alone... does it?' George's mother asked.

'Not that I'm aware of,' grumbled Mr Stryder as he turned to George and laid a firm hand on his shoulder. 'M'boy, tell me what happened. I need to know exactly what you heard.'

George tried to think of how to best explain, but before he could, his father pulled away in shock.

'Did you see that?' he asked. 'It looked like a ghost... a little girl... standing over there... in the corner?'

'I didn't see anything,' replied Mrs Stryder.

'I must be going mad,' said Mr Stryder, as he shook his head in disbelief, 'I swear that for just a moment I saw a young girl in the corner over there... wearing glasses... and a bright yellow raincoat.'

'Dad... that's Alicia, and she's a friend of mine,' said George as he took his father's hand in his own, 'but I think you can only see her when you're touching me.'

'Hi Mr Stryder,' said Alicia as she waved a little awkwardly, making her hand shimmer in and out of view. 'It's good to see you again.'

'L-likewise, I'm sure... but what do mean *again*? When have we met before?'

'Dear, who are you talking to?' asked George's mother as she reached out to her husband, but as soon as she touched his hand, Alicia shimmered into her view as well. Mrs Stryder let out a gasp, then struggled to compose herself. 'Oh my... are you a ghost?'

'No... well... I'm not dead, if that's what you mean,' said Alicia, a little defensively, 'and besides, I don't believe in ghosts.'

'What in blue bloody blazes is going on here?' Mr Stryder demanded as he let go of George's hand to rub his temples in frustration.

'Oh my,' said Mrs Stryder, 'where did the girl go?'

'I'm still here,' said Alicia.

'But Mum and Dad can't see you unless they're touching me.'

'This is too much to take in all at once,' said Mr Stryder, as he sat down on the sofa and leaned back to rest his head, 'I need a moment to think.'

'Georgie,' said Mrs Stryder, as she calmly reached out to take her son's hand, 'why don't you and your friend... Alicia, is it? Why don't the two of you tell us what you know?' She then sat down next to her husband and placed her other hand on his knee, and once again, they could both see Alicia.

'Ruddy unnatural, if you ask me,' muttered Mr Stryder.

'You're not from our time, are you, dear?' asked Mrs Stryder, noting Alicia's unfamiliar style of clothes.

'Um... no.'

'Then when are you from... when were you born?'

'Um,' Alicia hesitated as she looked at George and then back to Mrs Stryder, 'I was born in 2003.'

Mr Stryder sat up, 'But how could you possibly be here?'

'I think you called it accordance, or entanglement, or something,' said Alicia.

'Accordant entanglement? How... how could you possibly know about that?' asked Mr Stryder, almost as if the strangeness of the situation was a direct assault on his sensibilities. 'And you talk as if we've met before, but I have no memory of that.'

'Dad, back at the house, do you remember when I showed you your letters?' asked George, 'and how I thought what had happened was a dream? Only, now, I don't think it was. Well, Alicia was the one who found me... or will find me... alone on a beach in British Columbia... quite a few years from now.'

'Oh, Georgie,' said Mrs Stryder, her voice constricted by emotion, 'I don't understand... why were you there alone? I don't think that I could bear the thought of us being separated.'

'All right, then,' cut in Mr Stryder, 'm'boy, you must tell me what you can.'

So, George recounted what had happened, at least as far as he understood it, while Alicia helped with some of the missing details. '... Then you came and found me, living with Alicia's family in Canada, in 2014.'

'But how?' asked Mr Stryder in disbelief, 'The Council would never allow me to travel forward in time.'

'Well... you told me that you had to wait seventy-five years to see me again.'

George's mother gasped, 'But... I'm not like your father, I'm not from the same time as he is, so I just won't be able to live that long... I'll never see you again.'

Mr Stryder put his arm around his distraught wife as tears rolled down her cheeks.

'Um... actually... Mum,' George said, a little hesitantly, 'whatever took me to the future, it took you somewhere else... to some other time.'

'Oh that does it!' Mrs Stryder said with surprising energy, 'Alex, I simply must have one of those devices... I refuse to be separated from the two of you, with no way to write to either one of you!'

'Of course... you must take my node.' said Mr Stryder as he unbuckled his wristwatch. He then held it up and spoke directly into it, 'Alexiares Stryder[8], voiceprint authorization, edit ownership access: Add account, Emily Rose Stryder. Confirm.'

His watch chimed softly and a small message floated above it: 'New account added, please confirm additional voiceprint.' He handed the watch to his wife, 'now you must be holding it when you speak... just tell it your full name...'

Mrs Stryder spoke hesitantly to the watch, 'my name is Emily Rose Stryder.'

The watch chimed softly: 'Voiceprint confirmed. Would you like to review your new account settings?'

'That's all we need... for now,' said Mr Stryder, 'but keep it with you at all times... In fact, you best put it on right now so you don't lose it.'

'But Alex,' said Mrs Stryder, 'how will we be able to afford another one? I was too hasty... you should keep it, since without it, how will you ever be able to find George in the future again?'

'I'll manage,' said Mr Stryder. Then the ship's engines rumbled and the cabin swayed as the ship changed course again. 'One way or another... I'll keep us together... I promise.'

---

[8] **Alexiares** – (pronounced *Alex-ee-ARE-ees*)

Chapter Fourteen

Sinking Hope

'All right,' said Mr Stryder, 'just because things happened one way before, doesn't mean we can't change it for the better this time.' He looked at his wife and son, and then added, 'we need to dress warmly, and get out on deck... near the lifeboats.'

'This is really happening... isn't it?' George's mother spoke with a tremor in her voice, 'perhaps you could check the history records... maybe they'll have something that will help us.'

'I'm afraid,' said Mr Stryder, 'the time scanners are limited to land based targets and don't reach out to sea... budget priorities and all that. Besides, we've been changing events based on knowledge of the future, and the currents and eddies that it creates are impossible to predict.'

'I trust you, love,' said Mrs Stryder, as she adjusted her overcoat, then knelt down next to George to make sure that his coat was done up. She suddenly pulled him close and held him tight, 'I don't want to lose you.'

'Don't worry, Mum... Dad and I will come and find you.'

'Oh, dear, it's not me I'm worried about,' she said as she stood up, and quickly dabbed her eyes. She then distractedly brushed the front of her coat to straighten the fabric. 'I just want to be sure you'll be safe.'

'George will be safe with my family,' Alicia tried to reassure her, but only George could hear her.

'We best get a move on,' said Mr Stryder, 'I think the ship just changed direction again, and if there's a U-boat in the area, I have no doubt that it'll be tracking us already.' He paused, and then added, 'I want you to wait for me by the lifeboat... while I go see Sikes, and find out what the devil he's up to.'

Mr Stryder opened the cabin door and checked for any stewards who might try to stop them.

'Dad,' George whispered, 'let Alicia go first. Only, no one can see her.' He reached over and touched his father's hand, so once again Alicia came shimmering into his view.

'That really is unearthly,' muttered Mr Stryder, 'all right, young lady, after you.'

'No problem, Mr S.' said Alicia as she slipped by him and out into the corridor. She ran ahead to look around the corner to where the main staircase was, but saw a steward standing guard, so she signalled quickly for Mr Stryder to stay where he was. She then ran back to check the other direction, and that way was clear, so she beckoned the others to follow.

Out on deck, the wind was even colder and harsher, and the only light came from the gibbous moon above.[9] When Alicia noticed for a moment that no one was touching George, she quickly turned to him and said, 'don't say anything, but I'm going to follow your dad.' George made no reply, save for a very slight smile of agreement. Then, once Mr Stryder was sure that his family was safely in reach of the lifeboats, he headed up toward the bridge deck, with Alicia trailing invisibly behind him.

As he watched his father leave, a strange thought occurred to George, and it gave him an odd if somewhat desperate hope. He could not remember any of this happening before. Perhaps, this time, he thought, his mother would not be lost, perhaps his father would be able to stay with them both, and maybe, just maybe, they would make it safely to Canada. He squeezed his mother's hand to reassure her.

Meanwhile, Alicia followed Mr Stryder as he made his way up the stairs toward the dimly lit bridge, but then slipped past him as he entered. She was careful to squeeze herself against the frame so she

---

[9] The moon was not quite full on that night - October 23rd, 1939

didn't accidently touch him, just in case that would give away her presence.

Then the cold Atlantic wind caught the door, slamming it hard behind them. 'Sikes, what the devil is going on?'

A uniformed man stepped in front of Mr Stryder. 'Sir, you are not authorised to be here.'

The captain, however, glanced over and raised his hand. 'Thank you, commander, let him be... I take it, sir,' he added as he turned to face Mr Stryder, his voice gruff and strained, 'that you know this madman. I hope then, that you are here to talk some bloody sense into him.'

'He is my governor,' said Mr Stryder.

'Well then, sir,' said the captain, 'it would appear that we are in the same boat, so to speak, as the papers he carries make him my superior as well, at it seems that he is bound and determined to endanger us all.'

'Why?' asked Mr Stryder as he turned to Mr Sikes, 'why have you turned this ship into a running target?' but Mr Sikes did not answer.

'The purpose of this action,' the captain growled, 'is simple. It would seem that someone in Whitehall intends to use my ship as cannon fodder, and I can only presume that it is in hopes of drawing the Yanks into the war... that is, assuming enough of them die tonight. The only problem with that little plan,' said the captain as he turned directly to Mr Sikes, 'is that this is a British ship, and there are precious few Yanks onboard to sacrifice to your bloody cause!'

'As I have said before, captain,' Mr Sikes answered calmly, 'this has nothing to do with the Americans. They will join the conflict when they do, and the cost to them will be far greater than the loss of a few expatriates fleeing the war in Europe... This is something else entirely.'

The captain swore loudly. 'What the hell is it, then? You deliver orders that endanger my passengers, my crew, and my ship, and all you do is talk in riddles!'

Mr Sikes ignored the captain as he turned to Mr Stryder. 'Now, I trust that your wife and son are currently on deck near one of the lifeboats?'

'Y-yes,' Mr Stryder answered hesitantly. 'I thought it prudent... but why would you do this?'

The dim light used to read the navigational charts reflected ominously on Mr Sikes face as he spoke with a dead even calm. 'I do not undertake these things lightly, Stryder, but in times of war, things must be done that are... distasteful... and right now, I have neither the time, nor the desire, to explain myself.'

'But this isn't even our war. We're just supposed to be recording events...' Mr Stryder began to protest.

'This war? You are quite right, this is not our war, but this is not the war to which I was referring.'

The ship shuddered as a deep, booming, explosion rumbled below.

'We're hit!' The captain barked to his first officer, 'Commander, send out a distress signal and get the running lights on – and I need a damage report – NOW! And you,' he turned back to face Sikes directly, 'I want you off my bloody bridge, you damnable monster!'

'I assure you, captain, I have dealt with monsters before, and I am nothing like them,' said Mr Sikes. He then turned to George's father, 'we need to hurry, Stryder, but before we join your wife and son, there is something we must do.'

As the door opened, Alicia dashed out – she knew she had to warn George. People were running onto the deck, desperate to discover what had happened, and Alicia had to dart and weave through the crowds. More than once, she bumped into people and for a fleeting moment became visible to them, but in all the confusion, no one really seemed to notice. Then finally, she was able to make her way through the crush of people.

'George,' she cried out, 'Mr Sikes did this... it was him!'

'Where's my dad, why didn't he come back with you?' he asked as she drew nearer.

'I don't know... Sikes said that there was something he and your dad needed to do first. I thought he might be back by now.'

'Emily,' someone shouted. It was Mr Sikes, trying to be heard above the confusion of passengers. 'Emily Stryder... something terrible... your husband needs you now!'

'What happened?'

'No time to explain... you must hurry,' he shoved his way through the crowd. 'I will take care of your boy, but you must go now.'

'Where's Alex?'

'He's back in your cabin... You must go, before it's too late... your boy will be safe with me, but please... go now!'

'George, come with me,' his mother began.

'No!' Mr Sikes barked. 'Alex insisted that only you should go to him. It is safer for the boy to stay here. I will watch over him – Now go!'

George didn't want to let go of his mother's hand, but she turned to him with pleading eyes as she pulled away. He called out to her, but the crush of bodies deadened his voice and the thick smoke that billowed from below decks made it impossible to see where she had gone.

Suddenly, Mr Sikes was right in front of him.

'Quickly now, we don't have much time, Your father wants me to get you safely off the ship, and in order to do that, I'm going to have to do something that will seem very frightening – but I need you to trust me.' He brought his face uncomfortably close in order to speak in his strangely calm manner, 'your father needs you to trust me.'

The ship's crew was struggling to deploy a lifeboat, but one of the wire falls caught on something, and the boat jammed at an awkward angle in the davit tracks. With fire burning below, and the threat of an unusable lifeboat, the passengers were growing ever more panicked.

Mr Sikes pulled something from his pocket and then held it at arm's length as he tried to steady himself, but desperate people kept crashing into him. Suddenly, a thin beam of light shot out from his hand and struck the lifeboat, but the fear in his eyes told George that this was not what he had intended to do.

For just a second, it was as if nothing much had happened, but then a point of light formed on the hull of the lifeboat, and then, almost imperceptibly, the boat and its passengers began to shimmer. There were shouts and screams as the people, the lifeboat, and a large chunk of the ship's deck, all folded and crumpled into nothing.

Then there was a blinding explosion.

A sphere of crackling blue lightning now occupied the space, hovering over a round hole cut out of the ship's deck. The lightning began to spin as it formed into a vortex.

'It was you!' George shouted, but the noise of the terrified passengers drowned his voice. 'You separated us! It's all your fault!'

Mr Sikes grimaced as he reached over and roughly grabbed the collar of George's heavy overcoat, and then in one violent motion, threw him over the side of the ship toward the lightning.

It was only just before he let go, that Sikes saw the young girl in a yellow raincoat, clinging to George as the vortex swallowed them both.

This storm was different, and George knew it. It seemed to go on forever, tearing through time. This storm was not... his... and it had a malevolence at its core that he could feel reaching and clawing toward him. The darkness was so complete, it was as if light had never existed, and the cold hollow wind felt alien and violent as it tore across his body and twisted around him.

But just when he thought he couldn't fight it any more, there was an explosion of stars as he slammed into the ground. It was hot and burned his face, and as he opened his eyes, they were filled with dust and sand carried along by a hot wind. He stood up blindly as he furiously blinked to try to clear the grit from his eyes, but when he did, he could hardly believe what he was seeing.

A bleak landscape stretched out around him, and through a haze of heat, he could see rocky red hills shimmering in the distance. There were no trees to offer shade from the relentless sun, only sparse scrub and tufts of dry grass clustered at the base of the hills, and not a sign of humanity anywhere.

'Alicia?'

'Yeah... I'm here.'

He turned to see her fumbling for her glasses as she stood up and surveyed their new surroundings.

'Although,' she said with a resigned sigh, 'I really wish I wasn't.'

'This sun,' said George, as he took off his heavy overcoat and jersey, 'will be the death of us.'

Alicia pulled off her raincoat and sweater, and then tied them around her waist, but when George threw his heavy overcoat away, she warned him not to.

'You might need that... we gotta keep everything until we know what we need.... and right now, we really need to find shade,' she said as she scanned the horizon. A nearby rocky hill looked like it might offer some on its northern face, and it was toward this that she began to walk.

'Where do you think this is?' asked George as he ran to catch up.

'I don't know, but I don't see a single cactus anywhere.'

'Really... and what does that have to do with anything?'

'If we were in North America... or even South America... there'd be cactus in a desert like this... but there aren't any that I can see.'

'I suppose that narrows it down to just a couple of other continents,' said George, a little sarcastically. Then, after a moment, he said, 'what I don't understand, is why that blighter Sikes would send us here at all... wherever 'here' is.'

'Hey, I don't know... you're the one with the freaky watch,' said Alicia, 'so you tell me where 'here' is.'

'Yes, yes, of course,' said George as he fumbled to locate his watch, which he found it in the breast pocket of his overcoat.

'Wow... and you were going to throw that coat away.'

'Alright, alright,' he muttered as he flipped open the watchcase. 'Show current location,' The watch face glowed green, and a short message appeared above it.

'Wadi Rum, Arabian Desert

29°49'45.38" N 35°28'58.26" E'

'Wow,' said Alicia, 'I have *definitely* never been here before.'

'Neither have I, but – and call me impertinent, if you wish – but *are* you here? I mean... *really* here.'

'I don't know,' she said as she spun around and punched him in the shoulder. She cried out in pain, but he felt nothing. 'Ow... so... satisfied? I'm still stuck in this stupid in-between place... wherever that is.'

The heat was almost unbearable as they kept going. Soon they were walking were uphill.

'I'm completely... knackered,' George panted, 'I just need a moment... to catch my breath.'

'Yeah, okay,' said Alicia, as she found a place to sit in the shade of a low rock ridge. 'So anyway, shouldn't we find out *when* this is... like, the date?'

George leaned against a rocky outcrop at the base of the ridge and flipped open his watch. 'Good... question... but I've got a better one: Where might we find water hereabouts?'

The watch, however, was little help.

There are no detailed scans of this region for this time

'Well, that was ruddy useless, then wasn't it?'

'Okay, not great,' said Alicia, 'but remember, we don't stay in any one place too long, anyway... so we should zap out of here pretty soon, shouldn't we? We always have before.'

'Really, you think so? Only, this time I'm actually here, in the real world. It's not as if I'm in that blasted in-between place with you. This time, I might really be stuck here.'

'Okay, no need to panic,' said Alicia, 'let's find out what we can...'

'I'm not ruddy panicking!'

'Good... way to not panic. But you still haven't found out the date like I asked.'

George mumbled something incoherent and then requested the date. 'It says that it's the 27th of March, 1896,' he said, 'which is very peculiar, but I don't see what good knowing that does.'

'I don't either... just... give me a minute to think of something.'

'All right, and while you do that, since we're stuck in the middle of bloody nowhere with no water to drink, I think I *will* have myself a damn good panic.'

Chapter Fifteen

Abducted

The landscape turned brilliant orange as the dying rays of the sun fell on the sparse desert scrub, the light flaring against the background of blood red hills. The air was still and the heat of the day was beginning to relent, as the moon rose and stars became visible in the ever-darkening sky.

'Wow,' whispered Alicia, marveling at the harsh beauty of the place, 'if we weren't totally lost without food or water...'

'It's the waiting I can't stand,' said George, not really listening to what she was saying, 'being so utterly helpless... waiting until someone else does something.'

'Yeah, well,' said Alicia, 'we've been stuck here for hours, so who knows when that might be. We need to start making plans.'

'Hold on,' said George, as he caught the flash of a white tipped tail in the distance, 'I think help just might be on the way... finally.'

It was the little fox. But something was wrong, and she darted back and forth nervously as she hid in patches of scrub before carefully sniffing the air until she was sure that it was safe to run to the next bush. Finally, she ran up to greet George and Alicia.

'I am dashed thirsty,' said George, as he reached out to pet her, 'so if you could just bung us back to where we ought to be, that would be grand.' But the fox pulled away, and shook her head ever so slightly.

'I don't think she can,' said Alicia, to which the fox just looked down at the ground. 'I think she's just as lost and helpless as we are... aren't you?' The fox looked up with a little nod.

'Okay,' said Alicia, 'then like I said, we need a plan.'

'Don't be silly,' said George, his mouth getting dryer by the minute, 'she's always been able to get us out of trouble before... and if I don't get a drink soon...'

'Right. We need water,' said Alicia, 'can you sniff it out?'

'If I could do that,' snapped George, 'don't you think I'd have bloody done so?'

'I wasn't talking to you.'

'Oh... right.'

The fox seemed to shrug, but then nodded just a little before looking out across the desert. She then very carefully scanned the night sky, and after a few minutes, seemed to decide that it was safe. She flicked her head to signal that she wanted them to follow, and then led them back along the rock ridge, and down into a gully that had once been a river.

Even though the air was getting quite cool, George's thirst was only getting worse, and after almost an hour of hiking over rough ground, he stopped to check his watch. He just wanted to see how far they had come, but the fox jumped up and knocked the watch closed, growling at him.

'Oh, for pity's sake,' he protested, his voice thin and hoarse, 'I just wanted to see...'

But the fox let out another little growl and then nervously checked their surroundings again.

'Something's bugging her,' said Alicia as she looked around the moonlit desert, 'and it's starting to freak me out a little, too.'

The fox impatiently jerked her head toward the dark silhouette of a nearby hill, indicating that they should follow her there. It was further than it had looked, but once they reached the base of the rocky hill, the fox began to climb.

'Y-you've got to be joking,' George croaked, 'after all that slogging through the desert... you want us to start rock climbing?'

'Come on,' said Alicia, 'it's not that bad.'

'That's all well and good for you,' he grumbled, 'you're just a blasted ghost anyway, so you don't even get thirsty!'

'Whoa, I am *so* not a ghost!' she protested as she turned around so fast that she shimmered out of view, 'and anyway, I *am* getting thirsty... and really hungry, too.'

But that was ridiculous, thought George, she couldn't possibly know what it was really like there in the desert, she was just complaining for the sake of it. He, however, was really there, and his throat was hurting so badly that he didn't bother to argue with her any more.

They were walking over a sandstone plateau, smoothed by centuries of wind into rolling waves of rock. Eventually, they reached an ancient tree, near where two ridges met. The tree's bare branches were silver in the moonlight, and as they drew closer, Alicia could see that it was actually growing out of an ancient well.

The little fox ran down the stone steps, which led into the well's depths, and George followed closely, desperate for the cool water. The moist air filled his lungs, and as he knelt by the pool in the darkness, he drank handful after handful of water. And it seemed so much more delicious and refreshing than he ever remembered it being.

However, no matter how hard Alicia tried, she could not break the pool's surface, and so she could not drink the cool water herself. Thirsty, dejected, and even a little scared, she climbed back up the stairs and out into the desert night.

None of this made any sense to her, and she really hated things that made no sense. If she could breathe the air, then why couldn't she drink the water, eat the food or feel the softness of a human touch? This world was all too solid, too unforgiving, and within it, other humans felt like rocks and she was little more than a ghost. But she didn't believe in ghosts.

She walked slowly and not far from the mouth of the well, there was a natural alcove in the sandstone ridge, where she slumped down and hugged her knees. She thought about her own world, and how distant and lost it all seemed now, and although she wanted to cry, she refused to give in. She wasn't going to waste her time with something so useless and stupid.

And she almost made it.

The little fox seemed to know that something was wrong, and

came over to nestle beside her. The fox was not like the rest of this world, hard and immovable as stone. She was soft and her fur felt warm and silky, and even though she had never allowed anyone else to pet her before, she seemed to know that Alicia was desperate for the feel of life. So, in the end, it wasn't another harsh realization that finally broke down Alicia's defences, but this simple act of kindness.

When she heard George come back up the steps, she quickly wiped her eyes on her sleeve and made a point of looking away as she asked, 'had enough?' trying to keep her voice steady.

'Yes, thank you,' said George, 'though I do need to sit down a while... I think I might have had a tad too much water to drink.'

'Must be nice,' said Alicia, a little too sarcastically.

'So what's got your knickers in a twist?'

'Seriously?' she asked, still avoiding his gaze. 'This whole thing doesn't freak you out?'

'Well,' said George, in a way that he hoped was reassuring, 'now that the fox is here, things should get sorted out soon enough... she's done it before.'

'Oh wow,' said Alicia, 'then, like, it's all okay. Stupid me, 'cuz I was worried.'

'I'm sure it'll all turn out fine... just like it's worked out before.'

'But this isn't like before,' said Alicia. 'Like, the last time I was back home... it was really freaky, my parents didn't remember you at all.'

'I don't understand.'

'I woke up from this fever, and I was really sick... but the weird part was that my mom and dad couldn't remember you at all... it was like one of those stupid movies where the whole thing was just some stupid dream,' she said, and then, as an afterthought, muttered, 'I really hate those movies... they're so stupid.'

'Perhaps your parents were just having you on,' George suggested, 'besides, this is all turning into a rather grand adventure... isn't it? Rupert Bear has nothing on us.'

'Oh, by all means,' said Alicia, in a remarkably good imitation of an English accent, 'this has been a perfectly delightful diversion... what with burning up in the desert and slowly dying of thirst.'

'All right, then,' he laughed, 'I shall wring my hands and rend my garments in utter despair, if that makes you feel any better.'

'What-*ever*,' she said, turning to him, no longer trying to hide her tear-streaked face. 'You know, it's not just us... like, what about your parents, huh? They're probably still on that ship, and there's no way it wasn't going to sink after Mr Sikes blasted that hole in it!'

In one sudden moment, the pleasant fog of forgetfulness fell away from his mind as all the danger and fear came rushing back, and George felt as if the weight of the world had suddenly pummelled him in the chest. He could hardly breathe.

The fox jumped onto his lap, gently nuzzled him on the cheek, and then an unnatural sensation of calm came over him. He tried to fight it, if only because it somehow felt unnatural, and some part of him still wanted to keep the sharpness and reality of his fear, but whatever the fox had done, it was too strong to fight.

The fox then turned to Alicia, and before she knew what was happening, all of her own fears fell away in a cascade of relief.

'Whoa, sorry,' she said, 'what were we talking about?'

'I'm not really sure,' said George, rubbing the warm tingly spot on his cheek where the fox had nuzzled him. 'Oh, I know, you were complaining about the heat... weren't you? But it's pleasantly cool now.'

'Actually,' said Alicia as she shivered, 'it's getting cold... like really cold.'

'It is, rather, isn't it?' George agreed as he slipped on his jersey, and then decided that he needed his overcoat as well. Alicia put on her sweater and raincoat.

'I've read about this before,' she said, 'the desert can go down to freezing at night.'

'Well, I wish we had some matches, or a flint, so we could start a fire.'

'What about your watch?'

'I don't think it was meant to start fires.'

Alicia rolled her eyes. 'I meant you should use it to look up *how* to start a fire.'

'Oh... right, of course... I suppose it's worth a try,' replied George, a little embarrassed that he hadn't thought of it himself. He flipped the case open, 'Search, information, fire starting,' and there it was, all the information he could ever want, including instructions on how to use the watch's own infrared laser.

So, with a little effort and guidance from the fox on where to look, he found a few old branches and some dried scrub, and eventually had enough for a good stout campfire.

'About blooming time,' he said as he sat back down, 'I don't know about you two, but I was getting dashed cold.'

The fox nodded appreciatively, and then curled back up next to Alicia.

The fire crackled and glowed, and the stone alcove reflected the heat and kept them all comfortable and warm, protected from the cold desert night. So, in time, feeling safe and contented, they all drifted off to sleep.

Beyond the shelter of the alcove, beyond the warmth of the fire, far away on a jagged rocky ledge, a creature with giant bat-like wings watched, and waited.

Hours later, the creature was joined by two more of its kind, much larger and more mature looking. As they folded their large leathery wings, the creatures spoke amongst themselves, using faint clicks, whistles and barely audible grunts, all of which might have been mistaken for the normal sounds of the night.

Then, after a long exchange, the largest of the creatures stood up, unfolded its wings, and raised its arms toward the sky. As it did so, it seemed to command gusts of hot wind, laden with tropical moisture, to be pulled down from an inversion layer high above. These winds collided with the cold night air nearer the ground, and great billowing clouds were formed, rapidly pushing higher and higher, blotting out the moon and the stars, plunging the desert into total darkness.

Like the mad conductor of a deranged orchestra, the creature continued to direct the action, asserting its mastery over the weather, even as it beat its leathery wings and lifted into the roiling tempest. Then, with a flick of its clawed hand, the creature directed small red and blue sparks to trace along underneath the clouds, dancing and spiralling toward a central void that had formed where the conductor pointed. Suddenly, with a violent gesture, it brought its tempestuous symphony to a crescendo as it commanded lightning to explode over the desert.

Far below, the campfire sputtered and died in the driving rain.

'What... what's going on?' George yelped as he jolted awake.

'It's one of those storms,' cried Alicia, 'those things are back!'

'Run!' he shouted and the fox led the way, bounding down the smooth rock and out into the desert, followed closely by Alicia and George. They ran along the dry riverbed that had led them to the well, but now the heavy rain was rapidly filling it with streams of slick mud that ran down the shallow banks, making the uneven ground treacherous and slippery.

To his left, George saw one of the winged creatures, silhouetted against the dark clouds, and ahead he could see Alicia's bright yellow raincoat light up like a flare with each flash of lightning. To his right, he could just make out the shadow of a stone ridge. He was sure that they were being herded. His only hope was that once again, they might just be able to outrun the storm.

His chest ached, his lungs felt like they couldn't possibly expand enough to get all the air he needed, and his legs were growing heavy and unresponsive. But then, when he reached his breaking point, when he was sure he couldn't go any faster, something odd happened, something that he hadn't expected at all. Amazingly, he was able to breathe more easily, and the rhythm of his legs seemed to become almost comfortable. He had caught his second wind.

He was sure that there was no way they could catch him now. The storm seemed to be fading behind him as the wind weakened, and he knew that he was going to make it.

Then the fox and Alicia were suddenly right in front of him, trapped at the dead end of a stone canyon. There was nowhere for any of them to run. The wind and rain lashed at their faces as the power of the storm grew, and before they could turn back, the creatures flew down to block their only escape.

'They've trapped us,' Alicia shouted, 'we have to climb!'

The fox was able to navigate her way up the rock face easily, bounding from one impossibly narrow ledge to the next, but George fumbled for each handhold as his fingers became numb in the cold water that spilled down the cliff.

Then, behind him, he heard the beat of large leathery wings. Suddenly a clawed hand grabbed his shoulder, and pulled him away from the rock face. Bright stars exploded in his eyes as he crashed into the ground. The pain made him want to cry out, but the impact had driven away his breath, so he only sputtered and gasped, and couldn't move as the smallest of the gargoyles began to search through his clothes.

Running to protect him, the little fox jumped over George and sank her teeth into the creature's boney arm. The thing shrieked in pain and reflexively pulled away, throwing the little fox against the gully wall. She slammed hard against the rocks, and with a muffled crack of breaking bone, fell down into the mud, limp and unmoving.

One of the larger gargoyles shouted something, and the little one backed away, nursing its arm where the fox had bitten it. The larger gargoyle directed a tornado to come crashing down on top of George. The powerful wind seemed to suck the last vestige of air from his lungs, and he was sure he was going to suffocate. Then everything went black.

Alicia watched helplessly as he vanished into the blurring cloud, and she braced herself, fully expecting to be swept into the storm as well, but the wind only died away, leaving her behind.

Desperate to help the fox, she started to climb back down the rocks, but stopped when she saw the largest of the creatures pick up her little limp body. Alicia felt a surge of anger run through her as the creature callously threw the fox aside, but before she could do anything, the entanglement caught up with her, and she was pulled into the violent emptiness of the storm.

Chapter Sixteen

A Council of Creatures

Alicia straightened her glasses and looked around. She was in a desert, but one unlike any she had ever seen before.

A thin mist hung over the landscape, and through it, unearthly shaped silhouettes were visible, strange trees clinging to the craggy red granite slopes. She was standing in a wide gully, where two dry streambeds converged, and although the rocks beneath her feet were worn smooth as if by water, the ground was now dry, and the land looked as parched as she felt.

The few trees here looked like giant heads of broccoli, but topped with clusters of sharp green daggers instead of little round buds. One of the nearby trees had been damaged, and the sap that oozed from its trunk looked just like fresh blood.

Alicia was so intrigued by the strange new plant life that she ignored the large grey boulder next to the tree, until she heard the rock breathing. She froze.

She watched it until she was sure that the thing was sleeping, and then she allowed her curiosity to overrule her fear as she moved in closer for a better look.

The thing looked like a gargoyle statue that someone had put beneath the tree, but as she watched it carefully, she could see its chest moving ever so slightly with every breath it took. While this creature looked similar to the ones she and George had encountered before, those had been black and shadowy, while this one appeared to be carved out of ancient stone, grey, decaying, and flaking with age.

Even in a crouched position, the creature was taller than she was, and with the added height of its folded wings arching high over its head, it was an imposing sight.

The more she studied it, the more alien it seemed. She had learned enough to know that all the higher orders of animals have only four limbs, but this impossible creature had six: Two arms, two legs, and two very large wings, and it was these wings that truly fascinated her, since, as far as she knew, there was no other animal in the world like it.

As she looked at the creature more closely, she could see that in addition to the smaller shoulders that supported its boney arms, it had a peculiar secondary set that jutted out of its spinal column. These unusual shoulders arched high out of the creature's back, and were spread wide enough so that the huge muscles, clearly evident even under the thing's stony hide, connected its wings to its deeply barrelled chest. So, however impossible this gargoyle might have seemed, there was no question that it was capable of powerful flight.

Alicia moved even closer to study the thing's grotesque face, when she noticed a trickle of sweat that had run down its forehead, washing away a thin layer of clay, exposing the creature's true shadowy black skin beneath. It opened its yellow eyes, and stared directly at her.

Alicia tumbled backwards, bracing for an attack, but when there was none, she fumbled to get her glasses back on. She turned to look at the creature, and was surprised to see it patiently waiting for her.

There was something both familiar and strange about this gargoyle, but Alicia just could not quite understand what made her feel that way. Why had she expected its eyes to be glowing red? And distant memories of nightmarish ragged wings clawed at her mind as well, but never quite broke through to the present.

When she looked again, the creature was holding a ewer of water out to her, indicating that she should drink, and for a moment, she wasn't sure what to do, but she was so desperately thirsty that she accepted. However, like everything else in this world, the jug was as immovable for her as if it had been solid rock. The gargoyle appeared to be puzzled by this problem, but then, without looking away from her, it dashed the pitcher on the rocks.

Alicia was startled by this oddly indifferent act of violence, but then she noticed that the ewer, or at least a ghostly image of it, had actually remained in the gargoyle's hand. The creature now offered her the image of the ewer, and this time, when Alicia took only the ghostly image of the thing, she was able to take it in her own hands. She drank deeply, and the cool memory of the water cascaded refreshingly down her throat.

The creature then handed her the ghostly image of a small bowl of fresh figs, and their sweet juicy flesh melted in her mouth, but even though the water had quenched her thirst, and the figs had relieved her hunger, it was unlike anything she had ever experienced before. She wiped her mouth with her sleeve, but stopped, and then watched the gargoyle as carefully as it had been watching her.

The creature, apparently satisfied that she had eaten, then rose up as it spread its huge leathery wings and flew away.

When someone coughed behind her, Alicia spun around and saw George awkwardly getting to his feet, the right side of his head bloody from his impact with the ground.

'You need a bandage on that,' she said.

'We don't have time,' he replied, fighting the urge to retch, 'I'm sure that thing has gone to get more of its kind, so we need to get out of here.' He paused to steady himself. 'You know,' he added as he glanced over his shoulder, 'those things are supposed to eat people.'

'So why didn't it kill us, then?' asked Alicia. 'Birds of prey always kill what they catch as soon as they can... that way the prey doesn't escape... that is... unless...' she stopped as a terrible thought occurred to her.

'Unless what?' George prompted.

'Unless they want to teach their young how to kill,' she said quietly, 'then they just wound the animal and take it back to their nest.'

'Bloody hell...'

'But,' she added quickly, 'it wouldn't have bothered to give me food and water if all it wanted to do was kill us...'

'Still... not a great lot of bloody comfort in that.'

'Yeah, I know… we still need to get out of here.'

'How can you do it?' George asked, 'how can you be so calm? I thought girls were supposed to be so delicate.'

'What?'

'Only, you're not crying, or getting all… all… I don't know… girly'

'Seriously?' Alicia looked at him in disbelief, and then decided to ignore the remark, 'I think I see a way out.'

But it was too late. Their winged guard returned and landed on a nearby ledge. Then another gargoyle swooped low in front of them, only to rise up and land on the other side of the gully, followed by a third, a fourth and then a dozen more creatures.

They were surrounded.

No one moved, and the air once again became very still, with barely a sound, save for the occasional rustle of leathery wings. Each of the creatures had a distinct face and grotesque form, as if each one was from an entirely different species. Some had beaks like freakish birds, while others had the snouts of snarling dogs, and still others were quite beyond comparison, however, none had ragged wings or eyes that glowed red.

The largest of the creatures, one with four very large horns on its goat-like head, thrust its wings wide and let out a loud, low shriek. And then, only after the echo of its terrible cry had died away in the distance, did the other creatures begin to whisper in their strange language of clicks, whistles and barely audible grunts.

The conversation, if you can call it that, went on until the heavy early morning mist had lifted, and the mid-morning sun spilled into the rocky valley. Then, when all the gargoyles appeared to reach a consensus, the goat-headed one flew down from its high perch, followed by a second, much smaller creature, and the two of them landed in front of George. The large one then spoke in a way that suggested its mouth was not well suited to human speech.

'You have something that does not belong to you, mătu[10]. Return it now… or die.'

---

[10] **Mătu** – (pronounced *maw-TOO*)

'I... don't know what you're talking about,' protested George.

'But you speak Angle-ish, so you do understand.' The creature bellowed angrily as it drew itself up to its full height and spread its huge wings in a threatening display. 'It is a fool you take me for?'

'But I don't... I don't know what it is that you think I have.'

'You have with you a device of great power that was stolen from us – do not deny it – I can sense it even now.' But without waiting for George to respond, the creature slashed him across the chest with its claw, tearing his watch from the shreds of his shirt pocket.

The creature looked at the watch as its already terrifying face became distorted with rage. It then turned to the much smaller one, who cowered in anticipation of a beating, pleading piteously while the larger one bellowed. 'Speak Angle-ish, so even the lowly mătu might know of your pitiful excuses!'

'It must have had the amulet... you could sense it too... it must have had it,' the little one croaked, 'I followed it... it could not travel as it did, not without the amulet. It *must* have it.' The smaller creature then turned on George. 'Tell me what you did with it!' The little one's long bony hands easily fit around George's neck, and while George struggled to pull its scaly fingers away, he knew that the thing didn't really want to hear his answer, it only wanted to impress the others. 'I will kill you like I killed your little fox.'

The large goat-headed monster suddenly shrieked and slashed a talon across the smaller one's cheek, spraying George with some of its blood. The smaller creature cowered again as it hid its freshly wounded face.

'A fox?' the larger one bellowed, 'That was no simple fox you little fool! That was a Skogsrå[11], the Anzû[12] who owns this mătu!'

This revelation seemed to frighten the other creatures, and they let out wails and screeches that echoed through the valley and off the mountains above.

The noise and commotion seemed to attract many more

---

[11] **Skogsrå** – (pronounced *skogs-[g]rrr-UH*) The 'r' should be rolled in pronunciation to the point where it might even sound as if a second 'g' is in the name.

[12] **Anzû** – (pronounced *an-ZUH-who*)

creatures that came from all directions, circling overhead and landing among the rocks, while the screeches, clicks and whistles of their frantic conversation grew louder and more panicked. The goat-headed creature then threw the watch back at George, flexed its giant wings, and beat them hard as it lifted up from the ground to fly above all the others.

'Silence!' it commanded in a deep hollow voice. 'I speak to you in Angle-ish so that the mătu will understand. Its dead owner's clan will be coming to seek revenge, and the one who has brought this curse upon us must now face alone the wrath of the hated Skogsrå.'

Huddled pitifully on the ground, the wounded creature wrapped its wings around itself and whimpered in fear.

From high above, the large gargoyle continued to bellow. 'It is my own whose hope I now confiscate, and whose life I give to the Skogsrå in payment for the life of their child.' And with that, the goat-headed gargoyle rose higher into the morning sky only to fly away. Then, like vultures driven away by the approach of a predator, the others lifted from the surrounding rocks to follow their fleeing leader.

In all the confusion, one lone creature, an almost elegant looking bird-like gargoyle, fought against the rush of others as it climbed down the slope to approach the wounded one, but as it reached out with a trembling hand, a deep hollow shriek from above frightened it away, and it reluctantly took flight as well.

Then, all at once, the desert air was strangely empty except for the muffled sobs of the lone creature left huddled on the ground.

'I don't believe it!' said Alicia, 'those things just left that one to die!'

'What?' George turned to her in stark amazement. 'Those things were about to kill us, and that *particular* one just tried to strangle me... so you'll pardon me if I don't shed a tear for it... Anyway,' he said as he looked to the sky, 'we need to get out of this blasted place. I don't want to be anywhere near that thing when whatever it is that scared those monsters silly, comes for its revenge.'

'Do you even know where we are?' asked Alicia, defiantly.

'No... do you?' asked George, even more defiantly.

'Of course not. So even though you wanted to leave that poor thing to die, I think he might actually be our best chance of getting out of here.'

'Right!' said George with a new determination. 'I suppose there's only one thing for it.' He then muttered a command into his watch, and the image of a fully-grown lion appeared in front of him. 'All right, you!' he shouted, 'I want some answers... You may have killed my fox, but my lion will eat you alive if you don't tell me what I want to know!'

The creature looked up and shrieked, but as it turned to fly away, its claw caught the edge of its wing and there was a horrible ripping sound. It cried out in pain and fell backwards in the dust.

'George!' Alicia shouted, 'don't be cruel!'

'What? Are you going to defend this thing now? These monsters eat people, or did you forget that?'

'Look,' said Alicia as she ran up to George, 'there's no need to be that way. Let me try.'

George stood aside, shaking his head in disbelief as she cautiously approached the whimpering creature.

'My name is Alicia...'

'Oh... how rude of me,' said George sarcastically, 'of course, I should have started with formal introductions.'

Alicia ignored him and continued toward the creature, who was once again trembling and hiding within its bat-like wings.

'What's your name?' she asked. 'If you talk with me, I'll tell the Skogger that you tried to help us. If it owns us... then it will be pleased that you tried to help... won't it?'

The creature let its wing slip from in front of its face, and for the first time, Alicia could see that it was unmistakeably the face of a child. Its bright golden eyes watched her carefully as she approached.

As she drew nearer, Alicia could see that blood from the wound on its cheek had smeared the clay covering it, exposing a patch of soft looking shadowy black skin beneath.

'My name is Alicia... what's your name... what are you called?'

The creature narrowed its eyes as if uncertain of her motives, but then seemed to decide that it had nothing to lose.

'Årkigara,' it sputtered, 'I am Årkigara[13].'

'Hello, Årkigara. I'm a human... um... so, uh... what are you?'

'I... I am Anzû.'

Alicia took a moment to think about this answer, 'but isn't that what the other... the big one like you said the fox was... Anzû?'

'Yes,' Årkigara trembled as he answered, 'I am Anzû... the fox was Anzû... but I did not *know* that it was...'

'You killed one of your own?'

'No! Not my own! I am Pazoân[14], the fox was Skogsrå, we are not the same. The Skogsrå are cruel, the Pazoân are free.'

'You just said that you're An-zoo,' George said with renewed frustration, 'so now why are you saying you're a blasted paw-zo-an?'

'I am a Pazoân, we are the free Anzû.'

'Why do you say the Skogsrå are cruel?' asked Alicia. 'The little fox was never cruel to us...'

'You are ignorant...'

'Who are you calling ignorant, you foul thing?' demanded George.

'Don't!' snapped Alicia, 'we need his help!'

Årkigara narrowed his eyes as he appeared to carefully consider the situation, and when he spoke again, it was in a more measured tone. 'The Skogsrå own you, so of course they treat you well.'

'That's ridiculous, you stupid beast!' shouted George, 'no one owns us!'

'You do not call me stupid!' Årkigara got to his feet and rose up to his full height, which was taller than either George or Alicia. 'You need me to survive, so you do not talk to me like that! You are nothing but a Skogsrå pet! You are not free!'

'Stop it you two!' Alicia shouted, 'George, we need Årkigara's help... whether we like it or not.'

'You need me,' the creature laughed a strange, ugly laugh, 'because you will die without me!'

'And you will die,' said Alicia, very deliberately, 'unless we tell the

---

[13] **Årkigara** – (pronounced *are-KEY-gar-ah*)

[14] **Pazoân** – (pronounced *paw-ZO-uh-han*)

Skogger... the Skogsrå... that you actually tried to help us.'

Årkigara's smile faded as he sat back on his haunches, and then muttered, 'so I will help you.'

'Good,' said Alicia, 'then start by telling us what that thing is that you're looking for... the thing you mistook George's watch for.'

'I don't believe it,' said George, throwing his arms in the air, 'try asking something relevant, such as how to get the hell out of here!'

'Shut up, George,' she said, while never taking her eyes off the gargoyle. 'If you'd just listen a minute, you might learn something that could save us all.'

Årkigara tilted his head, looked at Alicia, then smiled faintly as if in admiration, and then spoke only to her. 'It is a device that is said to create the Galda-ḥamun[15],' he said, 'the storm that breaks time...'

'Like the storm that you trapped us with... in the Arabian Desert?' Alicia asked.

'No, not like that.'

'Then what in blue bloody blazes,' demanded George, 'was that storm that brought us here?'

Årkigara ignored him and smiled slightly at Alicia as he raised an eyebrow, suggesting that he would answer only her.

'Oh, for crying out loud!' grumbled George as he kicked a rock away in frustration.

'So, then,' prompted Alicia, not paying any attention to George, 'what was it?'

'That storm was a Mir-túm[16], which does not break time,' said the gargoyle, 'it is the only safe way to move mǎtu...'

'Safe? You call that blasted thing safe?' yelped George.

'Okay,' said Alicia slowly, trying to make sense of things, 'so, before we were in the desert, where you found us, we were on a boat, and there was a man there, and he made a storm that carried us back in time to the desert... was that the same type of storm?'

'You talk nonsense,' said Årkigara, his eyes wide with disbelief.

---

[15] **Galda-ḥamun** – (pronounced *gal-duh-CCHA-moon*) In Pazoân jargon the letter '**ḥ**' (h-breve below) is pronounced with a deep guttural sound, similar to clearing your throat when you have a particularly bad cough.

[16] **Mir-túm** – (pronounced *meer-TOMB*)

'No human can do such a thing.'

'Mr Sikes did,' said George, 'he made a ball of blue light and he threw us into it.'

'The Gal-ūd[17] has been awoken?' shouted Årkigara as he jumped up. 'I knew that you could not naturally fly across time as you did! Who is this muster-sikes? He must be the real thief! Take me to him!'

'And how are we supposed to do that?' asked Alicia. 'It's not like *we* can make any of those storms... can you?'

The gargoyle's excitement vanished suddenly and he sat back down. 'No... only the Lúmñíri[18] can command a Mir-túm... and they have fled with the others.'

'Oh that's just ruddy grand,' muttered George, 'so we are well and truly stuck in this blighted wasteland... well, then, there's nothing for it... we'll have to walk out.' He flipped open his watch and asked for the location map. The message read:

Unable to compile relevant path and travel maps, as the date is unknown. Geolocation is 12°34'10.36"N 54° 0'13.82"E at 910 meters above current sea level, and approximately 2,702.85 kilometers (1,679.47 statute miles or 1,459.42 nautical miles) from your last location request

'Well, that's no ruddy use,' he said as he looked around again. Then, after a few moments, he decided that the dry streambed was their best option. 'Come on,' he beckoned, 'if we follow this down through the mountains, it's bound to lead us to water...'

'No,' said Alicia.

'...or at least to a way out of here,' he turned to look at her. 'Sorry, what was that?

'I said no... I think we have more important things to do.' She pointed to a deep shadow on a high sheer cliff face, 'I saw a lot of Pazoân come out of there... there's a cave up there, isn't there?'

'There is,' said Årkigara, 'it is... it was... my home.'

---

[17] **Gal-ūd** – (pronounced *gal-OOD*). This was a tricky one to translate. See the entry in *'Appendix A – Glossary of Terms'*, for more details.

[18] **Lúmñíri** – (pronounced *loom-NYEAR-ee*)

'I don't see what that has to do with anything,' said George.

'Årkigara,' said Alicia, 'you said those loomy guys used storms to move people, didn't you? They used one to take George's dad from my house, didn't they?'

'I do not know what a jorjuss-ad is, but the Lúmñíri did capture another thief.'

'My dad never stole anything!'

'... and that thief is imprisoned within,' said Årkigara as he nodded toward the mouth of the cave.

George's eyes went wide with realization. 'Take me to him!' he demanded, but when the creature merely looked at him askance, George asked more quietly, 'please... take me... take us to him...'

The creature seemed to think about this for a long time, and then finally said, 'I will do it.'

'Brilliant!'

'And we promise,' added Alicia, 'that we won't let that Skogsrå thing kill you.'

'Oh, it will still kill me,' the gargoyle replied, matter-of-factly.

'Then why would you help us?' asked Alicia, 'I mean... like... if nothing's changed?'

'Because I hope,' said Årkigara as he turned toward the path leading up the mountain, 'to be granted the chance to die quickly.'

Chapter Seventeen

Descent into Darkness

'Hang on you two,' George called out as he stumbled over a large rock, 'I'm not nearly as light on my feet as you are!' He was having difficulty keeping up with Alicia, and the gargoyle Årkigara, as they easily scrambled over the rocks and up the steep terrain toward the base of the cliff.

'But we have reached the stair,' said Årkigara, 'so now you must climb.' However, what he called a stair was nothing more than a narrow crevice of sandstone, which extended vertically to the cave opening far above.

'You must be out of your bloomin' mind,' panted George in disbelief. 'There's no way that we can climb up that.'

'Then you go no further,' said Årkigara.

'Hey, it's not so bad,' Alicia tried to reassure him, 'I've done this before... we have a climbing chimney at the local community centre, and this is kinda like that.' She then demonstrated by bracing herself against the opposing walls of the crevice as she began to climb up.

George watched for a moment, and then reluctantly followed, carefully noting each handhold and foothold that she had used.

Far above, Alicia reached a narrow shelf on the cliff face, and once there, leaned back over to encourage him. 'Come on... you don't have that far to go.'

'It's easy for you... you weigh nothing right now!' snapped George, his arms and legs aching with tension. It was a strange sensation to be braced against the two walls with nothing directly beneath him. Sweat dripped from his forehead and stung his eyes, and he had to pause more than once to blink them clear.

'Keep going,' said Alicia, encouragingly, 'you're almost there.'

Startled by the sound of the intruders, a falcon burst from its perch, shrieking in alarm. Alicia instinctively ducked, losing her balance.

She may have felt impossibly light as she had climbed up, but now as she plunged toward the ground, the weight of reality had her sure that she was about to die.

Suddenly, she felt Årkigara's boney arms wrap around her, and then the two of them swept wide in a low arc, skimming just above the rocks, as the gargoyle's wings then caught the hot desert wind, lifting up and soaring high on the thermals that rose from the valley below.

George had instinctively reached out for Alicia when she had fallen, and had almost lost his grip. His legs were shaking with shock and exhaustion as he climbed the remaining few feet to the narrow stone shelf where she had just been, and when he looked back over the edge, he felt a sudden rush of fear that forced him back to press against the cliff face.

He watched nervously as Årkigara made a wide, lazy turn, expecting any second that he would pulled to his death if the Gargoyle flew too far away, and exceeded the limits of the bond between him and Alicia. When that limit was reached, he did indeed feel a slight pull, but it felt like nothing more than a kite tugging on a string. The gargoyle came drifting back around, gliding toward the cave's gaping mouth, and then beat his huge wings once or twice to slow his momentum, as they landed as softly as thistledown on the wind.

'Thanks,' Alicia muttered, embarrassed and grateful all at once.

'It would not do,' said Årkigara, 'to die while you are not whole.'

Alicia wondered what he meant by this, but before she could say anything, George asked, 'So, where do we go to get off this ruddy ledge?'

'We must go down there,' Årkigara said, pointing his boney claw toward the depths of the cave, 'to the labyrinth and then to the

Imaru[19], the Well of Lost Souls.'

'It's so dark,' said George, as they began their decent, 'how are we going to see?'

'Ah, I had forgotten,' said the creature, 'you do not see reflected time, only reflected light... that is a mătu weakness.'

'Bloody cheek,' muttered George, and then added, 'but I suppose I can use the light from my watch as a torch,' yet his watch cast little light ahead, and the deeper they went, the darker their surroundings became. The path was narrow and precarious, and although in some places it had uneven stairs carved into the sandstone, mostly it was little more than a sloping ramp.

Årkigara led the way, often bounding along on all fours, which somehow seemed easier for him when traveling over ground, and while George was completely preoccupied with maintaining his balance and not falling into the abyss, Alicia had other things on her mind.

'Årkigara, how old are you?'

'I do not understand.'

'Well,' Alicia tried to figure out the best way to word her question, 'what year were you born in?'

'I was not born in a year... I was born in the Túlgún[20], the place of my people.'

'But you must have some way of measuring time,' insisted Alicia.

'We are not bound by it the same way you are.'

However, Alicia was sure that Årkigara was still very young, and she was trying to get him to admit it. 'Okay, so like, how do you know when you're fully grown?' she asked.

'While a Pazoân fills with life, that is his youth. Then, he must hold on to his being in adulthood... but when he can hold it no more, it will drain away like all things.'

'Oh, wow, said Alicia, 'that sounds like you measure your life by volume?'

'I am not yet half full of being,' answered Årkigara.

---

[19] **Imaru** – (pronounced *EYE-mar-oo*) – The Forgotten Deep.

[20] **Túlgún** – (pronounced *TUL-gun*) – The home of the Imaru Pazoân

'So, you're just a kid like us, and you were sentenced to *death*?' asked Alicia, with unmistakable revulsion in her voice.

'I have brought shame to my clan.'

'But, you're just a kid... and, well, every kid deserves a chance,' Alicia said, almost pleading, and then she paused, a little uncertain if she really wanted to hear the answer to her next question. 'You didn't mean to kill the fox... did you?'

'No,' he replied with a sigh, 'it bit me, and... I did not think.'

'Alicia, you're not bloody defending what he did, are you?' George asked in disbelief, 'I was growing rather fond of that little fox... she was almost like a pet.'

'Foolish mătu,' Årkigara laughed, 'she was not your pet, you were hers.' Yet his tone quickly softened, 'I did not know that she was Skogsrå... had I but known that you were under their protection.'

Årkigara stopped, and then sat back on his haunches as he picked up a small shiny black stone and regarded it carefully. 'I was ordered to find the mătu thief, you see... but in that, I have failed, and so I am not worthy.' He then tossed the little stone into the abyss.

'But who would condemn you for that... like who was that guy with all the horns, anyway?' asked Alicia.

'He is the greatest of us.'

'Your leader?'

'Yes, Ulgara Lugal,[21] he is a great Pazoân,' Årkigara spoke the name with pride, but there was also tension in his voice.

'Great?' Alicia burst out, 'But... but if he's so great, why did he condemn you to death without a trial?' She shuddered with indignant rage, 'I mean... to sentence a child to death... I bet he wouldn't have done that if his own kid had screwed up.'

George nudged her and whispered, 'remember? That thing said it was giving up its *own* as an example. I think he jolly well did condemn his own son.'

'Is that true?' asked Alicia in total disbelief, 'are you his son?'

'I am.'

'That's... that's terrible.'

---

[21] **Ulgara Lugal** – (pronounced *OOL-gar-ah loo-GUL*)

'It is what it is,' said Årkigara, as he continued down the path while George and Alicia followed.

Trying to sound reassuring, not so much to quell the creature's fears, but to quiet his own, George asked, 'well, if the fox was a ruddy Skogsrå, then that's not the scariest thing in the world, is it? Really... how big could a blooming fox get?'

'You will see,' said Årkigara with a guttural laugh.

'Well,' said George, looking around, 'I wouldn't worry about the Skogsrå finding you, at least not while we're hidden down in this godforsaken place.'

'Did the fox ever have trouble finding you?' asked Årkigara, to which both George and Alicia mumbled that she hadn't. 'And she was nothing more than a Skogsrå child, so her elders will have no trouble finding me, wherever I am.'

'I don't get it, said Alicia. 'How could you be related... how could you both be Anzû? I mean... well... you don't look anything like a fox, and the fox didn't have wings or anything... it just doesn't make any sense.'

'Anzû wear the mantles of their clan, of their race. I am proud to wear the mantle of the Pazoân. Skogsrå children wear only the mantle of stupid foxes,' he laughed, but then his voice softened, 'but I did not look through the mantle to the Anzû beneath... so I thought it was just a common fox.'

'What's a mantle?' asked Alicia, 'is that like your body?'

'It is more than that... and less,' said Årkigara as he thought about this for a minute, then added, 'I do not have the words beyond what I have said, so I cannot tell you more.'

'Okay, so why did you call us Skogsrå pets?' asked Alicia, 'like, how could anything own us without us even knowing?'

'Mătu are either wild, or are owned by the Anzû. Most are wild, but *he*,' Årkigara nodded toward George, 'he is one of the owned.'

'Nobody bloody owns me.'

'If you keep a goldfish,' the creature asked George, 'does it know that it belongs to you?' He then made a sound that might have been a laugh, 'Mătu have been property since before they were mătu.'

'How do you know about ruddy goldfish?' asked George, feeling distinctly uncomfortable that such an alien creature would have this level of perfectly mundane, yet disturbingly intimate, knowledge of human beings.

'The Anzû know all about you, we speak your languages, we know your customs... your knowledge is our knowledge... you are owned.'

'Do *you* own anyone,' asked Alicia, 'like, a human... a mǎtu?'

'The Pazoân are not like other Anzû, we gather only the free mǎtu for our harvest.'

'Harvest?' asked Alicia, 'you mean you... you kill people?'

'We do not kill, we only harvest... from the wild.'

'What do mean you 'harvest' but you don't kill?' George asked uneasily.

'You harvest and eat apples, but you do not consume the trees they grow upon. We are like that; we gather only the ka-xi[22] from mǎtu who have fallen naturally, when they are still fresh...'

'That's rubbish!' George barked. 'Have you ever asked people if they mind you ruddy 'harvesting' them?'

'Um, so,' Alicia asked uneasily, 'when you say *fallen*... do mean, like... people who have died?'

'Yes.'

'Bloody beasts,' George growled under his breath.

'You are foolish and blind like all mǎtu. The Anzû have lived since before mǎtu walked the earth, and we will live long after you are gone.'

They continued down the narrow path in silence for a few moments more, but there were just too many other questions that Alicia still had to ask, and besides, part of her wanted to avoid thinking about what she had just heard. 'Okay, so about those freaky storms,' she began, 'what's the real difference between them, because they *are* different... like, really different... aren't they?'

'Yes,' said Årkigara, 'when the Mir-túm – the storm the Lúmñíri used to capture you – when it has done its work, it dies... but the Galda-ḥamun... it is the Great Breaker of Time, it is a terrible great

---

[22] **Ka-xi** – (pronounced *kah-X[z]EE* – a soft 'x' sound, similar to a 'z', but deeper in tone, and produced further forward in the mouth) See the entry in *'Appendix A – Glossary of Terms'*, for more details.

beast, and it is said that it will bind to its creator, both in life... and after.'

'Did that storm bind to me?' asked George. 'Is that why I've been bouncing around time for no good reason... because Mister Sikes threw us into that blasted tempest of his?'

'No,' said Årkigara as he stopped so suddenly that George almost bumped into him. 'Only the creator of the Galda-ḫamun is bound to it. Any others who might enter its vortex merely travel through it.'

'So what in blue blazes has been happening to us, then? Why have we been tossed about in time like a couple of ragdolls?'

'This... this I do not know' replied the gargoyle as he resumed his descent along the spiral path.

'Okay... but what did you mean,' asked Alicia, 'when you said *both in life, and after*... like, did you mean after death?'

'The Galda-ḫamun will never let its creator go,' replied Årkigara. 'It is said that in this way, he who uses the Anu-gìn-a-nir [23] to create the storm, will be both honoured and cursed by his creation.'

'Then what *has* been happening to me... to us?' asked George.

'As I said... I do not know... I thought that I could sense the traces of the Anu-gìn-a-nir on you... but alas... you did not have it, after all.'

'What's this *a-new* thing?' asked Alicia.

'The Anu-gìn-a-nir, the sacred relic that was stolen from us. It is the amulet that calls upon the Gal-ūd to create his terrible storm, the Galda-ḫamun,' explained Årkigara. 'I thought I could smell it on you.'

'You thought you could *smell* it?' asked George in disbelief.

'Yes,' said Årkigara, as he led them down a set of stairs that widened as they went, 'because you reek of ruptured time.'

For a while, they continued without speaking, but there were still too many questions that still needed answers, so Alicia asked, 'the little fox, she's Anzû right? So, is that why she could make the storms, too?'

'No,' Årkigara replied, almost mockingly, 'a Skogsrå could never create such a storm, let alone a foolish Skogsrå child...'

---

[23] **Anu-gìn-a-nir** – (pronounced *ah-NU-jeen-ah-near*) The **Tear of Anu.** See the entry in *'Appendix B – Notes'*, for more details.

'But she *could*,' insisted Alicia, 'she did it more than once.'

After a moment of thought, the gargoyle said, 'when I was very small, my mother told me stories of the Galda-ḥamun, and how the ancient heroes learned to tame it by riding on the crests of its waves... but that was just a story, a myth. No Skogsrå child could ever do such a thing.' He stopped abruptly at the base of the stairs, and then announced; 'Now we enter the labyrinth.'

George turned his watch to shine on what lay ahead, but he could see only black emptiness surrounding them. 'So where is the ruddy thing?'

'It is right in front of you,' said Årkigara as he climbed up and perched on a large rock nearby. 'If you cannot see it, you will surely die if you enter, as the labyrinth is treacherous, even for those who are able to see it.'

'Is it a tunnel, or a cave?' asked George, his frustration growing, 'where's the entrance?'

'It is right in front of you, and yet you are blind to it,' said the creature, sounding defeated, 'and it is far too dangerous for a blind mătu.'

As Alicia looked around, the darkness was not as complete as she had first thought. Before, she had wondered if she had just imagined this strange ability, but now she was sure that she could see shapes in the void. It reminded her of what she had seen when her father had shown her a pair of night-vision goggles that he had been testing. The goggles had produced images that were grainy and tinged green, but what she saw now was clear, and in colours that she had never before seen.

She began to walk around, studying her surroundings as Årkigara watched her carefully, suspicious of her ability to move so easily in the pitch-black cave.

'Hey George, come over here,' she called out, her voice clear and plain, with no hint of an echo, 'I think this might be a big torch.' She had found a tall pillar with a large shallow basin on top of it, and from the basin hung a tattered rope.

'Where the deuce are you?' his voice echoed back.

'Over here,' she replied, and once again, there was a disquieting absence of echo, 'just follow my voice.'

'That... that is *ruddy* peculiar,' said George, as he approached, 'how can your voice not have an echo?'

'Must be because I'm in the in-between place,' she said dismissively, then added, 'look at how this rope is glowing, like it's almost on fire... I bet if you used the laser in your watch, you could light it.'

George shone the light of his watch onto the rope, but it appeared as dull and plain as any old rope he had seen before. 'I see it, but it's not glowing,' he said as he felt the rope, it was greasy and reeked of rancid oil, 'but I think you're right.' He focused his watch's laser onto the rope, and within a few seconds, a small flame erupted and climbed toward the basin above.

Then, with an audible whump, the giant torch was ablaze, and for the first time, George could clearly see the cavern.

'It's all very impressive,' he said as he looked around, 'only, I still don't see any ruddy labyrinth.'

'It is there,' said Årkigara, as he pointed to a high arch over wide imperial steps that led down into nothingness.

'Look!' Alicia called out suddenly, 'up there...'

Flames raced along the high rope, away from the torch and into the darkness beyond the arch. Suddenly, there was a bright flash at the base of the imperial stairs, as an even larger torch exploded in a ball of flame.

Årkigara's yellow eyes grew wide with shock. 'The ùru[24] must have been prepared for the celebrations... for the return of the amulet,' he said, as he climbed down from his perch.

'Well, at least now,' said George, 'I just might be able to see this labyrinth of yours.'

In the glow of the torchlight, George could now see a stone platform that extended out from the base of the wide stairs, and from it, several bridges appeared to stretch into the darkness beyond.

Alicia, however, was able to see something more. 'Oh wow,' she whispered, her voice clenched with excitement, 'just wait 'til you see

---

[24] **Ùru** – (pronounced *OOR-oo*). A ceremonial fire.

what happens next.'

Suspended in the darkness, three more ropes burned, and three more torches burst into flames. Then, like a spider web glowing in the sunset, more ropes, and more torches, were alight. Further and further, the web of fire spread into the seemingly endless cavern. At first dozens, then hundreds, and then thousands of the giant torches burned, and beneath them, the labyrinth slowly became visible.

The labyrinth itself was an impossible filigree of twisting stone bridges and arches, which stretched hopelessly into an ever-expanding distance. This unlikely maze, this maddening confusion of rock and fire, did not bear any marks of having been created by human hands, but neither did it seem natural.

'At least now, you will be able to see,' said Årkigara as he started down the wide stairs, 'but you must follow me closely... the labyrinth will betray you if it can... and there is only one true path through it.'

The stone bridges led in many different directions, some narrow, some a wider, some going under, and others going over, but all tangled and seemingly leading nowhere, yet Årkigara never once hesitated to decide which path to follow.

While the first bridges were wide and easy, the deeper they traveled, the narrower and more twisted the path became, and high above them, the ropes were starting to burn through, dripping flaming debris onto the pathways below.

'Steady on,' said George, trying to keep his balance on the narrow bridges, 'only, we don't have ruddy great wings like you do, so we have to be a little more careful about falling.'

'But it is forbidden for me to fly within the Imaru,' replied the gargoyle, 'so if I fall... then I too, must die.'

'Well, if they're already going to kill you... what difference does it make if you fly in here?'

'There are worse things than dying,' said Årkigara.

'But who's to know if you *do* fly?' asked Alicia.

'You will see.'

Chapter Eighteen

The Well of Lost Souls

For hours, they walked, climbed, and crawled through the labyrinth, and George was weak from lack of sleep, lack of water, and, especially, lack of food.

The last time he had eaten was the lavish dinner on the ship, the night of the sinking, and now his mind was drifting back to it. He remembered the consommé, how delicious, salty, and wonderfully savoury it had been... and then the main course had been roast beef, and then...

'Hey!' Alicia shouted, 'Watch where you're going!'

The reality of the moment came rushing back as George found himself at the very edge of a stone platform, just beneath one of the giant torches. He looked down into the deep abyss and stepped back.

'I was... I was distracted,' he said, a little shaken. 'Only, I haven't eaten in ages, and... my mind was wandering.'

'Yeah... well,' said Alicia, stammering for something more profound to say, 'just don't do that again, okay?'

'I need a moment,' he answered quietly. 'You didn't bring any food with you, did you?'

'No... sorry... but it's not like I could give it to you, anyway.'

'And we do not have time to tarry,' said Årkigara, 'we still have far to go to get to the where the thief is kept.'

'I told you,' said George with frustrated exhaustion, 'my dad's not a thief.'

'But the Lúmñíri are never mistaken.'

'That's rubbish, and you know it!' snapped George. 'Those loomy blighters thought that I had the amulet… and I didn't, did I?'

'No,' said Årkigara as he looked sideways at George with just a hint of a smile, 'but it is a great crime to doubt the Mages of the Lúmñíri. Almost as great a crime as disappointing my father, the Lugal.'

'Whoa, I just thought of something,' said Alicia, 'if those Lúmñíri guys can make storms anyway, like without the amulet, then why are they so desperate to get it back?'

'Because the Anu-gìn-a-nir unleashes great forces that none can control,' said Årkigara.

'Okay,' said Alicia, 'that does sound kinda dangerous, but…'

'And any mătu who possess it, can use it to see the Pazoân, even when we do not want to be seen.'

'Well, that's not the worst thing in the world,' said George.

'But for us, it would be,' said Årkigara. 'And besides,' he added with a guttural laugh, 'can you imagine the chaos if your people were to realize that the shadows on the walls have minds of their own?'

'They'd be terrified,' said Alicia.

'And rightly so,' muttered George.

'So I will retrieve the amulet,' said Årkigara, 'and then the mătu need not be frightened of seeing the truth that lies around them. But now,' he said over his shoulder as he turned back to the labyrinth, 'we have other concerns, as we have yet to face the Guardian.'

Eventually, they came to a place in the labyrinth where all the bridges seemed to vanish into darkness. It was an emptiness that seemed to swallow everything around it. Suspended over this void was a massive rocky platform, accessible only by a single, narrow, stone bridge. Then, somewhere above the pall of smoke from the torches, came the sound of giant wings.

It was an immense dragon, trailing spirals of fume as it swooped down and landed on the platform in front of them. Despite its massive size, the creature moved with liquid smoothness, casually shaking itself from head to tail, as a bird does upon returning to its nest.

The giant creature's body was long and almost snake-like, while its head had the look of a vicious, hungry crocodile. It had a crest of metallic green feathers on its forehead, and a collar of long red feathers around its neck. Its limbs and claws were slender and bony, with razor-sharp talons that glinted in the firelight. This impossible beast, this thing seemingly made up from so many other creatures, carefully folded its giant bat-like wings, and then, and only then, turned around to look disdainfully at those who had dared to intrude into its realm.

The giant swung its head toward the visibly nervous little gargoyle, and spoke to him in the Pazoân language of strangely quiet clicks, whistles, and barely audible grunts. Then, Årkigara turned to George and Alicia, 'this is the Mušḫuššu[25],' he said uneasily, 'The Guardian of the Well, and he will not allow us to pass.'

The dragon suddenly pulled back as the feathers on its head sprang up into a large crest, and iridescent blood-red feathers flashed in a ruff around its neck. It then reared up on its haunches, and spoke in a booming voice, very unlike the one it had just been using. 'So, it is Angle-ish that these mătu understand, is it? Why would you, the son of a Lugal, be consorting with the likes of them?'

'I... I am taking them to see the thief,' said Årkigara, with a quaver in his voice. 'I... I thought... they might know...'

'You are as foolish as your father says you are,' the dragon growled, 'mătu are stupid... good only for the harvest... and yet these two are not even worthy of that... so insubstantial, so *unripe*... and that one,' it said, nodding toward Alicia, 'that one is incomplete, it has lost its husk... The tributes you have brought me are unsuitable.'

'Th-they are not tributes,' Årkigara stammered, 'they are here to help me.'

The dragon ignored him. It flexed its giant wings, turned its head upward, and then let out an unearthly howl before turning to face George, greedily licking the slobber from its scaly lips.

'But I have been guarding this place for too long, and have fed only on the rotten remains of those who would seek to escape my prison... so I have missed the taste of fresh meat...'

---

[25] **Mušḫuššu** – (pronounced *Mush-CHU-shish-uh*) The Dragon, the Guardian of the Well. See the entry in '*Appendix A – Glossary of Terms*' for more details.

'But that is not the way of our people!' Årkigara shouted. 'We take only the fallen...'

'I am the Mušḫuššu,' it snarled, 'and my word is Pazoân law, but my actions are my own business, and you must never presume to question me...' Before it could finish, the dragon was interrupted by a roar in the distance, and when it turned its head to listen, a second roar sounded much closer.

The Guardian spun around so fast that its long tail struck George full in the chest, knocking him into the pit, and before Alicia knew what was happening, Årkigara pushed her into the abyss as well, diving in after her.

Echoing down from far above, the dragon's voice came after them. 'Only I, the Guardian, may fly in here... for all your sins against me, son of Ulgara, I shall certainly kill you.'

Tumbling in the darkness, George heard the sound of leathery wings. The gargoyle came up beneath him, and George was able to grab Årkigara's shoulders.

'Hold on!' Alicia shouted. George clung on to Årkigara's back as best he could, but then, without warning, the gargoyle rolled over, and George was falling once again.

He felt the impact of cold water, driving all the air from his lungs. He was desperate for a breath, but he could only feel himself going deeper. It was impossible to tell which way was up, and just when he thought that his chest was about to burst for want of air, he broke the surface.

'Over here,' Alicia called out, 'there's solid ground over here.'

He swam toward the sound of her voice, and soon felt the rocky bottom beneath him as he stumbled toward the shore.

'Thanks,' he gasped as he fumbled for his watch.

Alicia's face glowed an unearthly blue in the light of the watch, but Årkigara was almost invisible now that the clay was washed away from his body. His shadowy black skin blended almost perfectly with the darkness, yet his yellow eyes shone eerily in the dim light.

George looked back up to the mouth of the well, which now appeared to be nothing more than a tiny glowing dot of orange firelight. 'Is there another way out?' he asked.

'There is not,' said Årkigara, 'but we are where we need to be. We are where the prisoners are kept.'

'Well, I can't see a ruddy thing down here.'

'I can,' said Alicia, 'kind of, but I'm not really sure what I'm seeing.' As she looked around, she could detect faint shadows in unfamiliar colours, but the stalactites and stalagmites seemed to grow and change right before her eyes. 'Like... what *is* this place?'

'It is the Imaru,' replied the gargoyle, 'a prison that confines and torments its inmates with endless confusion.'

High above, the dragon shrieked and something else roared.

'We'd better get going,' said George.

'But I have never been in these depths before,' said Årkigara, 'and I do not know my way... I cannot go on.'

'I know what you mean... just looking around at this place makes me sick,' said Alicia. 'It won't stop moving.'

George held up his watch, shone its dull light onto the wide fat cone of a nearby stalagmite, and looked at it carefully. 'What do you mean... what's moving?'

'Everything!' yelped Alicia, 'seriously... can't you see it?'

George continued to look around as he shone his watch light on the ground, and then onto some stalactites, all of which seemed perfectly still. 'What on earth are you blithering on about?'

At first, Alicia wanted to snap back, but then she looked where George was pointing the light from his watch, and she could see what he was seeing.

'This is a prison for your people,' she asked Årkigara, 'like, for the Anzû... right?'

'It is.'

'Of course,' she said to herself, 'it totally makes sense now.'

'Then, do you mind,' said George, 'explaining what you think makes so much blasted sense?'

'Yeah, yeah, right... okay, it's like this: You and I see with light, right? But the Pazoân, the Anzû see with... what did you say it was?' she asked the gargoyle, 'reflected time?'

'So what's your ruddy point?' asked George in growing

frustration.

'This place was totally set up to confuse Anzû prisoners… so,' she stopped and turned back to Årkigara. 'Okay, what do you see… like, where the light is?'

'It moves… nothing is solid… the walls move and rob my people of all hope,' he replied.

'See?' said Alicia, triumphantly, as if that had fully explained everything.

'I still don't have the foggiest notion what you're going on about?'

'Argh!' she rolled her eyes in frustration. She simply didn't have the words to adequately describe what she could see so clearly in her mind. But before she could begin again, the Guardian screeched as it entered the well and flew down toward them.

'No time!' she shouted, 'George, into that tunnel!' She then grabbed Årkigara, but he resisted.

'It is a wall!' he cried, 'we cannot go that way!'

'Just close your eyes and take my hand!' she snapped, 'George, hurry up, get in the tunnel!' In her hand, the gargoyle's claw felt boney and strange, but within it, she could feel the living being beneath, trembling with fear.

'It's okay,' she tried to reassure him, 'just keep your eyes closed… don't look at the walls.' She tried to pull him along, but found that she was just as unable to move him as any other part of the physical world. 'Crap! George, you're going to have to take him!'

'Not bloody likely!'

'Dammit, just do it! We don't have time!'

A deafening roar echoed through the cavern, followed by a massive thud of flesh and bone colliding with rock.

'Go, go, go!' Alicia shouted.

Reluctantly, George grabbed Årkigara's clawed hand and pulled him roughly toward the tunnel entrance as Alicia followed close behind.

In the pale glow of his watch, the cave seemed clear and steady, but there still were too many tunnels, and they seemed to branch and fork endlessly.

'So where should we go?' he asked.

'Just keep moving,' Alicia shouted back as she tried very hard to ignore the changing walls and focus only on the solid place where the light fell. It was there, and only there, that the way seemed clear to her, as everywhere else, the cave was moving, shifting and shaking, as if desperate to steal her attention.

They travelled deeper and deeper into the unknown while wretched, mournful cries echoed from the many small openings all along the tunnels. The air was choked with the stench of death, and as they moved deeper, the putrid reek filled George's nostrils and ran down the back of his throat.

In a thousand unknown languages, without source or direction, lonely wails wafted through the damp air, all desperately seeking ears to hear them. The farther the three ran, the more voices joined this haunted chorus.

Then, out of the depths, George thought he heard familiar words, and he stopped to listen. He called out, 'Who's there?' as he turned his light around the cavern where many tunnels converged. 'I thought I heard someone... crying out... in English.'

At the sound of his human voice, the chorus faded into silence, but then a weak voice reached out to him, 'I beg you...'

George turned his light to the small opening where the sound seemed to come from, and cautiously moved closer. When he shone his light inside, he saw a body, in an advanced state of decay, lying sprawled on the floor. He fought back the urge to vomit, 'bloody hell.'

'So much death,' whispered Alicia.

Something moved in the shadows. George flipped the light to the far corner, and there, propped up against the cell wall, was another body. It was hard to tell if it had once been one of the creatures, or if it had been a human being. A rat crawled out of the ribcage and scurried away. 'Poor beggar,' muttered George.

The rotten eyelids flicked open and one of the eyeballs fell out, dangling on the tattered remains of an optical nerve, '...h-help me...'

'Do not look upon them!' Årkigara cried, 'there is great evil here!'

'I-I beg you... help me...' The body stretched out a hand, but there was no arm connecting it. Then, as the thing struggled to stand, putrefied organs fell out of its rotten body cavity, 'I-I must... feed...'

'Food!' a strangled voice cried out from behind them, 'the son of the Lugal has brought us food!'

'Oh, blessed one,' another voice rasped, 'such mercy, such a feast you bring us!'

Unspeakable horrors, foul remnants of life, were now walking, scraping, dragging toward them in the dark. Everywhere George shone the pale light of his watch, there were dead body parts impossibly suspended in the air in a sick imitation of whole beings.

'I bring you nothing!' Årkigara cried out, his voice cracking with terror, 'you are evil and unworthy! Leave us!'

'Oh, Great One...'

'We *are* unworthy... but beg your mercy... do not torture us more.'

'G-George,' Alicia croaked, 'we gotta get out of here!'

Dozens, hundreds, of rotten corpses crowded in, and the stench was so thick that George could barely breathe, and he almost gagged.

'These mătu,' Årkigara shouted, 'these mătu belong to the Skogsrå, they are not for you!'

The very sound of the name of Skogsrå was enough to bring forth great wails of terror, and many of the dead stopped their approach, while still others struggled to retreat, and escape the threat. Yet, there were also a few that were not so easily driven away.

A large hulking creature, which was not nearly as decayed as the others, crashed through the hoard, crushing those that got in its way.

'I owe that treacherous, filthy Ulgara no allegiance,' it growled as it slammed an unfortunate fellow prisoner into the cave floor. 'And I do not fear the Skogsrå, those spoiled remnants of a failing foreign monarchy.' It then pointed to Alicia, 'and that one is already dead, so why do you even bother to defend it?'

'I am *so* not dead!' Alicia shouted.

George moved in front of her, but found that he was shaking so hard that it was difficult to get the words out. 'K-keep behind m-me,' he stammered, 'st- stay back.'

But in one swift motion, the monster threw him aside, and sank its teeth deep into the ghostly traces of Alicia's shoulder.

The pain was more intense than anything she had ever known, and her knees gave way. Something, some part of her, could see trails of tissue flowing from her body into the monster, and she felt it growing stronger with every passing second. She cried out in pain as George started to punch at the creature's flank, but the thing did not stop feeding. But then George's fist hit a particularly rotten spot on the beast's ribcage, and his arm sank deep as the thing howled in pain and dropped Alicia. It tried to pull away, but George's hand had caught on a jagged rib, and the two were locked together.

Adrenalin had taken over. There was no fear left in George, nor panic, nor even anger. He was left only with an intense clarity of mind, and he thrust his hand deeper into the creature's chest, reaching for its heart. Not its heart of dying flesh, but a deeper one – the very core of the thing's being. Suddenly the creature was truly aware of this new danger, and it howled in terror as it knocked George and away fled into the darkness.

George slammed hard into the cave wall, his watch went flying, and its lid snapped shut when it struck the ground, extinguishing its reassuring light. He quickly fumbled to retrieve it, but it was gone, lost in the darkness, and he could hear more dead things shuffling closer, driven toward him by their relentless hunger.

Årkigara continued to shout and plead, 'they are not for you... they belong to the Skogsrå!'

Alicia tried to stand up as she fought through her own pain. When she clasped her shoulder and felt where the creature had bitten her, she was surprised to find that it had somehow remained whole, although weakened and diminished.

As she looked around in the absence of the light from George's watch, she could see the prisoners more clearly now. They were different from what she had first seen. What she had thought was empty space between the chunks of putrefying flesh, was now filled with the silvery traces of the whole beings within, and it was only their rotten mantles that hung on them like ragged clothing. There were hundreds, if not thousands, of them there, blindly stumbling within the prison as the walls shifted around them. They were just as helpless in this place as she was.

She turned to Årkigara, his eyes tightly closed as he continued to plead and threaten, and when she reached out to him, he pulled away, terrified.

'It's okay... it's me... Alicia.'

'We are lost,' he muttered in a quiet, defeated voice, 'the evil here is too great.' He then sat back on his haunches and wrapped his wings tightly around himself as he rocked back and forth, moaning.

In that moment, Alicia felt an odd combination of compassion and revulsion. She couldn't believe that Årkigara, the son of a king, was giving up so easily, especially after he had seemed so calm when talking about his own impending death... it just didn't make sense. She then looked back at the other creatures, who were also giving up and abandoning hope once again.

Then a thought occurred to her – they weren't abandoning hope, it was being taken from them. It was as if the prison itself could actively drain its occupants of all hope. Perhaps, she thought, because she was human and this place had been designed to imprison Anzû, it did not have the same effect on her.

However, without the light from George's watch, the prison she saw shifted and moved in confusing and unnatural ways. She found herself wishing that her parents had allowed her to have a phone of her own, and then she wouldn't be in this situation. Well, okay, she thought, she *would* still be in this situation, but at least she'd be able to turn on her phone for a little light.

'George,' she called out, clear and without echo, 'where are you?'

'I'm over here,' his voice echoed back so profoundly that it was impossible to tell from which direction it came. 'I've lost my watch, I can't see.'

He continued to fumble for his watch, even as more of the dead abominations shuffled closer. How he craved the comfort, the sanctuary, of his watch's glow, but then froze when he heard one of the creatures drawing too near, its festering stench growing unbearable. Then, a slimy claw grabbed his hand and the thing's grip only increased as he tried to pull away. He could feel the thing's rotten flesh squishing out from between its boney fingers as its grip tightened.

Then he felt something else – the thing was pressing something into his hand. It was his watch. The claw let go, and George flipped open his watch and it glowed a reassuring blue. When he looked up, the corpse was just standing there, looking back at him.

'Wh-what,' George stammered, 'what do you want?'

'You are here for the mătu... the one they call the thief?' it asked through mangled, rotten lips. Its voice was soft and feminine, and what remained of this creature's face looked disturbingly human. 'You seek the lone mătu?'

'Y-yes.'

'Why?'

'He's my father... do you know where he is?'

'I do.'

'Could you take me to him?'

'I will... but in return you must do something for me.'

'I-I can't feed you... if that's what you want.'

'No, I seek something far more valuable from you... you must remember me... you must remember my name. I am Gešti.[26]'

---

[26] **Gešti** or **Gešti-nanna** – (pronounced *Gesh-TEE na-na*) Also known as 'She Who Weeps', or 'The Scribe of the Underworld'

Chapter Nineteen

The Prisoner

'You must follow me if you wish to find your father,' said Gešti as she turned away.

'Wait,' said George, 'I need to get Alicia.'

'No,' replied Gešti, 'that child has more important work to do where she is.'

George felt uneasy that this corpse was trying to separate them, and he feared that it might be a trap. 'But it's too dangerous for her.'

'She is safe... for now. You have driven away the only one who would harm her... you attacked him more deeply than he would have ever believed possible, so his new fear of you is far greater than his hunger.'

'But...'

'The dumu-lugal[27], the one you know as Årkigara, he is in greater need of Alicia's help right now, as she is his one true hope... and right now, your father's only hope, is with you.'

'Yes... yes, of course,' said George as he followed Gešti into the mouth of the tunnel. She led him through many passages and took many turns, but always seemed to know where she was going. 'How do you do it?' he asked, 'how are you not lost in here like the others?'

'I am here by choice... and this prison does not know how to steal the hope of one who would choose to be here.' She then turned to him and pointed to an opening, where George could see his father

---

[27] **Dumu-lugal** – (pronounced *do-MOO-loo-gul*) – Child of the king.

lying on the floor, and he ran to him.

'Dad! It's me, wake up!'

His father stirred and groaned, but did not look up.

'Dad, I've come to get you out of here!'

Mr Stryder only covered his ears and rocked back and forth, mumbling, 'go away... you're not real... I've never seen your cursed amulet.'

'What's wrong with him?' George demanded.

'Your father has delved into forces quite beyond his understanding... and the jailers sought to find out how deeply he had gone... and they can be very cruel when they are desperate.'

'Dad,' George pleaded, 'Dad, it's me... I've come to help get you out of here.' He then laid a hand on his father's shoulder, but the man cringed and then sprang to his feet and slammed George violently against the rock wall.

'Get out of my head you damnable monster!' Mr Stryder cried as he stumbled and held his head in his hands. Then, as if fighting demons both real and imagined, he leaned against the far side of the cell and banged his fist against the rock until it was bloody. 'How dare you assume the form of my son!'

In a defeated voice, George slumped to the floor and asked, 'why won't you believe... it's me... your boy, Arthur.'

At the sound of that name, a name so familiar, yet one that the jailors could not have known, Mr Stryder stopped and turned around slowly, his eyes wide with shock. He moved uncertainly toward his son, and then knelt down and touched George's cheek with his bloodied fingers.

'Is it really you? My dear boy... how... why? You mustn't be here.' He then wrapped his arms around his son, 'I'm so sorry... I didn't know... I didn't realize... Why would you come here?'

'I had to... I would have gone anywhere to find you.'

'No, m'boy, not here... you should never have come here... you'd have been better off if you'd just forgotten me.'

'I could never do that, dad.'

'Oh, m'boy...' his father said with a choked laugh as he wiped his eyes with his sleeve, 'you look like you've been through hell...' Then

Mr Stryder caught a glimpse of Gešti, almost hidden by the darkness. His demeanor quickly changed from joy to one of intense anger. 'What is that abomination doing here?'

'Dad, don't... Gešti helped me.'

At first, George's father just glared at the strange being that stood before him, but then she reached out and took his hand in the skeletal remains of hers, and something in him changed. He returned the gesture of apparent tenderness and touched the air where there ought to have been her other arm. 'My God,' he muttered, 'how could a woman of such beauty be trapped inside such a foul shell?'

'It was by my own choice,' said the corpse, 'but then I was betrayed.'

'Such cruelty,' Mr Stryder said, as he tenderly brushed the remains of her cheek.

'Cruelty?' Gešti asked, 'you speak so casually of cruelty, yet I know of the terrible things that you have...'

'Please,' he cut in, 'not in front of the boy... I am a changed man... I know now how wrong I was.'

'You will have much to answer for.'

'That... I well know,' said Mr Stryder, 'but now my only concern is for my boy. I must get him out of this accursed place.'

'Then we share a common purpose,' replied Gešti, 'but alas, it is beyond my ability to free him.'

'Perhaps it is beyond you, but I have my own resources,' said Mr Stryder as he turned to George, 'however, to access those, I will need to see your watch, m'boy, I need to contact Sikes.'

'Dad, you mustn't trust him,' said George. 'He's the one who caused our ship to be torpedoed, and he was the one who threw me into that blighted storm.'

'I know... but I'm afraid that he was only doing as I ordered...'

George felt a wrench inside his gut. Everything he thought he understood was falling apart. 'But he's your governor... you're not his.'

'I was granted a field promotion. Now be a good boy, and give me your watch.'

'But... then,' George struggled to understand, 'then, if you had

Mr Sikes throw me into the storm... what happened to Mum?'

'Things change over time... as do people,' said Mr Stryder, his patience visibly straining.

'But that doesn't answer...'

'Just give me the bloody acnode so we can get out of here!'

Almost reflexively, George handed his watch over to his father, even as more doubts clouded his mind. Mr Stryder snatched it roughly from his hand, and simply said, 'operation oversight: go.' He then casually tossed it back to George, 'the 'node requires physical contact for full verification, that's all... you needn't have been so worried, m'boy.'

'I fear,' said Gešti to Mr Stryder, 'that the role you play in this evil game is not the one you believe it to be.'

'I'm sure I don't know what you're talking about,' he replied, but George had the uneasy feeling that his father was lying.

'The Anu-gìn-a-nir does not contain the answers that you seek,' said Gešti, with a look of deep sorrow, 'it will only undo that which you have laboured to create.'

Before Mr Stryder could reply, a terrible howl echoed deep from within the tunnels.

'There is no time,' Gešti cried out, a look of panic in her eyes, 'the Guardian is losing his battle, and he will be seeking fresh bodies on which to feed.'

Alicia called out, but George did not answer. Without the glow from his watch, there was no reflected light for her to see by, only time reflecting off the illusion of the shifting walls. Knowing that it was merely a trick, a temporal illusion, should have been enough to protect her, but it wasn't. The prison was finally starting to seep into her mind as fear, and doubt, and blame, crowded into her thoughts.

What if George had found his father and then left without her?

How long could she last on her own?

What a stupid rule her parents had that she had to wait until she was twelve before she could have her own smart phone. Like, seriously, how stupid would they feel when they realized that she had died because they didn't get her a proper phone? Oh sure, they'd given her a basic flip-phone, like for emergencies and stuff, but that thing was so totally last century that she never carried it with her, anyway. And, yeah, okay, it's not like she could get a signal here, but at least she'd have a decent screen with real light to see by. So it was so totally her parents fault for not letting her have a phone with a proper screen…

Thoughts circled and repeated, growing louder in her head.

How stupid and thoughtless her parents were, how useless and pitiful this gargoyle was, how absolutely hopeless this place was.

'No,' she heard her own voice speaking to her. 'No,' her own voice repeated, 'think about it, Alicia, this place isn't like that.'

Could it be, she wondered, that hope is actually a tangible thing? And if that's true, then perhaps she and George had given Årkigara just enough real hope that he could then bring them this far, but now that the prison had robbed him of even that faint trace, he was once again lost, and she was bound to follow him into despair.

Then another unexpected and complex thought came flooding into her mind. She found herself reasoning that since the human understanding of reality could be argued to be little more than a construct of shared perception, it is therefore not entirely unreasonable to extend that concept to include the otherwise intangible concept of hope. If one then assumes that to be axiomatic, then one need only share hope with others to make it tangible…

Whoa, she thought, where did that come from? Was this just the prison trying to confuse her? No, that couldn't be… these thoughts were the exact opposite of what the prison would want her to think.

And it was then, in that moment alone in the dark, separated from her body and ungoverned by time, that Alicia realized that she had somehow reached out and touched the mind of herself as an adult. And just knowing that she was going to have the chance to *be* an adult, gave her hope. And although the connection had been only momentary, the hope that it had generated remained with her, and she knew what she had to do.

'Hey,' she said to Årkigara, 'we're going to get out of here and everything's going to be okay.' She looked at his face, which seemed softer and even younger with only time reflecting off it, yet she could also see that his eyes were strangely ancient.

'How can you still find hope in this place?' he asked.

'I don't know... I just know that we're going to make it out of here.'

'Thank you,' he said in a way that made Alicia realize that he wasn't used to receiving such kindness, and it was then that she saw in him something so wonderfully... human.

Alicia knew, almost instinctively, that they still had to wait for George to return, but the wait was not so bad, since at least now, she had hope. She sat down next to Årkigara and held him, offering him what comfort she could. They sat that way for a long time without saying anything, but then he turned to her and asked, 'why are you a ghost?'

'I am so not a ghost!' she almost shouted. 'Way to ruin the moment!'

'But you are here without your body, your mantle... so what are you, then? And what force could be strong enough to tear you from it?'

'I-I don't know,' she stammered, 'well, yeah, I guess I do... kinda... it's this thing called 'accordance'... it kinda stuck George and me together.'

'But without you inside your mantle to give it purpose, does it still live?'

'Of course it does,' she snapped, but the more she thought about it, the less sure she was of her answer. 'I mean... I guess, I think it does... like, okay, I *was* really sick last time I was back home... but that was just the flu... or something...'

'Yes,' he said as he seemed to peer inside her, 'I see great potential in you, you do attain a full life... so perhaps all of this has not been in vain... perhaps you are to be the first living being to escape this inescapable place.'

'Whoa, hang on,' said Alicia, 'what do you mean *this inescapable place*? Like, why would you bring us here if you knew that there's no way out?'

'Because I thought George might wish to die with his father,' he explained, but when he saw the look of shock on her face, he added, 'George and his father had already been sentenced to death... and then your kindness... the kindness you showed to me... That inspired me. When you promised to ask the Skogsrå to give me a good death, you gave me hope enough to carry on.'

'No way! I said that I'd ask it to spare your life... and besides, why didn't you mention that George and his dad had been sentenced to death? Like, that's kind of important.'

'Not if knowing it only serves to crush your own hope.'

'Whoa,' she said, shaking her head in disbelief, 'you so-o-o don't get humans! Look, I'm sure we're all going to make it out of here... okay? I mean, seriously, I'm totally stuck with George, so how else would I get out of here and grow up?'

'True,' agreed the gargoyle, but then he stopped to think about it for a moment more, and added, 'however... if he does die, then you will no longer be anchored to him, and so you will be free to return to your mantle, will you not? That is almost certainly the only way that you, and you alone, will escape this cursed place.'

Unearthly howls and the sounds of crashing stone echoed through the tunnels.

'For me, however,' said Årkigara as he stood up, 'it is only a matter of how I die.'

An impossibly deep roar echoed around them.

George steadied himself as the ground shook and the cell walls cracked with the impact of something huge. Even in the dampness of the cave, dust rose up in the glow of his watch.

Outside of the prison cell, he could see broken bodies scattered everywhere in the tunnel, some still shifting and moaning under the weight of their dead comrades. The sounds of panicked prisoners echoed from the unseen depths. Hidden within the clouds of dust, he heard an immense body dragging across stone. Suddenly, from within the murk, the claw of the Guardian reached out and tore away the wall.

George cried out to warn his father, and at the sound of his voice, the claw tensed and then the creature drew itself closer, until its massive head was directly in front of him.

The voice of Gešti called out from the ruins of the prison cell, 'Leave the boy! These mătu are now under my protection, and by the laws of lord Anu, you may not harm them!'

'I care not for the foolish tenets of your dead religion,' the Guardian roared, 'my will is the sole authority here... before me, there are no other laws!' With that, the monster reached into the cell and wrapped its claw around the body of Gešti.

'Run!' she called out, even as she struggled to free herself, 'save yourselves and run!'

The Guardian coiled its huge body into the small space as it tightened its grip and growled at her, 'I have consumed your story and spat it out as a myth... but now, to finally devour the remains of your life... I shall savour that greatly.'

'I will not fight you,' cried Gešti, even as the dragon tightened its grip on her, 'but nor will I allow your attack to continue.' Her body glowed, and then there was an explosion of white light. The dragon shrieked as its claw was torn apart, and it writhed in pain so violently that more of the cave was shattered, exposing a vast honeycomb of prison cells above and below.

George grabbed his father's hand and dashed for the tunnel, searching for a way out.

'Alicia,' he called out, 'Alicia, where are you?' George ran with his father close behind, both following the faint glow of his watch. At first, there was no answer, but then, between the echoes of his own cries, he could hear traces of her voice, coming through the darkness, faint and clear, but without echo.

'We're here,' her voice grew louder as they drew nearer, 'what happened?'

'The mush-what-ever-it-is came after us... it's in the tunnels!'

Mr Stryder stepped back and shouted, 'bloody hell! So it *was* all just another damned illusion!'

George turned to look at his father, who was keeping his eyes tightly closed as he shook and mumbled to himself.

'Dad...? W-what's wrong?' but his father did not answer. 'Dad... it's me... your boy Arthur.'

Mr Stryder slowly opened his eyes. 'I-I'm sorry m'boy... this place plays cruel tricks on the mind... I could have sworn I just saw the young Henderson girl with you. What was her name, Alice?'

'Alicia,' said George in disbelief, 'you just heard me calling her name... why wouldn't you remember that?' George then reached out to take his father's hand again, 'and you didn't imagine her... she's right over there.'

'Hi, Mr Stryder,' said Alicia a little uncertainly, 'it's good to see you again.'

'Right... right, of course,' said Mr Stryder, mumbling to himself, 'must be temporal dissonance... really bloody disconcerting.' Then his face clouded with anger when he saw Årkigara in the shadows. 'And just what is that damn sapper doing here?'

'He helped us,' Alicia began to explain, but then crashing echoed up through the tunnels.

'Alright, then... You! Sapper!' Mr Stryder barked at Årkigara, 'do you know the way out?'

The gargoyle looked up in surprise, 'I can return you to the pool at the base of the well, but...'

'Then do it! Our time here is limited.'

The prison was now broken, and its ability to confuse and ensnare its inmates was quickly fading, so all along the way, corpses were moving slowly toward the central cavern below the mouth of the well.

It would have been, should have been, too crowded for the outsiders to move, but something strange was happening: the corpses maintained their distance. They kept just outside the glow of George's watch, murmuring in their many languages and dialects, but always with whispers of Gešti, Gešti-nanna.

'What's going on?' Alicia asked, 'what are they saying?'

Årkigara's golden-yellow eyes were wide with disbelief, 'they're saying that "She Who Weeps" has returned.'

'Who's that?'

'A rumour... a myth,' he replied in an uncertain voice.

'I just met someone by that name... Gešti,' said George, 'though I hardly would have thought she would be the cause of all this fuss.'

'That cannot be!' snapped Årkigara. 'I was always told that she was not real, the imagined redeemer of the lost and forgotten, and the usurper of kings... kings like my father... but she cannot be real.'

As they entered the main cavern, a cold light now bathed the cave's interior, and for the first time, George and Alicia could see the immensity of the place. It was a natural rock dome, one vast enough to contain an entire city, and it was where hundreds of thousands of Anzû corpses were now gathering, chanting whispers of the name Gešti-nanna.

Without ever looking at the four outsiders, the crowd separated to let them through, only to close in again as they passed.

'What are all the prisoners coming here for?' whispered Alicia, her unease growing, 'that redeemer of theirs?'

Indistinct at first, but then with increasing intensity, a chant was cutting through the whispers of 'Gešti-nanna' and growing louder – 'Skogsrå... Skogsrå...'

'No, they are not,' said Årkigara, matter-of-factly. 'They are here to see the child of a despised king butchered for their amusement. They have come to see me die.'

Chapter Twenty

The Skogsrå

Far above, at the mouth of the well, George could see something new was approaching. At first, it was just a blur of gold, white, and black, but as it drew closer, he could see a golden Barbary lion, with its distinctive black mane. Out of its back, however, sprouted an immense pair of white wings, like those of a royal swan.

Far below it, the teaming hordes of undead continued to chant, their ragged voices growing louder and more insistent, 'Skogsrå... Skogsrå...'

'Wow,' said Alicia, 'that thing is huge.'

'But not nearly as big as the dragon,' said George as he watched the magnificent creature glide down in wide sweeping circles.

'What in blue bloody blazes *is* that?' asked Mr Stryder. 'Is it another type of sapper... or something else entirely?'

George shook his head, and Alicia just shrugged.

'The Skogsrå feed on humans just as we do,' said Årkigara with a sneer, 'yet they think that they are better than the Pazoân because their humans are domesticated, not wild and free...'

'But... what's it doing here?' asked Mr Stryder, still watching in awe as the creature circled in its decent.

'Well, dad,' George began awkwardly, 'it's all really a bit of a mess.'

'It's here to kill Årkigara,' said Alicia, 'and we've got to stop it.'

The lion swooped low and then landed majestically nearby, as the crowd of corpses still chanting parted so that there was nothing between the newcomer and the four outsiders. Several times larger than a natural lion, the Skogsrå looked particularly grand as he held his wings up regally, the way a falcon does when diving toward its prey. He then surveyed the vast gathering of prisoners with some distaste, but when he saw Årkigara, the lion roared with such force that the ground shook. And the crowds of undead fell silent.

With regal bearing, the lion approached George and addressed him in deep, fluid tones, which sounded oddly like someone speaking Russian with a Norwegian accent. 'Is that him?' the lion asked, nodding toward Årkigara, 'is that the níðhöggr [28] who attacked our child?'

'Um... yes,' said George, but before he could say anything more, the lion had turned on the gargoyle, and with a single blow, knocked him unconscious against a stalagmite. A ripple of whispers ran through the crowd, punctuated by occasional cheers from those eager for blood.

'Don't!' Alicia shouted in anger. 'He's just a kid!'

'And he saved our lives!' added George. Then, just as the lion was about to strike again, George stood in his way and the lion stopped, looking at him in astonishment. 'What are you doing? Why should you care about this filthy little höggr?'

'He saved our lives,' said George, 'more than once... and I never would have found my dad without his help.'

'He didn't mean to kill her,' pleaded Alicia.

The lion stared at Alicia with great puzzlement. 'What? No, our child is not dead, only her mantle was damaged... but this filthy little höggr must pay for attacking one of its betters.'

When Alicia moved next to George, the lion looked even more confused. 'We have heard of you,' he said, 'but did not expect you to be as incomplete as you are. You appear as a mind without a body.'

'I have a body!' she snapped, but then added a little hesitantly, 'I-I just don't have it with me.'

'Your spirit is strong... especially for an uadelig[29],' the lion said as

---

[28] **Níðhöggr** – (pronounced *neezth-WHO-ger*) the pejorative name the Skogsrå use for the Pazoân, usually shortened to **höggr** (the plural is **níðhöggär** – pronounced *neezth-WHO-gaar*)

[29] **Uadelig** – (pronounced *OO-ah-duh-lig*) – This is a Skogsrå word, similar to the Pazoân term mătu, but in this case, it refers only to humans not owned by any particular Skogsrå clan. It roughly translates as 'commoner'

he appeared to almost smile. 'You have the force of will to stand up to us, guarding this filth, even though we could tear you asunder with a single blow.'

'He is not filth,' insisted Alicia, 'he's just a kid... like us.'

'In that, you are wrong, little ghost,' said the lion in an almost grandfatherly way. He then looked to where Årkigara lay and added, 'the níðhöggär are unclean scavengers, tricksters and deceivers, and certainly not worthy of your protection.' The lion then turned back to Alicia with a smile, 'however, you intrigue us, and we have decided not to sully ourselves with that filthy höggr's blood. We shall instead leave it here to face the justice of its own kind. Does that offer you some comfort?'

Without waiting for a reply, he shook his immense mane and returned his attention to George, 'But we are wasting time. We must remove you from this foul place.' He then crouched low to the ground, as if preparing to pounce, 'you and your strange little ghost must climb on our back.'

'What about my dad?' asked George.

'The one who sired you?' The lion seemed genuinely surprised as it stood up and turned to Mr Stryder. 'So, you are the one!' He furrowed his brow and regarded George's father carefully. 'We have heard tell of you. You have endangered many with your actions, and you have much to answer for...'

Suddenly there were screams and howls of terror from the crowds as the Guardian exploded from the mouth of the tunnel. It angrily swept its tail in a wide arc, clearing a path for itself and throwing a rain of rotten body parts into the hordes of undead. It then let loose a howl that seemed to come from the depths of hell itself.

The Skogsrå roared in angry reply, and bounded over to the mouth of the tunnel, where the two giants clashed, indifferent to the terrified prisoners crushed as they fought.

'Damn and blast,' cursed Mr Stryder as the panicked corpses rushed away from the battle, and directly toward them. 'Arthur! Get back... get out of the way!'

'I'm not leaving you, dad!'

'Damn it! Do as I say... I can't hold them off... so get bloody... going!'

'Aren't they supposed to be leaving us alone,' shouted George, 'because of Gešti?' As soon as he uttered her name, the corpses seemed to freeze, and then withdrew, pushing back any others who may not have heard, until once again, the Pazoân undead were giving the outsiders a wide berth, reverentially repeating the sacred name of their redeemer.

'Damned handy name that, eh what?' said Mr Stryder, looking somewhat stunned. He then looked at the rotten limb that one of the creatures had left in his grasp, and realizing what it was, threw it away in disgust.

However, the two giants continued to fight, and soon took to the air as each tried to gain the advantage. With their wings fully extended and their talons locked together, they tumbled through the air like a couple of eagles, each straining to throw the other against the jagged stalactites that hung from the roof of the cavern.

'Wow, do you think the lion has a chance?' asked Alicia.

'I don't know,' said George as he felt his gut tighten, 'the dragon is more than twice the size of the lion...' There was a roar of pain as the lion slammed into a dagger-like stalactite, and then crashed to the ground with a heavy thud, and sickening crack of bone. 'But I'm pretty sure that if the lion dies... so do we.'

Badly wounded, the lion struggled to get up, and stumbled as his right wing dragged uselessly behind him. He tried to fold his damaged wing, but the effort seemed too much, and he collapsed in exhaustion and remained still, while high above, the dragon screeched triumphantly overhead.

Several corpse prisoners approached the lion, testing to see if he would respond to their probes, and when he did not, they grew bolder and, perhaps trying to win favour with the Guardian, they began to poke and prod the dying beast.

The dragon circled lower and lower.

Alicia fought back tears of anger, but then she noticed the lion tense ever so slightly just as the dragon made a particularly low pass. What if he had been faking, she wondered, like a bird does to distract a predator from its young.

On the dragon's next pass, the lion leapt up, and in one swift motion, flipped over in mid-air, locked his front paws around the astonished dragon's neck, and sank his teeth deep into its throat. The Guardian screeched and beat its wings in desperation as the two giants fell to the ground, crushing a group of hapless corpses beneath them.

Without letting go, the lion quickly twisted himself onto the dragon's back, and shook his head violently, trying to force his teeth deeper, but the scales were tough and resistant to puncture. The dragon spun around and kicked out with its talons, tearing a gash in the lion's flank. The lion let go as he roared in pain, and the dragon pulled free, holding its wounded throat with its one good fore-claw as it scrambled back to the sanctuary of the tunnels.

The Skogsrå lion did not pursue his enemy, but only watched, and when reassured that his foe was not soon returning, he turned and trotted back to where George and Alicia stood. The Skogsrå acted as if he had no wound at all, despite the bloody gash on his flank, exposing the glint of pinkish-white ribs beneath.

'We must get you out of here,' he rumbled in his thick accent, 'quickly now, you and your ghost must climb on our back.'

'I am *so-o-o* not a ghost,' protested Alicia, but the lion ignored her. 'So how can you do it?' she asked, 'how can you act like you're not injured at all?' The lion looked at her as though he didn't quite understand her question.

'I am not injured,' he said, but then added, 'my mantle may bear the marks of battle, but the níðhöggär has been unable to harm me within.' The lion offered no further explanation as he coaxed George to climb onto his back. Alicia followed, and was surprised to find that like the fox, the lion did not feel like stone, but instead, felt like a living thing.

When Mr Stryder moved to join them, the Skogsrå quickly turned away, 'No – we will have to return for you.'

The lion then leapt into the air, beating his wings hard as he lifted up with surprising grace. George and Alicia clung to his back as he rose up out of the Imaru, and then landed on the huge stone platform at the edge of the well.

'You're not used to carrying passengers, are you?' George asked as he could sense the lion's unease.

'We do not believe we have ever allowed such a thing before. We found it greatly interfered with our flight... and a strangely demeaning experience.' Then, when George and Alicia had slid off his back, the lion dove back into the depths of the well.

'Really rather a regal fellow, wouldn't you agree?' George said as he watched the Skogsrå lion disappear.

'Maybe,' said Alicia, 'but totally arrogant, too... I still have to convince him to save Årkigara.'

George's watch suddenly made an unfamiliar noise, and when he pulled it from his pocket, and flipped it open, it displayed an unexpected message: 'Remote override authorized – Temporal geo-locator activated.'

'Did you ask it to do that?' asked Alicia.

'No,' said George as the watch face went dark, and then, when he tried to retrieve the message, the device refused to respond to any of his commands. 'Bloody hell,' he muttered as he then tried every command he could think of.

'Oh wow,' said Alicia, 'what if it's a computer virus?'

'These blasted things can get sick?' George looked at her in disbelief, 'well then, that's rotten timing, isn't it?' His watch chimed again, and this time the message read '*Tracking...*'

'What the devil is with this thing?' he asked in growing exasperation. 'Display map: Current location,' he commanded, but the watch still refused to work. 'Damn and blast... so how could this thing possibly catch a cold?'

'A virus, I said a virus.'

'So what will make it better? A spot of beef tea and a mustard plaster?'

'What? ... No, it's like a computer virus, so, you're just going to have to run some sort of security program, or something.'

'Oh, and I suppose you just happen to have one of those on hand?'

'No, of course not,' she said, resisting the temptation to roll her eyes. 'You need to download it from the 'Net... or whatever that thing connects to.'

'Well that's just bloody grand, isn't it?' George growled as he resisted the urge to smash his watch on the ground.

Just then, the lion returned, rising out of the darkness of the well, circling the platform, and then landing majestically. Mr Stryder slid off the Skogsrå's back easily, but then staggered like a drunken man.

'Dad!' George rushed to support his father before he fell, 'what's wrong with you?'

'I'm fine,' he snapped, 'just a little unsteady... that's all.' But he continued to stumble, and finally had to sit down.

The lion looked concerned. 'This will not do. Your sire is weak from his imprisonment, and in no fit state to enter the labyrinth. You will need to proceed without him.'

'No, we blasted-well will not!' protested George. 'We're not bloody leaving him. Why can't you fly him out and then come back for us?'

'We cannot,' replied the lion. 'The fume hangs heavy in here, and we fear that the smoke above has grown too thick for your kind to survive.'

'Then you can walk... carry him on your back, and lead us out,' said George as his watch chimed again. The new message read, '*Searching...*'

'We cannot do that, either,' said the Skogsrå, 'we still have an enemy to battle, and so you must enter the labyrinth without us. You must make your own way out.'

'But we don't know the way!' cut in Alicia, 'we'd be totally lost – we need Årkigara to show us the way out... so you totally need to go back for him!'

'That filthy little höggr is not our concern,' replied the lion.

'Well, I'm not leaving here without my father – or Årkigara – for that matter,' said George. Then his watch chimed yet again, and this time the message read '*Localizing*'.

'I won't hear of it,' said Mr Stryder as he cursed and struggled to his feet, 'we're not going to put our lives in the hands of some bloody sapper... anyway, I have the situation well in hand...' He stumbled again, and sank back to his knees.

'You see?' said the lion, 'even your sire knows the folly of trusting a höggr... But we fear that your father is still too unsteady, and will be a danger to you on the narrow bridges... so you must leave him as well.'

'I will not!' shouted George.

'I have a man,' said Mr Stryder, standing up very slowly and carefully, 'coming for us... and he should be here any minute now.' George's watch chimed and the new message read, '*Contact*'.

Then, on the far side of the large stone platform, red and blue sparks spiralled out of the darkness, and a man stepped out from the vortex.

'Sikes!' called out Mr Stryder, 'it's about time you got here! I need you to get us out of this godforsaken place. Do you still possess the device?'

'I do, sir, but it's not what we thought it was... it's not what we were told.'

'Don't be a fool! Clearly you were able to use it to get my son off the ship, so I need you to use it again.'

'I-I can't sir... you don't know how soul-destroying it is.'

'Damn it, man! Pull yourself together!' Mr Stryder spoke like someone familiar with commanding legions, and George watched dumbfounded, unable to recognize the man his father had become.

'Dad,' he pleaded, 'what's going on?'

Mr Stryder looked at his son only briefly, but then turned back to Mr Sikes. 'You told me that you could handle this,' George's father snapped, 'and I took you at your word.'

As Mr Stryder berated his subordinate, Alicia turned to the lion, 'you have to go back for Årkigara. He's the only one who can take us through the labyrinth.'

'You try our patience,' rumbled the lion. 'We can tarry no longer. The dragon will be feeding now, and so his strength will soon be restored... It is better for all if we just leave the little höggr with his own kind.'

'His own kind condemned him to death!' protested Alicia.

'Your concern for lesser beings does you credit, little ghost,' said the lion as he surveyed the vast labyrinth for a moment or two.

'Besides,' added Alicia, 'he brought us through the labyrinth, and he'll know the way out.'

'Perhaps,' rumbled the lion, seeming to finally consider the idea, 'that filthy little höggr may prove some value after all... I shall return presently.' He bounded off the platform, and dove back into the mouth of the well.

Deep below and unseen, waiting for just such a moment, the dragon started to slither slowly, carefully, up the steep rock wall and toward the dark side of the platform. It surveyed it's surrounding, and then eased out of the shadows.

'Your protector has left you vulnerable,' the Mušḫuššu hissed as it uncoiled toward them, but then stopped suddenly. It tilted its head and snarled in anger as it recognized Mr Sikes. 'Traitor! You dare return?' The dragon reared up and then lunged, seizing him in its claws.

Sikes struggled to free himself, pleading, 'it wasn't me, tell him, sir, please... tell him... it wasn't me.' But Mr Stryder only clasped his hands behind his back, like a General at ease, and rocked back and forth on his heels once or twice.

'If you kill him,' said Mr Stryder, speaking to the dragon with a very cold, very even tone, 'all your plans will be for naught.'

The Guardian's eyes darted to George's father. 'What do you know of these things?'

But, before Mr Stryder could reply, the lion returned, rising up out of the well, roaring at the sight of the dragon. Tossing the limp body of Årkigara onto the platform, the lion then flew at the dragon. Although not quite as large as his foe, the Skogsrå lion was able to deliver blow after blow, driving the serpent back. The Mušḫuššu dragon twisted and coiled defensively, trying to avoid the lion's attack, but having lost the advantage, retreated into the well. Mr Sikes still firmly in its grasp.

When the lion was certain that his enemy was safely gone, he limped over to where George and Alicia were trying to revive Årkigara.

'Is it alive?' he asked, almost indifferently.

'Yes,' said Alicia, 'but not conscious.'

'This will not do,' rumbled the lion, 'the Guardian of the Well will return soon, and we need him to lead you out of here now.'

'No!' cut in Mr Stryder, 'we need Sikes to get out of here. Go and get him back, now!'

'If he still lives,' replied the lion, 'we will see what we can do later.'

'Now,' demanded Mr Stryder, 'you need to get him now.'

The lion turned to Mr Stryder and growled, 'we know that your interest in Sikes is only for the stolen device that he carries, but you would do well to leave him... and it. That accursed amulet is a filthy höggr artefact that is too dangerous for the likes of humans to possess.'

'It is precisely because of its dangerous nature,' said Mr Stryder, defiantly, 'that we need to keep it out of Pazoân hands.'

'Your kind would do well to show more humility in the face of things you do not understand,' rumbled the lion. 'We have heard that it was on your orders that the device was used to unleash the Galda-ḥamun, the breaker of time.'

'Then you misheard.'

'You take us for a fool, you arrogant little man?' the lion roared. 'Your life is already very nearly forfeit for what you have ordered done... and for endangering the life of our child!'

'I don't understand,' said Mr Stryder, 'what has any of this to do with your child?'

'No, indeed you do not understand,' the lion growled, 'but our child has been fighting to save your son, and trying to repair that which was broken, by riding the crests of the storm that was created on your orders.'

'You cannot seriously hold me accountable for the irresponsible actions of your own child.'

'Irresponsible?' the lion roared. 'It is only by the actions of *our* child that your child continues to live! Indeed, your son has almost been torn asunder by the Galda-ḥamun.'

'I didn't know,' protested Mr Stryder, 'how could I?'

'Precisely,' snapped the lion, 'you did not know... because humans simply do not possess the capacity to understand such things! Now, we have wasted much time,' said the lion as he turned back to where

George and Alicia had been working to revive Årkigara. 'Is the höggr awake yet?'

'Yes,' said Alicia, 'but only just.'

The lion then addressed Årkigara directly. 'Can you understand Angle-ish?' to which the gargoyle nodded, and braced himself for another blow, but the lion did not strike. 'You may yet earn a reprieve from our wrath... you must lead our subjects safely out of the labyrinth. Your life depends upon it.' The lion then turned to George, 'quickly now, there is no time to tarry.'

Just then, a shrieking roar echoed out of the well, and the dragon burst up through it, shooting high above them, and then circling overhead, with Mr Sikes no longer in his claws.

'So, you truly value these mătu, do you?' it taunted as it landed next to a giant torch on a high perch. 'They seem important to you... some of your best breeding stock, perhaps?' The dragon then carefully inspected the flaming cauldron of oil next to it as it sneered, 'although, I am sure that by now, your need to revive your strength, by eating one of them, outweighs your desire to protect them.'

'You still hide yourself in fear-mongering and lies,' the lion roared in reply, 'yet your weakness ultimately betrays you.'

Enraged, the dragon hurled the cauldron at the outsiders, but the lion launched himself up and blocked the stone basin, shattering it as the burning oil sprayed over him. Then, hardly slowed by the impact, the lion landed on the startled serpent, knocking it from its high perch. Blackened and still dripping with fire, the lion pursued the dragon as they clashed again and again, smashing more bridges and torches as they went, roaring and shrieking deep into the vast cavern.

'Did you understand any of that?' asked Alicia.

'Not a word,' said George as he looked over to his father, who was standing on the far side of the platform, and while his father seemed steadier on his feet now, everything else about the man seemed cold and distant. 'But then again, I'm not really sure that I understand anything anymore.'

Chapter Twenty-one

The Mangled Maze

If the labyrinth had been dangerous before, it was nothing to what it was now. After the first battle between the Skogsrå lion and the Mušḫuššu dragon, the narrow bridges that remained were covered in loose rubble and patches of burning oil, and the heat was becoming almost unbearable. The smoke from the many torches had nowhere to go, and so hung heavy overhead, like an oppressive cloud, growing ever lower as the oil continued to burn.

'We must go... now,' said Årkigara as he led the way.

George hesitated.

'Are you okay?' asked Alicia.

'I just wish I understood more,' George replied, 'don't you?'

'What in blazes is holding you up?' Mr Stryder called back over his shoulder, 'hurry up, boy!'

'Yes sir,' he mumbled as he ran to catch up.

They had been traveling for hours, over many miles, and although in some places, the bridges had smashed together, allowing them to take a short cut, in other places, they had to backtrack to find usable paths. George was growing weak from hunger and thirst, and the further he pressed, the more he stumbled.

'Come on,' said Alicia, encouragingly, 'I know we can do this.'

'Oh that's easy for you to say, you're not really here,' said George as he struggled to stand. 'Just like with the rain in India, the smoke and heat can't get to you.'

'Actually,' said Alicia, 'the smoke is totally getting to me.'

'How could that be?'

'I don't know,' she mused, but then burst out, 'hey, maybe the reason the rain didn't get to us was because of the surface tension of water, or something like that.'

'You never cease to amaze me,' said George, 'always thinking about things.'

'Actually,' she said, 'I was wondering about the storm... you know, the one Mr Sikes made on the ship... Like Årkigara said, that type of storm is supposed to totally trap the guy who makes it... but that doesn't explain what's been happening to us... and I think your dad knows more about it than he's saying...'

'Get a move on,' barked Mr Stryder, 'stop talking to yourself, boy... and stop your ruddy dawdling!'

'That's it! This is so totally stupid!' said Alicia as she ran ahead and grabbed Mr Stryder's hand. The surprised look on his face told her that she had made herself known. 'George was talking to *me*, okay?'

'It really is dreadfully unnerving,' said Mr Stryder, 'when you pop out of thin air like that.'

'Well, it's time you heard me,' said Alicia, 'I was saying that the storm Mr Sikes made doesn't make sense... like, not for what's been happening to George and me... and I think you know more about it than you're saying.'

'I really don't think it's any business of yours,' said Mr Stryder as he pulled away and she became invisible to him again. 'You would do well to keep out of matters that do not concern you.'

'But it does concern her,' protested George, 'and it concerns me, too.'

'Listen, Arthur,' said Mr Stryder, 'I've always tried to be honest with you.'

'Have you?' George asked defiantly. 'Only, you had no trouble lying to the Hendersons. You told them that you didn't know what happened on the ship... but clearly you did.'

'That's enough,' barked Mr Stryder, as his expression went cold. 'Some things were... broken... and now we're doing our damnedest to get them back in order... but the less you know about all that, the better.'

'What are you not telling me, then?' George persisted, 'why don't you at least tell me what happened to Mum!'

'Even if I knew, I couldn't tell you.'

'No!' George shouted, as he turned on the narrow bridge to confront his father directly. 'That's not right... it's not fair!' But as he did so, he lost his footing, and it was only Mr Stryder's quick reactions that prevented him from falling. Far below, he could see jagged stalagmites illuminated by pools of burning oil, spilled from the shattered torches.

'Grow up, boy! This is neither the time, nor the place,' Mr Stryder growled as he helped his son back onto the narrow bridge. He then turned to Årkigara, and demanded, 'how much further?'

'We are almost free,' replied the gargoyle as he pointed to the large torch that marked the entrance, just visible in the distance through the pall of smoke. 'But the one true way is not as short as it may first appear.'

'Damn and blast,' Mr Stryder grumbled, 'we'd be out of here by now if Sikes hadn't been so damn insubordinate.'

'The one you call Sikes is here?' asked Årkigara as he stopped dead. 'The real thief?'

Mr Stryder did not answer, but only glared at the gargoyle distrustfully. Alicia, however, did speak up, although George's father could not hear her.

'Yeah,' she said, 'I guess you were still pretty out of it then, but he's the guy that came to get us out of here, but then the dragon took him down into the well...'

Before she could finish, Årkigara spread his wings wide and dropped off the edge. He flew quickly through the tangled bridges and soon disappeared in the haze of smoke.

'You can't just leave!' shouted George in disbelief, 'you're supposed to lead us out of here!'

'Typical ruddy sapper,' said Mr Stryder, 'can't trust 'em with anything... well, there's nothing for it, boy, we'll have to make our own way out of this infernal place.'

'No, we can't,' said George, shaking his head as doubt and betrayal swept over him, 'it's impossible to tell which bridges are safe.'

'Hey,' said Alicia, 'I can do it... I can see what's safe.'

'But can you see the real path?' asked George, still feeling defeated. 'Only, it's all so ruddy confusing.'

'Look, we're close,' she said as she pointed to the large torch in the distance, 'and I can find the way.'

'What are you talking about?' asked Mr Stryder.

'I said,' snapped Alicia as she grabbed Mr Stryder's hand, 'that I can see the way out... at least... I can see which bridges are safe.'

'Bloody hell,' said Mr Stryder, caught off guard by her sudden appearance. 'Alright then, let's get going... come on, boy, snap out of it! Get a move on!'

Alicia led the way while Mr Stryder kept a firm hand on George's shoulder so he wouldn't lose sight of her again, and it was in this way that they slowly traced their way across bridge after bridge, looking for a safe route out.

Some of the bridges spiralled high into the choking smog, where it became difficult to breathe, while others tangled deep below the level of the torches, where the flickering shadows made it almost impossible to see. They had entered a part of the labyrinth that was not broken, and no burning oil had spilled into its depths to illuminate the hidden places.

Alicia froze. Something moved in the shadows. 'Wait,' she whispered, 'did you see that?'

'No,' said George, 'I can't really see much of anything.'

There was the rustle of folding leather wings and a something moved toward her. Alicia felt a sense of relief.

'Årkigara! I knew you'd come back!'

'That useless dumu-lugal?' asked a much larger creature as it stepped out of the shadows. George recognized the ragged hole in its chest as several more gargoyles moved to surround them, but the large one held up its clawed hand, signalling the others to hold their ground.

'It would not do for us to feed upon these mătu... not ones with such powerful...' it paused, as if searching for the right word while looking intently at George, 'friends.'

'Indeed,' said Mr Stryder, 'then you would do well to help get us out of here.'

'You?' the creature sneered at him, 'I was not referring to you. I know what you are: a meddler who cannot be trusted. No, it is the one who fought me so bravely... and his ghost.'

'I am so totally not a ghost!'

The creature turned to George, 'you are the one who the Skogsrå protects, *and* the one whom Gešti has chosen.' The other gargoyles stepped back and whispered her name reverently, which seemed to anger the large one. 'She may be the redeemer of your dying faith,' he snapped at his companions, 'but her refusal to embrace armed insurrection has led to too many of our brethren dying!'

'Say this you must not,' croaked a dog-faced creature, but this only seemed to inflame the large one's anger even more.

'I am tired of waiting for a savior who refuses to fight!' he growled, but then stopped suddenly and looked around. 'But then... where is that useless dumu-lugal Årkigara who brought you into the Well?'

'He abandoned us!' said George.

'Ha! I am not surprised. You are well to be rid of him. He is nothing more than a privileged little princeling who thinks only of himself.'

'Hey, that's not fair!' protested Alicia. 'He saved our lives more than once.'

'... And like all of his class, he is a coward,' the gargoyle added, glaring at her.

'No way!' she snapped back, 'he was totally ready to face his death!'

'No matter,' the gargoyle replied dismissively, 'he and all his kind will soon be swept aside by our glorious revolution... and as for you,' he said as he turned back to George. 'It is strange for me to owe a mătu anything, but I see now that it is only by your actions that we have been able to gain our freedom.'

'Tarry we must not,' cut in the dog-faced gargoyle, 'the Mušḫuššu will soon return.'

'True,' said the large one, 'so we must leave you.'

'Damn and blast,' barked Mr Stryder, 'if you owe us so much, then at least fly us out of this blighted hell!'

The large gargoyle turned to him menacingly. 'My men have not the strength to carry the likes of you, so heavy with the terrible things that you have done...' But then the gargoyle stopped, and added thoughtfully, 'that is, unless... you are willing to make a sacrifice and allow my men to feed on you... so that they will have the strength to save the boy.'

Mr Stryder hesitated, as he seemed to consider the offer.

'No!' shouted George.

'Then we must go,' said the gargoyle as he signalled the others to leave, but just before he left, he turned to Alicia. 'You are their guide, are you not?' She nodded. 'Then I am glad that I did not feed too deeply... and would have foiled our escape by my own ignorance.'

'You really hurt me,' said Alicia.

'Indeed?' asked the gargoyle, genuinely surprised by this revelation. Then, with a slightly bemused look, he added, 'odd the things one learns when one takes the time to talk to one's food... No matter,' he said dismissively, 'you will recover.' He then leaned in close, 'now, as I was about to tell you, if you keep to the lower bridges, you will find the path much shorter.'

'Whoa, so there *is* more than one way?'

'There is always more than one way,' he replied as he turned and flew away.

For just a moment, Alicia and George stood and watched the creatures as they disappeared into the dark tangle of bridges, but then Mr Stryder said, 'enough, boy... we need to get cracking.'

'At least your dad seems to be getting better,' said Alicia.

'Yes... but better than what?' asked George as he turned to follow.

So, on they went, and as the large gargoyle had advised, Alicia did keep to the more hidden bridges and soon discovered that even though these routes might have been harder to see, there were so many more of them to take. Once or twice, she had to climb up to a high platform to check that they were still headed in the right direction, but in the end, she was able to lead the others and make the remaining journey much faster than even Årkigara had been able to.

At last, they emerged onto one of the stone platforms overlooking the great chasm at the edge of the labyrinth, but before they set foot on the final bridge, there came the sound of approaching wingbeats.

'Hey, look,' said Alicia, as she pointed to a blur coming through the haze of smoke, 'it's Årkigara, it's really him this time! I told you he'd come back!'

'What are you doing here?' George shouted as the gargoyle landed, 'you abandoned us, but we've managed to make it all this way without you, so go away, we don't need you anymore!'

'I had no choice,' Årkigara protested, 'I had to...'

'I don't care!' snapped George, 'we saved you and then you bloody abandoned us!'

'Hey, give him a chance,' pleaded Alicia, 'he saved *us* more than once, too... let's at least hear what...'

'No! I don't want to hear his excuses!'

'Muster-sikes was the real thief, and from him I have retrieved the Anu-gìn-a-nir,' he said as he held out a small wooden box for George to see.

Mr Stryder suddenly pulled George back and said, 'I agree with you, boy, I don't think that there's anything that little Sapper can say to make things right. However,' he added as he turned back to Årkigara, and spoke in a calm, but strangely desperate, way. 'There is something you *could* do to show your good intent and regain our trust... for instance... if you were to give me the amulet...'

'It is not mine to give,' said Årkigara.

'My dear fellow,' said Mr Stryder, almost losing his forced calm, 'I have no intention of keeping it. However, just handing it to me now would go a long way to rebuilding a trust you so carelessly broke.'

'The dragon!' cried Alicia, 'it's back!'

The dragon's giant wings cut through the heavy smoke above as it circled overhead. It then glided to the grand stairs on the far side of the chasm. After it landed, it was limping noticeably as it turned to face them, but then, with surprising force, it swung its tail in a wide high arc, and brought it down so heavily that the bridge in front of it shattered. The dragon then moved slowly and deliberately as it destroyed each of the remaining bridges across the great chasm, before it finally turned to face them once again.

'So, son of Ulgara,' its voice boomed across the void, 'you thought you could defy me and escape with the Skogsrå's pets... but of course, I cannot allow that.' The dragon shifted painfully, clearly suffering from the many injuries inflicted by the lion. 'Yet I cannot simply kill you, either, since you do not fear your own death, but then, what punishment *is* suitable?'

When Årkigara did not reply, the dragon continued, speaking almost casually. 'You know, there are far too many petty Pazoân kings, and it's all becoming an administrative nightmare... I think I shall make a few cuts... What do you think?'

'What's he playing at?' George asked his father, but Mr Stryder did not respond.

'Playing at?' asked the dragon, who clearly had overheard. 'I am not playing at anything... I am merely seeking a suitable punishment for this dumu-lugal who has sinned against me... No,' said the dragon as it carefully inspected the bloody remains of its right front claw. 'Death is not good enough for what pain he has caused me. Instead, I think I shall make him watch as I kill his father, the Lugal, and then I shall sell his people into slavery. What do you think of that, little princeling?'

Still, Årkigara did not say anything, but only stood and glared at the dragon across the chasm. The Mušḫuššu then paused, as if surprised by this lack of reaction.

'Oh, my,' it said in false civility, 'I see now that your taste for revenge runs deeper than I ever imagined... I know how your people abandoned you when your father, the king, condemned you... but I had no idea that you held them in such contempt for their loyalty to their Lugal. I must say, that sort of cold-bloodedness can be very useful in a future king, and now I'm starting to think that killing you would indeed be a great waste.' The dragon turned to look at the little gargoyle directly, and suddenly flared out the blood-red feathers around its head. 'But still, you must be punished... So what of that lowly little concubine, the one who gave you birth? I should make you watch as I destroy her... slowly... and painfully.'

'No!' Årkigara cried out, quickly regretting his outburst.

'Ah, good,' said the Mušḫuššu, 'then it is settled. I was starting to despair that I would ever find a suitable punishment... But first, I must rebuild my strength.'

With unexpected speed, the dragon launched off the stone steps and flew directly at them, seizing George's father.

'Dad!' George shouted, but there was nothing he could do.

The dragon circled back to the far side of the chasm, where it landed further up on the grand stairs and looked at them defiantly.

'Don't... please don't,' cried George.

'My, my,' said the dragon, ignoring George's pleas and speaking to Mr Stryder. 'You are truly a meal worthy of the great Mušḫuššu, so laden with the delicious weight of the terrible things you have done.' The creature then dragged its giant claw across Mr Stryder's chest, and pulled away from his body what looked like a strip of smoke. It then coiled the delicate tendril of fume around an outstretched talon, and with a revolting smirk, held it above its gaping mouth and slobbered with delight as it began to feed.

George's father called out weakly, 'Get out of here, boy... run!'

'Dad, I'm not leaving without you!'

George looked around desperately for anything he could throw, but there was nothing. He turned to Årkigara, and through gritted teeth whispered, 'give me the amulet! I saw what it did on the boat... give it to me!'

Årkigara's eyes narrowed, 'you do not know what you ask... it will tear you apart.'

'If Sikes can bloody take it, so can I... give it to me and I'll show that damnable beast what's what!'

Årkigara looked over George's shoulder toward the dragon, to see if it was aware of what was about to happen, but the monster only continued to feed slowly, tauntingly. So Årkigara pulled the wooden box out from under the fold of his wing, and opened it to expose a dark blue teardrop-shaped jewel.

'What do I do?' asked George, under his breath, 'how do I make it work?'

'Hold it,' Årkigara whispered in reply, 'and point it at the Mušḫuššu. Do it now!'

Alicia was terrified by what she was hearing. 'If you make a new storm,' she pleaded, 'you'll never get things back to the way they were.' George looked at her and hesitated for just a second, but then his father cried out as the dragon pulled another strand of smoke from his chest. George grabbed the amulet from Årkigara and held it up with its point aimed at the dragon's head. His hand began to shake.

'What do I do now?' he whispered desperately.

'Imagine,' replied Årkigara under his breath, 'that the jewel does for you what it did for the thief, imagine that it makes the lightning.'

George closed his eyes and tried to remember just what Mr Sikes had done on the ship, and then, all at once, his felt his fear and anger focus.

'George!' Alicia shouted.

He opened his eyes.

He had missed the dragon's head, and the only evidence that he had done anything was a small point of light that rested on the creature's tail. But then the light flickered and grew, and the air around it began to shimmer. The Mušḫuššu howled in terror and tried to pull itself free, but it was pinned in place and in its rage and fear, the dragon cast Mr Stryder aside. The shimmering air around the beast's tail began to crumple and fold.

'You fools,' it rasped, 'you don't know what you've done...' The dragon seemed to want to say more, but gurgled into silence as gore erupted from its mouth and it thrashed helplessly, sputtering and fighting for breath as its body was crushed in the growing light.

George was repulsed by what he saw, and yet unable to turn away, triumphant but also sickened. His head was spinning, and he felt like he was going to vomit. The creature was dying horribly, and there was nothing he could do to change that.

There was a deafening crash of thunder as a spinning vortex of light erupted where half the dragon had been crushed into oblivion.

'George,' Alicia whispered in awe, 'you slew the dragon.'

'You only did what needed to be done,' said Årkigara as he snatched the amulet back, 'but I fear you will pay a terrible price for waking the Gal-ūd and creating the Galda-ḫamun.'

For George it seemed that there was too much pain, too much

revulsion, to think clearly, but then something deep inside him broke, and all that confusion tumbled away, leaving only cold determination.

'That's almost a sheer rock wall on the far side,' he said, 'and it must be hundreds of feet down… yet we have to find a way across.'

'I cannot carry you,' said the gargoyle.

'But you *can* carry *her*,' said George. 'Alicia, go with Årkigara and check on my dad… and I'll try to work out a way over for myself.' He then looked around and saw something that gave him hope, 'Årkigara, once you've dropped her off, come back and meet me up there,' he said, pointing to a small observation platform, high above the labyrinth, and almost obscured by thick clouds of smoke. It appeared to be a small lookout that was accessible only by a very narrow and twisted stair.

George was sure that there wasn't time to share his plan, so he headed straight toward it, but then stopped suddenly as he shouted back to the others, 'I forgot to ask; is this path safe?'

'Yeah, it's safe,' Alicia shouted in reply, 'at least, it doesn't look like it's going to fall apart,' but before she could say anything more, Årkigara wrapped his arms around her. He then spread his wings wide and launched off the edge of the shattered bridge.

Chapter Twenty-two

The Storm

The path wound precariously upward, and more than once, George was overcome by fits of coughing. Smoke billowed down around him, carried by the ever-shifting air currents in the cavern. As he stopped to catch his breath, he could see Årkigara easily fly across the void with Alicia in his arms, safely below the choking fumes and when they landed, Alicia ran to Mr Stryder's side.

'He's still breathing!' she called back across the chasm.

With renewed urgency, George climbed up the rest of the steeply twisting bridge, his eyes burning and lungs aching. But when he finally reached his destination, Årkigara was already there, waiting for him, and seemingly unaffected by the smoke.

'I cannot bear your weight when I fly.'

'You don't... need to fly,' George coughed as he struggled to breathe, 'we're just... going to... try to glide.'

'I will not be able hold you,' said the gargoyle as he spread his wings wide, and then braced them with his arms, 'so you must cling to my back.'

George, almost blind from the smoke, and wracked by painful coughs, fumbled for Årkigara's back, and then held on as tightly as he could. In the next moment, he could feel that they were falling, and the rush of cool air was a relief, but he also knew that they were falling too fast.

Årkigara was not able to hold his wings out against the onrush of wind, so George braced himself and forced the gargoyle's wings back out, so together they were able to glide more than fall toward the broken edge of the stairs. They landed awkwardly, and George tumbled hard against the stone steps, but picked himself up and quickly ran to where Alicia knelt beside his father.

'Dad!' he coughed.

'He's unconscious,' said Alicia, 'but at least he's breathing.'

'Dad, please wake up!' George pleaded as he shook his father.

'We must go now,' said Årkigara.

'I can't wake my dad,' George protested, 'dad… please…'

'The Mušḫuššu was greedy, and fed too deeply… but your father lives, and he will heal… in time.'

'We don't have time!' shouted George, 'we need to get out of here *now*, and there's no way we can carry him up the stairs.'

'I thought you understood,' said Årkigara, once the storm is awakened, there is no choice but to enter it.'

'George,' Alicia cut in, 'something weird is happening… look at the torches.'

A strange wind had arisen, a gale that was whipping through the burning cauldrons of oil and fanning them into even greater infernos.

'The Galda-ḫamun must consume its creator,' Årkigara shouted over the roar of the spiralling winds, 'or else it will feed until it swallows the world.'

The spiraling vortex continued to expand, driving the winds even faster. Numerous small funnel clouds danced around the giant cavern as the wind roared and the fires swirled and grew. Shards of lightning flickered and stabbed out from the centre of the vortex as the storm began to devour everything around it.

Årkigara was the first to be swept away, and then Alicia, while George threw himself over the body of his father as they too were carried into the gaping maw of the vortex.

Right away, George could feel that this was not like the other storms. This storm was his, and his alone. At once, it surrounded him as it drilled deep inside him. And then, it was as if his life shattered into a million pieces as his own memories blasted by the unnatural wind, tore through him like shards of broken glass.

Even his warmest and sweetest Memories, some long forgotten, came forward in his mind, and cut through him before forever disappearing into the void of the storm.

He was taking his first steps. His mother was holding his hands above his head, and gently encouraging him... gone.

He was with his parents in a little rowboat on a lake, and he was laughing and pointing at the swans that glided along with their young on their backs... but then that moment was lost as well.

His father was holding the seat of his first bicycle as he wobbled along the promenade in Blackpool, while down on the beach his mother unpacked a picnic lunch... that memory shattered and fell away.

The sharpness of the pain then became oddly fluid as the storm changed how it attacked. It was as if the nature of time itself was battering him, and he tried to shield himself from the painful impacts, but it was relentless.

Moments of joy were now drowned in waves of sadness, pulled into the depths by the weight of their loss in time. Helplessness and hopelessness wrapped around him in a sick competition for his attention, while desperation enveloped his every thought. The darkness around him was not the absence of light, but an emptiness of hope that was far greater.

It was not just that it had abandoned him in the present; it was that every moment of hope that had ever entered his life was now torn away, leaving only suffocating regret for every precious second that was lost. Every inch of his body ached, every cell of his brain cried for release, but the emptiness only grew to swallow more of him.

The storm would not let go. Its violent winds of loss continued to tear through him. Images blurred into one another, and the raw emotions of life cut through him unrelentingly. Not just of his life, but of the others he loved, indistinct for not originating in his own experience, yet no less painful in their nature.

Within the storm, he could see his mother grieving at a funeral. It had been back when he was only seven, but now, more than ever before, he could feel her own loss explode inside him.

Then he could see his father's rustication at Oxford, when he was sent down for crimes that he had not committed, and now the turmoil of that day, and all the pain that his parents had tried to shield him from back then, was laid bare in his mind.

The scene changed again. It was a country lane outside Oxford, on a sunny autumn day, and Roger, his Golden Retriever, was excitedly barking as he chased rabbits back into the hedgerows. All should have been right with the world, but George knew the moment that was coming, and much as he desperately wanted to, he couldn't escape it.

He was reliving every painful moment as the motorcar came roaring around the corner, screeching to a halt in front of him, then the driver shouting and swearing at him, berating him, and telling him that he was damn lucky that it was only his dog that was dead. And that his father had damn-well better pay for the damage to his precious car.

The storm was now seeking out his worst memories and making them more vivid, physically battering him with their strength. It now reached deep into him and found the moment when he had learned that his best friend had died. How the headmaster at his school had told him with forced indifference how he had struck a rock in the shallows, and drowned.

Just as it had happened then, within the storm, George experienced the rushing in his ears, the disbelief and despair as all other sounds became muffled and distant, and once again, he felt how his heart raced and sank while he was left weak and utterly bereft of hope.

Yet the storm did not let up. Days, months, years flashed by, all filled with images of a life known and unknown, events familiar and strange, days both great and terrible came crashing down, crushing him.

In a rapid succession of terrible images, he saw his mother pull away from him on the ship, and then his father carried away by the spinning black cloud in the Henderson's back yard, followed by the sight of the little fox, hurled against the rock. And then, slowly and painfully, he could see the dragon smirking as it began to consume his father's life essence. Finally, it was too much, and George lost consciousness.

When he awoke, everything was quiet, and when the stillness did not end, he wondered if this is what it was like to be dead.

He was lying on the ground, and very slowly, he opened his eyes. For just a moment, he thought he was back in the garden, as he had landed on a small rosemary bush, but as he stood up and looked around, he could see that this was a completely different place. It was an old parish churchyard, and he was standing next to an open grave. When he thought he saw a shadow with ragged wings and blazing red eyes on the roof of the church, he backed away suddenly, only to collide with a coffin. He had knocked the lid partially open, and he turned away as quickly as he could, not wanting to see inside – and he forgot about the shadow completely as other thoughts clouded his mind.

What if it was his father, having succumbed to the terrible wounds the dragon had inflicted? Or what if it was the body of his mother, drowned when the ship had sunk? And then he was consumed by the many thoughts of what he would have, should have, said to his parents if only he had known it would be the last time he would ever see them.

He quickly became convinced that if he looked inside the coffin, the moment would then become fixed in time, but if he did not look inside, then there still might be a chance for him to change things. In fact, he found that he did not even want to think about who might be in there, lest that was enough to seal their fate.

So, to distract himself, he looked around more carefully at his new surroundings, trying desperately to occupy his mind with the mystery of where he was, rather than think about the possible why of it all.

He did not recognize the church, which was an ancient and irregular building, distinctive yet anonymous like so many others that had been constructed over the centuries. Beside it, stood a yew tree of incalculable age, and both were surrounded by numerous gravestones, some ancient and covered with lichen, while others were newer, with rosemary bushes planted beside them.

He almost caught a glimpse of one of the names deeply etched into one of the gravestones, but then stopped himself before he could truly see it. He did not want to be responsible for sealing the fate of anyone by carelessly reading their names. He did not want to know anyone who might be buried here.

As time dragged on, the mist turned into rain, yet the light in the dull grey sky never seemed to change, and whether it was minutes or hours that had passed, George did not know. Loss and regret overtook his thoughts, spinning around in his mind, his heart, and his soul, and it was then that he realized that the storm still raged inside him.

The rain became heavy, and he sought shelter in the church's porch, where he watched it come down as he fought to distract himself from thoughts that could change things for the worse. But with no one else there, to help distract him such things, his mind wandered back into thoughts of the people he missed.

He wondered if the storm brought him to this place to see his parents one last time, and he wondered where Alicia was. She had been his one constant in all this, and now he wondered if this was the final cruel trick of the storm, to bring him here to see her end.

Then, after mulling it over for some time, he came to the inescapable conclusion that, whatever else might have been true, all the people he cared about in his life would have been better off without him. But then he was struck by another thought: The body in the coffin must be his, because the storm had brought him to his own mortal end. This was not the end of someone else, but his own natural conclusion.

With this one realization, the relief that crashed over him was so great that he fell to his knees and laughed. And then he wept.

Eventually though, he got up, wiped his eyes, and looked across the churchyard, to where the coffin lay. He knew then that all he had to do was to look upon his own mortal remains, and then he would be done with it. He would be free, but more importantly, those he loved would be free as well.

The cold rain was pouring down now, and it soaked deep into his clothes as he walked toward the open coffin, which only served to confirm the reality of his situation.

'Of course I'm getting wet,' he thought, 'it's not like before, not the same as when Alicia and I were bouncing around in time… because this time, I'm really here. After all,' he chuckled to himself, 'it simply wouldn't do to miss my own funeral.'

But the storm inside him refused to let him go, and as he began to walk to where the coffin lay, doubts once again swirled around inside him.

Was he just giving up?

What if he was mistaken, and what if it really was his mother… or his father?

What if it was *Alicia*? Or the little fox? Now you're just being silly, he thought, the lion had said that she still lived, and besides, no one would bury a fox in a church graveyard… No, it simply had to be his own body, and all he had to do was to find the courage to go over there and look at himself and be done with it. Get it over with. Move on…

But move on to where… and why?

The rain came down even harder and the wind picked up as, without even realizing that he was doing it, he continued to walk slowly toward the coffin.

His mother had once told him that death was a great mystery, a secret that people were never meant to know, at least, not until their own time came. But then his father had replied that those ideas were all rubbish, and that once you're dead, you're dead. Nothing more to it. Finished. Gone.

So, then, why not get it over with?

Time to let go.

Do it.

No.

Not bloody likely.

He wouldn't… he couldn't give in. Not now… not ever.

The storm might have brought him here, pushed him to the brink, but no one, and no thing, was going to push him over the edge.

He felt a new defiance growing inside him.

He wasn't going to the coffin to look at himself and die, he was bloody well going to go over there to stare death in the face. And live, damn it.

George walked up to the coffin with a new determination, and when he reached for the precariously balanced lid, it fell to the ground, exposing the body within.

He didn't really know what he had expected, but certainly not this: It was the body of a strangely dressed man, a man that he did not know, or recognize. It was impossible to tell the man's age, because despite the mortician's best efforts, his face was battered and bruised beyond recognition.

'Poor blighter,' George muttered to himself.

The heavy rain ran off the body's damaged face, and George knew that he couldn't leave things this way. It was up to him to make things right again, so he struggled to get the lid back in place, even as the rain pounded down harder, and the wind grew stronger.

The lid was large, and awkward to manage in the wind, but then a powerful gust caught it, and George instinctively hung on. The ground beneath him tumbled away, and once again, he was flying through the storm as it battered him. He reflexively shielded himself behind the lid, pressing himself more deeply into its satin covered interior, seeking what little refuge it offered from the violence around him.

He could feel himself rising up within the spiralling wind, the force of it pushing him higher and yet deeper into the heart of the nightmare. Then, quite unexpectedly, the wind above him seemed so light that he risked raising his head to have a better look. It simply took his breath away.

He was inside a giant tunnel of cloud, like a moving, rolling cave, large enough to swallow a city, a country, a world. It was as if he were inside a hurricane that was spinning on its side, and he was somehow gliding on the eye-wall of the storm on the coffin lid.

The heavy grey clouds rose up behind him so fast that it was impossible to tell if he was falling, or the cloud was rising up like a massive reverse waterfall. Far above him, could see the storm wall arch high overhead, and almost a mile away through the mist of distance, he could see the far side of the storm barreling down, before racing back toward him.

He wanted to stand, to get a better view, and as he moved to get to his feet, he wobbled to the right ever so slightly. The coffin lid dug in and turned sharply, but he was able to steady himself before he lost control. He was facing the narrower end of the lid, away from the wall of the storm, and as he skimmed across the surface, he carefully stood up straight.

He felt something rising up in his chest, expanding to the point of bursting, and then he let out a wild whoop and laughed in utter amazement. He knew this. He had done this before. This was just like Matt's mountain-board, only bigger, wilder, and a bit more coffin-y.

Ever so slightly, he shifted his weight to his right foot as he leaned toward the wall, and so carved a sweet curve across the rushing cloud, but then the back of the lid almost slid out from under him, so he quickly steadied himself. Safe from the violence beneath him, he could now appreciate the true majesty of this storm. His storm. He saw it now for what it was: a thing of great and terrible beauty.

The eye-wall formed a vast tunnel that tilted sharply down to his left, where far below he could see the ocean, and then, to his right and far above, it opened to deep blue sky, faintly splashed with stars, and edged with the glow of oncoming dawn.

Then the top of the hurricane shifted down ever so slightly, and sunlight spilled across the surface in shades of red, yellow, and gold, against the deep blue and purple of the storm clouds.

Far away, through the haze of distance, he saw something flying, and as it drew closer, he recognized Årkigara. The gargoyle seemed dumbfounded by what he was seeing, and called out, but his voice was drowned in the rush of the wind. George didn't care, he just laughed as he carved a long lazy sweep across the face of the storm.

Årkigara shouted again, but when George did another long sweep, the gargoyle just appeared to laugh and did a loop of his own in reply in the air above. George took this as a challenge, and so tried an even more daring maneuver; he shifted his weight to his back foot and angled the lid to dig in just enough that he swept high up the wall, and then, with a slight lean forward, he came racing down in a wide sweeping carve.

For just an instant, he wished Alicia could see him, he wished that she were there, and in that moment, he lost focus and came down too hard, so the back of the coffin lid slipped out from under him, and was swept away by the wind.

Tumbling back into the storm, without anything left to shield him, the pain of loss and regret once again wrapped itself around him, and the control that riding above it had ever so briefly given him, was gone.

The storm stretched him wide and thin against the sky, almost beyond existence across the fabric of space. It became part of him, he became part of it, and the difference between memory and experience was torn away. The life he had known seemed so distant one moment, but then the storm would bring him back, tantalizingly close, as if to return him to the life he once had. Yet like a flat stone thrown across the smooth surface of a pond, he would glance off, unable to break the surface and return to himself.

Now, the moments of his life that passed before him were from his time with the Hendersons, but he was watching it all from new and different angles. He could see Alicia and himself in India, then together with Matt in London, and then they were all watching a movie in the great room...

But George could see something else there now, something that seemed to be just out of view... something lurking in the dark. A shadow moving across the ceiling of the officers' club in Bombay, or down Regent Street in London, or even across the wall in the Hendersons' house. And it was a shadow that moved with a mind of its own.

He felt dread and loathing rise up as he saw this thing wrap itself around Alicia when the storm had carried them away from India. Then he watched as it captured him when they were swept out of

London… and then he saw it again, crawling up the wall toward his bedroom window. What was it, and what was it doing?

Was it Årkigara, stalking him in hopes of recovering the amulet? After all, he had seen the Pazoân fade into shifting shadows before, but this thing was different – larger, stranger, with ragged wings and blazing red eyes.

The storm was different now, much more violent, and stranger than it ever had been before. The darkness that swirled around him was broken by streaks of light that pulsed and broke open, then closed and vanished in the wind. Within these streaks of reflective time, he could see new images, strange visions of destruction and change.

It was night. In the woods at Drysdale School. The dragon was coming after him… and he ran up the street toward the Hendersons', but the Mušḫuššu was gaining on him. He sought refuge in an old abandoned house… a shadow crawled down the wall.

The sun was blazing hot.

There were dozens… no hundreds… of people around him, hewing blocks of stone out of the ground, while hundreds more worked with odd wooden devices to move the large rocks across the sandy ground.

The shadow drew nearer.

The scene changed and heavy grey clouds hung low in the sky, the air was cold and full of the stench of death. Bodies – human, Pazoân, Skogsrå, and others – all lying strewn about the ancient fens, with bloody spears and battle-axes at their sides, while in the distance, impossible machines of metal and glass marched toward an unseen destination.

The shadow crouched low, ready to pounce.

George awoke in a nothingness that was both incredibly small, and infinitely vast. And he was alone. Except for the shadow.

The thing wrapped its cold, dead, ragged wings around him, while its blazing red eyes stared into his own, penetrating his thoughts and forcing its way into his mind.

He could feel it rifling through his thoughts and digging deep. Each memory of itself that it encountered, and then touched, decayed and dissolved into nothingness.

It was erasing all recollection he might have of it.

George fought to save what he could, trying desperately to hide his remaining memories by burying what he could, willing himself to forget, with the desperate hope that he would remember them later. Within his mind, he ran from room to room, slamming closed what doors he could, and secreting away his remaining thoughts of the creature.

He was determined to deny the thing the chance to erase itself, but even as he tried, the memories of it still continued to dissolve. The fight was exhausting, and the thing was relentless.

Then George crashed into something hard, he felt his right shoulder crack, and everything went black.

The wind drove the waves against the shore, rolling them high up the beach as Årkigara struggled to land. The storm was at the height of its power, and it pummelled the gargoyle with wind and rain as he crouched low, clawing his way over to where George lay face down at the edge of the surf. Årkigara rolled him onto his back and tried to wake him.

'The Mušḫuššu did not die,' he shouted, struggling to be heard over the roar of the wind. He then removed the watch from George's coat pocket and placed it within a little wooden box. It was the hand-hewn vessel that has once hidden the Anu-gìn-a-nir. 'You must keep your watch in this… it will block the traces of your device… and make you invisible to the Mušḫuššu and his Lúmñíri…'

Årkigara suddenly tensed, hearing some danger within the storm. 'I cannot stay – Alicia will be crushed by a tree if I don't reach her soon.' He then spread his wings wide, caught the wind, circled high above, and then vanished.

Chapter Twenty-three

Strange Memories

Halfway between sleep and wakefulness, George rolled over. He could hear birdsong, much as he had for many a morning back in Oxford, before his family moved to London. The sound was sweet but oddly unfamiliar, but he didn't feel like getting up to investigate, because the bed was so warm and comfortable. He opened his eyes.

He was back. Back in the room at the top of the stairs. In the Hendersons' house, just as it had been the first time, but now things were different. This time, he could remember all the terrible things that had torn his family apart. He could recall how they had travelled from London, their time on the ocean liner, the seeming betrayal of Mr Sikes, and how his father had changed. He could remember the cave, and the shadows... something about the shadows.

He looked to the nightstand for his watch, grabbed it, flipped it open and spoke quickly. 'New message, direct link: Alex Stryder, Dear Dad; Please write to me as soon as you can... please tell me that you and Mum are safe. Send.' Almost instantly, a reply came as a new sheet of paper unrolled above the watch, and his heart leapt as he recognized his father's distinctive handwriting.

My Dear Boy,

I am well, but there is much we need to talk about. I shall write to you with more details as soon as I am able.

— As ever, your father

It wasn't much, no news of his mother, and no news of when his father might arrive, but it was enough for the moment. George fell back onto his bed, laughing in a wave of relief. But then a thought occurred to him, and he quickly retrieved his father's letter and checked the timestamp. It was sent on the 16th of July 2014, the morning after his father's abduction. Even though it had felt like days, or even weeks since all that had happened, the watch said it was only the next morning, and his father had replied from the present.

He ran down the stairs to Alicia's door, one floor below.

'Hey,' he whispered, not wanting to wake the rest of the family, 'Alicia... wake up, do,' but there was no answer. He knocked a little louder, and called again, but still there was no response. He felt panic and opened her door just to peek in, but her bed was empty. The covers were in a complete mess as if she had tossed violently during the night.

He then ran down the stairs to the kitchen, and there she was, seated at the table, eating bowl after bowl of cereal.

She nodded her head and mumbled something that sounded vaguely like 'G'morning,' and continued to eat as if she had gone without food for days.

'Good morning, to you too,' he said, 'you seem a mite peckish this morning.'

She rolled her eyes and poured herself another bowl of cereal, carelessly slopping the milk over it.

'Would you like some?' she asked through a very full mouth.

'Don't mind if I do,' he replied as he quickly poured himself a bowl of cornflakes, 'I must admit... I *am* famished.'

In fact, George was very, very hungry, and he had a couple of bowlfuls of cereal before he finally paused long enough to ask, 'so... what happened... how'd you get back?'

'I dunno, same as before... I guess. Like, I just woke up in my bed,' she explained, but then, with a guilty smile added, 'but I was so totally hungry... I had to get something to eat before checking on you... sorry. But at least now, everyone won't think I just imagined you.'

'So, you're quite serious about that? No one could remember me before?'

'Nah, but they will now.'

'I do hope so,' said George as he helped himself to yet another bowl of cereal.

Alicia sat back and watched as George ate as ravenously as she just had.

'So… like… how are you doing?' she asked when she thought he was slowing down a little. A simple question, even an innocent one, but then the memories of the cavern slammed into him, and George had to stop. He looked at his hand, which was shaking so badly that he dropped his spoon.

'I've… I've never killed anything before.'

'You didn't have a choice,' she said as she reached over to steady his hand, 'that thing was eating your dad,' she whispered, but then fell silent when her mother came in with the baby.

'Good morning Alicia, Matt,' Dr Henderson said, but then she turned to have a better look. 'Sorry… you're not Matt, do I know you?'

'Mom,' said Alicia, 'this is George… he lives here, remember?'

The smile on Dr Henderson's face faded and she turned away distractedly, fumbling to get the baby's formula ready, but she did not reply.

'Mom, are you okay?'

'Yes,' her mother said as she stopped and seemed to build up her resolve, 'yes, I'm fine… it's early, and my memory must be playing tricks on me.' She then pulled a bottle out of the refrigerator and set about warming it up. 'So,' she said, regaining her composure and trying to sound conversational, 'I'm glad you're here, George… I'm glad that you're safe.'

'So you *do* remember me?'

'No… not yet, dear,' she replied, a certain tension in her voice, 'but I will in time.' However, before George or Alicia could ask what she meant, her father came bounding into the kitchen, a particular spring in his step.

'Good morning everyone,' he said, 'another beautiful day in paradise. So, who's the new kid?' He turned to his wife and gave her a quick peck on the cheek. 'Don't tell me you've decided to take in another stray... Nessa's enough of a handful as it is...'

'Dad,' said Alicia, 'this is George.'

'A friend of Matt's, eh? I'm his dad, Gil Henderson.' He held out his hand for George to shake, 'and you are?'

'Stryder... George Stryder...'

As they shook hands, the colour drained out of Mr Henderson's face.

'Dad, are you okay?'

'Yeah, sure... I'll be fine...'

'Gil, I think you'd better sit down.'

'You really don't remember me, do you?' asked George.

'Stryder... you know... that name rings a bell,' said Mr Henderson as he let go of George's hand, 'now that you mention it... I do remember hearing... or reading... something about a kid with that name... really mysterious... washed up on a beach somewhere.'

'Gil... seriously, sit down!' Dr Henderson insisted. Her husband, looking quite dazed and disoriented, sat down on one of the bar stools by the kitchen island.

'What... the... hell... is happening to me?' he asked. 'It's as if I can remember too many things... like the strangest case of déjà vu,' he clutched his head, as if to keep it from physically spinning, and then, after a moment, turned to George, his eyes wide with realization. 'You're that kid, aren't you? But why couldn't I remember that before?'

'I... I'm not entirely sure,' said George, 'but I think my dad called it 'Temporal Dissonance'... although I really couldn't tell you precisely what that is.' He pulled out his watch and flipped it open, 'but I think that I'd best ask him what he knows.'

'Cool,' said Mr Henderson, 'I haven't seen that before... a flip-phone that looks like a pocket watch...'

When a sheet of paper appeared to roll out of thin air above the device, Mr Henderson's eyes went wide in amazement.

'New message,' said George, 'direct link, Alex Stryder, Dear Dad... things seem to be getting rather a bit complicated... Still waiting to hear from you. Please reply as soon as you can.'

Mr Henderson reached out to test the reality of the floating paper.

'That's... that's impossible,' he said. Then, without thinking, he placed his hand on George's shoulder to steady himself. Suddenly, it was as if he truly remembered. 'Wow, it's the weirdest thing,' he said, 'it's just as Allie said it was... last week, when she had the fever... My God, kid... the lightning... what about your dad, is he okay?'

'Yes,' said George, 'at least, I think he is.' He closed the watchcase slowly, but then remembered message protocol and quickly flipped it open again. 'Send,' he said, but the watch did not behave as he expected, and made an odd noise as a blunt notice appeared:

Your message cannot be sent. Your credit limit for this billing period has been exceeded. Service will resume upon payment of the outstanding balance. If you believe this statement to be in error, please contact a service representative for assistance...

'Fine,' said George, with some exasperation, 'then, by all means, please put me in touch with a service representative.'

Such contact would require a new message, which currently cannot be sent, as your credit limit for this billing period has been exceeded...

'Bloody hell,' he muttered.

'So who's the new kid?' asked Matt as he came into the kitchen.

'This is George,' said Alicia with a note of triumph in her voice, 'and he's not just my imagination.'

'Yeah... so?' asked Matt as he went to pour himself a bowl of corn flakes, but found all the cereal boxes empty.

'*So*,' said Alicia, defiantly, 'he's living here now, and you need to remember him.'

Matt looked at her with that sort of disbelieving contempt that is unique to older brothers. 'No, I don't.'

'Alright then,' said Mr Henderson, 'but at least have the decency to shake hands with him, and introduce yourself.'

'Gil, don't...' protested Dr Henderson, but relented when her husband gave her a knowing look, as if to say, 'this has to be done.'

'Seriously?' Matt asked as he noticed his father's odd smile, and sensing that he was somehow being set up, turned to George. 'Like, you've got some stupid buzzer in your hand or something... that's so last century.'

'I have nothing,' said George, as he held his hand out, palm up, so Matt could see. 'My name is Stryder, George Stryder.'

'Yeah, whatever,' said Matt, cautiously taking George's hand, but as soon as he did, he found the experience so exhilarating that he didn't want to let go. 'Whoa... that's a total head-rush.'

'Yes, well... be that as it may,' said George, after a minute or two, 'Do you mind letting go? I rather need my hand back.'

'Right... yeah... sure... but, I mean, like, your watch, like only the sickest tech I've ever seen... how could I have forgotten that?'

'Sick indeed,' agreed George, 'and I haven't the foggiest notion of how to get it to start working again... I say, do you mind?'

'What?' asked Matt, with a certain false innocence.

'I'm trying to concentrate on what's wrong with this infernal device, but you keep jabbing me as if something more is going to happen.'

'Whoa, dude,' said Matt, 'what's eating you?'

'What?' George spun around in a near panic, 'where?'

'Hey kid,' said Mr Henderson, 'take it easy, kid, it's just an expression.'

'Yes... yes, of course it is,' said George, who was just as surprised by his reaction as anyone. 'I... I thought that there was something... but for the life of me I can't quite remember what it was.'

'Can't remember what?' asked Chella, rushing in to fix herself a quick bite before heading out to work.

'This is Allie's imaginary friend,' said Matt, 'you know, the one she was telling us about the other day... and you totally have to shake his hand.'

'Uh, yeah, whatever,' said Chella, dismissively, but then she stopped and looked at George more carefully. 'Okay, right... so, like, you're my kid sister's very own Harry Potter?'

'Well, I can't say as I know who he is.'

'Seriously, what planet are you from?' she almost laughed. 'You know, you kinda look like him, except you don't have the scar and glasses, but you totally have the accent.'

'Stryder, George Stryder,' said George as he held out his hand for her to shake, because in spite of everything, he was starting to enjoy people's reactions. 'And you are?'

'Chella... that is, Rachael, Henderson,' she said as she took his hand and smiled slightly, but then pulled away suddenly as if hit with an electric shock. 'NO! Stop it! You had no right to do that! You can't just come in here and take away part of my life like that!'

'I-I'm sorry,' he stammered, 'I didn't mean...'

'Chella, honey,' said Dr Henderson, 'it's just a few days different...'

'No, it isn't, Mom,' Chella snapped, 'don't you get it? He's changed everything!'

'Hey, Princess,' said Mr Henderson, 'go easy...'

'This is so stupid!' Chella almost shouted, but when the baby began to cry, she lowered her voice and rolled her eyes in a sort of frustrated defeat. 'I can't deal with this now... I have to go to work.' She then turned to George, 'that is, if you haven't gone and changed that, too!' She stormed past Simon Toliver as he came into the kitchen.

'Hi George,' he said, which surprised both Alicia and George.

'Toliver... you know who George is?' asked Alicia, in complete disbelief. 'But... before... when no one else could remember him, why didn't you say anything?'

'Because,' he answered very quietly, 'you never asked me.'

The front doorbell rang, and when no one else seemed inclined to do anything, Mr Henderson went to answer it, and when he returned to the kitchen a minute later, he was carrying a small parcel and distractedly reading the letter that had come with it.

'Hey dad,' asked Matt, 'is that the new smart phone?'

'No... no, not exactly,' he muttered, almost to himself, as he went into his office, and closed the door.

At best, the morning had been confusing, and George just wanted to get away and be alone, but of course, that was impossible, as he and Alicia were still bound to one another.

Although, he thought, as he helped her weed and water her garden, at least she knows what it was like.

As they worked, they hardly spoke a word to one another. It wasn't that there wasn't anything to talk about... it was just that there was nothing they *wanted* to talk about. The memories of the cave were still too fresh, too real, and far too painful. George tried to convince himself that he had only done what had to be done, but that was not enough to keep him from seeing the blood gushing out of the dragon's mouth time and again. And more than once, he had to stop what he was doing to fight of the nausea, as he saw his father suffering and almost dying.

'Hey... are you okay?' asked Alicia, 'I was just saying we should go in and get some lunch.'

'Oh... right, yes... let's do that,' agreed George. 'You know... I just can't get that damn beast out of my mind.'

'I know... neither can I,' she mumbled, and although there was so much more that she wanted to say, in the end, she only said, 'let's go in, Dad usually has lunch ready about now.'

George picked up the basket of berries and vegetables that they had gathered, and followed Alicia back into the house. When they entered the kitchen, Mr Henderson was not fixing lunch as Alicia had expected, but was still in his office, having a rather heated discussion with someone.

'... This is a big risk you're asking us to take,' he bellowed from behind the closed door, 'and I don't think my request is out of line one damn bit...'

George looked awkwardly at Alicia, 'I hope I'm not the cause of this.'

'Nah, it's just dad's business. His company grew really fast... like, I don't think he expected it to be such a success, and I think it's kinda stressing him out.'

'Gil, drop it,' came Dr Henderson's angry voice from the office, and Alicia cringed. 'If he can't do it, then he can't, and that's that... it doesn't change anything else, as far as I'm concerned...'

'Dammit, Gayle, why won't you back me up on this? I'm just asking for your sake... to help you get your life back... your health...'

'Gil, there's no way I would ever promise to keep that a secret. It would go against everything I believe as a doctor...'

George had always felt trapped when his own parents argued, but this strangely familiar scene, playing out in someone else's home, seemed all the more awkward. He shared an uncomfortable glance with Alicia, and then, in unspoken agreement, they quietly headed for the back door, but when George heard a third voice, he froze.

'As I've said before, cures are global catalysts... events that have profound repercussions...'

It was his father.

George ran.

He didn't knock, didn't wait, he just burst into Mr Henderson's office, and his heart leapt as he saw his father, looking older and more haggard, but there in person, and there for him. He ran to embrace him... but clutched only thin air, and in that instant, George was overcome by a profound emptiness.

His father had been nothing more than a hologram. An illusion projected from the new acnode disguised as a cell phone sitting on Mr Henderson's desk.

'Blast it all, Henderson,' Mr Stryder's hologram barked, 'you told me that he was out for the day!' But then the hologram turned to look at George with deeply sad eyes, 'I'm sorry, m'boy, this is not how I wanted you to see me.'

'Dad... where are you?'

'I am where I need to be... and I'm afraid that I can't tell you anything more than that... except to say... I won't be able to come back for you.' Mr Stryder's hologram then turned to face the Hendersons once again. 'It would appear that we are out of time, which is just as well, as we have nothing more to discuss.' With that, his image simply blinked out of existence.

Whether it was from fear or anger, or a profound sense of abandonment, George didn't know, but he began to shake. His heart pounded, and there was a rushing noise in his ears. He was only vaguely aware of Mr Henderson pulling him in, and holding him tight.

'It's okay, kid... you're gonna be okay...'

It had been a very long, very strange day, and it was late when George finally made his way upstairs to go to bed, but when he reached the first landing, he found Alicia sitting alone, on the seat under the big window, looking out onto her garden in the moonlight.

'Hey,' she said, although she didn't turn to look at him. 'I thought you were already in bed.'

'No,' George replied quietly as he sat down next to her. 'Your dad wanted to talk to me about some things. How about you... aren't you tired?'

'Nah,' she said, trying to sound casual, 'I just wanted to think a while.'

'Sorry... then, did you want to be alone.'

'No... please stay,' she said as she glanced over to him. 'I'm glad that you're here... like, not just here, here... but, like, you know... here, living with us now.'

'I'm glad, too, but I only wish my parents could be here as well.'

'Yeah, that totally sucks.'

'You know,' said George, with a slight blush, 'I'm still not quite used to the way you talk.'

'Oh, as if you talk like a normal kid,' she chuckled, but then the smile faded from her face and she fell silent. After a few minutes, she said, 'I haven't told my mom and dad about what happened in the desert... or the cave.' She glanced back at George with a pleading look, 'you won't tell them, will you? I don't want to, like, you know, worry them or anything.'

'No... no, of course not,' said George, avoiding her gaze by looking out at the moonlit garden. 'Although, to be honest, my memories are such a ruddy jumble that I'm not really sure *what* happened... I can remember the lion... and the dragon. In fact, I only wish I could forget that ruddy great beast,' said George, 'but what happened in the desert? It was as if something attacked us... yet I can only recall shadows.'

'Yeah, I know what you mean... Hey, wasn't there more than one desert... and like, in the second one, wasn't there that kid who helped us... what was his name... Archie?'

'By Jove, you're right... Årkigara, wasn't it? But for the life of me, I couldn't tell you what he looked like.'

'Whoa, yeah,' said Alicia, 'it's so weird... kinda like the images are all blurry... I know this is going to sound stupid, but it's almost as if someone didn't want us to remember.'

'It's bit of a relief to hear you say that,' said George. 'I thought I was going mad, but I'd swear that there's more to it... so much I can't quite recall.' His voice trailed off, 'sorry... what were we talking about?' he asked, but Alicia didn't answer, so he asked another question, 'what of the little fox... do you remember her?'

'Yeah... yeah, of course,' said Alicia, trying hard to piece together her own broken recollections, 'but, didn't she die... wasn't she killed?'

'I do believe you're right,' he sighed, but then he recalled a vague reason to hope. 'Although... you know, didn't the lion say that she had survived? I do so hope that at least that memory is real.'

The night was still black when George awoke from a troubled sleep. Memories of the dragon kept clawing at him, dominating his thoughts, as fears and fragments cluttered his mind. But there was something else, something deeper that tore at his memory as well, yet the pieces were too shattered, too damaged to make any sense, so there he lay, alone in the dark, unable to sleep, and unwilling to dream.

When he rolled over restlessly for the umpteenth time, he caught a glimpse of something odd. At first, it just looked like the moonlight, spilling through his bedroom window and pooling on the floor, but then the light began to ripple.

He sat up and watched as the air shimmered, and then silently, gracefully, the pool of light rose up and formed into the little red fox. She looked up at him pleadingly, and then, without a sound, hopped onto his bed and curled up next to him. When he gently stroked her soft fur, she made no attempt to pull away, and he could feel that she was whole, real, and warm.

She nestled in closer to him.

'I still don't know just who you are… not really,' he whispered, 'but when you're here, all seems right with the world…'

The Appendices
(the extra bits that almost nobody reads)

Appendix A

Glossary of Terms

Anu – (pronounced *ah-NU*)
The Great Sky God – See *'Appendix B – Notes'* for more details.

Anzû – (pronounced *an-ZUH-who*)
There is some confusion about the origin of the word *Anzû*, since it is more commonly known to human scholars as the Akkadian name for a mythical winged griffin-like demigod, Imdugud.
However, some scholars (Landvættir *et al*) have suggested that the name Anzû is much more ancient than either the Akkadian or the Sumerian cultures, and that the term actually means 'The People of Anu'. There are many races and cultures of Anzû, of which the Pazoân and Skogsrå are only two.

Anu-gìn-a-nir – (pronounced *ah-NU-jeen-ah-near*)
The Tear of Anu – See *'Appendix B – Notes'* for more details.

Årkigara – (pronounced *are-KEY-gar-ah*)
The Dumu-lugal and son of Ulgara Lugal.

Dumu-lugal – (pronounced *do-MOO-loo-gul*)
Son of the king. This does not imply the same meaning as the word prince, since in Pazoân society there is apparently no special status or privilege by birth for the sons of the various kings. Merit and status may only be gained by deeds, not rank of birth.

Galda-ḫamun – (pronounced *gal-duh-CCHA-moon*)
In the Pazoân argot, as written by human scholars, the letter ḫ (h-breve below) is a consonant that is pronounced with a deep guttural sound, similar to clearing one's throat. This term appears to be composed of three Sumerian words: **gal**, 'great'; **dal**, 'to fly'; and **ḫa-mun**, 'conflict or contradiction'

Gal-ūd – (pronounced *gal-OOD*)
This was a tricky one to translate. Although initially it appears to be two distinct words: **gal**, which, when used as an adjective, means great or mighty and **ūd**, which often refers to time, but the term's meaning is more complex than that, as it may also refer to weather, the sun, or even a storm demon. My best guess is that, in this case, the term Gal-ūd means 'great time storm'. However, if the adjective had followed the noun, which is a more common practice in Pazoân jargon, then I would say it meant 'great sun-storm demon'. However, the uncommon word order suggests an ambiguous, although possibly intended, multiple meaning.

Gešti-nanna – (pronounced *Gesh-TEE na-na*)
A legendary redeemer of the Pazoân, sometimes referred to as simply Gešti.

Imaru – (pronounced *EYE-mar-oo*)
This word was quite difficult to translate. The literal translation to English is 'deep', but it also means hidden, forgotten, and may even refer to the mythical netherworld of the Pazoân.

Imaru Pazoân – (pronounced *EYE-mar-oo paw-ZO-uh-han*)
This is the Pazoân kingdom that Ulgara Lugal rules over, and the society from which Årkigara was banished.

Ka-xi – (pronounced *kah-X[z]EE*)
There is a soft 'x' sound, similar to a 'z' sound, but deeper in tone, and produced further forward in the mouth. This word appears to be related to the ancient Egyptian **ka** or **kau** (soul) and the even more

ancient Sumerian **zi** (the breath of life). The Anzû see **Ka-xi** as a 'life force', but all evidence suggests that it is actually temporal mass, and removing this from humans (or anything else, living or otherwise) will shorten the existence of an object, or the life of a person, from whom it has been taken.

Lóðarr – (pronounced *lawz-THAR*)
This is the name the Skogsrå call themselves. The letter '**ð**', called 'eth', might look like an '**o**' with a tail, or a '**d**' that got bent out of shape, but it's actually an unrelated letter that's pronounced 'zz-th'. Just think of it as sounding a little like a bumblebee with a lisp.

Lúmñíri – (pronounced *loom-NYEAR-ee*)
Likely Sumerian in origin. Composed of **lú** (the one who does) + **im** – (storm) + **ñíri** – (lightning). This is the title of the summoners of storms, the Pazoân Time Mages (priests, of a sort) who produce storms for transporting physical beings through space and time.

Mătu – (pronounced *maw-TOO*)
This is what the Pazoân call humans, and it is the same word whether referring to one human, or to many humans, and is generally regarded as quite derogatory.

Mir-túm – (pronounced *meer-TOMB*)
This is the name of the specific storms generated and used by the Pazoân Time Mages, or Lúmñíri, to move humans and other physical beings through space and time.

Mušḫuššu – (pronounced *Mush-CHU-shish-uh*)
The Guardian of the Well. This is the imperial title of the holder of absolute power, both spiritual and political, over the many Pazoân kingdoms. [30]

---

[30] Some scholars (Landvættir et al) have suggested that the personal name of the current holder of this title is *Huwawa*, but this has not yet been independently confirmed.

Níðhöggr – (pronounced *neezth-WHO-ger*)
Proto-Nordic in origin, meaning 'malice striker'. The pejorative name the Skogsrå use for the Pazoân, usually shortened to **höggr** (the plural is **níðhöggär** – pronounced *neezth-WHO-gaar*)

Pazoân – (pronounced *paw-ZO-uh-han*)
Of uncertain linguistic origin. See entry under *'Appendix B – Notes'*

Skogsrå – (pronounced *skogs-[g]rrr-UH*)
The 'r' should be rolled so it sounds as if there is a second 'g' in the name. This is one of the few known examples of a human attempt to express subsonic intonations in Anzû languages. For further information, see the entry in *'Appendix B – Notes'*

Túlgún – (pronounced *TUL-gun*)
This is the home of the Imaru Pazoân, Årkigara's people.

Uadelig – (pronounced *OO-ah-duh-lig*)
This is a Skogsrå word, similar to the Pazoân term mătu, but is more specific in that it refers only to humans not owned by any particular Skogsrå clan. It roughly translates as 'commoner'.

Ulgara Lugal – (pronounced *OOL-gar-ah loo-GUL*)
The current king of the Imaru Pazoân, and Årkigara's father. Lugal is a title meaning 'one who shines' or 'great one' while Ulgara is his personal name.

Ùru – (pronounced *OOR-oo*)
A ceremonial fire or the basin in which the fuel for the fire is kept. It is important to note that the Pazoân do not require visible light to see (as they are able to see primarily with reflected time), so these fires are only lit for ceremonial reasons.

Appendix B

Notes

Anu – (pronounced *ah-NU*)
The Great Sky God

The Pazoân origin myth is currently the only one known to human scholars, and in it, we learn of how the Great Sky God Anu wrote each supreme law to allow the universe to come into being. The legend says that without these laws, the universe would be featureless, meaningless,  and therefore non-existent. In other words, the laws themselves do not merely define the universe, but that they are the very essence of the universe itself.

It is interesting to note that the majority of Anzû scholars, at least those that this author has had the privilege of speaking with, hold that there are only five major Anzû religions (although with numerous schisms and a number of minor faiths), that hold Anu as the central or sole deity.

Many of these same scholars regard the Pazoân belief system as primitive superstition and not a true religion. However, recent works by some human scholars suggest that this view is reductionist and the result of strong prejudices between Anzû cultures.[31]

---

[31] '*Pazoân Culture – A Brief Overview*' by A. G. Henderson *et al*; pgs. 20, 465, 1181-1196, Lindenleaf Academic Press, pub. September, 2067

Anu-gìn-a-nir – (pronounced *ah-NU-jeen-ah-near*)
The Tear of Anu

The Legend

After the world had been destroyed by a great war, the sky god Anu tried to recreate the earth as a beautiful garden. But when he realized that his newly perfect world was still subject to the machinations of the creatures within it, and therefore destined to change over time, he was overcome by a profound sense sorrow, and so wept. A young mătu woman came across Anu in his grief, and tried to console him, and even though she did not succeed in relieving his sorrow, to show his gratitude that she would even try, Anu took the last tear that fell from his cheek, and gave it to her as a gift. (It is important to note the concept of grief here: Anu did not cease to grieve, but only ceased to weep, indicative of a sad resignation to the supremacy of his laws, even over himself.)

The Physical Object

The actual jewel appears to be a small (2.5×1.4×4.2 cm) teardrop shaped piece of lapis lazuli, flecked with gold and marked with three distinctive gold streaks running diagonally across its face. It is alternately referred to as a 'jewel' or an 'amulet'. The stone is not pierced, but some scholars have suggested that the term 'amulet' arose from a time when the stone may have been mounted in a (now lost) gold setting, and worn around the neck on a chain (also lost).

It is interesting to note that there is an obscure Pazoân legend that within the stone the Gal-ūd resides, which is the force or deity responsible for creating the time storms known as the Galda-ḥamun. While this may seem entirely fanciful, it nonetheless has been noted, in numerous written reports, that the device appeared to have a sentience of its own, since it has reacted to situations in ways that suggested an awareness of its place in time, space, and circumstance.

The Anzû Argots
The Hidden Languages

One of the great difficulties in researching the Pazoân and Skogsrå argots, or hidden languages, is that no written records exist. While it may be tempting to think that these words form a true language, they are, in fact, a jargon or argot, a half-language that arose as a means of communication between two very different species.

All Anzû argots appear to have developed in the Paleolithic and Neolithic ages, as a means of communication between the species, when such interaction was believed to have been more common.

For instance, the Pazoân argot will often use words that appear to have origins in human languages of the ancient Levant, or Middle East, with words tracing back to Sumerian, Akkadian, Babylonian and, in a few cases, ancient Egyptian, while the Skogsrå use words derived from the (relatively speaking) more recent proto-Nordic languages.

It is important to note that the Anzû words used in this book are derived from these argots, these hidden languages, and not the Anzû native tongues. This is critical to a scholarly understanding of their culture, as the Anzû native languages are actually composed of sounds and actions that do not readily translate into *any* human language.

The Pazoân
The Outlaw Kingdoms, The Eaters of the Dead

The Pazoân are Anzû who wear mantles of bat-winged, demon-faced creatures, which are intended to strike fear into the hearts of both Anzû and humans alike.[32]

Pazoân kingdoms, unlike other Anzû societies, are strictly patriarchal and tend to be located in remote areas, such as the Island

---

[32] *'Pazoân Culture – A Brief Overview'* by A. G. Henderson *et al*; pgs. 45, 1291-1298, Lindenleaf Academic Press, pub. September, 2067

of Socotra, where the Imaru Pazoân (the loyal servants of the Mušḫuššu) live. In such intensely hot and sunny locations, the Pazoân often smear their bodies with a clay slip that acts as a sunscreen. When this dries and cracks, it gives them the rather remarkable appearance of being made of stone, however, their natural skin colour is generally blue-grey.

The Pazoân feed only on very recently deceased humans, consuming their temporal mass while it is still 'fresh', and for this reason, the Pazoân believe themselves to be morally superior to the other Anzû races.

However, they are considered social outcasts and even outlaws by most other Anzû societies, which almost universally regard the consumption of the recently dead to be an exceedingly distasteful, even criminal, activity, as virtually all other Anzû races feed only on living things, which includes, but is not limited to, humans.

The Skogsrå
The House of Lóðarr

The Skogsrå, or the House Lóðarr as they are formally known, are a proud and distinctive race, although their influence among other Anzû cultures is declining, as is their overall population.

Traditionally and historically, the Skogsrå maintain European royalty, a line of rarefied humans that they are believed to have domesticated sometime in the early Greco-Roman period. Although, some scholars believe (Landvættir et al) that the current House of Lóðarr was not established until well into the Eighth Century, AD, when the otherwise obscure northern family of Anzû rose to particular prominence. However, this does not adequately explain why the Skogsrå argot is predominantly proto-Norse in origin, and although there are a number of theories, none is any more likely than any other.

The Skogsrå, like many older traditional Anzû societies, maintain rather fanciful mantles, favouring unicorns, griffins and any number of other mythological creatures, as are often depicted in many royal coats of arms.

The Skogsrå regard the Pazoân as not true Anzû, but an inferior race, with many believing the Pazoân to be an entirely different species. One of the most contentious issues between the two cultures concerns their respective harvesting practices. The Pazoân believe in collecting Ka-xi only when it has naturally fallen – that is to say from humans who have recently died. The Skogsrå, by contrast, insist on extracting the hamingja[33] from living subjects – their well-tended domestic stock. This allows them to 'milk' a far more refined essence than might otherwise be obtained from humans left to their own devices in the wild.

Young Skogsrå, particularly the children of the royal court of Lóðarr, are often assigned as a guardian, or vörðr[34], to a particular human child selected from the Lóðarr's most prized stock.

However, the practice of human husbandry in general is somewhat controversial among other Anzû societies, as there are many who insist that simple creatures such as humans should never be subjected to the sort of extreme captivity, public scrutiny, and rigidly controlled lives that European royalty have historically had to endure.

---

[33] **Hamingja** (pronounced *haa-MING-gya*) While conceptually this is practically the same thing as the Pazoân Ka-xi, the Skogsrå regard it somewhat differently, treating the 'spirit' as distinct from the 'breath of life'.

[34] **Vörðr** (pronounced *VOOR-zther*) plural **varðir** (pronounced *VAR-ztheer*) The guardian, warden, or watcher of a chosen individual human.

Appendix C

The Paradoxical Grandfather

In this thought-experiment, time is treated as a conserved value, and therefore has several dimensions of its own. It exists in linear, plasmatic, and spatial states, and when in a spatial state, it is called *temporal mass*, which is offered here as an extended property of matter. While normal mass *may* be expressed as a dimension, along with the standard three volumetrics of height, width, and depth, in this story, time is presented as several dimensions, which includes temporal mass and its associated temporal volumetrics... but explaining all that would be really boring, so I won't.

Instead, I offer you the previously missing part of the conversation between Mr Henderson and Mr Stryder, as originally recorded on Mr Stryder's acnode:

'Take M-Theory, for instance,' said George's father. 'Admittedly it contains some peculiar ideas, but at the core of it, it is arguably the first truly valid exploration of a poly-dimensional universe. And yet,' he paused, 'it has been abandoned by its originator, and generally dismissed by most quantum physicists as untestable, unprovable, and therefore, unimportant.

'In fact, these days,' he added, 'many of those very same physicists are now focusing their collective efforts on particle accelerators... Which, as far as I'm concerned, is akin to cavemen studying the finer points of email by hurling computers off a cliff, and then trying to understand how to reply to a message by studying the patterns left in the shattered remains.' He chuckled at his own joke.

'That,' said Mr Henderson, sounding more than a little indignant, 'is a gross over-simplification. Particle research involves a hell of a lot more than just accelerators...'

'Indeed it does,' Mr Stryder replied calmly, 'and eventually all such efforts that will lead to the discovery that what is currently known is but a minute fraction of what will be known, and what has yet to be uncovered, far out-weighs what has so far only been guessed at.' He took a moment to thoughtfully savour his ale, and then added, 'so, ultimately, there really is no chance of you screwing up the timeline, as you so colourfully put it, with revelations of fanciful nonsense like temporal mass and accordant gravitation.'

'Yeah, but someone's bound to pay attention at some point, and that would potentially create a research feedback loop... wouldn't it?' Mr Henderson asked. 'Sort of like the Grandfather Paradox.'

'Ah, right,' said Mr Stryder, 'that old myth. The one whereby you go back in time and cause the death of your own grandfather, thus making your own birth impossible...'

'Yeah, that,' said Mr Henderson, confident that he had made an irrefutable argument.

'Time simply does not work like that,' sighed Mr Stryder. 'However, rather than going into a long explanation, before dinner, and on an empty stomach no less, I offer you only this to ponder while we eat:

'Think of yourself as a creature made of sentient energy, existing at the speed of light, hurtling away from the exploding star that gave you birth. Now, if it were at all possible for you to look back at your point of origin, that very star would seem immutable and unchanging to you, even though it continues to disintegrate. To you, locked as you are in linear light, that star will appear to be frozen in the very moment you left it...

'And that is exactly the way history appears to people like you... people who are actually trapped in linear time...'

Time is a Relative

Gil Henderson was true to his word, and made several attempts at communicating what he had learned from his talks with Alex Stryder. Presented here for the first time is the opening to one of his more philosophical efforts, loosely based on a re-imagining of Plato's *Allegory of the Cave.*

You have been kidnapped... struck on the head, tied up, thrown in the back of a van, and left with no memories of your life before.

The van you are in is now speeding toward an unknown destination, and your limited view of the world is through a window in the rear door. You see only a narrow strip of asphalt, lined with street lamps endlessly racing away from you as they disappear into the distance.

But at least you do not have to face this fate alone. There are others trapped in the van with you, and together, after many years of captivity, you and your fellow passengers resolve to make the best of a bad situation. You make new lives for yourselves.

Only the very oldest passengers still keep their memories of the world as it was before. They speak of oceans, deserts, forests, and mountains, a world they wistfully call the Dreamtime. But the rest of you are more sensible than that. You dismiss any such ideas as primitive and superstitious, and you conduct your lives according to the new rules – the rules of the road.

Ah, yes, the road, the only world that you can see, and therefore, the only world that truly exists: A narrow strip of pavement that only allows you to see the past clearly, while it carries you blindly toward the future. A path that never varies.

However, one lonely night, when all the other passengers are asleep, an old man approaches you, a relative of yours whom the others mockingly call Father Time. He leans uncomfortably close, and whispers in your ear, 'I know the truth.'

Over the years, you have grown weary of his inane ramblings, not to mention his bad breath, so you decide to put an end to this nonsense, once and for all.

'Then tell me,' you demand, 'tell me your great truth, you foolish old man, or else leave me be!' Yet, he does not turn away as you expect, but instead he slaps you across the face – hard.

You awake with a start, and find yourself standing at the side of a mountain highway. The air is fresh, the sun warm and welcoming, and you wonder at the beauty of this strange land, a world in which you can see in many different directions at once.

As you look around, you see that your fellow passengers are gone, carried away by the countless vehicles that race along the highway, and it is only the old man who remains by your side. He is taller and more self-assured than you remember him being.

'If I had done nothing more than tell you, you would never have believed me,' he chuckles. 'Indeed, if I were to tell you another truth... that time is not merely a single dimension, but several dimensions intertwined, you would think me utterly mad, which, of course,' he smiles at you in a grandfatherly way, 'you already do... So, instead, I have decided to *show* you... but in order to do that,' he says as he waves his hand in front of your eyes, 'you will need to see not only with reflected light, as you already do, but also with reflected time.'

Suddenly, the spatial and temporal dimensions diverge around you, and you see your life, and the lives of others, known and unknown, stretching out before you, intimately woven into the very fabric of space itself.

Yet there is too much information to process, and your mind reels as your world seems to spin out of control. You close your eyes, struggling to return to your simpler existence, but your efforts are in vain, and the nightmare does not end.

'Perhaps you are not ready,' you hear the old man saying, 'so instead, I shall tell you a little parable of mine about shadows in a cave...'

'Plato, you old fool,' you cry out through the growing chaos in your head, 'you couldn't have just *started* with that?'

The End of the Beginning

It was near the end of the summer of 2014. Two young boys were playing on the wide sandy beach at Tribune Bay on Hornby Island, and they had just built themselves a truly impressive driftwood fort. It was their way of making the island safe from invasion by space aliens, zombie hordes, or whatever other terrible danger their vivid imaginations could dream up. However, proud as they were of their construction, the fort still didn't feel quite complete, so they decided that an expedition was needed to acquire more materials. They began their quest by heading south-west along the wide beach until it narrowed into a rocky shore, and there they could see a ragged collection of shore pine and arbutus growing at the top of the bluff.

'Hey, look,' said the taller boy as he pointed up to the trees, 'it looks like an old flag.'

'Cool,' said the other, 'we totally need that.'

They began their difficult climb, but since the large rocks offered good cover for lurking enemies, the going was slow. They took turns laying down cover fire from their imaginary weapons as they moved from rock to rock, but eventually, they reached their destination safely.

Weary from their many battles, and proud of their hard-won victory, they stood majestically at the top of the bluff, their hair heroically wind-tousled as they surveyed their newly conquered lands.

The younger boy went to retrieve the goal of their mission, the tattered flag, and he soon found it among the trees, attached to an ancient weatherworn slab of wood. The old slab was jammed upright between two rocks, and it looked to the boy as though the fabric had once covered the wood on one side, but had torn free over time, and now flapped in the wind like a flag. 'Hah,' he laughed, 'this'll be perfect.'

'What do you think it is?'

'I dunno… it kinda looks like an old Halloween decoration… you know, like the lid from a coffin or something.'

'Hey… I bet it's real… and from some old pioneer's grave,' said the taller boy as he rubbed the dirt off an engraved brass plaque. 'And I'll bet you anything that this is the guy's name…'

The engraving simply read:

Arthur George Edward Stryder

J. W. Kingsley has been writing for many years, far more than would be decent to mention, and yet this is his first published novel.

It's about time.

www.ingramcontent.com/pod-product-compliance
Lightning Source LLC
Chambersburg PA
CBHW071124170626
46809CB00002B/493